Dr Robin Cook, a graduate of the Columbia University medical school, finished his postgraduate medical training at Harvard. The author of many bestselling novels, most recently *Chromosome 6*, *Invasion* and *Contagion*, he lives and works in Florida.

## ALSO BY ROBIN COOK

CHROMOSOME 6

INVASION

CONTAGION

ACCEPTABLE RISK

FATAL CURE

TERMINAL

BLINDSIGHT

VITAL SIGNS

HARMFUL INTENT

MUTATION

MORTAL FEAR

OUTBREAK

MINDBEND

GODPLAYER

FEVER

BRAIN

SPHINX

COMA

THE YEAR OF THE INTERN

# ROBIN COOK

# TOXIN

MACMILLAN

First published in Great Britain 1998 by Macmillan
an imprint of Macmillan Publishers Ltd
25 Eccleston Place, London, SW1W 9NF
and Basingstoke

Associated companies throughout the world

ISBN 0 333 73035 6

1 3 5 7 9 8 6 4 2

A CIP catalogue record for this book is available
from the British Library.

Printed and bound in Great Britain by
Mackays of Chatham PLC, Chatham, Kent

THIS BOOK IS DEDICATED TO
THOSE FAMILIES WHO HAVE SUFFERED
FROM THE SCOURGE OF E. COLI 0157:H7
AND OTHER FOOD-BORNE ILLNESSES.

I would like to acknowledge:

Bruce Berman, for his suggestions at the outset of this project as well as his insightful critique of the outline for *TOXIN*;

Nikki Fox, for sharing with me her extensive research on food-borne illness;

Ron Savenor, for helping me overcome a particular barrier in my own research;

and Jean Reeds, for her invaluable comments and suggestions on the work in progress.

# TOXIN

The sky was an immense, inverted bowl of gray clouds that arched from one flat horizon to the other. It was the kind of sky that hovered over the American Midwest. In the summer the ground would be awash in a sea of corn and soybeans. But now in the depths of winter it was a frozen stubble with patches of dirty snow and a few lonely, leafless, skeletonized trees.

The leaden clouds had excreted a lazy drizzle all day—more of a mist than a rain. But by two o'clock the precipitation had abated and the single functioning windshield wiper of the aged, recycled UPS delivery van was no longer necessary as the vehicle negotiated a rutted dirt road.

"What did old man Oakly say?" Bart Winslow asked. Bart was the driver of the van. He and his partner, Willy Brown, sitting in the passenger seat, were in their fifties and could have been mistaken for brothers. Their creased, leather faces bore witness to a lifetime of labor on the farm. Both were dressed in soiled and tattered overalls over layered sweatshirts and both were chewing tobacco.

"Benton Oakly didn't say much," Willy answered after wiping some spittle off his chin with the back of his hand. "Just said one of his cows woke up sick."

"How sick?" Bart asked.

"I guess sick enough to be a downer," Willy said. "Has the runs bad."

Bart and Willy had evolved over the years from mere farmhands to become what the local farmers referred to as 4-D men. It was their job to go around and pick up dead, dying, diseased, and disabled farm animals, particularly cows, and take them to the rendering plant. It wasn't a coveted job, but it suited Bart and Willy just fine.

The van turned at a rusted mailbox and followed a muddy road that ran between barbed-wire fences. A mile beyond the road opened up at a small farm. Bart drove the van up to the barn, made a three-point turn, and backed the vehicle to the open barn door. By the time Bart and Willy had climbed from the truck, Benton Oakly had appeared.

"Afternoon," Benton said. He was as laconic as Bart and Willy. Something about the landscape made people not want to talk. Benton was a tall, thin man with bad teeth. He kept his distance from Bart and Willy as did his dog, Shep. Shep had been barking until Bart and Willy got out of the truck. With his nose twitching from the scent of death, Shep shrank back behind his master.

"In the barn," Benton said. He motioned with his hand before leading his visitors into the depths of the dark barn. Stopping at a pen, he pointed over the rail.

Bart and Willy ventured to the edge of the pen and looked in. They wrinkled their noses. The area reeked of fresh manure.

Within the pen an obviously sick cow was lying in its own diarrhea. Raising its wobbly head, she gazed back at Bart and Willy. One of her pupils was the color of gray marble.

"What's with the eye?" Willy asked.

"Been that way since she was a calf," Benton said. "Got poked or something."

"She only been sick since this morning?" Bart asked.

"That's right," Benton said. "But she's been down on her milk for almost a month. I want her out'a here before my other cows get the runs."

"We'll take her, all right," Bart said.

"Is it still twenty-five bucks to haul her to the renderer?" Benton asked.

"Yup," Willy said. "But can we hose her off before putting her in the truck?"

"Be my guest," Benton said. "There's hose right over there against the wall."

Willy went to get the hose while Bart opened the gate to the pen. Trying to be careful where he put his feet, Bart gave the cow a few swats on its rump. Reluctantly it rose to its feet and tottered.

Willy came back with the hose and squirted the cow until it looked relatively clean. Then he and Bart got behind the cow and coaxed it out of the pen. With added help from Benton they got the animal outside and into the van. Willy closed the truck's back door.

"What'd ya got in there—about four head?" Benton asked.

"Yup," Willy said. "All four dead this morning. There's some kind of infection over at the Silverton Farm."

"Criminy," Benton said with alarm. He slapped a few wrinkled greenbacks into Bart's palm. "Get them the hell off my spread."

Bart and Willy both spat as they rounded their respective sides of the truck. The tired engine let out a belch of black smoke before propelling the vehicle out of the farm.

As was their habit Bart and Willy didn't speak again until the truck reached the pavement of the county road. Bart accelerated and finally got the van into fourth gear.

"You thinkin' what I'm thinkin'?" Bart asked.

"I imagine," Willy said. "That cow didn't look half bad after we hosed her down. Hell, it looks a mite better'n that one we sold to the slaughterhouse last week."

"And it can stand and even walk a little," Bart said.

Willy glanced at his watch. "Just about the right time too."

The 4-D men did not speak again until they pulled off the county road onto the track that ran around a low-slung, almost windowless, large commercial building. A billboard-sized sign said: HIGGINS AND HANCOCK. At the rear of the building was an empty stockyard that was a sea of trampled mud.

"You wait here," Bart said, as he pulled to a stop near the chute that lead from the stockyard into the factory.

Bart got out of the van and disappeared down the chute. Willy got out and leaned up against the van's rear door. Five minutes later Bart reappeared with two burly men dressed in bloodstained long white coats, yellow plastic construction helmets, and yellow midcalf rubber boots. Both sported a name tag. The heavier man's name tag said: JED STREET, SUPERVISOR. The other man's said: SALVATORE MORANO, QUALITY CONTROL. Jed had a clipboard.

Bart gestured to Willy, and Willy unlatched the van's rear door and opened it. Salvatore and Henry covered their noses and peered inside. The sick cow raised its head.

Jed turned to Bart. "Can the animal stand?"

"Sure can. She can even walk a little."

Jed looked at Salvatore. "What do you think, Sal?"

"Where's the SME inspector?" Salvatore asked.

"Where do you think?" Jed said. "He's in the locker room, where he goes as soon as he thinks the last animal has come through."

Salvatore lifted the tail of his white coat to get at a two-way radio attached to his belt. He switched it on and held it up to his lips. "Gary, did that last combo bin that's going to Mercer Meats get filled?"

The answer came back accompanied by static: "Almost."

"Okay," Salvatore said into the radio. "We're sending in one more animal. That will more than do it."

Salvatore switched off his radio and looked at Jed. "Let's do it."

Jed nodded and turned to Bart. "Looks like you got a deal, but as I said, we'll only pay fifty bucks."

Bart nodded. "Fifty bucks is okay."

While Bart and Willy climbed into the back of the van, Salvatore walked back down the chute. From his pocket he pulled out a couple of earplugs that he put in his ears. As he entered the slaughterhouse, his mind was no longer concerned about the sick cow. He was concerned about the myriad forms he still had to fill out before he could think of going home.

With his earplugs in place, Salvatore wasn't troubled by the noise as he traversed the kill-floor area of the slaughterhouse. He approached Mark Watson, the line supervisor, and got his attention.

"We got one more animal coming through," Salvatore yelled over the din. "But it's only for boneless beef. There'll be no carcass. Got it?"

Mark made a circle with his thumb and index finger to indicate he understood.

Salvatore then passed through the soundproof door that led into the administrative area of the building. Entering his office, he hung up his bloodied coat and construction helmet. He sat down at his desk and went back to his daily forms.

Concentrating as hard as he was, Salvatore wasn't sure how much time had passed when Jed suddenly appeared at his door. "We got a slight problem," Jed said.

"Now what?" Salvatore asked.

"The head of that downer cow fell off the rail."

"Did any of the inspectors see it?" Salvatore asked.

"No," Jed said. "They're all in the locker room with the SME for their daily chitchat."

"Then put the head back on the rail and hose it off."

"Okay," Jed said. "I thought you should know."

"Absolutely," Salvatore said. "To cover our asses I'll even fill out a Process Deficiency Report. What's the lot and head number of that animal?"

Jed looked down at his clipboard. "Lot thirty-six, head fifty-seven."

"Got it," Salvatore said.

Jed left Salvatore's office and returned to the kill floor. He tapped José on the shoulder. José was a sweeper whose job it was to sweep all the filth from the floor into one of the many grates. José had not been working there very long. It was a chronic problem keeping sweepers because of the nature of the job.

José didn't speak much English and Jed's Spanish wasn't much better, so he was reduced to communicating by crude gestures. Jed motioned that he wanted José to help Manuel, one of the skinners, to heft the skinned cow's head from the floor onto one of the hooks on the moving overhead rail.

Eventually José caught on. Luckily José and Manuel could communicate without difficulty, because the job required two steps and significant effort. First they had to get the hundred-plus-pound head up onto the metal catwalk. Then, after climbing up there themselves, they had to hoist the head up high enough to secure it on one of the moving hooks.

Jed gave a thumbs-up sign to the two panting men, who at the last second had almost dropped their slippery burden. Jed then trained a jet of water on the soiled skinless head as it moved along on the rail. Even to the hardened Jed the appearance of the cataractous eye gave the skinned head a gruesome aura. But he was pleased with how much of the filth came off with the high-pressure water, and by the time the head passed through the aperture in the kill-floor wall on its way into the head-boning room, it looked relatively clean.

# CHAPTER 1

The Sterling Place Mall was aglow with the marble, bright brass, and polished wood of its upscale shops. Tiffany competed with Cartier, Neiman-Marcus with Saks. Mozart's piano concerto number 23 was piped in through hidden speakers. Beautiful people milled about on this late Friday afternoon in their Gucci shoes and Armani coats to survey the offerings of the post-Christmas sales.

Under normal circumstances Kelly Anderson wouldn't have minded spending a part of the afternoon at the mall. As a TV journalist it was a far cry from the gritty beats she was usually assigned around the city while putting together in-depth pieces for the six or eleven o'clock news. But on this particular Friday, the mall had not provided Kelly with what she wanted.

"This is a joke," Kelly said irritably. She looked up and down the expansive hall for a likely candidate to interview but no one looked promising.

"I think we've gotten enough," Brian said. Brian Washington, a lanky, laid-back African-American, was Kelly's cameraman of choice. In her mind he was the best WENE had to offer, and Kelly had maneuvered, cajoled, and even used threats to get the station to assign him to her.

Kelly puffed up her cheeks before blowing out her breath in an expression of exasperation. "Like hell we've got enough," she said. "We've got diddly-squat."

At thirty-four, Kelly Anderson was a no-nonsense, intelligent, aggressive woman hoping to break into national news. Most people thought she had a good chance if she could find a story that would catapult her into the spotlight. She looked the part with her sharp features and lively eyes framed by a helmet of tight, blond curls. To add to her professional image she dressed fashionably and tastefully, and groomed herself impeccably.

Kelly transferred her microphone to her right hand so that she could see her watch. "And to make matters worse, we're running out of time. I'm going to have to pick up my daughter. Her skating lesson's over."

"That's cool," Brian said. He lowered his camcorder from his shoulder and unplugged the power source. "I should get my daughter from day care."

Kelly bent down and stowed her microphone in her sizable shoulder bag, then helped Brian break down the equipment. Like a couple of experienced pack rats, they hoisted everything over their shoulders and started walking toward the center of the mall.

"What's becoming obvious," Kelly said, "is that people don't give a damn about AmeriCare's merger of the Samaritan Hospital and the University Med Center unless they've had to go to the hospital during the last six months."

"It's not an easy subject to get people fired up about," Brian said. "It's not criminal, sexy, or scandalous, and there are no celebrities involved."

"They ought to be concerned," Kelly said with disgust.

"Hey, what people ought to do and what they actually do has never been related," Brian said. "You know that."

"All I know is that I shouldn't have scheduled this piece for tonight's eleven o'clock news," Kelly said. "I'm desperate. Tell me how to make it sexy."

"If I knew that, I'd be the talent rather than the cameraman," Brian said with a laugh.

Emerging from one of the radiating corridors of the Sterling Place Mall, Kelly and Brian arrived at the spacious epicenter. In the middle of this vast area and beneath a three-story-high skylight was an oval skating rink. Its frosted surface glowed under the glare of klieg lights.

Dotted around the rink were a dozen or so children along with several adults. All were careening across the ice in various directions. The apparent chaos resulted from the recent conclusion of the intermediate lesson and the imminent commencement of the advanced lesson.

Seeing her daughter's bright red outfit, Kelly waved and called out. Caroline Anderson waved back but took her time skating over. Caroline was very much her mother's daughter. She was bright, athletic, and willful.

"Shake a leg, Chicken," Kelly said when Caroline finally neared. "I gotta get you home. Mom's got a deadline and a major problem."

Caroline stepped out of the rink, and walking on the toes of her figure-skate blades, she moved to the bench and sat down. "I want to go to the Onion Ring for a burger. I'm starved."

"That's going to be up to your father, sweetie," Kelly said. "Come on, chop, chop!"

Kelly bent down and got Caroline's shoes out of her knapsack and put them on the bench next to her daughter.

"Now, there's one hell of a skater," Brian said.

Kelly straightened up and shielded her eyes with her hand from the bright lights. "Where?"

"In the center," Brian said, pointing. "In the pink outfit."

Kelly looked where Brian indicated, and it was immediately apparent whom he was referring to. A girl, around the same age as Caroline, was going through a warm-up exercise that had now caused some of the shoppers to pause and watch.

"Whoa," Kelly said. "She is good. She looks almost professional."

"She's not that good," Caroline said, as she gritted her teeth in an attempt to pull off one of her skates.

"She looks good to me," Kelly said. "Who is she?"

"Her name is Becky Reggis." Having given up trying to yank off her skate, Caroline was back to loosening the laces. "She was the junior state champion last year."

As if sensing she was being watched, the girl then executed two double axels in a row before arcing around the end of the rink, heel to heel. A number of the shoppers broke out in spontaneous applause.

"She's fantastic," Kelly said.

"Yeah, well, she's been invited to the Nationals this year," Caroline reluctantly added.

"Hmmm," Kelly murmured. She looked at Brian. "There could be a story there."

Brian shrugged. "Maybe for the six o'clock. Certainly not for the eleven."

Kelly redirected her attention to the skater. "Her last name is Reggis, huh?"

"Yup," Caroline said. She had both skates off now and was looking in her knapsack for her shoes.

"Could that be Dr. Kim Reggis's daughter?" Kelly asked.

"I know her father's a doctor," Caroline said.

"How do you know?" Kelly asked.

"She goes to my school," Caroline said. "She's a year ahead of me."

"Well, bingo!" Kelly murmured. "This must be serendipity calling."

"I recognize that beady look in your eye," Brian said. "You're like a cat ready to pounce. You're plotting something."

"I can't find my shoes," Caroline complained.

"I just had a brainstorm," Kelly said. She picked up Caroline's shoes from the bench and put them in her daughter's lap. "Dr. Kim Reggis would be perfect for this merger story. He was chief of cardiac surgery at the Samaritan before the merger and then, bang, he became one of the Indians. I'd bet he'd have something saucy and sexy to say."

"No doubt," Brian said. "But would he talk to you? He didn't come off too good in that 'Poor Little Rich Kids' piece you did."

"Oh, that's water over the dam," Kelly said with a wave of dismissal.

"That might be the way you feel," Brian said, "but I doubt he'd feel the same way."

"He had it coming," Kelly said. "I'm sure he's figured that out. For the life of me I can't understand why cardiac surgeons like him don't realize their moaning about Medicare reimbursement rates strikes a hollow chord with the public when they're earning six-figure incomes. You'd think they'd be more street-smart."

"Deserved or not, I can't imagine he wasn't pissed," Brian said. "I doubt if he'd talk to you."

"You're forgetting that surgeons like Kim Reggis love publicity," Kelly said. "Anyway, I think it's worth the risk. What do we have to lose?"

"Time," Brian said.

"Which we don't have much of," Kelly said. Bending down to Caroline, she added: "Sweetie, would you know if Becky's mother were here?"

"Sure," Caroline said. She pointed. "She's over there in the red sweater."

"How convenient," Kelly said, as she straightened up to peer across the ice. "This truly is serendipitous. Listen, Chicken, finish getting your shoes on. I'll be right back." Kelly turned to Brian. "Hold the fort."

"Go for it, girl," Brian said with a smile.

Kelly walked around the end of the skating rink and approached Becky's mother. The woman appeared to be about her own age. She was attractive and well groomed, although her clothes were conservative. Kelly hadn't seen a crew-neck sweater over a white collared shirt on a woman since she'd been in college. Becky's mother was deeply absorbed in a book that couldn't have been bestseller fiction. She was carefully underlining with a yellow felt-tipped pen.

"Excuse me," Kelly said. "I hope I'm not disturbing you too much."

Becky's mother looked up. She was a dark brunette with auburn highlights. Her features were chiseled but her demeanor was gentle and her spirit immediately empathetic.

"It's quite all right," the woman said. "Can I help you?"

"Are you Mrs. Reggis?" Kelly asked.

"Please call me Tracy."

"Thanks," Kelly said. "That looks like serious reading for the skating rink."

"I have to take advantage of every moment I get," Tracy replied.

"It looks like a textbook," Kelly said.

"I'm afraid it is," Tracy said. "I've gone back to school in my early middle age."

"That's commendable," Kelly said.

"It's challenging," Tracy said.

"What's the title?"

Tracy flipped the book over to show its cover. *"The Assessment of Child and Adolescent Personality."*

"Whoa! That sounds heavy," Kelly said.

"It's not too bad," Tracy said. "In fact it's interesting."

"I've got a nine-year-old daughter," Kelly said. "I probably should read something about teenage behavior before all hell breaks loose."

"It can't hurt," Tracy said. "Parents need all the help they can get. Adolescence can be a tough time, and it's been my experience that when difficulties are anticipated, they happen."

"Sounds like something you know a bit about," Kelly said.

"Some," Tracy admitted. "But you can never be complacent. Before going back to school last semester, I was involved with therapy, mostly with children, including adolescents."

"Psychologist?" Kelly asked.

"Social worker," Tracy said.

"Interesting," Kelly said to change the subject. "Actually, the reason I came over here was to introduce myself. I'm Kelly Anderson of WENE News."

"I know who you are," Tracy said with a touch of scorn.

"Uh-oh!" Kelly said. "I have the uncomfortable feeling that my reputation precedes me. I hope you don't hold it against me that I did that segment on cardiac surgeons and Medicare."

"I felt it was underhanded," Tracy said. "Kim was under the impression that you were sympathetic when he agreed to do the interview."

"I was to an extent," Kelly said. "After all, I did present both sides of the issue."

"Only in regard to falling professional incomes," Tracy said. "Which you made the focus. In reality that's only one of the issues that concern cardiac surgeons."

A pink blur raced past Kelly and Tracy and drew their attention to the rink. Becky had increased her speed and was now tensing as she streaked backward. Then, to the delight of the impromptu audience of shoppers, she executed a perfect triple axel. More applause erupted.

Kelly let out a faint whistle. "Your daughter is a phenomenal skater."

"Thank you," Tracy said. "We think she is a phenomenal person."

Kelly regarded Tracy in an attempt to interpret her comment. Kelly couldn't quite decide if it were meant to be disdainful or merely informative. But Tracy's face gave little hint. She stared back at Kelly with a soulful but undecipherable expression.

"Did she get her skating talent from you?" Kelly asked.

Tracy laughed freely, letting her head fall back in true amusement. "Hardly," she said. "I've never had a pair of skates on my clumsy feet. We don't know where she got her talent. One day she just said she wanted to skate, and the rest is history."

"My daughter says Becky's going to the Nationals this year," Kelly said. "That might make a good story for WENE."

"I don't think so," Tracy said. "Becky was invited, but she's decided not to go."

"I'm sorry," Kelly said. "Gosh, you and the good doctor must be crushed."

"Her father's not terribly happy," Tracy said. "But to be honest, I'm relieved."

"Why is that?" Kelly asked.

"That level of competition extracts a high price from anyone, much less a prepubescent child. It's not always mentally healthy. It's a lot of risk without a lot of payoff."

"Hmmm," Kelly said. "I'll have to give that some thought. But, meanwhile, I've got a more pressing problem. I'm trying to do a piece for tonight's eleven o'clock news since today's the sixth-month anniversary of AmeriCare's merger of the Samaritan with the University Med Center. What I wanted was the community's reaction, but I've run into a lot of apathy. So I'd love to get your husband's feelings on the issue since I know he'd have an opinion. By any chance is he coming here to the rink this afternoon?"

"No," Tracy said with a giggle, as if Kelly had suggested an absurdity. "He never leaves the hospital until six or seven on weekdays. Never!"

"Too bad," Kelly commented, while her mind rapidly processed various contingencies. "Tell me, do you think your husband would be willing to talk with me?"

"I really have no idea," Tracy said. "You see, we've been divorced for a number of months, so I couldn't guess how he feels about you at the moment."

"I'm sorry," Kelly said with sincerity. "I didn't have any idea."

"No need to be sorry. It was best for everyone, I'm afraid. A casualty of the times and a clash of personalities."

"Well, I can imagine being married to a surgeon, particularly a cardiac surgeon, is no picnic. I mean, they think that everything pales in importance compared to what they do."

"Hmmm," Tracy responded noncommittedly.

"I know I couldn't stand it," Kelly said. "Egotistical, self-centered personalities like your former husband and I don't mix."

"Maybe that's saying something about you," Tracy suggested.

"You think so?" Kelly said. She paused for a moment, recognizing she was dealing with a gentle but quick wit. "Maybe you're right. Anyway, let me ask you this: would you have any idea where I might find your former husband right now? I'd really like to talk with him."

"I can guess where he is," Tracy said. "He's probably in surgery. With all the fighting for OR time at the med center, he's had to do all three of his weekly cases on Friday."

"Thank you. I think I'll head right over there and see if I can catch him."

"You're welcome," Tracy said. She returned Kelly's wave and then watched the woman walk swiftly back around the rink. "Good luck," Tracy murmured to herself.

# CHAPTER 2

All twenty-five of the University Medical Center's operating rooms were identical. Having been recently renovated and re-equipped, they were up-to-the-minute in every way. The floors were a white composite that gave the impression of granite. The walls were gray tile. The lights and fittings were either stainless steel or gleaming nickel.

OR twenty was one of two rooms used for open-heart surgery and at four-fifteen it was still in full operation. Between the perfusionists, anesthesiologists, circulating and scrub nurses, the surgeons and all the necessary high-tech equipment, the room was quite crowded. At that moment the patient's still heart was in full view, surrounded by a profusion of bloodstained tapes, trailing sutures, metal retractors, and pale green drapes.

"Okay, that's it," Dr. Kim Reggis said, as he handed his needle holder to the scrub nurse and straightened up to relieve the stiffness in his back. He'd been operating since seven-thirty that morning. This was his third and final case. "Let's stop the cardioplegia solution and get this ticker going."

Kim's command resulted in a minor flurry of activity at the console of the bypass machine. Switches were flipped. "Warming up," the perfusionist announced to no one in particular.

The anesthesiologist stood and looked over the ether screen. "How much longer do you estimate?" she asked.

15

"We'll be closing here in five minutes," Kim said. "Provided the heart cooperates, which looks promising."

After a few erratic beats, the heart picked up its normal rhythm.

"Okay," Kim said. "Let's go off bypass."

For the next twenty minutes there was no talk. Everyone on the team knew his job, so communication wasn't necessary. After the split sternum had been wired together, Kim and Dr. Tom Bridges stepped back from the heavily draped patient and began removing their sterile gowns, gloves, and plastic face shields. At the same time the thoracic residents moved into the vacated positions.

"I want a plastic repair on that incision," Kim called to the residents. "Is that understood?"

"You got it, Dr. Reggis," Tom Harkly said. Tom was the Chief Thoracic resident.

"But don't make it your life's work," Kim teased. "The patient has been under long enough."

Kim and Tom emerged from the OR into the operating-room corridor. Both used the scrub sink to wash the talc off their hands. Dr. Tom Bridges was a cardiac surgeon like Kim. They had been assisting each other for years and had become friends although their relationship remained essentially professional. They frequently covered for each other, especially on weekends.

"That was a slick job," Tom commented. "I don't know how you manage to get those valves in so perfectly and make it look so easy."

Kim's practice over the years had evolved into mostly valve replacement. Tom had gravitated more toward bypass procedures.

"Just like I don't know how you can sew those tiny coronary arteries the way you do," Kim answered.

Leaving the sink, Kim interlocked his fingers and stretched them high over his six-foot-three-inch frame. Then he bent down and put his palms on the floor, keeping his legs straight to stretch out his lower back. Kim was an athletic, trim, sinewy type who'd played football, basketball, and baseball for Dartmouth as an undergraduate. Because of the demands of time his current exercise had been reduced to infrequent tennis and lots of hours on a home exercise bike.

Tom, on the other hand, had given up. He, too, had played football in college, but after years of no exercise, the muscle bulk that he'd not lost had turned mostly to fat. In contrast to Kim, he had a beer belly despite the fact that he rarely drank beer.

The two men started down the tiled corridor, which at that time of day was relatively peaceful. Only nine of the OR's were in use, with two more available for emergencies. It was about standard for the three-to-eleven shift.

Kim rubbed his stubbled, angular face. Following his normal routine, he'd shaved that morning at five-thirty, and now, twelve hours later, he had the proverbial five-o'clock shadow. He ran a hand through his long, dark brown hair. As a teenager in the early seventies he'd let his hair grow beyond shoulder length. Now, at forty-three, it was still on the long side for someone in his position, though it was nowhere near as long as it had been.

Kim looked at his watch pinned to his scrub pants. "Damn, it's five-thirty already, and I haven't even made rounds. I wish I didn't have to operate on Friday. Invariably it cuts into any weekend plans."

"At least you get to have your cases run consecutively," Tom said. "It's sure not like it used to be when you ran the department over at the Samaritan."

"Tell me about it," Kim said. "With AmeriCare calling the shots and with the current status of the profession, I wonder if I'd even go into medicine if I had it all to do over again."

"You and me both," Tom said. "Especially with these new Medicare rates. Last night I stayed up and did some figuring. I'm afraid I'm not going to have any money left after I pay my office overhead. I mean, what kind of a situation is that? It's gotten so bad Nancy and I are thinking of putting our house on the market."

"Good luck," Kim said. "Mine's been on the market for five months, and I haven't even had a serious offer."

"I already had to pull my kids out of private school," Tom said. "But hell, I went to public school myself."

"How are you and Nancy getting along?" Kim asked.

"To be honest: not great," Tom said. "There've been a lot of bad feelings."

"I'm sorry to hear that," Kim said. "I sympathize since I've been through it. It's a stressful time."

"This is not how I expected things to be at this stage in my life," Tom said with a sigh.

"Me neither," Kim said.

The two men stopped just beyond the OR desk at the entrance to the recovery room.

"Hey, are you going to be around for the weekend?" Tom asked.

"Yeah, sure," Kim said. "Why? What's up?"

"I might have to go back in on that case you helped me with Tuesday," Tom said. "There's been some residual bleeding and unless it stops, my hand is forced. If that happens, I could use your assistance."

"Just page me," Kim said. "I'll be available. My ex wanted the whole weekend. I think she's seeing someone. Anyway, Becky and I will be hanging out together."

"How is Becky doing after the divorce?" Tom asked.

"She's doing fantastic," Kim said. "Certainly better than I am. At this point she's the only bright light in my life."

"I guess kids are more resilient than we give them credit for," Tom said.

"Apparently so," Kim agreed. "Hey, thanks for helping today. Sorry that second case took so long."

"No problem," Tom said. "You handled it like a virtuoso. It was a learning experience. See you in the surgical locker room."

Kim stepped into the recovery room. Hesitating just beyond the threshold, he scanned the beds for his patients. The first one he saw was Sheila Donlon. She'd been his immediately preceding case and had been particularly difficult. She'd needed two valves instead of only one.

Kim walked over to the bed. One of the recovery-room nurses was busy changing an almost empty IV bottle. Kim's experienced eye first checked the patient's color and then glanced at the monitors. The cardiac rhythm was normal, as was the blood pressure and arterial oxygenation.

"Everything okay?" Kim asked as he lifted the recovery-room chart to glance at the grafts.

"No problems," the nurse said without interrupting her efforts. "Everything's stable and the patient's content."

Kim replaced the chart and moved alongside the bed. Gently he raised the sheet to glance at the dressing. Kim always instructed his residents to use minimal dressing. If there was unexpected bleeding, Kim wanted to know about it sooner rather than later.

Satisfied, Kim replaced the sheet before straightening up to look for his other patient. Only about half the beds were occupied, so it didn't take long to scan them.

"Where's Mr. Glick?" Kim asked. Ralph Glick had been Kim's first case.

"Ask Mrs. Benson at the desk," the nurse responded. She was preoccupied putting her stethoscope in her ears and inflating Sheila Donlon's blood pressure cuff.

Mildly irritated at the lack of cooperation, Kim walked over to the central desk but found Mrs. Benson, the head nurse, equally preoccupied. She was giving detailed instructions to several housekeeping workers who were there to break down, clean, and change one of the beds.

"Excuse me," Kim said. "I'm looking . . ."

Mrs. Benson motioned to Kim that she was busy. Kim thought about complaining that his time was more valuable than the housekeepers', but he didn't. Instead he rose up on his toes to look again for his patient.

"What can I do for you, Dr. Reggis?" Mrs. Benson said as soon as the housekeepers headed off toward the recently vacated bed.

"I don't see Mr. Glick," Kim said. He was still scanning the room, certain he was overlooking the man.

"Mr. Glick was sent to his floor," Mrs. Benson said curtly. She pulled out the controlled-substance log and opened it to the appropriate page.

Kim looked at the nurse and blinked. "But I specifically asked he be kept here until I finished my final case."

"The patient was stable," Mrs. Benson added. "There was no need for him to remain and tie up a bed."

Kim sighed. "But you have tons of beds. It was a matter of . . ."

"Excuse me, Dr. Reggis," Mrs. Benson said. "The point is Mr. Glick was clinically ready to go."

"But I had requested he be kept," Kim said. "It would have saved me time."

"Dr. Reggis," Mrs. Benson said slowly. "With all due respect, the recovery-room staff doesn't work for you. We have rules. We work for AmeriCare. If you have a problem with that, I suggest you talk to one of the administrators."

Kim felt his face redden. He started to talk about the concept of team-work, but he quickly changed his mind. Mrs. Benson had already directed her attention to the loose-leaf notebook in front of her.

Murmuring a few choice epithets under his breath, Kim walked out of the recovery room. He yearned for the old days back at the Samaritan Hospital. Stepping across the hall, he stopped at the OR desk. With the aid of the intercom, he checked on the progress of his last case. Tom Harkly's voice assured him the closure was proceeding on schedule.

Leaving the operating suite, Kim marched down the hall to the newly constructed family lounge. It was one of the few innovations AmeriCare had instituted that Kim thought was a good idea. It had come from AmeriCare's concern for amenities. The room was specifically designated for the relatives of patients in the operating or delivery rooms. Prior to AmeriCare's purchase of the University Medical Center, there had been no place for family members to wait.

By that time of day it was not crowded. There were a few of the omnipresent expectant fathers pacing or nervously flipping through magazines while waiting for their wives to have Caesareans. In the far corner a priest was sitting with a grieving couple.

Kim glanced around for Mrs. Gertrude Arnold, the wife of Kim's last patient. Kim wasn't looking forward to talking with her. Her peppery and truculent personality was hard for him to bear. But he knew it was his responsibility. He found the late-sixties woman in the opposite far corner away from the grieving couple. She was reading a magazine.

"Mrs. Arnold," Kim said, forcing himself to smile.

Startled, Gertrude looked up. For a nanosecond her face registered surprise, but as soon as she recognized Kim, she became visibly irritated.

"Well, it's about time!" Mrs. Arnold snapped. "What happened? Is there a problem?"

"No problem at all," Kim assured her. "Quite the contrary. Your husband tolerated the procedure very well. He's being . . ."

"But it's almost six o'clock!" Gertrude sputtered. "You said you'd be done by three."

"That was an estimate, Mrs. Arnold," Kim said, trying to keep his voice even despite a wave of irritation. He'd anticipated a strange response, but this was more than he'd bargained for. "Unfortunately the previous case took longer than expected."

"Then my husband should have gone first," Gertrude shot back. "You've kept me waiting here all day not knowing what was happening. I'm a wreck."

Kim lost control and in spite of a valiant effort, his face twisted into a wry, disbelieving smile.

"Don't you smile at me, young man," Gertrude scolded. "If you ask me, you doctors are too high and mighty, making us normal folk wait all the time."

"I'm sorry if my schedule has caused you any distress," Kim said. "We do the best we can."

"Yeah, well, let me tell you what else happened," Gertrude said. "One of the AmeriCare administrators came to see me, and he told me that AmeriCare wasn't going to pay for my husband's first day in the hospital. They said he was supposed to be admitted this morning on the day of surgery and not the day before. What do you say to that?"

"This is an ongoing problem I'm having with the administration,"

Kim said. "When someone is as sick as your husband was before his surgery, I could not in good conscience allow him to be admitted the day of surgery."

"Well, they said they weren't going to pay," Gertrude said. "And we can't pay."

"If AmeriCare persists, then I'll pay," Kim said.

Gertrude's mouth dropped open. "You will?"

"It's come up before and I've paid before," Kim said. "Now, about your husband. Soon he'll be in recovery. They'll keep him there until he's stable, and then he'll go to the Cardiac floor. You'll be able to see him then."

Kim turned and walked from the room, pretending not to hear Mrs. Arnold calling his name.

Retreating back up the hall, Kim entered the surgical lounge. It was occupied by a handful of OR nurses on their breaks and a few of the staff anesthesiologists and anesthetists. Kim nodded to those people he recognized. Having been working at the University Medical Center only since the merger six months previously, Kim didn't know all the staff, particularly the evening and night people.

Pushing through the door into the men's surgical locker room, Kim pulled off his scrub top and threw it forcibly into the hamper. He then sat on the bench in front of the bank of lockers to unpin his watch from the waistband of the pants. Tom, who'd taken a shower, was busy putting on his shirt.

"It used to be when I finished a case I felt a certain euphoria," Kim commented. "Now I feel a vague, unpleasant anxiety."

"I know the feeling," Tom said.

"Correct me if I'm wrong," Kim said. "This all used to be a lot more fun."

Tom turned from facing the mirror and chuckled. "Excuse me for laughing, but you say that as if it were a sudden revelation."

"I'm not talking about the economics," Kim said. "I'm talking about the little things, like getting respect from the staff and appreciation from patients. Nowadays you can't take anything for granted."

"Times are a-changing," Tom agreed. "Especially with managed care and the government teamed up to make us specialists miserable. Sometimes I fantasize about one of the responsible bureaucrats coming to me for a bypass, and I make him get it from a general practitioner."

Kim stood up and pulled off his scrub pants. "The sad irony is that all this is happening when we cardiac surgeons have the most to offer the public."

Kim was about to toss his pants into the hamper by the door, when the door opened and one of the women anesthesiologists, Dr. Jane Flanagan, stuck her head in. Catching sight of Kim's skivvy-clad body, she whistled.

"You came mighty close to having these sweat-soaked pants draped over your noggin," Kim warned.

"For such a view it would have been worth it," Jane joked. "Anyway, I'm here to inform you that your public awaits you out here in the lounge."

The door closed and Jane's perky face disappeared.

Kim looked at Tom. "Public? What the hell is she talking about?"

"My guess is you have a visitor," Tom said. "And the fact that no one has come in here leads me to believe it must be female."

Kim stepped over to the cubbyholes filled with scrub tops and bottoms and took a clean set. "What now?" he questioned irritably.

At the door Kim paused. "If this is Mrs. Arnold, the wife of my last case, I'm going to scream."

Kim pushed out into the lounge. Instantly he saw it wasn't Gertrude Arnold. Instead, Kelly Anderson was at the coffee urn, helping herself to a cup. A few steps behind her was her cameraman with a camcorder balanced on his right shoulder.

"Ah, Dr. Reggis," Kelly exclaimed, catching sight of the surprised and none-too-pleased Kim. "How good of you to come to talk with us."

"How the hell did you get in here?" Kim asked with indignation. "And how did you know I was here?" The surgical lounge was like a sanctuary that even nonsurgical doctors were hesitant to violate. For Kim the idea of being confronted by anyone here, much less Kelly Anderson, was too much to bear.

"Brian and I knew you were here thanks to your former wife," Kelly said. "As for how we got up here, I'm happy to say we were invited and even escorted by Mr. Lindsey Noyes." Kelly gestured toward a gray-suited gentleman standing in the doorway to the hall who'd hesitated to come in himself. "He's from the AmeriCare–University Med Center PR department."

"Evening, Dr. Reggis," Lindsey said nervously. "We just need a moment of your time. Miss Anderson has graciously decided to do a story commemorating the six-month anniversary of our hospital merger. Of course, we'd like to assist her in any way we can."

For a moment Kim's dark eyes darted back and forth between Kelly and Lindsey. On the spur of the moment he wasn't certain who irritated him more, the muckraking journalist or the meddlesome administrator. Ultimately he decided he didn't care. "If you want to help her, then you talk to her," Kim said before turning to go back into the locker room.

"Dr. Reggis, wait!" Kelly blurted. "I've already heard the prepared AmeriCare side. We're interested in your personal view, from the trenches, so to speak."

With the locker-room door open a crack, Kim paused and debated. He looked back at Kelly Anderson. "After that piece you did on cardiac surgery, I vowed never to talk to you again."

"And why is that?" Kelly said. "It was an interview. I didn't put words in your mouth."

"You quoted me out of context by editing your questions," Kim fumed. "And you left out most of the issues I said were of primary importance."

"We always edit our interviews," Kelly said. "It's a fact of life."

"Find another victim," Kim said.

Kim pushed open the locker-room door and had taken a step within, when Kelly called out again: "Dr. Reggis! Just answer one question. Has the merger been as good for the community as AmeriCare contends? They say they did it for purely altruistic reasons. They insist it's the best thing that's happened to medical care in this city since the discovery of penicillin."

Kim hesitated again. The absurdity of such a comment made it impossible for him not to respond. Once again he turned back to Kelly. "I

have trouble understanding how anyone could say such a ludicrous statement and have a conscience clear enough to sleep at night. The truth is
that the entire rationale for the merger was to benefit AmeriCare's bottom line. Anything else they may tell you is rationalization and pure bull."

The door closed behind Kim. Kelly looked at Brian. Brian smiled and
gave Kelly the thumbs-up sign. "I got it," Brian said.

Kelly smiled back. "Perfect! That was just what the doctor ordered."

Lindsey coughed politely into a closed fist. "Obviously," he said, "Dr.
Reggis has given his personal view, which I can assure you is not shared
by other members of the professional staff."

"Oh really?" Kelly questioned. She let her eyes roam the room. "Anybody here wish to make a comment concerning Dr. Reggis's statement?"

For a moment no one moved.

"Pro or con?" Kelly prodded.

Still no one moved. In the sudden silence, the hospital page could be
heard like the backdrop of a TV melodrama.

"Well," Kelly said brightly, "thank you all for your time."

○    ○    ○

Tom slipped on his long white hospital coat and arranged the collection
of pens, pencils, and flashlight in its upper front pocket. Kim had come
into the locker room and, after removing his clothes and throwing them
into the hamper, had gotten into the shower. He'd not said a word.

"Aren't you going to tell me who was out there?" Tom said.

"It was Kelly Anderson from WENE News," Kim said from the
shower.

"In our surgical lounge?" Tom questioned.

"Can you believe it?" Kim said. "She was dragged up here by one of the
AmeriCare admin guys. Apparently my ex told her where to find me."

"I hope you told her what you thought of that piece she did on cardiac
surgery," Tom said. "After my car mechanic saw it, I swear he raised his
rates. I mean talk about backwards; my income's plummeting and service
people are upping their charges."

"I said as little as I could," Kim said.

"Hey, what time were you supposed to pick up Becky?" Tom asked.

"Six o'clock," Kim said. "What time is it now?"

"You'd better get a move on," Tom said. "It's already heading toward six-thirty."

"Damn," Kim said. "I haven't even done my rounds yet. What a life!"

# CHAPTER 3

By the time Kim did his rounds and checked Mr. Arnold in the recovery room, another hour had passed. En route to his former wife's house in the University section of town, he pushed his ten-year-old Mercedes and made record time. But it was still going on eight when he pulled up behind a yellow Lamborghini directly in front of Tracy's house.

Leaping from the car, Kim jogged up the front walk. The house was a modest affair built around the birth of the twentieth century, with a few Victorian gothic touches, like pointed arch windows in the second-floor dormers. Kim took the front steps in twos to reach the columned porch, where he rang the bell. His breath steamed in the wintery chill. While he waited he fanned his arms to keep warm. He wasn't wearing a coat.

Tracy opened the door and immediately put her hands on her hips. She was plainly anxious and irritated. "Kim, it's almost eight. You said you'd be here by six at the latest."

"Sorry," Kim said. "It was unavoidable. The second case took longer than anticipated. We ran into an unexpected problem."

"I suppose I should be used to this by now," Tracy said. She stepped out of the way and motioned for Kim to step inside. She closed the door behind him.

Kim glanced into the living room and saw a smart, casually dressed,

27

mid-forties man in a suede fringe jacket and ostrich cowboy boots. He was sitting on the couch, with a drink in one hand and a cowboy hat in the other.

"I would have fed Becky if I'd had any idea it was going to be this late," Tracy said. "She's starved."

"That's easy to remedy," Kim said. "I mean, we are planning on going out to dinner."

"I wish you would have at least called," Tracy said.

"I was in surgery and didn't get out until five-thirty," Kim said. "It's not like I was out golfing."

"I know," Tracy said with resignation. "It's all very noble. The problem is, you were the one who picked the time, not me. It's a matter of consideration. Every second I thought you were about to arrive. Luckily we're not flying commercial."

"Flying?" Kim questioned. "Where are you going?"

"Aspen," Tracy said. "I've given Becky the number where I can be reached."

"Aspen for two days?"

"I feel it's time for me to have a little fun in my life. Not that you would know what that is, apart from your surgery, of course."

"Well, as long as we're being nasty and sarcastic," Kim said, "thanks for sending Kelly Anderson to the surgical lounge. That was a pleasant surprise!"

"I didn't send her," Tracy said.

"She said you did."

"I just told her I thought you were in surgery," Tracy said.

"Well, it's the same thing," Kim said.

Over Kim's shoulder, Tracy saw her guest stand up. Sensing he was uncomfortable from undoubtedly overhearing her exchange with her former husband, Tracy motioned to Kim to follow her into the living room.

"Enough of this bickering," she said. "Kim, I'd like you to meet a friend of mine, Carl Stahl."

The two men shook hands and eyed each other warily.

"You two entertain yourselves," Tracy suggested. "I'll run upstairs and make sure Becky has everything she needs. Then we can all go our separate ways."

Kim watched Tracy disappear up the stairs. Then his gaze returned to Tracy's apparent boyfriend. It was an uncomfortable situation, and Kim couldn't help feel some jealousy, but at least Carl was several inches shorter, with significantly thinning hair. On the other hand, the man was tanned despite its being mid-winter. He also appeared in reasonable physical shape.

"Can I get you a drink?" Carl suggested, motioning toward a bottle of bourbon on a side table.

"Don't mind if I do," Kim said. Kim had never been much of a drinker, although over the last six months a nightly cocktail had become a habit.

Carl put down his cowboy hat and stepped over to the sideboard. Kim noticed he seemed to have a proprietary manner.

"I saw that interview Kelly Anderson did with you a month or so ago," Carl said as he shoveled several ice cubes into an old-fashioned glass.

"I'm sorry," Kim said. "I was hoping most people missed it."

Carl splashed a generous dollop of liquor over the ice and then handed the drink to Kim. He sat back down on the couch next to his cowboy hat. Kim lowered himself into a facing club chair.

"You have a right to be angry about it," Carl said condescendingly. "It wasn't fair. TV news has an irritating way of twisting things."

"Sad, but true," Kim agreed. He took a sip of the fiery fluid and inhaled before swallowing. He felt a comfortable warm feeling course through his body.

"I certainly didn't buy her premise," Carl said. "You guys earn every penny you get. I mean, I personally have a lot of respect for you doctors."

"Thank you," Kim said. "That's very reassuring."

"Seriously," Carl said. "In fact I was premed for a couple of semesters in college."

"Really? What happened? Didn't you like it?"

"It didn't like me," Carl said with a laugh that ended with a peculiar snorting sound. "It was a wee bit too demanding, and it began to cut into my social life." Carl laughed again as if he'd just told a joke.

Kim began to wonder what Tracy saw in the guy.

"What do you do?" Kim asked to make conversation. Besides, he was interested. Considering the lower-middle-class neighborhood, the yellow Lamborghini outside had to belong to Carl. Plus there was Tracy's comment about not flying commercial. That was even more worrisome.

"I'm CEO of Foodsmart," Carl said. "I'm sure you've heard of us."

"I can't say that I have," Kim said.

"It's a large agricultural business," Carl said. "Really more of a holding company. One of the largest in the state, actually."

"Wholesale or retail?" Kim asked, not that he knew much about business.

"Both," Carl said. "But mainly export wholesale involving grain and beef. But we're also the major stockholder in the Onion Ring burger chain."

"I've heard of them," Kim said. "I even own some stock."

"Good choice," Carl said. Then he leaned forward, and after furtively looking around as if he thought there were a chance of hidden eavesdroppers, he whispered: "Buy some more Onion Ring stock. The company's about to take the chain national. Consider it an insider tip. Just don't tell anyone where you heard it."

"Thanks," Kim said. Then he added sarcastically: "I've been wondering what to do with all my discretionary income."

"You'll be thanking me a thousandfold," Carl added, insensitive to Kim's tone of voice. "The stock is going to go through the roof. In a year's time the Onion Ring will be out there challenging McDonald's, Burger King, and Wendy's."

"Tracy mentioned you two are flying to Aspen on a private plane," Kim said, changing the subject. "What do you fly?"

"Me personally?" Carl questioned. "I don't fly. Hell, no! I'd be the last person to get into a plane with me behind the controls."

Carl laughed again with his peculiar style, making Kim wonder if the guy snored when he slept.

"I've a new Lear jet," Carl added. "Well, technically it's Foodsmart's, at least according to the IRS. Anyway, as you undoubtedly know, for such an aircraft the FAA mandates we have two highly qualified pilots."

"Of course," Kim said as if he were intimately aware of the rule. The last thing he wanted to do was reveal his ignorance of such things. Nor did he want to let on how angry it made him feel that a businessman who did nothing but shuffle paper could have such perks while he, who worked twelve hours a day on people's hearts, was having trouble keeping his decade-old Mercedes on the road.

A clatter of footfalls on the uncarpeted stairs heralded Becky's arrival. She had an overnight bag and her skates thrown over her shoulder. She dumped both onto a chair in the front hall before racing into the living room.

Kim hadn't seen Becky since the previous Sunday when they'd spent a happy day at a nearby ski area, and Becky acted accordingly. She made a beeline into Kim's arms and gave him an enthusiastic hug, momentarily making him lose his balance. With his face pressed up against her head, Kim could feel that her brunette hair was damp from a recent shower. The remnant odor of the shampoo made her smell like an apple orchard in bloom.

Without letting go of Kim, Becky leaned back and assumed a mock reproving expression. "You're late, Daddy."

Kim's aggravations of the day melted as he regarded his darling, precocious ten-year-old daughter who, in his mind, glowed with grace, youth, and energy. Her skin was flawless, her eyes large and expressive.

"I'm sorry, pumpkin," Kim said. "I understand you're hungry."

"I'm starved," Becky said. "But look!"

Becky turned her head from side to side. "See my new diamond earrings? Aren't they gorgeous? Carl gave them to me."

"Just chips," Carl said self-consciously. "Sort'a late Christmas present, and something for letting me borrow her mom for the weekend."

Kim swallowed. He was taken aback. "Very impressive," he managed.

Becky let go of Kim and went out into the foyer to gather her things and get her coat out of the front closet. Kim followed and went to the door.

"Now, I want you in bed at your normal time, young lady," Tracy said. "You understand? The flu's making the rounds."

"Oh, Mom!" Becky complained.

"I'm serious," Tracy said. "I don't want you missing school."

"Chill out, Mom," Becky said. "You have fun and don't be so nervous about . . ."

"I'll have a great time," Tracy said, interrupting her daughter before she could say something embarrassing. "But I'll have a better time if I don't have to worry about you. You have the phone number I gave you?"

"Yeah, yeah," Becky intoned. Then, brightening, she added: "Ski the Big Burn for me."

"Okay, I promise," Tracy said, as she took Becky's coat from her daughter's arms. "I want this on."

"But we'll be in the car," Becky complained.

"I don't care," Tracy said, helping her daughter into the coat.

Becky ran to Carl, who was standing in the doorway to the living room. She gave him a hug and got her mouth close to his ear. "She's real nervous, but she'll be okay. And thanks for the earrings. I love them."

"You're welcome, Becky," Carl said nonplussed.

Becky ran to Tracy and gave her a quick hug before dashing out the door held open by Kim.

Outside Becky ran down the stairs and waved to Kim to hurry up. Kim broke into a trot.

"Call if there's a problem," Tracy yelled from the porch.

Kim and Becky waved as they got into Kim's car.

"She's such a worrywart," Becky said, as Kim started the car. Then she pointed ahead, through the windshield. "That's a Lamborghini. It's Carl's car, and it's awesome."

"I'm sure it is," Kim said, trying not to sound as if he cared.

"You should get one, Dad," Becky said. She turned her head to look at the vehicle as they drove by.

"Let's talk about food," Kim said. "I was planning on picking up Ginger. I thought all three of us could go to Chez Jean."

"I don't want to eat with Ginger," Becky said poutingly.

Kim drummed his fingers on the steering wheel. The stress of the day at the hospital, even the meeting with Carl, had him on edge. He wished he'd had time to play some tennis. He needed some form of physical outlet. The last thing he wanted was a problem between Becky and Ginger.

"Becky," Kim began. "We've been through this before. Ginger likes your company."

"I just want to be with you, not your receptionist," Becky complained.

"But you will be with me," Kim said. "We'll all be together. And Ginger is more than my receptionist."

"I don't want to eat at that stuffy old restaurant either," Becky said with emotion. "I hate it."

"Okay, okay," Kim said, struggling to control himself. "How about we go to the Onion Ring on Prairie Highway. Just you and me. It's just up the road."

"Fabulous!" Becky perked up, and despite her seat belt, she managed to lean over and give Kim a peck on the cheek.

Kim marveled at how adroitly his daughter could manipulate him. He felt better now that she had reverted to her normal, vivacious self, but after a few miles Becky's comment began to gnaw at him again. "For the life of me," Kim said, "I don't understand why you have this thing against Ginger."

"Because she made you and Mom break up," Becky commented.

"Good gravy," Kim snapped. "Is that what your mother says?"

"No," Becky said. "She says it was only part of it. But I think it was Ginger's fault. You guys hardly ever argued until Ginger."

Kim went back to drumming his fingers on the steering wheel. Despite what Becky had said, he was certain Tracy had to have put the thought in her mind.

As he turned into the Onion Ring parking lot, Kim shot a glance in Becky's direction. Her face was awash in color from the huge Onion Ring sign. She was smiling in anticipation of their fast-food dinner.

"The reason your mother and I got divorced was very complicated," Kim began, "and Ginger had very little . . ."

"Look out!" Becky cried.

Kim redirected his gaze through the windshield and saw the blurry image of a preteen on a skateboard off the right front fender. Kim jammed on the brakes and threw the steering wheel over to the left. The car lurched to a stop but not before colliding with the rear of a parked car. There was the unmistakable sound of breaking glass.

"You smashed the car!" Becky shouted as if it were a question.

"I know I smashed the car!" Kim shouted back.

"Well, it's not my fault," Becky said indignantly. "Don't yell at me!"

The skateboarder, who'd momentarily stopped, now passed in front of the car. Kim looked at the child, and the boy irreverently mouthed: "Asshole." Kim closed his eyes for a moment to control himself.

"I'm sorry," he said to Becky. "Of course it wasn't your fault. I should have been paying more attention. And I certainly shouldn't have yelled at you."

"What are we going to do?" Becky said. Her eyes anxiously scanned the parking area. She was terrified lest she see one of her schoolmates.

"I'm going to see what happened," Kim said as he opened his door and got out. He was back in seconds and asked Becky to hand him the registration packet from the glove compartment.

"What broke?" Becky asked as she handed over the papers.

"Our headlight and their tail light," Kim said. "I'll leave a note."

Once inside the restaurant, Becky immediately forgot the mishap. It being Friday night, the Onion Ring was mobbed. Most of the crowd were young teenagers in a ridiculous collection of oversized clothing and punk hairstyles. But there were also a number of families with lots of small children and even infants. The noise level was considerable thanks to fussy babies and competing ghetto blasters.

The Onion Ring restaurants were particularly popular with children mainly because the kids could doctor their own "gourmet" burgers with a bewildering display of condiments. They could also make their own sundaes with an equivalent number of toppings.

"Isn't this an awesome place?" Becky commented as she and Kim got into one of the order lines.

"Just delightful," Kim teased. "Especially with the quiet classical music in the background."

"Oh, Dad!" Becky moaned and rolled her eyes.

"Did you ever come here with Carl?" Kim asked. He really didn't want to hear the answer because he had an inkling she had.

"Sure," Becky offered. "He took Mom and me here a couple of times. It was cool. He owns the place."

"Not quite," Kim said with a certain satisfaction. "Actually the Onion Ring is a publicly owned company. Do you know what that means?"

"Sort of," Becky said.

"It means a lot of people own stock," Kim said. "Even I own stock, so I'm one of the owners too."

"Yeah, well, when I was here with Carl we didn't have to stand in line," Becky said.

Kim took a deep breath and let it out. "Let's talk about something else. Have you thought any more about skating in the Nationals? I know the entry deadline is coming up."

"I'm not going to enter," Becky said without hesitation.

"Really?" Kim questioned. "Why not, dear? You are such a natural. And you won the state junior championship last year so easily."

"I like skating," Becky said. "I don't want to ruin it."

"But you could be the best."

"I don't want to be the best in competition," Becky said.

"Gosh, Becky," Kim said. "I can't help but be a little disappointed. I'd be so proud of you."

"Mom said you would say something like that," Becky said.

"Oh, great!" Kim exclaimed. "Your know-it-all therapist mother."

"She also said that I should do what I think is best for me."

Kim and Becky found themselves at the front of the line. A bored teenage cashier gazed at them with glassy eyes and asked them what they wanted.

Becky looked up at the menu mounted over the bank of cash registers. She screwed up her mouth and stuck a finger in her cheek. "Hmmm . . . I don't know what I want."

"Have a burger," Kim said. "I thought that was your favorite."

"Okay," Becky said. "I'll have a burger, fries, and a vanilla shake."

"Regular or jumbo?" the cashier asked in a tired voice.

"Regular," Becky said.

"And you, sir?" the cashier asked.

"Oh, hell, let me see," Kim said. He too looked up at the menu. "Soup du jour and salad, I guess. And an iced tea."

"Comes to seven ninety," the cashier said.

Kim paid, and the cashier handed him a receipt. "Your number is twenty-seven."

Kim and Becky turned around and left the order area. It took some hunting, but they found a couple of empty seats at one of the picnic-style tables near the window. Becky squeezed in, but not Kim. He handed her the receipt and told her he had to use the men's room. Becky nodded absently; she had her eye on one of the cute boys from her school who happened to be sitting at the next table.

It was like a broken-field run for Kim to make his way across the restaurant to the anteroom leading to the restrooms. There were two phones, but both were tied up by teenage girls. Behind each was a line. Kim reached into his jacket pocket and extracted his cell phone. He punched in the numbers, leaned back against the wall, and held it to his ear.

"Ginger, it's me," Kim said.

"Where the devil are you?" Ginger complained. "Have you forgotten our reservations at Chez Jean were for seven-thirty?"

"We're not going," Kim said. "I've had to change the plans. Becky and I are grabbing a bite at the Onion Ring on Prairie Highway."

Ginger didn't respond.

"Hello?" Kim said. "Are you still there?"

"Yeah, I'm still here," Ginger said.

"Did you hear what I said?"

"Of course I heard," Ginger said. "I haven't eaten, and I've been waiting. You haven't called, and besides, you promised me we'd eat at Chez Jean tonight."

"Listen," Kim growled. "Don't you give me a hard time too. I can't please everybody. I was late picking up Becky, and she was starved."

"That's nice," Ginger said. "You and your daughter have a nice dinner together."

"You're irritating me, Ginger!"

"Well, how do you expect me to feel?" Ginger asked. "For a year your wife was your convenient excuse. Now I suppose it's going to be your daughter."

"That's enough, Ginger," Kim snapped. "I'm not going to get into an argument. Becky and I are eating here, and then we'll come by and pick you up."

"Maybe I'll be here and maybe I won't," Ginger said. "I'm getting tired of being taken for granted."

"Fine," Kim said. "You decide."

Kim cut off the connection and jammed the phone back into his jacket pocket. He gritted his teeth and cursed under his breath. The evening was hardly progressing as he would have liked. Kim's eyes involuntarily strayed to the face of a teenage girl waiting for one of the wall phones. Her lipstick was such a dark red it bordered on brown. It made her look like someone who'd succumbed to the elements on the north face of Mount Everest.

The girl caught Kim staring at her. She interrupted her cowlike gum-chewing long enough to stick out her tongue. Kim pushed off the wall and went into the men's room to splash water on his face and wash his hands.

The level of activity in the kitchen and service area of the Onion Ring was commensurate with the number of customers in the restaurant proper. It was controlled pandemonium. Roger Polo, the manager who regularly worked a double shift on Fridays and Saturdays, the Onion Ring's two busiest days, was a nervous man in his late thirties who drove himself and his staff hard.

When the restaurant was as busy as it was while Kim and Becky awaited their order, Roger worked the line. He was the one who gave the burger and fries order to the short-order chef, Paul; or the soup and salad orders to the steam-table and salad-bar worker, Julia; or the drink orders to Claudia. All the restocking and the routine, on-going cleanup was done by the "gofer," Skip.

"Number twenty-seven coming up," Roger barked. "I want a soup and salad."

"Soup and salad," Julia echoed.

"Iced tea and vanilla shake," Roger called out.

"Coming up," Claudia said.

"Regular burger and medium fries," Roger ordered.

"Got it," Paul said.

Paul was considerably older than Roger. His face was leathered and deeply creased; he looked more like a farmer than a cook. He had spent twenty years as a short-order chef on an oil rig in the Gulf. On his right forearm was a tattoo of a gusher with the word: *Eureka!*

Paul stood at the grill built into a central island behind the row of cash registers. At any given time, he had a number of hamburger patties on the cooktop; each one was in response to an order. He organized the cooking by rotation so that all the burgers got the same amount of grill time. In response to the most recent wave of orders, Paul turned around and opened the chest-high refrigerator directly behind him.

"Skip!" Paul yelled when he realized the patty box was empty. "Get me a box of burgers from the walk-in."

Skip put his mop aside. "Coming up!"

The walk-in freezer was at the very back of the kitchen, next to the walk-in refrigerator and across from the storeroom. Skip, who'd only been working at the Onion Ring for a week, had found that a significant portion of his job was to carry various supplies from storage to the preparation area.

He opened the heavy freezer door and stepped within. The door was mounted with a heavy spring and closed behind him. The interior was about ten feet by twenty feet and illuminated by a single light bulb in a wire cage. The walls were surfaced in a metallic material that looked like aluminum foil. The floor was a wooden grate.

The space was almost full of cardboard containers except for a central aisle. To the left were the large cartons full of frozen hamburger patties. To the right were the boxes of frozen french fries, fish fillets, and chicken chunks.

Skip flapped his arms against the subzero chill. His breath came in frosted clouds. Wishing to get back to the warmth of the kitchen, he scraped away the frost from the label of the first carton to his left to make sure it was ground meat. It read: MERCER MEATS. REG. 0.1 LB HAMBURGER PATTIES, EXTRA LEAN. LOT 6 BATCH 9-14. PRODUCTION: JAN 12; USE BY APR. 12.

Reassured, Skip tore open the carton and lifted out one of the inner boxes that contained fifteen dozen patties. He carried them back to the refrigerator behind Paul and put them in.

"You're back in business," Skip said.

Paul didn't respond. He was too busy setting up the cooked burgers, while his mind kept a running account of the new orders Roger had given him. As soon as he could, he turned to the refrigerator, opened the patty box and extracted the number of burgers he needed. But as he was about to close the door, his eye caught the label.

"Skip!" Paul yelled. "Get your ass back here!"

"What's wrong?" Skip questioned. He'd not left the area, but had bent down to change the trash bag under the central island's rubbish disposal opening.

"You brought the wrong goddamn patties," Paul said. "These just came in today."

"What difference does it make?" Skip asked.

"Plenty," Paul said. "I'll show you in a second." He then called: "Roger, how many burgers you looking for after order twenty-six?"

Roger checked his tickets. "I need one burger for twenty-seven, four for twenty-eight, and three for twenty-nine. That's eight total."

"That's what I thought," Paul said. He tossed the eight patties he had in his hand onto the grill and turned around to get the box of patties out of the refrigerator. As preoccupied as he was, he didn't notice that the first patty he threw ended up partially covering another patty that was already on the grill.

Paul motioned for Skip to follow him and spoke while he walked. "We get shipments of frozen hamburger once every couple of weeks," he explained. "But we have to use the older ones first."

Paul opened the door to the walk-in freezer and was immediately confronted by the carton Skip had opened. Paul wedged the box he was carrying back into the carton and closed the lid.

"See this date?" Paul asked while pointing to the label.

"Yeah, I see it," Skip said.

"Those other cartons back there have an older date," Paul said. "They have to be used first."

"Somebody should have told me," Skip complained.

"I'm telling you now," Paul said. "Come on, help me move these new ones to the back and the ones in the back to the front."

○   ○   ○

Kim had returned from the restroom and had managed to squeeze his six-foot-plus frame into the seat next to Becky. There were six other individuals at the same table, including a two-year-old whose face was smeared with ketchup. He was busy beating his half-eaten hamburger with a plastic soupspoon.

"Becky, please be reasonable," Kim said while trying to ignore the two-year-old. "I told Ginger that we'd pick her up after we finished eating."

Becky took a breath and exhaled, slumping her shoulders. She was sulking, which was uncharacteristic for her.

"I mean, we've done what you wanted," Kim said. "We're eating together, just you and me, and it's not at Chez Jean."

"Well, you didn't ask me if I wanted to pick up Ginger," Becky said. "When you said we were coming here, I thought you meant we didn't have to see her tonight at all."

Kim looked off and tightened his jaw muscles. He loved his daughter, but he knew she could be frustratingly willful. As a cardiac surgeon, he was accustomed to people on his team following his orders.

○    ○    ○

Paul returned from the rearranging in the walk-in freezer to face an exasperated Roger.

"Where have you been?" Roger demanded. "We're way behind."

"Don't worry," Paul said. "Everything is under control."

Paul picked up his spatula and began slipping the fully cooked burgers into their respective buns. The patty that had been leaning up against another was pushed aside so that the one beneath could be removed.

"Ordering thirty," Roger barked. "Two regular burgers and one jumbo."

"Coming up," Paul said. He reached behind into the refrigerator to get the meat. Turning back around he tossed them onto the grill. He then used his spatula to pick up the patty that had been draped over another. Flipping it back onto the grill, it again landed so that it was leaning on another and not flat against the cooktop. Paul was about to adjust it when Roger got his attention.

"Paul, you screwed up!" Roger snapped. "What's wrong with you tonight?"

Paul looked up with his spatula suspended over the grill.

"Number twenty-five is supposed to be two jumbos not two regulars," Roger complained.

"Shit, sorry!" Paul said. He turned back to the refrigerator to get two jumbo patties. After he tossed them onto the grill he used his spatula to press them down. Jumbos needed twice the cook-time of the regular burgers.

"And number twenty-five was supposed to have a medium fries," Roger said irritably. He waved the ticket as if he were threatening Paul with it.

"You got it," Paul said. He quickly filled a paper cone with the potatoes.

Roger took the fries and put them on the number twenty-five tray and shoved it over to what was called the distribution counter. "Okay," Roger said to Paul. "Number twenty-seven's ready to go. Where's the burger and fries? Come on Paul, let's get on the ball."

"All right, already," Paul said. Paul used his spatula to scoop up the patty that had spent most of its grill-time on top of two other patties. He slipped it into a bun and placed it on the paper plate Roger had put on the countertop in front of him. Paul shoveled on some grilled onions, then filled another paper cone with french fries.

Within seconds the teenager on the distribution counter leaned over his goosenecked microphone and said: "Pick up, number twenty-five and number twenty-seven."

○   ○   ○

Kim stood up. "That's us," he said. "I'll get the food. But after we eat, we're going to pick up Ginger, and that's final. And I'm going to expect you to be pleasant. Okay?"

"Oh, all right," Becky said reluctantly. She stood up.

"I'll get the food," Kim said. "You stay put."

"But I want to fix my own burger," Becky said.

"Oh, yeah," Kim said. "I forgot."

While Becky dressed her burger with an impressive layer of various toppings, Kim picked out what he hoped would be the least offensive salad dressing. Then father and daughter returned to their seats. Kim was happy to see the ketchup-besmeared toddler had departed.

Becky perked up considerably when the boy from her school asked for some of her french fries. Kim picked up his soupspoon and was about to sample the soup when his cell phone rang against his chest. He took the phone out and put it to his ear.

"Dr. Reggis here," he said.

"This is Nancy Warren," the nurse said. "I'm calling because Mrs. Arnold demands that you come in to see her husband."

"What about?" Kim asked.

Becky used both hands to pick up her burger. Even so, a couple of sliced pickles fell out from beneath the layers of bread. Undaunted, she got her mouth around the behemoth and took a bite. She chewed for a moment, then examined the bitten surface.

"Mr. Arnold is very anxious," Nancy said. "And he says his pain medication isn't holding. He's also had a couple of PVC's."

Becky reached out and tugged on Kim's arm, trying to get him to look at the bitten surface of her burger. Kim motioned for her to wait while he continued his cellular phone conversation: "Has he had a lot of PVC's?"

"No, not a lot," Nancy said. "But enough so that he's aware of them."

"Draw a potassium and double-up on his pain meds. Is the intensivist there?"

"Yes, Dr. Silber is in the hospital," Nancy said. "But I think you should come in. Mrs. Arnold is insistent."

"I'll bet she is," Kim said with a dismissive chuckle. "But let's wait for the potassium level first. Also check and make sure there isn't any marked abdominal distension."

Kim disconnected his call. Mrs. Arnold was turning into a bigger pain in the neck than he'd imagined.

"Look at my hamburger," Becky said.

Kim glanced at Becky's burger and saw the ribbon of pink in the middle of the meat patty, but he was preoccupied and none too happy about the call he'd just gotten from the hospital. "Hmmm," he said. "That's the way I used to eat my hamburgers when I was your age."

"Really?" Becky questioned. "That's gross!"

Deciding it was best he speak directly to the intensivist himself, Kim dialed the hospital page number. "That was the only way I ate my hamburgers," he said to Becky as the call went through. "Medium rare, with a slice of raw onion, not with those reconstituted grilled onions, and certainly not with all that slop."

The hospital page operator answered, and Kim asked for Dr. Alice Silber. He said he'd hang on.

Becky looked at her burger, shrugged her shoulders, and then took another, more tentative bite. She had to admit, it tasted fine.

# CHAPTER 4

Kim's car rounded the bend in his street and approached his house. It was a large Tudor-style home sited on a generous wooded lot in a comfortable suburban township. At one time it had been an admirable house. Now it looked neglected. The previous fall none of the leaves had been raked up, and they now covered the lawn area with a layer of wet, dirty brown debris. Most of the house's trim was badly peeling and sorely in need of paint, and some of the window shutters were awry. On the roof a few of the slate shingles had slipped out and were angled into the gutters.

It was nine o'clock on an overcast, wintery Saturday morning; the neighborhood seemed deserted. There was no sign of life as Kim turned into his drive and pulled up to the garage door. Even the next-door neighbor's morning paper had yet to be retrieved from the front walk.

The interior of Kim's house reflected the exterior. It had been mostly stripped of rugs, accessories, and furniture since Tracy had taken what she wanted when she moved out. In addition, the house hadn't been cleaned in months. The living room in particular had a dance-hall feel, with only one chair, a tiny scatter rug, a side table with a telephone on it, and a single floor lamp.

Kim tossed his keys onto a built-in console table in the foyer before passing through the dining room into the kitchen/family room combination. He called out Becky's name, but she didn't answer. Kim glanced into the sink. There were no soiled dishes.

Having awakened a little after five that morning, which was his custom, Kim had gotten up and gone to the hospital to make his rounds. By the time he got home he'd expected Becky to be up and ready to go.

"Becky, you lazy bum, where are you?" Kim called out while mounting the stairs. As he crested the top he heard Becky's bedroom door open. A moment later Becky was standing in the doorway, still dressed in her flannel nightgown. Her hair was a dark mop of tangled curls, and her eyes were heavy-lidded.

"What's going on?" Kim asked. "I thought you'd be raring to get to your skating lesson. Let's move it."

"I don't feel so good," Becky said. She rubbed her eye with her knuckle.

"Oh?" Kim remarked. "How come? What's wrong?"

"I have a stomachache."

"Well, it's nothing, I'm sure," Kim said. "Does the pain come and go or is it steady?"

"It comes and goes," Becky said.

"Where exactly do you feel it?" Kim asked.

Becky made some vague movements with her hand around her abdomen.

"Any chills?" Kim asked. He reached out and put his hand on Becky's forehead.

Becky shook her head.

"Ah, nothing but a few cramps," Kim said. "It's probably your poor stomach complaining about last night's junk food. You shower up and get dressed while I see to some breakfast for you. But snap it up; I don't want your mother complaining to me about you being late for your skating."

"I'm not hungry," Becky said.

"I'm sure you will be after your shower," Kim said. "I'll see you downstairs."

Back in the kitchen Kim got out cereal, milk, and juice. Returning to the base of the stairs, he was about to call out to Becky when he could hear the unmistakable sound of the shower. Returning to the kitchen, he used the wall phone to call Ginger.

"Everybody's okay at the hospital," Kim said as soon as Ginger answered. "All three post-ops are sailing along fine, although the Arnolds, particularly Gertrude Arnold, are driving me bananas."

"I'm glad," Ginger said tartly.

"What's wrong now?" Kim asked. He'd had another minor run-in with one of the nurses on rounds that morning and was looking forward to a stress-free day.

"I wanted to stay over last night," Ginger said. "I don't think it is fair . . ."

"Stop right there!" Kim snapped. "Let's not get into this again, would you please. I'm tired of this nonsense. Besides, Becky is a little under the weather this morning."

"What's the matter with her?" Ginger asked. Her concern was genuine.

"Nothing much, just a stomachache," Kim said. He was about to elaborate when he heard Becky coming down the stairs. "Uh-oh," he intoned. "Here she comes. Listen, meet us at the rink at the mall. Bye!"

As Becky came into the room, Kim hung up the phone. She was dressed in Kim's bathrobe, which was so big it dragged on the floor and the arms came down to midcalf.

"There's cereal, milk, and juice on the table," Kim said. "Feel any better?"

Becky shook her head.

"What do you want to eat?"

"Nothing," Becky said.

"Well, you have to have something," Kim said. "How about a shot of Pepto-Bismol?"

Becky screwed up her face into an expression of pure disgust. "I'll have a little juice," she suggested.

The stores in the mall were just beginning to lift their shutters to start the day as Kim and Becky made their way along the corridor toward the skating rink. Kim hadn't asked again, but he was certain Becky was feeling better. She'd ended up eating some cereal after all, and in the car she'd been her usual, talkative self.

"Are you going to stay while I have my lesson?" Becky asked.

"That's the plan," Kim said. "I'm looking forward to seeing that triple axel you've been telling me about."

As they approached the rink, Kim handed Becky her skates that he'd been carrying. A whistle sounded, indicating the end of the preceding intermediate class.

"Perfect timing," Kim said.

Becky sat down and started to unlace her sneakers. Kim glanced around at the other parents, mostly mothers. Suddenly he found himself locking eyes with Kelly Anderson. Despite the early-morning hour she was dressed as if she were about to go to a fashion show, and her hair looked as if she'd just emerged from a beauty salon. She smiled. Kim looked away.

A young girl about Becky's age skated over and exited the rink. She sat down next to Becky and said "hi." Becky returned the greeting.

"Ah, my favorite cardiac surgeon!"

Kim turned, and to his distaste he found himself face-to-face with Kelly.

"Have you met my daughter?" Kelly asked.

Kim shook his head.

"Caroline, say hello to Dr. Reggis," Kelly said.

Despite his reluctance to get into a conversation with Kelly, Kim greeted the young girl and introduced Becky to Kelly.

"What a delightful coincidence running into you again," Kelly said to Kim as she straightened up from shaking hands with Becky. "Did you see my segment last night on the eleven o'clock news about the hospital merger anniversary?"

"Can't say that I did," Kim responded.

"Shucks," Kelly said. "You would have enjoyed it. You got some good airtime, and the consensus is that your 'bottom line' quote stole the show. It lit up the phone lines, which the station manager loves."

"Remind me not to talk to you again," Kim said.

"Careful, Dr. Reggis," Kelly said happily. "You'll hurt my feelings."

"Kim!" a voice called from the other side of the rink. "Kim, over here!"

Ginger had arrived and was enthusiastically waving as she started around the end of the rink on her way toward Kim and Kelly. She was in her early twenties, with pixie-like features, flowing blond hair, and spidery legs. When she wasn't at the office, she made it a point to dress in her interpretation of a casual, sexy manner. That morning she had on a tight pair of jeans, a cutoff top that exposed her narrow, firm midriff, and a workout headband and wristbands as evidence of her fondness for aerobics. On her feet were cross-trainer shoes. She wasn't wearing a coat.

"Oh, my!" Kelly whispered while watching Ginger approach. "What do we have here? I'm smelling tabloid material: the renowned cardiac surgeon and the aerobics instructor."

"She's my receptionist," Kim said in an attempt to downplay the imminent confrontation.

"I wouldn't doubt that for a minute," Kelly said. "But look at that body. And look at that girlish enthusiasm. I get the feeling she thinks you are the living end."

"I'm telling you she works for me," Kim snapped.

"Hey, I believe you," Kelly said. "And that's what interests me. Even my internist and ophthalmologist divorced their wives to marry their receptionists. I'm smelling a story here. What is this, the typical male medical midlife crisis scenario?"

"I want you to stay away from her," Kim growled.

"Oh, come on, Dr. Reggis," Kelly said. "You cardiac surgeons think of yourselves as celebrities. This is the kind of thing that comes with the turf, especially if you date people half your age."

Becky leaned over to Caroline and whispered: "I'll see ya. Here comes my father's dorky girlfriend." Becky stood up, entered the rink, and quickly skated off.

Ginger came straight to Kim, and before he knew what she intended, she managed to plant a forceful kiss on his cheek. "Sorry, darling," she said. "I know I was out of sorts on the phone this morning. I was just missing you."

"Hmmm! Not very businesslike," Kelly remarked. "Lipstick evidence."

Kim used the back of his hand to wipe his cheek.

"Uh-oh!" Ginger commented when she saw the red imprint of her lips on Kim's skin. "Let me get it off."

Ginger licked two of her fingers, and before Kim could react again, she smeared the lipstick.

"This is perfect," Kelly commented.

Ginger turned to Kelly and immediately recognized her as a local celebrity. "Kelly Anderson!" she gushed. "What a treat. I adore you on the news."

"Why, thank you," Kelly said. "And you are . . ."

"Ginger Powers."

"Nice to meet you, Ginger," Kelly said. "Let me give you one of my cards. Perhaps we could get together."

"Why, thank you," Ginger said. She took the card and smiled with true glee. "I'd love to get together."

"Good," Kelly said. "I do a number of health-related stories, and I'm always looking for the opinions of those in the business."

"You'd want to interview me?" Ginger questioned. She was surprised and flattered.

"Why not?" Kelly said.

Ginger pointed to Kim. "He's the one you should interview, not me. He knows everything about medicine."

"Sounds like you have a high opinion of the good doctor," Kelly said. "Would that be safe to say?"

"As if there's a question," Ginger said with fake indignation. "He's the best cardiac surgeon in the world. And he's the best-looking too." Ginger tried to tweak Kim's cheek, but this time he evaded her.

"With that, I think I'll take my leave," Kelly said. "Come on, Caroline. Let's get your coat on and get the show on the road. And Ginger, give me a call! I'm serious about talking to you. And Kim, I can certainly understand why you have Ginger for your receptionist and companion."

Kelly and Caroline walked away, with Kelly carrying her daughter's skates and backpack. Caroline was having trouble getting into her long, down-filled coat.

"She's really nice," Ginger said, watching Kelly's figure recede.

"She's a shark," Kim said. "And I don't want you talking with her."

"Why not?" Ginger said.

"She's given me nothing but grief," Kim said.

"But it would be fun," Ginger whined.

"Listen," Kim spat. "You talk to her and you're out of a job and my life. Understand?"

"All right!" Ginger snapped back. "Gosh, what a grouch. What's wrong with you?"

Becky, who'd been doing some warm-up exercises, skated over to where Kim and Ginger were standing.

"I can't take a lesson," Becky said. She stepped off the ice, sat down, and began quickly removing her skates.

"Why not?" Kim asked.

"My stomach is worse," Becky said. "And I have to use the bathroom, bad!"

# CHAPTER 5

Kim lifted out Harvey Arnold's hospital chart and cracked it open. It was before eight in the morning and the day-shift nursing crew was busy having its report. Consequently Kim had the nurses' station to himself save for the ward clerk.

He turned to the nurses' notes to read what had transpired during the previous day and during the night. He suppressed a smile. It was apparent from some of the entries that Mrs. Arnold was bothering the nursing staff as much as she bothered him. It was also apparent Mr. Arnold was doing fine. This impression was confirmed by the grafts of his vital signs, the input and output sheet, and the previous day's laboratory values. Satisfied, Kim slipped the loose-leaf chart back into its slot and walked down to his patient's room.

Mr. Arnold was sitting up in his bed, eating his breakfast and watching TV. Kim silently marveled at the progress cardiac surgery had made over the last couple of decades as evidenced by this individual. Here was a seventy-year-old man who less than forty-eight hours previously had been gravely ill and had had open-heart surgery. His heart had literally been stopped, opened, and repaired, and yet he was already relatively happy, mostly pain-free, and enjoying a significant improvement in the quality of his life. Kim couldn't help but feel a keen disappointment that such a miracle was being devalued in the current economic environment.

"How are you feeling, Mr. Arnold?" Kim asked.

53

"Pretty good," Mr. Arnold said. He wiped his chin with his napkin. When he was by himself, Mr. Arnold was a pleasant gentleman. It was when the husband and wife were together that the sparks began to fly.

Kim interrupted his patient's breakfast long enough to check on the dressing and the amount of drainage. Everything was progressing on schedule.

"Are you sure I'll be able to play golf?" Mr. Arnold asked.

"Absolutely," Kim said. "You'll be able to do whatever you want."

After a few more minutes of banter, Kim took his leave. Unfortunately he ran into Gertrude Arnold on her way in.

"There you are, doctor," Mrs. Arnold said. "I'm glad I caught you. I want a private-duty nurse in here around the clock, you hear?"

"What's the problem?" Kim asked.

"The problem?" Mrs. Arnold echoed. "I'll tell you what the problem is. The nurses on this floor are never available. Sometimes hours go by before we see one. And when Harvey rings his call button they take their sweet time."

"I imagine that's because they believe Mr. Arnold is doing well," Kim explained. "And that they are devoting their time to patients who are not doing quite so well."

"Now, don't you start making excuses for them," Mrs. Arnold said. "I want a nurse in here all the time."

"I'll have someone come to talk to you about it," Kim said.

Momentarily mollified, Mrs. Arnold nodded. "Don't make me wait too long."

"I'll see what I can do," Kim said.

Back at the nurses' station Kim told the ward clerk to page the Ameri-Care administrator and have him come up to talk to Mrs. Arnold. Kim couldn't help smiling as he waited for the elevator. He would have loved to hear the conversation that would ensue. The idea of causing the Ameri-Care administrators a little grief was enormously entertaining.

The elevator arrived and Kim squeezed on. It was remarkably crowded for a Sunday morning. Kim found himself pressed up against a tall, bony resident dressed in the typical "whites" and whose name tag read: JOHN MARKHAM, M.D., PEDIATRICS.

"Excuse me," Kim said. "Are there any enteric viruses making the rounds these days in school-age kids?"

"Not that I'm aware of," John said. "We've been seeing a pretty nasty strain of the flu, but it's all respiratory. Why do you ask?"

"My daughter's got a GI upset," Kim said.

"What are the symptoms?" John asked.

"It started with cramps yesterday morning," Kim said. "Then diarrhea. I've treated her with some over-the-counter antidiarrheal agents."

"Has it helped?" John asked.

"I thought so at first," Kim said. "But then last night the symptoms returned."

"Any nausea and vomiting?"

"Some mild nausea but no vomiting. At least not yet, but she hasn't had much appetite either."

"Fever?"

"Nope, none at all."

"Who's her pediatrician?"

"It was George Turner. After the merger, he was forced to leave town."

"I remember Dr. Turner," John said. "I rotated over to the Samaritan. He was a good man."

"For sure," Kim said. "He's now back in Boston at Children's Hospital."

"Our loss," John said. "Anyway, about your daughter. It would be my guess she's got a touch of food poisoning and not a virus."

"Really?" Kim questioned. "I thought food poisoning generally came on like gangbusters. You know, like the proverbial staph in the picnic potato salad."

"Not necessarily," John said. "Food poisoning can be present in countless ways. But whatever the symptom complex, if your daughter has had acute onset diarrhea, chances are it's food poisoning. Statistically it's the most likely cause. To give you an idea of its prevalence, the CDC estimates there are two to three hundred million cases a year."

The elevator stopped and John disembarked.

"I hope your daughter feels better," John said as the doors closed.

Kim shook his head. He turned to another resident. "Did you hear that? Two to three hundred million cases of food poisoning every year! That's crazy!"

"That would mean that just about everyone in the entire country gets it each year," the resident said.

"That can't be true," a nurse getting off duty said.

"I think it is," another resident said. "Most people take the symptoms in stride and attribute it to the 'stomach flu.' Of course, there isn't any such thing as the stomach flu."

"It seems astounding," Kim said. "It makes you think twice about eating out."

"People get food poisoning in their own homes just as easily," a woman from the back of the elevator said. "It comes from leftovers to a large degree, although inappropriate handling of raw chicken is another major source."

Kim nodded. He had the uncomfortable feeling that everyone else on the elevator knew more about the issue than he did.

When the elevator reached the ground floor, Kim got off and left the hospital. As he drove home, he couldn't help but ponder about food poisoning. He continued to marvel at the shocking idea of there being two to three hundred million cases a year in the United States. If such a statistic were true, it seemed incredible that he'd not come across it in any of his medical reading.

Kim was still mulling all this over as he came through his front door and tossed his keys on the console table in the foyer. He thought he'd get on the Internet and see if he could substantiate the food-poisoning statistic, when he heard the sound of the TV coming from the kitchen. He walked in.

Ginger was at the kitchen counter, struggling with the wall-mounted can opener. She was dressed in a spandex workout suit that left little to the imagination. Both Saturdays and Sundays she did aerobics religiously. Becky was sprawled on the couch in the family room, watching cartoons.

She had a blanket drawn up around her neck. She looked slightly pale against the dark green wool.

They'd spent the previous evening at home because of Becky's condition. Ginger had made a chicken dinner, of which Becky had eaten very little. After Becky had gone to bed early, Ginger had stayed over. Kim hoped they'd gotten along okay while he was at the hospital. He'd expected them still to be in bed by the time he got back from rounds.

"Hello, everybody," Kim called out. "I'm home."

Neither Becky nor Ginger responded.

"Damn!" Ginger exclaimed. "This thing is a piece of trash."

"What's the trouble?" Kim asked as he stepped over to Ginger. Ginger had abandoned her efforts with the can opener and had her hands on her hips. She looked exasperated.

"I can't get this can open," she said petulantly.

"I'll do it," Kim said. He picked up the can, but before putting it under the opener, he looked at the label. "What is this?" he questioned.

"It's chicken broth just like it says," Ginger replied.

"What are you doing with chicken broth at nine o'clock in the morning?" Kim questioned.

"It's for Becky," Ginger said. "My mother always gave me chicken broth when I had the runs."

"I told her I wasn't hungry," Becky called from the couch.

"My mother knew what she was doing," Ginger said.

Kim put the can of broth back on the counter and walked around the central island and into the family room. When he got to the couch, he put his hand on Becky's forehead. Becky moved her head to try to keep the TV in view.

"Feeling any better?" Kim asked. She felt warm, but he thought it might have been because his hand was cold.

"About the same," Becky said. "And I don't want anything to eat. It makes my cramps worse."

"She's got to eat," Ginger said. "She didn't eat much dinner."

"If her body is telling her not to eat, she shouldn't eat," Kim said.

"But she threw up," Ginger added.

"Is that right, Becky?" Kim asked. Vomiting was a new symptom.

"Just a little," Becky admitted.

"Maybe she should be seen by a doctor," Ginger said.

"And what do you think I am?" Kim responded hotly.

"You know what I mean," Ginger said. "You're the best cardiac surgeon in the world, but you don't have much chance to deal with children's tummies."

"Why don't you go upstairs and get me a thermometer," Kim said to Ginger.

"Where would I find it?" Ginger asked agreeably.

"In the master bath," Kim said. "The top drawer on the right."

"How about your cramps?" Kim asked.

"I still get them," Becky admitted.

"Are they any worse?"

"About the same," Becky said. "They come and go."

"What about your diarrhea?" Kim asked.

"Do we have to talk about this?" Becky asked. "I mean, it's like embarrassing."

"Okay, Pumpkin," Kim said. "I'm sure you'll be feeling your old self again in a few hours. But what about eating?"

"I'm not hungry," Becky said.

"Okay," Kim said. "Just let me know when you want something."

It was dark by the time Kim turned into Tracy's street and pulled to the curb at the base of her lawn. He got out and went around to the passenger side to open Becky's door. Becky had herself wrapped up inside a blanket so that it formed a hood over the top of her head.

Kim helped his daughter out of the car and up the walkway to the front door. She'd spent the entire day on the family-room couch in front of the TV. Kim rang the bell and waited. Tracy opened it and started to say hello to her daughter. She stopped in midsentence and frowned.

"What's the blanket for?" she asked. Her eyes shot to Kim for an explanation and then back to Becky. "Come in!"

Becky stepped inside. Kim followed. Tracy closed the door.

"What's going on?" Tracy asked. She turned back the edge of the blanket from Becky's face. "You're pale. Are you sick?"

Single tears formed in the corners of Becky's eyes. Tracy saw them and immediately enveloped her daughter in a protective hug. As she did so, she locked eyes with Kim.

"She's feeling a little punk," Kim admitted defensively.

Tracy pushed Becky out to arm's length so she could again look at her face. Becky wiped her eyes. "You're very pale," Tracy said. "What's the matter?"

"It's just a minor GI upset," Kim interjected. "Probably just a touch of food poisoning. At least that was the opinion of a pediatric resident I spoke with."

"If it's so minor, why is she so pale?" Tracy questioned. Tracy put her hand to Becky's forehead.

"She doesn't have a fever," Kim said. "Just some cramps and diarrhea."

"Have you given her anything?" Tracy asked.

"Sure," Kim said. "She's had Pepto-Bismol, and when that didn't seem to do the trick, I gave her some Imodium."

"Did it help?" Tracy asked.

"Some," Kim said.

"I have to go to the bathroom," Becky said.

"Okay, dear," Tracy said. "You go on upstairs. I'll be up in a minute."

Becky hoisted the edge of her blanket and hurried up the stairs.

Tracy turned to Kim. Her face was flushed. "My God, Kim! You've only had her for less than forty-eight hours and she's sick. What did you do with her?"

"Nothing out of the ordinary," Kim said.

"I should have known better than to leave town," Tracy snapped.

"Oh, come off it," Kim said, becoming angry himself. "Becky could have gotten sick whether you left town or not. In fact if she's got a virus, she could easily have contracted it before the weekend when you were here."

"I thought you said it was food poisoning," Tracy said.

"That was just a statistical guess by a pediatric resident," Kim said.

"Did Ginger make food this weekend?" Tracy asked.

"As a matter of fact she did," Kim said. "She made a wonderful chicken dinner last night."

"Chicken!" Tracy exclaimed. "I could have guessed. That must have been it."

"So you're already blaming Ginger," Kim said mockingly. "You really dislike her, don't you?"

"No, I don't dislike her," Tracy said. "Not anymore. At this point, I'm indifferent to her. But the fact of the matter is, she's young and undoubtedly hasn't had much experience in the kitchen. Those of us who have, know that you have to be very careful with chicken."

"You think you know everything," Kim said. "Well, for your information Becky hardly touched the chicken. Besides, she'd been feeling punk since Saturday morning. That means that if she's got a touch of food poisoning, then she got it from the Onion Ring out on Prairie Highway, the place that your new boyfriend bragged to Becky that he owned."

Tracy reached around Kim and opened the door. "Goodnight, Kim!" she said sharply.

"There's something else I'd like to say," Kim spat. "I resent you implying to Becky that I'm some kind of ogre for encouraging her to compete in the Nationals."

"I never made a value judgment about your wishes for our daughter," Tracy said. "When Becky informed me of her reluctance to face that kind of competition, I supported her. I also told her that you might try to change her mind. That was all I said."

Kim stared daggers at his former wife. The air of psychological superiority she assumed whenever they argued enraged him, especially in this instance when she felt she had to warn their daughter about what he might say to her.

"Goodnight, Kim!" Tracy repeated. She was still holding the door open.

Kim spun on his heels and left.

# CHAPTER 6

Kim's alarm was set to go off at five-fifteen in the morning, but it was rarely needed. He usually awoke just before the alarm, which allowed him to turn it off before it could shatter the early-morning peace. Kim had been getting up before dawn ever since he'd been a first-year surgical resident. And this particular morning was no exception. He climbed out of his warm bed in the pitch black and dashed stark naked into the bathroom.

Following a routine that needed no thought, Kim pulled open the heavy glass door of the shower and turned on the water full-blast. Kim and Tracy had always preferred showering to bathtub bathing, and the bathroom was the only room they'd wanted renovated back when he and Tracy had first purchased the house ten years earlier. They'd had the tub pulled out, as well its attached tiny shower stall. In their place a generous five-by-nine-foot custom shower was constructed. Three sides were marble slab. The fourth was half-inch glass, including the door that had vertically oriented, bright brass, U-shaped handles mounted as if they pierced the thick, tempered glass. In Kim's estimation it was a bathing extravaganza worthy of a spread in a design magazine.

Breakfast was a donut and a cup of half-milk half-coffee that Kim stopped for at a Dunkin' Donuts shop near his home. He ate while he drove through the morning darkness. He also used the time to listen to medical tapes. By six he was already in his office dictating consult letters

61

and writing checks for various overhead expenses. At six-forty-five he was in the hospital for teaching rounds with the thoracic surgery residents at which time he made it a point to see his own patients. By seven-thirty he was in the conference room for the unavoidable, daily hospital meeting. That morning it concerned hospital credentials and admitting privileges.

After the administrative meeting, Kim met with the thoracic surgery fellows whose research he supervised and participated in. That meeting went over, so he was a few minutes late to surgical grand rounds, where he presented a case of triple-valve replacement.

By ten o'clock Kim was back at his office and already behind schedule. He found out that Ginger had booked emergency patients for nine-thirty and nine-forty-five. Cheryl Constantine, Kim's office nurse, had the patients already in the two examining rooms.

The morning passed with nonstop patients. Lunch consisted of a sandwich that Ginger had ordered in. Kim ate while he went over cath results and X-rays. He also found time to return a semi-emergency phone call to a Salt Lake City cardiologist about a patient who needed a triple valve replacement.

The afternoon was a mirror image of the morning, with back-to-back patients, including a few emergencies that Ginger slipped into the schedule. At four o'clock Kim took a short break to dash over to the hospital to handle a minor problem with one of his inpatients. While he was there he quickly did afternoon rounds.

Back at the office Kim vainly tried to catch up, but he never could. Several hours and a number of patients later, he paused for a moment to catch his breath before pushing into what was called examine room A. He used the brief respite to glance at the chart. He was relieved to see it was merely a routine post-op check. That promised the visit would most likely be a "quickie." The patient's name was Phil Norton, and as Kim entered the cubicle, Phil was already obligingly sitting on the examination table with his shirt off.

"Congratulations, Mr. Norton," Kim said, lifting his eyes from the chart. "Your stress test is now normal."

"Thank God!" Phil said.

And thank modern-day cardiac surgery, Kim mused. He bent over and examined the incision that ran down the center of Phil's chest. Gently Kim palpated the raised ridge of healing tissue with the tips of his fingers. By such observation and touch Kim could accurately tell the internal state of the wound.

"And the incision looks great," Kim added. He straightened up. "Well, as far as I'm concerned you can start training for the Boston Marathon."

"I don't think that's in my future," Phil joked. "But come spring I'll certainly be out on the links."

Kim gave the man a pat on the shoulder and then shook his hand. "Enjoy yourself," he said. "But remember to maintain the change we've made in your lifestyle."

"Don't worry about that," Phil said. "I read all the material you sent home with me. And I've taken it to heart. No more smoking for this fellow."

"And don't forget the diet and exercise," Kim added.

"Don't worry," Phil said. "I don't want to go through this again."

"Now, it wasn't that bad," Kim joked.

"No, but it was scary," Phil said.

Kim gave Phil another pat on the back, jotted a quick note on the chart, and left the examination room. He stepped across the hall to examine room B but noticed there was no waiting chart in the rack on the door.

"Mr. Norton was the last patient," Cheryl said from behind Kim.

Kim turned around and smiled at his office nurse. He ran a tired hand through his tussled hair. "Good," Kim said. "What time is it?"

"It's after seven," Cheryl said.

"Thanks for staying," Kim said.

"You're welcome," Cheryl said.

"I hope this chronic overtime doesn't cause you any trouble at home," Kim said.

"It's not a problem," Cheryl said. "I'm getting used to it and so is my husband. He knows now to pick my son up from day care."

Kim reversed direction and went into his private office. He collapsed into his desk chair and eyed the stack of phone messages he'd have to respond to before leaving. He rubbed his eyes. He was exhausted yet on edge. As per usual the stresses of the day had accumulated. He would have loved to play some tennis, and he vaguely thought about stopping in at the athletic club on his way home. Maybe he could at least use a StairMaster.

The door to his office opened and Ginger leaned in.

"Tracy just called," she said with an edge to her voice.

"What about?" Kim asked.

"She wouldn't say," Ginger reported. "All she said was to have you call."

"Why are you upset?"

Ginger exhaled and shifted her weight. "She's just rude. I try to be nice and all. I even asked how Becky was."

"And what did she say?"

"She said just to have you call."

"Okay, thanks," Kim said. He picked up the phone and started to dial.

"I'm leaving for aerobics class," Ginger said.

With a wave, Kim acknowledged that he'd heard.

"Call me later," Ginger said.

Kim nodded. Ginger left and closed the door behind her. Then Tracy answered.

"What's up?" Kim asked with no preamble.

"Becky is worse," Tracy said.

"How so?"

"Her cramps are worse to the point of tears and there's blood in her diarrhea."

"What color?" Kim asked.

"For chrissake, what do you mean what color?" Tracy demanded.

"Bright red or dark?" Kim asked.

"Chartreuse," Tracy said impatiently.

"I'm serious," Kim said. "Bright red or dark red, almost brown?"

"Bright red," Tracy said.

"How much?"

"How am I to tell?" Tracy responded irritably. "It's blood, and it's red, and it's scary. Isn't that enough?"

"It's not so abnormal to have a little blood in diarrhea," Kim said.

"I don't like it," Tracy said.

"What do you want to do?"

"You're asking me?" Tracy questioned with disbelief. "Listen! You're the doctor, not me."

"Maybe I should try to call George Turner in Boston," Kim said.

"And what is he going to do a thousand-plus miles away?" Tracy complained. "I want her seen, and I want her seen tonight!"

"Okay, okay," Kim said. "Calm down!"

Kim paused for a moment to gather his thoughts. With George gone, he didn't have any handy contacts in pediatrics. He considered having one of his internal medicine acquaintances take a peek at Becky but was reluctant. It seemed excessive to call someone out at night because of mild diarrhea of a couple days' duration even if it were tinged with a small amount of bright red blood.

"I'll tell you what," Kim said. "Meet me over at the University Med Center emergency room."

"When?"

"When can you be there?" Kim asked.

"I guess in about a half hour," Tracy said.

"I'll see you then," Kim said.

Since he was only about ten minutes away from the hospital now that peak traffic time had passed, Kim used the intervening twenty minutes to return as many phone calls as he could. When he got to the emergency room, he discovered he'd still beat Tracy, so he stood out on the receiving dock and waited. While he stood there, several ambulances pulled up to the platform with their screaming sirens trailing off. Hurriedly the EMT's unloaded a couple of patients in dire need of emergency care. One of them was being given CPR. Kim watched them disappear inside, and it made him nostalgically recall his days as a surgical resident. Kim had worked hard and had been rewarded by being told repeatedly he was one of the best residents who had ever come through the program. It had been a heady time and in many ways more fulfilling than now.

Kim was just about to use his cell phone to try to contact Tracy when he saw Tracy's Volvo station wagon round the corner and pull to a stop. Kim dropped to the pavement and trotted over to the car as the doors were being opened. He went directly to the passenger side and helped Becky. She smiled at him weakly as she got out.

"Are you okay, Pumpkin?" Kim asked.

"My cramps are worse," Becky said.

"Well, we'll get them taken care of," Kim said. He glanced at Tracy, who'd come around the car. Kim noticed she looked as irritated as she had the night before.

Kim led the way back to the platform and up the half dozen steps. He pushed open the swinging doors, and they entered.

As the major emergency room in a large, sprawling, Midwestern city, the unit was so jammed it looked like a busy, urban bus station. Monday nights tended to be particularly busy because of a leftover effect from the weekend.

With his arm around his daughter, Kim steered her through the throng in the anteroom where the main admitting desk was located and past the crowded waiting room. He was almost past the nurses' desk when an enormous, Brunhild-type nurse stepped out from behind the counter. Her bulk effectively blocked Kim from proceeding any further. Her name tag read: MOLLY MCFADDEN. Her height was such that she just about looked Kim in the eye.

"Sorry," Molly said. "You can't come in here on your own. You have to check in at the receiving desk."

Kim tried to push by, but Molly held her ground.

"Excuse me," Kim said. "I'm Dr. Reggis. I'm on the staff here, and I'm bringing my daughter in to be seen."

Molly gave a short laugh. "I don't care if you're Pope John whatever," she snorted. "Everyone, and I mean everyone, checks in at the front desk unless they're carried in here by the EMT's."

Kim was so shocked he was rendered momentarily speechless. He could not believe that not only wasn't he being deferred to, he was being openly challenged. Kim stared disbelievingly into the woman's defiant blue eyes. She seemed as formidable as a Sumo wrestler dressed in white. If she'd heard Kim identify himself as a member of the professional staff she gave no indication whatsoever.

"The sooner you check in, Doctor," Molly added, "the sooner the girl will be seen."

"You did hear me, didn't you?" Kim questioned. "I'm a senior attending in the department of cardiac surgery."

"Of course I heard you, Doctor," Molly said. "The question is: did you hear me?"

Kim glared at the woman but she was not to be intimidated.

Tracy sensed an impasse. Having an all-too-good idea of her former husband's temper, she took it upon herself to defuse the situation.

"Come on, dear," Tracy said to Becky. "Let's follow orders and get you checked in." She guided Becky back the way they'd come.

Kim shot one more nasty look at Molly, then turned and caught up to Tracy and Becky. Together they joined the ragtag line of patients waiting to check in. But Kim was still fuming.

"I'm going to complain about that woman," Kim said. "She's not going to get away with that kind of insolence. The nerve! I can't believe it."

"She was only doing her job," Tracy replied, content to let the incident drop. She was relieved that Kim hadn't caused more of a scene.

"Oh really?" Kim snapped. "Does that mean you're trying to defend her?"

"Calm down!" Tracy said. "She's undoubtedly just following orders. You don't think she makes up the rules, do you?"

Kim shook his head. The line inched ahead. At the moment there was only one clerk taking admissions. It was her job to fill out the check-in sheet with all the pertinent information, including insurance coverage if the patient was not a member of AmeriCare's health plan.

Becky's face suddenly contorted in pain. Pressing her hand into her abdomen, she whimpered.

"What's the matter?" Kim asked.

"What do you think?" Tracy said. "It's another cramp."

Perspiration appeared on Becky's forehead and she became pale. She looked pleadingly at her mother.

"It'll pass like the others, dear," Tracy said. Tracy stroked Becky's head and then used her hand to remove the moisture from Becky's face. "Do you want to sit down?"

Becky nodded.

"Keep our place!" Tracy said to Kim.

Kim watched Tracy lead Becky over to one of the molded-plastic chairs along the wall. Becky sat down. Kim could tell that Tracy was talking with her because Becky was nodding her head. Becky's color returned. A few minutes later Tracy came back.

"How is she?" Kim asked.

"She feels better for the moment," Tracy said. Tracy noted how little the line had advanced since they'd joined it. "Can't you think of an alternative to this?"

"It's Monday night," Kim said. "A tough night anywhere."

Tracy exhaled noisily. "I certainly miss Dr. Turner."

Kim nodded. He rose up on his tiptoes to see if he could figure out why the queue wasn't moving, but he couldn't.

"This is ridiculous," he exclaimed. "I'll be right back!"

With his mouth set in a grim line, Kim skirted the people in front of him to reach the counter. Immediately he could see why they had not moved forward. An inebriated man in a soiled and wrinkled business suit was struggling through the process of checking in. All his credit cards had fallen from his wallet. On the back of his head was an angry scalp laceration.

"Hello!" Kim called out, trying to get the receptionist's attention. She was an African-American woman in her mid-twenties. "I'm Dr. Reggis. I'm on staff in the department of cardiac surgery. I have my . . ."

"Excuse me," the receptionist said, interrupting Kim. "I can only deal with one person at a time."

"Listen!" Kim ordered. "I'm on the staff here . . ."

"It doesn't matter," the woman interjected. "We're an equal-opportunity server. It's first-come first-served for all routine emergencies."

"Routine emergencies?" Kim questioned. It was a ridiculous oxymoron. All at once the idea of trying to talk to this clerk reminded him of the frustration of having to deal with medically untrained people when he called insurance companies or managed-care plans to get clearance for patients. That chore had become one of the truly exasperating problems of modern office practice.

"Please wait at the end of the line," the receptionist said. "If you'll allow me to concentrate and get these people before you signed in, I'll be able to take your information sooner." She then directed her full attention to the drunk. In the interim he'd managed to gather the contents of his wallet.

Kim started to protest, but it was all too obvious it was a waste of time to try to talk with this woman. It occurred to him that she might not even know what the term "on staff" meant. With growing frustration, humiliation, and irritation, Kim returned to Tracy.

"I don't know where they find these people," Kim complained. "They're like automatons."

"I'm impressed by how your exalted position in this hospital has greased the skids for us."

"Your sarcasm doesn't help one iota," Kim snapped. "It's all because of the merger. I'm not known down here. In fact, I can't remember ever coming to this ER."

"If you'd taken Becky's complaints seriously over the weekend, we probably wouldn't have to be here now," Tracy said.

"I took them seriously," Kim said defensively.

"Oh, sure," Tracy said. "By giving her some over-the-counter diarrhea medications. That's really an aggressive approach! But you know something? I'm not surprised you didn't do more. You've never taken seriously any symptoms Becky has ever had. Or mine either, for that matter."

"That's not true," Kim said hotly.

"Oh, yes, it is," Tracy said. "Only someone married to a surgeon would know what I'm talking about. From your perspective, any symptom less than what would call for immediate open-heart surgery is a kind of ma-lingering."

"I resent that," Kim said.

"Yeah, well, so do I," Tracy said.

"All right, Miss Know-It-All," Kim snapped. "What would you have had me do with Becky over the weekend?"

"Have her be seen by somebody," Tracy said. "One of your many colleagues. You must have a thousand doctor friends. It wouldn't have been too much to ask."

"Wait a second," Kim said, struggling to control himself. "All Becky had was just simple diarrhea and some cramps, both of short duration. And it was the weekend. I wasn't going to bother someone with such symptoms."

"Mommy!" Becky called. She'd come up behind Kim and Tracy. "I have to go to the bathroom!"

Tracy turned and, reminded of her daughter's discomfort, her anger immediately mellowed. She put her arm over Becky's shoulder. "I'm sorry, dear. Sure! We'll find you a bathroom."

"Wait," Kim said. "This could be helpful. We'll need a sample. I'll get a stool-sample container."

"You must be joking," Tracy said. "I'm sure she has to go now."

"Hold on, Becky," Kim said. "I'll be right back."

Kim walked deliberately and quickly into the depths of the ER. Without Becky and Tracy, he wasn't challenged as he passed the nurses' desk. For the moment the mammoth Molly McFadden was nowhere to be seen.

The interior of the ER was a series of large rooms divided into separate cubicles by curtains that hung from overhead tracks. In addition, there were individual trauma rooms replete with state-of-the-art equipment. There were also a handful of examination rooms used primarily for psychiatric cases.

Like the outer waiting area, the ER proper was packed and chaotic. Every trauma room was occupied and staff physicians, residents, nurses, and orderlies swirled between them in continuous motion.

As he walked, Kim searched for someone he recognized. Unfortunately he didn't see anyone he knew. He stopped an orderly.

"Excuse me," Kim said. "I need a stool-sample container ASAP."

The orderly gave Kim a rapid once-over with his eyes. "Who are you?"

"Dr. Reggis," Kim said.

"You got an ID?"

Kim produced his hospital identification card.

"Okay," the orderly said. "I'll be right back."

Kim watched the man disappear through an unmarked door that apparently led to a storeroom.

"Coming through," a voice called.

Kim turned around in time to see a portable X-ray unit bearing down on him. He stepped to the side as the heavy machine was trundled past by an X-ray technician. A moment later the orderly reappeared. He handed Kim two clear plastic bags with plastic containers inside.

"Thanks," Kim said.

"Don't mention it," the orderly said.

Kim hurried back the way he'd come. Tracy and Becky were still in line although they had moved up a few feet. Becky had her eyes shut tight. Tears streaked her face.

Kim handed one of the plastic bags to Tracy. "Cramps?" he questioned.

"Of course, you lunkhead," Tracy said. Tracy grabbed Becky's hand and led her back to the restroom.

Kim held their place in line as it advanced by one more patient. Now there were two check-in clerks. Apparently the other had been off on break.

By nine-fifteen the ER waiting room was filled to overflowing. All the molded-plastic chairs were occupied. The rest of the people were leaning up against the walls or sprawled on the floor. There was little conversation. In one corner, a television hung suspended from the ceiling. It was tuned to CNN. A number of unhappy infants drowned out the newscaster. Outside it had started to rain; the smell of wet wool filled the air.

Kim, Tracy, and Becky had eventually found seats together and had not moved, except for Becky, who'd made several more trips to the restroom. Kim was holding the stool-sample container. Although there had been some spots of bright red blood originally, now the contents appeared a uniform light brown. Becky was miserable and mortified. Tracy was exasperated. Kim was still seething.

"I don't believe this," Kim said suddenly. "I truly don't believe this. Every second I think we'll be called, but it doesn't happen." He glanced at his watch. "We've been here an hour and a half."

"Welcome to the real world," Tracy said.

"This is what Kelly Anderson should have done her merger story about," Kim said. "This is ridiculous. AmeriCare closed the ER at the Samaritan to cut costs and make everyone come here. It's all just to maximize profits."

"And maximize inconvenience," Tracy added.

"It's true," Kim agreed. "AmeriCare definitely wants to discourage emergency-room usage."

"I can't think of a better way," Tracy said.

"I can't believe that not one of the staff people has recognized me," Kim growled. "It's incredible. Hell, I'm probably the best-known cardiac surgeon in the department."

"Isn't there something you can do?" Tracy pleaded. "Becky's miserable."

Kim stood up. "All right," he said. "I'll try."

"But don't lose your temper," Tracy admonished. "It might make everything worse."

"How can it be worse?" Kim replied.

Kim walked out of the waiting room on his way to the nurses' desk. He'd gone only a few steps when the wailing of an ambulance siren reverberated through the main swinging doors to his left. A moment later a flashing red light was seen through the doors' glass panels. The siren died off and soon the doors burst open. Several bloodied people—apparently auto-accident victims—were rolled in and whisked into the ER proper.

Kim could not help but wonder if these new arrivals meant Becky would have to wait that much longer.

Kim approached the nurses' desk. Again he looked for Molly McFadden, but she was still out of sight. The people there were a clerk, who was on the phone transcribing laboratory values, and a solitary nurse doing paperwork while sipping coffee. Her name tag read: MONICA HOSKINS, ER Staff Nurse.

Forcing himself to be civil, Kim got her attention by gently tapping the countertop.

"Good evening," he said when she looked up at him. "Perhaps you recognize me?"

Monica narrowed her eyes slightly as she gazed at Kim.

"No, I don't think I do," she said. "Should I?"

"I'm on the surgical attending staff," Kim said. "But right now I'm here with my daughter, and we've been waiting for over an hour and a half. Could you tell me when she'll be seen?"

"It's been a busy night especially with auto accidents," Monica explained. "What's the name?"

"Dr. Reggis," Kim said. He squared his shoulders.

"No, the patient's name," Monica said.

"Rebecca Reggis," Kim said.

Monica picked up a stack of ER sign-in sheets. After wetting the tip of her index finger with her tongue she rapidly flipped through the papers.

"Okay," she remarked as she withdrew one of them. "Here it is." She read the chief complaint and then raised her face to Kim. She arched her eyebrows.

"Diarrhea, two days' duration," she commented. "Not exactly a four-plus emergency."

Kim lifted the stool-sample container to bring it into her line of sight. "She's been passing a little bit of blood this afternoon," Kim said.

Monica leaned forward. "Doesn't look like blood."

"It did earlier," Kim said. "And it has her mother upset."

"Well, we'll get to her as soon as we can," Monica said noncommittedly. "That's about all I can say." She replaced Becky's sign-in sheet to its former location in the stack.

"Listen," Kim said in a deliberately controlled voice. "As a member of the staff, I expect some consideration, and after waiting this long already, I want her to be seen shortly. I hope I'm making myself clear. She's in considerable discomfort."

Monica treated Kim to a patently false smile. "As I said a moment ago, we'll get to her as soon as we can. We have limited resources. If you've been here for an hour and a half, I'm sure you've seen the auto accidents that have come in, and now the police have alerted us a shooting victim is on his way."

No sooner had these last words escaped from Monica's lips than the familiar sound of an arriving ambulance could be heard.

"In fact, I'd wager that's them now," Monica said as she got to her feet. She moved over to an intercom and pressed a button. Talking to someone in one of the trauma rooms she informed them to get ready. Then she herself disappeared back into the depths of the ER.

With little satisfaction for his latest efforts, Kim headed back to the waiting room. As he passed by the main entrance doors, a team of EMT's rushed in with the shooting victim on a gurney. The patient had an oxygen mask strapped over his face and an IV running. His color was ashen.

"Well?" Tracy asked as Kim reclaimed his seat.

"They said they'd see her as soon as they could," Kim said. He was embarrassed to relate the rest of the conversation. He noticed that Becky had curled up in her seat as best she could and had her eyes closed.

"That's pretty vague," Tracy said. "What does it mean? Fifteen minutes, an hour, tomorrow morning?"

"It means exactly as soon as they can," Kim snapped. "A shooting victim just came in and victims from an auto accident came in a few minutes ago. It's a busy night."

Tracy sighed and shook her head in frustration.

"How's Becky doing?" Kim asked.

"She just had another bout of cramps," Tracy said. "So you guess. You're the doctor."

Kim looked away, gritting his teeth. It was hard not to lose his temper. And on top of everything else, he was hungry.

For the next hour Kim was sullenly silent. He was busy brooding over this ridiculous ER experience and eager to complain to his colleagues about it. They would understand. Tracy and Becky seemed more resigned to the wait.

Every time one of the nurses or residents came to the waiting-room threshold to call out a name, Kim expected it to be Rebecca Reggis. But it never was. Finally Kim looked at his watch.

"It's been two and a half freaking hours." He stood up. "I truly can't believe this. If I were the slightest bit paranoid, I'd think it was some kind of screwy conspiracy. This time I'm going to make something happen. I'll be right back."

Tracy glanced up at her former husband. Under more normal circumstances, she'd be concerned about Kim's temper, but after having been kept waiting so long, she didn't care. She wanted Becky seen. She didn't comment as Kim stalked off.

Kim marched directly back to the nurses' desk. A number of the ER staff was scattered about the station, engaged in desultory conversation punctuated by laughter.

Upon reaching the counter, Kim scanned the group for a recognizable face. No one looked familiar and none seemed to recognize him. In fact, the only person to notice his presence was the clerk, a young college-aged boy who was most likely a student at the university.

"I'm Doctor Reggis," Kim said. "What's happening?" He motioned to all the people.

"They're just taking a breather," the clerk said. "The shooting victim and the last car-accident patients just went up to surgery."

"Who's the acting head of the emergency department for the evening shift?" Kim asked.

"That would be Dr. David Washington," the clerk said.

"Is he here at the moment?" Kim asked.

The clerk glanced around the area to be sure. "No," he said. "I believe he's back with an orthopedic case."

"How about a head nurse or nurse supervisor?" Kim asked.

"That would be Nora Labat," the clerk said. "She's with a psych patient."

"I see," Kim said. "Thanks."

Kim proceded down the counter until he was at the very center. Raising his hand, he called out: "Excuse me, everybody! Hello!"

No one acknowledged Kim's voice or gesture.

For another moment he glanced around, trying to make eye contact with anyone. It was impossible. Instead he reached across the counter and lifted a metallic in-and-out basket from the desk top. Holding it above his head for a moment, he thought someone might notice. They didn't.

Kim brought the metal basket down to crash onto the Formica counter. He smashed it down twice again, each time with more force until the basket became distorted to the shape of a three-dimensional parallelogram.

That got everyone's attention. Conversations stopped in midsentence. Residents, nurses, and orderlies all stared at Kim. A security man who'd been standing over near the bank of elevators came running over, his hand holding the clutch of keys attached to his belt.

Having worked himself up to a fury, Kim's voice was tremulous. "I know you all are busy, but you certainly don't look busy at the moment. I've been waiting here for two and a half hours with my daughter. As a professional man myself, my time could be spent in much more valuable ways."

"Excuse me, sir," the security man said. He took hold of Kim's arm.

Kim yanked his arm free and spun around on the man. "Don't you touch me," Kim snarled. The security man wisely stepped back while he grappled for his two-way radio. Kim was not only a half a foot taller but also significantly more muscled.

"No need to contact anyone," Kim said. He pulled out his hospital ID and held it up to the security man's face. "I'm on the staff here, even though no one here in the emergency department seems willing to concede it."

The security man's eyes narrowed as he read Kim's ID card. "Sorry, Doctor," he said.

"That's quite all right," Kim said with a controlled voice. He turned back to the desk. Monica Hoskins had stepped forward.

"I'd like to talk with Dr. David Washington," Kim said.

"I'm sorry you've had to wait," Monica said. "We're doing the best we can."

"Nonetheless I'd like to speak to the acting head of the department," Kim said.

"Dr. Washington is tied up with a pneumothorax," Molly explained.

"I want to see him now," Kim said evenly. "I'm sure there must be at least one resident competent to handle a pneumothorax."

"Just a moment," Monica said. She stepped back, and out of earshot from Kim, conferred with Molly and several of the other staff. In less than a minute, she returned to Kim. In the background one of the nurses she'd been talking with picked up a phone.

"We'll have someone here in authority to talk with you momentarily," Monica said.

"It's about time," Kim remarked.

Kim's mini-tantrum had unnerved the staff and most of them vacated the nurses' desk for the interior of the ER. Monica took the in-and-out basket Kim had bent and tried to bend it back. She was unsuccessful.

Kim's pulse was racing. A sudden commotion behind him made him turn around. A teenage girl was being escorted by a vanguard of EMT's. She was sobbing. Both wrists were bound with bloody dishtowels: a clear suicide attempt, no doubt in this young woman's case a desperate cry for help.

Kim looked expectantly into the ER depths after the teenager was taken in. He expected to see the doctor-in-charge appear at any moment. Instead he felt a tap on his shoulder.

Turning around, he was surprised to see Tracy.

"Where's Becky?" Kim asked.

"In the restroom," Tracy answered. "It's a routine visit this time, but I have to get right back. I just came in here to beg you not to have one of your narcissistic rages. When you stood up in the waiting room to come in here, I didn't think I cared whether you got into a furor or not, but I do. I'm convinced it won't improve an already bad situation. In fact it might cause Becky to have to wait even longer."

"Spare me your psychobabble," Kim spat. "All I'm planning on is a sane but pointed conversation with the man who runs this place. I mean, this is unacceptable. Plain and simple."

"Just try to control yourself," Tracy said icily. "When you're done, you'll know where to find us." Tracy turned around and walked back toward the waiting room.

Kim drummed his fingers impatiently on the counter. After a while he looked at his watch. Another five minutes had passed. Once again he leaned out into the corridor to peer back into the ER depths. He saw plenty of staff but no one came striding in his direction. Kim's eyes met the clerk's who immediately averted his gaze. The rest of the ER staff avoided looking at Kim, instead busying themselves with paperwork.

A muffled bell sounded to herald the arrival of an elevator. Kim looked over to see a hefty man dressed in a conservative gray business suit disembark. To Kim's surprise, he came directly up to him.

"Dr. Reggis?" the man inquired. His voice was robust and commanding.

"I'm Dr. Reggis," Kim agreed.

"I'm Barclay Bradford," the man said stiffly. "I'm a vice president of the hospital and the acting chief administrator for the evening shift."

"How convenient," Kim said. "What I'd advise you to do is to go back into the ER, locate the asshole acting head of the department, and drag him out here. He and I have something to talk about. You see, I've been waiting for two and a half hours to have my daughter seen."

"Dr. Reggis," Barclay began as if Kim had not even spoken. "As a member of our professional staff, particularly a surgeon, you of all people know that triage is necessary in a busy ER. Life-threatening problems have to take precedence over simple juvenile diarrhea."

"Of course I understand triage," Kim shot back. "I've worked in ER's all through my training. But let me tell you something. When I walked in here ten minutes ago, there had to be a dozen ER staff hanging out behind this counter drinking coffee and chitchatting."

"Appearances never tell the whole story," Barclay commented condescendingly. He fluttered his eyelids. "They were probably conferring with each other over particularly difficult cases. But regardless, your childish behavior of pounding a letter box on a countertop cannot be tolerated. It's entirely inappropriate for you to demand special treatment."

"Special treatment!" Kim sputtered. "Childish behavior!" His face reddened and his eyes bulged. The administrator in front of him suddenly embodied his frustrations about the present emergency-room experience, the hospital merger, AmeriCare, and modern medicine in general. With a sudden fit of fury and losing all semblance of control, Kim struck the administrator with a lightning blow to the chin.

Kim shook his hand and clasped it with his other in response to the sudden pain in his knuckle. At the same time, Barclay rocked back on his heels, teetered, then fell heavily to the floor. Kim was stunned by his violent reaction. Taking a step forward, he looked down at Barclay and felt an impulse to help the man up.

A collective gasp arose from the staff behind the desk. The security guard came running. The clerk grabbed the intercom to announce: "Mayday at the nurses' desk."

From the depths of the ER, residents, nurses, and orderlies came streaming out. Even Tracy appeared after hearing the announcement. A crowd gathered around Kim and Barclay. The hospital VP had pushed himself up to a sitting position. He touched a hand to his lip. It was bleeding.

"Damn it, Kim!" Tracy said. "I warned you!"

"This is totally unacceptable," Monica said. She turned to the clerk. "Call the police!"

"Hold up, don't call anybody!" a deep, resonant voice called. The crowd parted. A powerfully built, handsome African-American man appeared. He snapped latex gloves from his hands as he walked into the cen-

ter of the ring. The name tag pinned to his scrub top read: DR. DAVID
WASHINGTON, ACTING CHIEF EMERGENCY DEPARTMENT. His eyes went
from Kim down to Barclay. "What's going on here?"

"Mr. Bradford was just struck by this man," Monica said, pointing at
Kim. "And that was after he destroyed a letter box by bashing it against
the counter."

"Believe it or not, he's a doctor on the hospital staff," Molly added.

David put out a hand and got Barclay to his feet. David glanced at the
man's split lip and palpated along the line of his jaw.

"Are you all right?" David asked the administrator.

"I think so," Barclay said. He got out a handkerchief and dabbed at his
bloodied lip.

David turned to Monica. "Take Mr. Bradford back and get him
cleaned up. And have Dr. Krugger take a look at him to see if we should
get an X-ray."

"Sure," Monica said. She grasped Barclay's arm above the elbow to
guide him through the crowd. Barclay glared at Kim before allowing
himself to be led away.

"Everyone else, back to work," David said, with a wave of his hand.
Then he turned to Kim, who'd recovered his senses.

"What is your name?" David asked.

"Dr. Kim Reggis."

"Did you really hit Mr. Bradford?" David asked incredulously.

"I'm afraid so," Kim said.

"What on earth could have provoked you?" David asked.

Kim took a deep breath. "That prig condescendingly accused me of demanding special treatment when my sick child has been waiting for two
and a half hours."

David stared at Kim for a beat. He was mystified at such behavior
from a colleague. "What's the child's name?" he asked.

"Rebecca Reggis," Kim said.

David turned to the clerk and asked for Rebecca's sign-in sheet. The
clerk fumbled through the stack.

"Are you really on staff here at the University Med Center?" David asked while he waited for the sheet.

"Since the merger," Kim said. "I'm one of the cardiac surgeons, although you'd never know it the way I've been treated here in the ER."

"We do the best we can," David said.

"Yeah, I've heard that excuse several times tonight," Kim said.

David eyed Kim again. "You know, you should be ashamed of yourself," he said. "Punching people out, smashing letter boxes. You're acting like some malcontent teenager."

"Screw you," Kim said.

"For the moment I'm going to chalk that remark up to stress," David said.

"Don't be patronizing," Kim said.

"Here it is," the clerk said. He handed the sign-in sheet to David.

David glanced at it, then looked at his watch. "At least you're right about the time. It's been close to three hours. That's certainly no justification for your behavior, but it's too long to wait."

David looked at Tracy. "Are you Mrs. Reggis?" he asked.

"I'm Rebecca Reggis's mother," Tracy said.

"Why don't you get the young lady. I'll personally see to it she's seen immediately."

"Thank you," Tracy said. She hurried out to the waiting room.

David went behind the desk to get a clipboard for the sign-in sheet. He also used the intercom to get a nurse to come out. When he reemerged, Tracy was back with Becky in tow. A moment later a nurse appeared. Her name tag identified her as Nicole Michaels.

"How are you feeling, young lady?" David asked Becky.

"Not too good," Becky admitted. "I want to go home."

"I'm sure you do," David said. "But first let's check you out. Why don't you go ahead with Nicole. She'll get you situated in one of the examination cubicles."

Tracy, Becky, and Kim started forward. David reached out to restrain Kim.

"I'd prefer that you wait out here, if you don't mind," David said.

"I'm going with my daughter," Kim stated.

"No, you are not," David said. "You've proved yourself emotionally stressed. You're acting like a loose cannon."

Kim hesitated. As much as he didn't want to admit it, David had a point. Still, it was irritating and demeaning.

"Come on, Doctor," David said. "Surely you understand."

Kim cast a glance at the receding image of Becky and Tracy. He looked back at David, who was not about to be intimidated, physically or otherwise.

"But . . ." Kim began.

"No buts," David said. "Don't make me call the police, which I'll do if you don't cooperate."

Reluctantly Kim turned around and walked back to the waiting room. There were no seats, so he leaned up against the wall by the entrance. He tried to watch the television but couldn't concentrate. He raised his hand and looked at it; he was trembling.

A half hour later Tracy and Becky emerged from the treatment area. It was by chance that Kim happened to see them as they pushed through the exit door. They were leaving without even having tried to find him.

Kim quickly gathered his coat and gloves and hurried after them. He caught up to them just as Tracy was helping Becky climb into the car.

"What are you going to do?" Kim demanded. "Just ignore me?"

Tracy didn't say anything. She shut the door behind Becky and then walked around to the driver's-side door.

Kim followed and put his hand on the door to keep it from opening.

"Please, don't cause any more trouble," Tracy said. "You've already embarrassed both of us."

Taken aback by this new and unexpected affront, Kim took his hand away. Tracy got into the car. She reached for the door but then didn't close it. She looked up into Kim's surprised and hurt face. "Go home and get some sleep," she said. "That's what we're going to do."

"What happened in there?" Kim asked. "What did they say?"

"Not much," Tracy reported. "Apparently her blood count and electrolytes, whatever they are, are fine. I'm supposed to give her broth and other fluids and lay off the dairy products."

"Is that all?" Kim asked.

"That's it," Tracy said. "But, by the way, they said the culprit could very well have been Ginger's chicken. They see a lot of food poisoning secondary to chicken."

"It wasn't," Kim shot back. "No way! Ask Becky! She was feeling sick the morning before the chicken." Kim leaned over to talk directly to his daughter. "Isn't that right, Pumpkin?"

"I want to go home," Becky said, staring out through the windshield.

"Good night, Kim," Tracy said. She pulled the door shut, started the car, and drove away.

Kim watched the car until it had disappeared behind the corner of the hospital. Only then did he start walking toward the doctors' parking area. He felt alone, more alone than he'd ever felt in his life.

# CHAPTER 7

The OR door burst open, and Kim and Tom entered the scrub area outside OR number 20. As they did so, they untied their face masks and let them drop down over their chests. They rinsed off the talc from their hands.

"Hey, thanks for lending a hand on such short notice," Tom said.

"Glad to help," Kim said flatly.

The two men started walking up the corridor toward the recovery room.

"You seem down in the dumps," Tom said. "What happened? Did your accountant just call you about your bottom line in response to the new Medicare reimbursement rates?"

Kim didn't laugh. He didn't respond at all.

"Are you all right?" Tom asked, seriously this time.

"I suppose," Kim said without emotion. "Just a lot of aggravation." Kim then told Tom what had happened in the ER the night before.

"Whoa!" Tom commented when Kim was finished. "What a God awful experience! But don't be down on yourself for taking a poke at that Barclay Bradford character. I had a mini run-in with him myself. Administrators! You know, I read in a journal last night that in the United States there's currently one administrator for every one and a half doctors or nurses. Can you believe that?"

"Yeah, I can," Kim said. "That's a big part of why our healthcare costs are so high."

"That was exactly the point of the article," Tom said. "But anyway, I can understand why you popped Bradford. If it had been me, I know I would have been bullshit. Three hours! Hell, I'd a punched him out as a minimum."

"Thanks, Tom," Kim said. "I appreciate your support. But the worst part of the whole episode is that after all that wait and aggravation, I never got a chance to talk with the doctor who examined Becky."

"How's she doing today?"

"I don't know yet," Kim said. "It was too early for me to call when I got up, and Tracy hasn't called me. But she's got to be doing better. Her blood-work was fine, and she's been afebrile."

"Dr. Reggis!" a voice called.

Kim turned to see Deborah Silverman, the OR head nurse, beckoning toward him. Kim detoured to the OR desk.

"Dr. Biddle called while you were in surgery," Deborah said. "He left a message for you to stop into his office as soon as you were out."

Kim took the message slip. It was punctuated with a number of exclamation points. Apparently it was serious.

"Uh-oh!" Tom commented over Kim's shoulder. "Sounds to me like the chief is planning on adding to your aggravation."

Kim and Tom parted ways at the recovery-room door. Kim went into the surgical locker room. Despite the implied urgency of Forrester Biddle's message, Kim took his time. It wasn't hard to guess what Forrester wanted to see him about. The problem was that after a point, Kim wasn't sure he understood his own behavior.

Kim took a shower and mulled over in his mind the previous evening's experience. He didn't reach any epiphany beyond admitting he'd been unduly stressed. After dressing in a clean set of scrubs, Kim used the phone in the surgical lounge to call Ginger at the office to discuss the afternoon schedule. Only then did he make his way over to the chief's office in the administration wing.

Dr. Forrester Biddle was the quintessential New England conservative.

He had the gaunt look of a Puritan preacher and the acerbic personality to go with it. His only redeeming quality was that he was an excellent surgeon.

"Come in and close the door," Forrester said as Kim stepped into his cramped, journal-filled office. "Take a seat."

Kim sat down. Forrester made him wait while some paperwork was being completed. Kim's eyes roamed the room. Kim noted he'd had a much better office as chief over at the Samaritan.

After adding his signature with a flourish, Forrester slapped down his pen on his desk top so that it sounded like a distant report of a firearm. "I'll get right to the point," he said, assuming an expression more stern than usual. "Your behavior last night in the emergency room is an embarrassment to this department as well as to the entire medical staff."

"My daughter was in pain," Kim said simply. It was an explanation not an excuse. He was not inclined to sound remorseful.

"There's no excuse for violence," Forrester remarked. "Mr. Bradford is considering filing charges, and I wouldn't blame him if he did."

"If anybody gets sued it should be AmeriCare," Kim said. "I waited over three hours mostly so that AmeriCare can maximize profits."

"Assaulting an administrator is no way to make social commentary," Forrester said. "Nor, I might add, is appealing directly to the media. I wasn't going to say anything about your quote Kelly Anderson gave during the Friday night news until this inexcusable episode of battery. Saying publicly that the rationale for the merger of the University Medical Center and the Samaritan was to benefit AmeriCare's bottom line hurts the reputation of this hospital."

Kim stood up. The meeting was not going to be a discussion, and there was no way Kim would sit there and absorb reprimands like a delinquent schoolboy. "If that's all, I have patients to see."

Forrester pushed his chair back and stood up as well. "I think you should keep in mind, Dr. Reggis," he said, "this department seriously considered hiring a full-time, salaried surgeon to cover your area of valve replacement prior to the merger. Your behavior of late is making us reevaluate that issue."

Kim turned around and left without responding. He wasn't about to validate such a comment. It was hardly the threat that Forrester intended. In reality Kim was being repeatedly recruited to take over a number of prestigious departments around the country. The only reason he was still at the University Medical Center was because of shared custody of Becky and the fact that Tracy couldn't move because of her metriculation in the liberal arts college.

But Kim was again angry. Of late it seemed to be his constant state of mind. Striding out of the administrative area of the hospital, he practically ran head-on into Kelly Anderson and her cameraman, Brian.

"Ah!" Kelly squealed with apparent delight. "Dr. Reggis! Just the man I've been hoping to see."

Kim flashed a nasty glance at the TV journalist and continued down the corridor at a brisk pace. Kelly reversed directions and ran after him. Brian kept pace despite his burden of equipment.

"My God, Dr. Reggis," Kelly panted. "Are you in training for a marathon? Slow down. I need to talk with you."

"I've no intention of talking with you," Kim said.

"But I want to hear your side of last night's ER episode," Kelly said.

Kim pulled up short, forcing Brian to collide with him. Brian apologized effusively. Kim ignored him and peered at Kelly in surprise. "How in God's name did you hear about that and so quickly?"

"Surprised you, huh!" Kelly remarked with a sly, self-satisfied smile. "But I'm sure you understand that I can't reveal my sources. You see, I do so many medical-related stories that I've developed a kind of fifth column here at the med center. You'd be surprised about the gossip I get. Unfortunately it's usually as prosaic as who's screwing whom. But once in a while, I get a real tip, like your episode in the ER last night. Cardiac surgeon punches out administrator: that's news!"

"I don't have anything to say to you," Kim responded. He recommenced walking.

Kelly caught up to him. "Ah, but I think you do," she said. "Having to wait three hours in an emergency room with a sick child must have been a major aggravation that I'd love to discuss."

"Too bad," Kim said. "Among other things I was just reprimanded for giving you that bottom-line quote. I'm not talking with you."

"So the administration hates the truth," Kelly said. "That in itself is interesting."

"I'm not talking to you," Kim repeated. "You might as well save your breath."

"Oh, come on!" Kelly said. "Your having to wait hours to be seen in the emergency room will strike a familiar chord with my viewers, especially with the ironic twist that it's a doctor doing the waiting. We don't even have to discuss the assault and battery part if you don't want."

"Yeah, sure, as if I could trust you," Kim said.

"You can," Kelly said. "You see, I think having to wait so long relates to the merger story. I believe it has something to do with AmeriCare's interest in profits. What do you think?"

Kim looked at Kelly as they walked. Her bright blue-green eyes sparkled. Kim had to admit that although she was a pain in the neck, she was also smart as a whip.

"You said it, not me," Kim remarked. "So no quotes. My life right now is sufficiently screwed up that I don't need you to make it worse. Goodbye, Miss Anderson."

Kim went through a pair of swinging doors leading back into the operating area. Kelly pulled to a stop to the relief of Brian. Both were out of breath.

"Well, we tried," Kelly said. "The sad irony is that this time I'm sincerely sympathetic. A month ago I had to wait almost the same amount of time with my own daughter."

○ ○ ○

Kim entered his office complex by the back door. It gave him a chance to get into his private office without having to go through the waiting room. As he struggled out of his suit jacket he picked up his phone and got Ginger at the reception desk.

"I'm back," Kim said. With the receiver caught in the crook of his neck, he walked over to his closet. The telephone wire was just long enough.

"You've got a waiting-room full of patients," Ginger said. "Thanks to Tom's emergency surgery, you're about two hours behind schedule."

"Any phone messages of import?" Kim asked. He managed to get his jacket hung up and grabbed his short white doctor's jacket.

"Nothing that can't wait," Ginger said.

"No calls from Tracy?"

"No," Ginger said.

"Okay, have Cheryl start moving the patients into the examining rooms," Kim said.

After slipping on the white jacket and collecting the pens and other paraphernalia he kept in his pockets, Kim dialed Tracy's number. While the call went through, he draped his stethoscope around his neck.

Tracy answered on the first ring as if she were right next to the phone.

"Well, how's the patient doing?" Kim asked. He tried to sound upbeat.

"Not a lot of change," Tracy said.

"Any fever?"

"No."

"How about cramps?" Kim asked.

"Some," Tracy said. "But I was able to get her to take some chicken broth."

Kim was tempted to say that Ginger had tried to get her to eat chicken broth on Sunday, but then he thought better of it. Instead he said: "It sounds like you're making progress. I'll bet Becky will be feeling herself in no time."

"I certainly hope so," Tracy said.

"It stands to reason," Kim said. "With no fever and no elevated white count, her body's obviously handled the infection. But keep me posted, okay?"

"I will," Tracy said. Then she added: "I'm sorry if I was mean last night."

"You don't have to apologize," Kim said.

"I feel I said some nasty things," Tracy said. "I was very upset."

"Please," Kim said. "I was the one out of line, not you."

"I'll call if there's any change," Tracy said.

"I'll either be here or at home," Kim said.

Kim hung up the phone. For the first time all day he felt relatively content. Walking out into the corridor, he smiled at Cheryl and took the first chart.

When Kim turned off the headlights of his car in front of his garage door, he found himself in pitch dark. It was only eight o'clock, but it could have been midnight. There was no moon, and the only light was a slight smudge on the eastern horizon, where the city lights reflected off the low cloud cover. The house was so dark it appeared like a hunk of rock.

Kim opened the car door, and the interior lights came on. That gave him an opportunity to collect the cartons of Chinese takeout he'd picked up on the way back from his office. The last patient had left at seven-fifteen.

With his arms full of food containers and paperwork he hoped to complete that evening, Kim made his way from the driveway toward the front door. He had to move by feel along the flagstone walkway. As dark as it was, it was difficult to comprehend that during the summer at that very time of the evening, the sun would have still been in the sky.

Kim heard his phone even before he got to the door. It was jangling insistently in the darkness. Without knowing why, Kim felt a stab of panic. In the process of getting his keys out, he dropped the paperwork. Then he couldn't find the right key, which forced him to put down the food cartons so that he could use both hands. Finally he got the door open and rushed inside.

With the help of the foyer light, Kim dashed into the cavernous, mostly empty living room and answered the phone. He was irrationally terrified that whoever was calling would hang up before the connection went through. But it didn't happen. It was Tracy.

"She's worse," Tracy blurted. She sounded desperate and on the verge of tears.

"What's happened?" Kim demanded as his heart skipped a beat.

"She hemorrhaged," Tracy cried. "The toilet's full of blood."

"Is she lucid?" Kim asked quickly.

"Yes," Tracy said. "She's calmer than I am. She's on the couch."

"Can she walk?" Kim asked. "Is she dizzy?"

"She can walk okay," Tracy said, getting more in control of herself. "I'm glad you answered the phone. I was about to call 911."

"Get her into the car and back to the ER," Kim said. "Provided you think you can drive okay. Otherwise, we can call 911 for an ambulance."

"I can drive fine," Tracy said.

"I'll meet you there," Kim said. He hung up the phone. Then he raced into the library and tore open the central drawer of his desk. Roughly he searched through the contents, looking for his address book. When he found it, he opened it to the T's and ran his finger down until he came to George Turner. Taking out his cell phone, he entered the number and pressed SEND.

With the phone pressed to his ear, Kim retraced his route to the car. He stepped over the Chinese takeout, leaving the cartons and the paperwork strewn over the doormat.

Mrs. Turner answered just as Kim opened the car door. Without any pleasantries, he asked if George were available. By the time George was on the line, Kim was already backing out the driveway.

"Sorry to bother you," Kim said.

"No bother," George said. "What's up? Nothing, I hope."

"I'm afraid so," Kim said. "I mean it's nothing earth-shattering. It's just that Becky's sick with dysentery-like symptoms: cramps, diarrhea, and now some bleeding, but no fever."

"I'm sorry to hear that," George said.

"We never got another pediatrician after you left," Kim explained guiltily. "And the few I knew, including yourself, all left town. Last night we took her to the emergency room at the University Med Center and ended up waiting for three hours."

"God! That's terrible," George said.

"I'm embarrassed to say I punched out one of the AmeriCare administrators over it," Kim said. "Anyway, Becky was sent home with nothing. No medications. Tracy just called me to tell me she hemorrhaged. I don't know how much, but Tracy was a bit hysterical. I'm on my way to meet them at the ER. Who should I have see her?"

"Hmmmm," George intoned. "I don't think a pediatrician would be best. I guess I'd recommend either an infectious-disease specialist or a GI person."

"Well, which?" Kim asked. "And would you recommend one? The consults I deal with don't see kids as a rule."

"You've got a lot of superb people," George said. "I guess I'd recommend an infectious-disease guy, at least initially. Try to get Claude Faraday. You can't do better than Claude anyplace."

"Thanks, George," Kim said.

"My pleasure," George said. "Sorry I'm not around."

"Me too," Kim said.

"Keep me posted," George said.

"I will," Kim said.

Kim disconnected, then used speed-dialing to get the hospital. He had the hospital operator patch him through to Claude Faraday. To Kim's relief, the man was at home.

Kim explained the situation much as he did to George. Claude listened, asked a few pertinent questions, and then graciously agreed to come to the ER directly.

Kim pulled into the hospital. On this occasion he drove directly around to the parking area reserved for the emergency room. He looked briefly for Tracy's Volvo. When he didn't see it, he went up the steps to the ER platform and pushed inside.

The emergency room appeared to Kim nearly as busy as it did the night before, although he saw some empty chairs in the waiting room. He bypassed the reception and went directly to the nurses' desk. Both Molly and Monica happened to be sitting there as he came in. They exchanged nervous glances.

"Has my daughter come in yet tonight?" Kim asked.

"I haven't seen her," Molly said. She seemed disinterested and a tinge wary at the same time.

"Nor I," Monica said.

"Is she supposed to come in again?" Molly asked.

Kim didn't bother to answer. He left the desk and headed directly back into the emergency room proper.

"Hey, where are you going?" Molly demanded. She stood up with the idea of coming around the edge of the desk to bar Kim's passage as she'd done the previous night, but Kim was already beyond. Molly hurried after him.

Monica snapped her fingers to get the security man's attention. When he looked over, she pointed frantically at Kim's disappearing figure. The security man nodded and started after him as well. As he trotted, he slipped his two-way radio out from its holster.

Kim walked the length of the first room, sticking his nose into each cubicle as he went along. Molly caught up to him. "Just what do you think you are doing?" she demanded.

Kim ignored the woman, who was joined by the security man. They trailed after Kim. "What should I do?" the security man asked Molly. "I mean, he is a doctor."

"I haven't the slightest idea," Molly said.

Kim ran out of cubicles on one side of the room and started on those on the opposite side. Finally he found David Washington suturing a laceration on a child's hand. A nurse was assisting him. David was wearing two-plus oculars, and he regarded Kim over the top of them.

"My daughter's on her way in," Kim announced. "Now she's apparently passing frank blood."

"I'm sorry to hear that," David said. "What's her blood pressure and pulse?"

"That I don't know," Kim said. "My ex-wife is bringing her in. I haven't seen her yet."

With his sterile, gloved hands raised in the air, David turned to Molly and asked her to get a room ready with a crash cart and plasma expanders in case they were needed. Molly nodded and disappeared.

"I want my daughter seen immediately," Kim ordered. "And I want her to have an infectious-disease consult."

"Dr. Reggis," David said. "Let's try to be friends. It would help if you recognize I'm in charge here."

"I've already talked with Dr. Claude Faraday," Kim said as if he'd not heard David. "He's on his way. I presume you know him?"

"Of course I know him," David said. "That's not the point. The usual protocol is for us to order the consults if the patient does not have an AmeriCare gatekeeper. AmeriCare is very clear on this issue."

"I want Dr. Faraday to see her," Kim averred.

"All right," David said. "But at least understand we are doing you a favor. This is not the way things are usually done here."

"Thank you," Kim said. He turned and walked back the length of the room. He scanned the reception area, and when he didn't see Tracy and Becky he went out onto the receiving platform. He stood waiting just as he'd done the evening before.

He didn't have long to wait. Within minutes Tracy's station wagon appeared and drove practically up to the platform itself. Kim jumped down and was at the back door by the time Tracy was pulling on the emergency brake.

He opened the door and leaned in. Becky was lying on the backseat on her side. Kim could see her face with the help of the floodlights on the receiving platform. Although she appeared pale, she smiled at him, and he felt relieved.

"How do you feel, Pumpkin?" Kim asked.

"Better now," Becky said. "The cramp went away."

"I'm glad," Kim said. "Come on, let me carry you."

"I can walk," Becky said.

"I'll carry you just the same," Kim said.

He got his right arm under her knees and slid her out so that he could get his left arm under her upper body. He hoisted her up. She put her own arms around his neck and buried her face under his chin.

"Okay," Kim said soothingly. "Daddy has you."

"She's not too heavy, is she?" Tracy asked.

"Not at all," Kim said.

Kim led the way: first up the stairs and then backing through the swinging doors. As he walked past reception with Tracy directly behind him, one of the clerks called out that they had to check-in. Kim ignored her. Although Tracy felt uncomfortable, she didn't say anything.

Monica was sitting at the nurses' desk when she heard the clerk call out. Looking up, she saw Kim approaching. Immediately she leaped to her feet and stepped into the hall to bar the way. But she was not Molly.

"No, you don't," Monica said. "You're not bringing that child in without a sign-in sheet."

Kim continued walking. Monica took several steps backward. "You can't do this," she protested.

Tracy tugged on Kim's arm. "Let's not have a scene," she said.

Relentless as a steamroller, Kim continued forward. Monica did not have Molly's bulk and was forced to the side.

"You can get the information from last night's sign-in sheet," Kim called over his shoulder.

Monica rushed back into the desk area to page David Washington.

Kim carried Becky into the first available cubicle. He laid her on the gurney. Tracy came in to stand on the opposite side and hold Becky's hand. Kim took the blood-pressure cuff and wrapped it around her other arm. Monica reappeared after putting in her page and tried to take over, but Kim would not hear of it. He put a stethoscope in his ears and started to inflate the cuff.

David Washington and Molly McFadden entered. David had a white jacket thrown over his scrubs. He nodded a greeting to Tracy and waited for Kim to finish taking the blood pressure. He also motioned to Monica that she could leave.

"You have no respect for protocol," David commented as Kim took the stethoscope from his ears.

"Her blood pressure is ninety over fifty," Kim said. "Let's get an IV going. I want her typed and cross-matched just in case. Also . . ."

"Hold up!" David yelled, raising his hand for emphasis. Then in a calm voice he added: "Dr. Reggis, with all due respect, you've already forgotten that you are not in charge here."

"I'm just covering the basics," Kim said. "Miss McFadden, how about getting me a twenty-one-gauge catheter, and I'll need a tourniquet and some tape."

David motioned for Molly to stay where she was, while he went up to Kim. He wrapped one of his sizable hands around Kim's forearm.

"I'm only going to ask you once," David said in his calm but commanding voice. "I want you to walk out of here and wait outside. It's in your daughter's best interest. I'm sure that if you just stop and think for a moment, you'll understand."

Kim's eyes narrowed as he stared at David. Slowly he looked down at David's hand clasped around his arm. For a moment no one said a word. The only sound came from a cardiac monitor in another cubicle.

Tracy sensed the electricity in the air. For her it was like the explosive calm just prior to a sudden summer thunderstorm. To avert an undoubtedly unpleasant scene, she dashed around the foot of the gurney and put her arm over Kim's shoulder and tugged on him. "Please, Kim!" she pleaded. "Let's let them do their thing."

Gradually Kim responded to Tracy's urging, and he visibly relaxed a degree. David took his hand away.

Kim nodded to Tracy. "Okay," he said. Then, turning back to Becky, he gripped her tiny arm. "Daddy will be right outside, Pumpkin."

"I don't want any needles," Becky said plaintively.

"They want to give you some fluid," Kim said. "But it will be only one stick. It will be over in a second. I know it's no fun, but you've got to be strong so you can get back to normal. Okay?"

"Okay," Becky said reluctantly.

Tracy gave Becky's hand a squeeze and told her that she would be with Kim and that they would be back in to see her in a few moments. Becky nodded but she clearly wasn't happy. She looked scared.

Tracy followed Kim out through the curtain surrounding Becky's gurney. She could hear that he was breathing fast. She didn't say anything until they had passed the nurses' desk.

"Kim, you have to calm down," Tracy said. She put her hand gently on his arm. "You're so tense."

"David Washington drives me up a wall," Kim snapped.

"He's doing his job," Tracy said. "If the situation were reversed and you were taking care of his child, I'm sure you'd act the same way he has. You wouldn't want him giving orders."

Kim pondered this as he pushed through the swinging doors to the outside. The blast of cold air felt good on his face. He stopped on the platform and took a deep breath. He slowly let it out. Tracy still had a hold of his arm.

"I guess you're right," he said finally. "It's hard for me to see Becky lying there and so vulnerable."

"I can imagine," Tracy said. "It must be very difficult."

Their eyes met.

"You can understand?" Kim asked. "Seriously?"

"Absolutely," Tracy said. "You're a surgeon. You are trained to act. And who would you want to take care of more than your own child. For you the hardest thing in the world is to see Becky in need and not do something."

"You're right," Kim said.

"Of course I am," Tracy said. "I'm always right."

In spite of himself, Kim smiled. "Now, I'm not going to go that far. Frequently maybe, but not always!"

"I'll accept that, provided we go back inside," Tracy said with a smile. "I'm freezing."

"Sure, I'm sorry," Kim said. "I just needed a breath of cold air."

O   O   O

"Does the IV bother you?" Kim asked Becky.

Becky raised her left hand which was taped to a flat wristboard. A length of clear plastic tubing dove into the gauze covering the back of her hand. "I can't feel it at all," she said.

"That's the way it's supposed to be," Kim said.

"Does it feel cold?" Tracy said. "That's what I remember when I was in the hospital having you."

"It does feel cold!" Becky remarked. "I didn't know it until you said it. My whole arm is cold."

David had carefully examined Becky, had started the IV, had done routine bloodwork and urinalysis, and had a flat plate and an upright X-ray taken of her abdomen. Although he'd yet to see the X-rays since they were not yet available, the blood and urine results were all normal, suggesting the blood loss had been minimal. At that point, he'd sent for Kim and Tracy to keep Becky company while they waited for Dr. Claude Faraday.

The infectious-disease specialist arrived a few minutes later. He introduced himself to Kim and Tracy, and then to Becky. He was a slender, dark-complected man with an intense manner. He listened to a full recounting of Becky's problem, from the very first symptoms Saturday morning until the episode of hemorrhage that evening. He nodded every so often, especially when Becky herself added specific details.

"Okay, Miss Reggis," he said to Becky. "Would you mind if I looked you over a bit?"

Becky looked at Tracy as if she had to get permission.

"Dr. Faraday is asking you if it's all right for him to examine you," Tracy translated for Becky.

"It's okay," Becky said. "I just don't want any more needles."

"No more needles," Claude assured her.

Claude started his rapid but thorough examination by feeling Becky's pulse and checking the turgor of her skin. He looked into her mouth and ears. He used an ophthalmoscope to peer into her eyes. He listened to her chest and checked her skin for rashes. He gently poked into her abdomen, which was tender. He searched for enlarged lymph nodes.

"You seem okay to me, except for that slightly sore belly," he said at last. "Now, I'm going to step outside and talk to your parents. Okay?"

Becky nodded.

Tracy leaned over and gave her daughter a kiss on the forehead before following Claude and Kim out through the curtain. The corridor was busy, so the group drew to the side to avoid the bustle. David happened to see them and walked over. He introduced himself to Claude.

"I was just about to give a summary to the parents," Claude said to David.

"Mind if I listen in?" David asked.

Claude looked at Kim and Tracy.

"That's fine," Tracy said.

"All in all, she looks good to me," Claude began. "She's a little pale, of course, and a bit dehydrated. There's also some generalized abdominal tenderness. Otherwise, on physical exam she's quite normal."

"But the hemorrhage?" Tracy questioned. She was afraid Claude was about to dismiss the case.

"Let me finish," Claude said. "I also went over her laboratory work. Compared to last night, there is a slight drop in her hemoglobin. It's not statistically significant, but in view of the mild dehydration, it might be important, considering the history of the hemorrhage. There's also a slight drop in her platelets. Otherwise, everything is within normal limits."

"What's your presumptive diagnosis?" Kim asked.

"I'd have to say food-borne bacterial illness," Claude said.

"Not viral?" Kim asked.

"No, I think it's bacterial," Claude said. He looked at David. "I believe that was your feeling last night as well, wasn't it?"

"Yes it was," David said.

"But why no fever?" Kim asked.

"The fact that there has been no fever makes me think this has been more a toxemia than an infection," Claude said. "Which also goes along with the normal white count."

"What about last night's culture?" Kim asked. "Is there a preliminary twenty-four-hour reading?"

"I didn't see a culture," Claude said. He looked at David.

"We didn't do a culture last night," David said.

Kim shook his head in disbelief. "What the hell are you talking about?" he demanded. "I even gave you the sample."

"We don't do routine stool cultures for simple diarrhea here in the ER," David said.

Kim slapped his hand to his forehead. "Wait a sec! You just said you'd made a presumptive diagnosis of a bacterial infection. Why wouldn't you do a culture? It just stands to reason, much less being good medicine. How else could you treat rationally?"

"AmeriCare utilization rules proscribe routine cultures in this kind of case," David said. "It's not cost-effective."

Kim's face reddened. Tracy was the only one who noticed. She reached out and gripped Kim's arm. He pulled it free. "Cost-effective! What kind of screwball excuse is that? What the hell kind of emergency room are you running here? You're telling me that to save a few measly dollars you failed to do a culture?"

"Listen, you prima donna," David snapped. "I just told you, it's standard operating procedure not to do them. Not for you, not for anybody."

Losing control as he'd done the night before, Kim grabbed David by the lapels of his white jacket. "Prima donna, am I? Well, your goddamn screwed-up operating procedure has lost us a whole damn day!"

Tracy grabbed Kim's arm. "No, Kim!" she cried. "Not again!"

"Take your hands off me, you arrogant son-of-a-bitch," David growled.

"Calm down!" Claude said as he insinuated himself between the two much larger men. "It's okay. We'll run some cultures stat. We haven't lost that much, because I doubt we'd treat anyway."

Kim let go of David. David smoothed his jacket. Each man glared at the other.

"What would you expect to see in the culture?" Tracy asked, hoping to defuse the situation and get the conversation back on track. "What kind of bacteria do you think is involved?"

"Mainly salmonella, shigella, and some of the newer strains of E. coli," Claude said. "But it could be a lot of other things as well."

"The blood scared me," Tracy said. "I guess it looked like more than it was. Will she be admitted?"

Claude looked at David. "It's not a bad idea," he said. "But it's not my call."

"I think it is a good idea," David said. "She needs fluids. Then we can evaluate the possibility of anemia and make sure there's no more bleeding."

"What about antibiotics?" Tracy asked.

"I wouldn't recommend it," Claude said. "Not at this juncture. Not until we have a definitive diagnosis."

"Which is why the goddamn culture should have been done last night!" Kim growled.

"Please, Kim!" Tracy urged. "We have to deal with the current situation. It would be nice if you'd try to be helpful?"

"All right," Kim said resignedly. "If we don't have a culture, why not use a broad-spectrum antibiotic. It can always be changed once the organism and its sensitivities are known."

"It would not be my recommendation," Claude repeated. "If the offending agent turns out to be one of the aberrant strains of E. coli, antibiotics can make the situation worse."

"Now, how can that be?" Kim said. "That's ridiculous."

"I'm afraid not," Claude said. "Antibiotics can decimate the normal flora and let the renegade E. coli more room to flourish."

"Will she be admitted to your care?" Tracy asked Claude.

"No, that's not possible," Claude said. "AmeriCare requires a gatekeeper. But I'll be happy to look in on her, especially if whoever handles the case requests an infectious-disease consult."

"Since Becky does not have a staff pediatrician, she'll be admitted under the care of Claire Stevens," David said. "It's her rotation. I can give her a call."

"You can't do much better than Claire," Claude remarked.

"You know her?" Tracy asked.

"Very well," Claude said. "You're lucky it's her rotation. She takes care of my kids."

"Finally something seems to be going right," Kim said.

# CHAPTER 8

Kim turned into the hospital parking lot a little after six in the morning. He'd skipped stopping at his office, as he normally did. He was eager to look in on Becky and make sure everything was okay.

The previous night things had gone well after the unpleasant episode with David Washington. Dr. Claire Stevens had come into the ER within a half hour of being paged. In the interim, Kim had phoned George Turner for the second time that evening. This gave him a chance to ask George's opinion about the pediatrician. George had echoed Claude's sentiments, and both Kim and Tracy had felt relieved.

Claire was a tall, thin woman—nearly Kim's height. Her features were sharp but they were belied by her gentle, reassuring manner. Kim's personal impressions of her added to the professional testimonials. She was about his age, which suggested years of clinical experience under her belt. What's more, her competence was immediately apparent and reassuring. Of equal importance, she established immediate rapport with Becky.

Kim pushed into Becky's room. There was a night-light near the floor that reflected off the ceiling, casting a gentle glow over the entire room. Kim advanced silently to the bedside and looked down at his sleeping daughter. Her halo of dark hair made her face appear the color of ivory. Its translucency gave her a fragile look as if she were made of porcelain.

Kim knew that under the circumstances it was appropriate for Becky to be in the hospital. At the same time her being there gave him great anx-

105

iety. His vast experiences in hospitals reminded him that it was an environment where horror could lurk.

Becky's breathing was regular and deep. Her IV was running slowly. Happy to see her resting so well, Kim quietly backed out. He did not want to disturb her.

Back at the nurses' station, Kim withdrew Becky's chart. He glanced through the admitting notes that Claire had dictated, then turned to the nurses' notes. He noticed Becky had been up twice during the night with continued diarrhea. There had been some blood reported but only by Becky. None of the nurses had seen it.

Kim then turned to the order sheet and was pleased to see that Claire had followed up on her word: she'd requested a pediatric gastroenterology consult for that day.

"Now, that's one delightful child," a lilting voice said.

Kim looked up. Glancing over his shoulder was a plump nurse with a face red from exertion. Her blond hair was permed into a multitude of tight ringlets. Her cheeks were dimpled. Her name tag indicated she was Janet Emery.

"Have you been looking in on her?" Kim asked.

"Yup," Janet said. "Her room's in my area. Cute as a button, that one."

"How has she been doing?" Kim asked.

"Okay, I guess," Janet said without a lot of conviction.

"That doesn't sound too positive," Kim said. A minute sliver of fear eked its way up his spine, giving him an involuntary shiver.

"The last time she was up, she seemed weak," Janet said. "Of course, it might have been because she was sleeping. She rang for me to come help her back to bed."

"I understand from the chart that you didn't get to see how much blood she might have passed," Kim said.

"That's right," Janet said. "The poor thing is embarrassed to beat the band. I tried to tell her not to flush after she uses the toilet, but she does anyway. What can you do?"

Kim made a mental note to talk to Claire about that problem and to

Becky as well. It would be important to know if the blood was mere spotting or worse.

"Are you a consult on the case?" Janet asked.

"No," Kim said. "I'm Dr. Reggis, Becky's father."

"Oh my goodness," Janet said. "I thought you were a consult. I hope I didn't say anything out of line."

"Not at all," Kim said. "I certainly got the feeling you care for her."

"Absolutely," Janet said. "I just adore children. That's why I work this floor."

Kim went off to see his inpatients and then attend the series of hospital conferences scheduled for that morning. Like Mondays, Wednesdays were particularly busy with respect to his administrative responsibilities. Consequently, he didn't get back to Becky's floor until almost ten. When he did, the ward clerk informed him that Becky was off to X-ray. He was also told that Tracy had come in and was with her.

"Can you tell me about the status of the gastroenterology consult?" Kim asked.

"It's been ordered," the clerk said. "If that's what you mean."

"Any idea when it will be?" Kim asked.

"Sometime this afternoon, I'd guess," the clerk said.

"Would you mind giving me a call when it does happen?" Kim asked. He handed the clerk one of his cards.

"Not at all," the clerk said.

Kim thanked him and hurried off to his office. He would have preferred to see Becky and talk to her, even if for a moment, but he didn't have the time. He was already behind schedule, a fact that he was philosophical about, since it tended to happen more often than not.

"Well, Mr. Amendola," Kim said, "do you have any questions?"

Mr. Amendola was a heavyset plumber in his early sixties. He was intimidated by modern medicine and horrified by Kim's verdict: he needed

a valve in his heart replaced. A few weeks earlier, he'd been blissfully unaware he even had valves in his heart. Now, after experiencing some scary
symptoms, he knew that one of them was bad and had the potential to kill
him.

Kim ran a nervous hand through his hair as Mr. Amendola pondered
the last question. Kim's eyes wandered out the window to the pale wintery sky. He had been preoccupied ever since Tracy had called an hour
earlier to say she thought Becky didn't look good, that she was glassy-eyed
and listless.

With a waiting-room full of patients, Kim's response had been to in-
struct Tracy to page Claire and to tell her Becky's status. He also told
Tracy to remind the clerk to call him when the gastroenterology consult
arrived.

"Maybe I should talk to my children," Mr. Amendola said.

"Excuse me?" Kim said. He'd forgotten what he'd asked the man.

"My children," Mr. Amendola said. "I got to ask them what they think
the old man should do."

"Good idea," Kim said. He stood. "Discuss it with your family. If you
have any questions, just call."

Kim walked Mr. Amendola to the door.

"You're sure the tests you've done are right?" Mr. Amendola asked.
"Maybe my valve isn't so bad."

"It's bad," Kim said. "Remember, we got a second opinion."

"True," Mr. Amendola said with resignation. "Okay, I'll get back to
you."

Kim waited in the corridor until it was certain Mr. Amendola was on
his way to reception. Then Kim lifted the heavy chart of the next patient
out of the chart rack on the back of the door to the second examining
room.

Before Kim had even read the name, Ginger appeared at the end of the
corridor. She had to move out of the way for Mr. Amendola to pass.

"I just got a call from the ward clerk on Becky's floor," she reported.
"I'm supposed to tell you that the gastro something-or-other doctor is
seeing Becky at this very moment."

"Then I'm out of here," Kim said quickly. He replaced the chart into its rack and stepped into his private office. While he was getting his suit jacket from the closet, Ginger came in.

"Where are you going?" she asked.

"Back to the hospital," Kim said.

"When will you be back?" Ginger asked.

"I don't know," Kim said. He pulled on his winter coat. "Let Cheryl know, so that the patient doesn't sit and wait in the examining room."

"What about the other patients?" Ginger said.

"Tell them there's been an emergency," Kim said. "I'll be back but probably not for an hour and a half or so."

Kim picked up his car keys and went to his rear door.

Ginger shook her head. She was the one who would have to face the patients. From past experience she knew how upset they were going to be, especially the ones coming from out of town.

"Just do the best you can," Kim said as if reading her mind.

Kim dashed to his car. He jumped in, started it, and drove out into the congested street. Leaning on his horn, he weaved in and out of the traffic. He felt desperate. Particularly after Tracy's comments, he did not want to miss talking directly to the GI consult.

In the hospital lobby, Kim repeatedly hit the elevator button as if such action would bring a car sooner. Several visitors eyed him suspiciously.

Once on Becky's floor, Kim literally ran down the hall. When he entered Becky's room, he was panting. He saw Tracy standing off to the side, talking with a woman in a long, professorial white coat. Even a quick glance told him that Tracy was distraught.

Becky was in her bed on her back with her head propped up against the pillow. Her dark eyes stared ahead. At the moment, the only apparent motion was the relentless drip of fluid in the millipore chamber of the IV line.

Kim stepped over to the side of the bed. "How are you doing, Pumpkin?" he asked. He grasped her hand and lifted it. There was little resistance.

"I'm tired," Becky offered.

"I'm sure you are, dear," Kim said. Instinctively he felt her pulse. Her heart rate was on the high side of normal. By gently pulling down one of her eyelids, he checked her conjunctiva. It was pale but not significantly paler than it had been. He felt her skin. It was not particularly hot or moist, and her level of hydration seemed better than it had been the night before.

Kim's own pulse began to race. He could tell what Tracy had meant. There had been a change in Becky, and Tracy's description of glassy-eyed and listless was accurate. It was as if part of Becky's incredible life force was in abeyance. She'd become lethargic.

"I'm going to talk to Mom," Kim said.

"All right," Becky answered.

Kim stepped over to Tracy. He could see she was subtly trembling.

"This is Dr. Kathleen Morgan," Tracy said.

"Are you the GI specialist?" Kim asked.

"I am indeed," Kathleen said.

Kim eyed the woman. In many ways she was the physical antithesis of Claire Stevens, although they were about the same age. Kim estimated that she couldn't have been much over five feet in height. Her face was round and her features were quite soft. She wore wire-rimmed glasses that gave her the aura of a schoolmarm. Her dark hair was prematurely streaked with silver.

"Dr. Morgan has told me she thinks Becky's case is serious," Tracy managed.

"Oh, that's a great comment," Kim remarked with obvious derision. "Serious, huh? I don't need someone to tell me it's serious. She wouldn't be in the goddamn hospital if it weren't serious. I need someone to say what it is that she has and how to treat and cure it."

"The lab will call me the moment they have a positive," Kathleen said warily. She was taken aback by Kim's response. "Until then our hands are tied."

"Have you examined her yet?" Kim demanded.

"Yes, I have," Kathleen said. "And I've gone over the laboratory results that are available."

"And . . . ?" Kim remarked impatiently.

"So far I agree with Dr. Faraday," Kathleen said. "Food-borne bacterial illness."

"She looks worse to me," Kim said.

"To me too," Tracy added. "She's changed just since last night. She's not herself; she's not as alert."

Kathleen cast an uncomfortable glance over at Becky. She was relieved to see the child was not paying attention to their conversation. Nonetheless she suggested they move out into the hallway.

"Having just seen her, I can't comment on any change," Kathleen said. "And there wasn't anything in the nurses' notes to that effect."

"I want her more closely monitored," Kim said. "How about moving her into one of the isolation rooms in the ICU?"

"I'm only a consult," Kathleen said. "Becky is officially under the care of Dr. Claire Stevens, the pediatrician gatekeeper."

"Then how about your convincing her?" Kim said. "Last night I suggested as much on admission, but I got the feeling she's on AmeriCare's side and worried about costs."

"That doesn't sound like Claire to me," Kathleen said. "But, to be truthful, I don't think your daughter needs the ICU. At least not yet."

"That's an encouraging statement," Kim snapped. "In other words, you expect her to get worse while the lot of you sit around and do nothing."

"That's unfair, Dr. Reggis," Kathleen said, taking offense.

"The hell it is, Dr. Morgan," Kim spat. He pronounced her name with more scorn than he felt. "Not from my point of view. As a surgeon I make a diagnosis, then I go in and I fix it. In other words, I do something, whereas now I have this sickening sense my daughter is slipping downhill in front of my eyes and no one is doing anything."

"Stop it, Kim!" Tracy said, fighting tears. As anxious as she was about Becky, she didn't want to have to deal with Kim's contentiousness.

"Stop what?" Kim challenged.

"Your bickering!" Tracy managed. "This constant fighting with the doctors and the nurses is not helping. It's driving me to distraction."

Kim glared at Tracy. He couldn't believe that she could turn on him so quickly, especially since the issue involved Becky's care.

"Dr. Reggis, come with me!" Kathleen said suddenly. She made a motion with her hand as she started toward the nurses' station.

"Go!" Tracy encouraged. "Get a grasp on yourself."

As Tracy went back into Becky's room, Kim caught up with the striding Kathleen. She had her mouth set and was moving at a surprising clip with her relatively short legs.

"Where are you taking me?" Kim questioned.

"To the chart room behind the nurses' station," Kathleen said. "I want to show you something, and I think we should talk, just you and me, doctor to doctor."

The nurses' station was a beehive of activity. The day shift was preparing to leave and the evening shift was just coming on duty. Kathleen walked through the congestion with practiced ease. She held open the chart-room door and motioned for Kim to step inside.

Once the door closed against the hubbub, relative quiet ensued. The chart room was a windowless nook with built-in desks and X-ray view box. The communal coffeemaker stood on the countertop in the corner.

Without speaking, Kathleen slipped some X-rays from their folder and snapped them up onto the light box. She turned the unit on. The films were of a child's abdomen.

"Are these Becky's?" Kim asked.

Kathleen nodded.

Kim leaned forward to study the details as he allowed his trained eye to scan the X-rays. He was more adept at reading chest films, but he knew the basics.

"The bowel looks uniformly edematous," he said after a moment.

"Exactly," Kathleen said. She was impressed. She'd thought she'd have to point out the pathology. "The mucosal lining is swollen for most of its length."

Kim leaned back. "What does that tell you?" he asked. He did not like what he was seeing but had no way of relating it to clinical symptoms.

"It makes me worry specifically about E. coli O157:H7," Kathleen said.

"You could see about the same X-ray with shigella dysentery, but the patient would probably have fever. As you know, Becky doesn't have any fever."

"What about antibiotics?" Kim asked. "Claude Faraday advised against them for fear of disturbing the normal flora. Do you agree?"

"I do," Kathleen said. "Not only so as not to disturb the normal flora, but they might very well be useless. With no fever, there is a good chance the offending organisms are already gone from Becky's gut."

"If we're dealing with a potential toxemia," Kim said, "how do we make the diagnosis then?"

"There is the possibility of testing for the toxin itself," Kathleen said. "Unfortunately AmeriCare has not authorized our lab to do the test."

"Don't tell me it's a money issue," Kim warned.

"I'm afraid so," Kathleen said. "It's one of those tests which is not used often enough for AmeriCare to justify its expense. AmeriCare feels it is not cost-effective."

"Jesus H. Christ!" Kim exploded. He pounded the countertop with his fist in frustration. "If I hear that phrase 'not cost-effective' one more time I'm going to have a fit. From the moment Becky became sick, AmeriCare's bottom line seems to be haunting me."

"Unfortunately managed care is a reality we all must face," Kathleen said. "But in this case I took it upon myself to have a sample sent out to Sherring Labs. We'll have the results in twenty-four to forty-eight hours."

"Hallelujah!" Kim commented. "Thank you, and I apologize for saying you weren't doing anything. I mean, money should not be a consideration when Becky's health is concerned."

"What do you know about this particular E. coli and its toxin?" Kathleen asked. "Assuming that it is indeed what Becky has."

"Not much," Kim said. "I didn't even know antibiotics weren't helpful. E. coli isn't something I've had to deal with in my practice. But vancomycin-resistant enterococcus is another matter. We cardiac surgeons are terrified of it."

"I get your point," Kathleen said. "I'm not familiar with the enterococcus problem, but I am with E. coli O157:H7. Maybe even a little too familiar. I think you and your wife should know that it can be a very bad bug."

"How so?" Kim asked nervously. He didn't like the sound of Kathleen's voice nor the implications of what she was saying. Kim didn't even bother to correct her misconception that he and Tracy were still married.

"Maybe you should sit down," Kathleen said. She was struggling with how best to explain her fears without unduly unsettling Kim. She could sense he was only in marginal control of his emotions.

Kim dutifully sat down in one of the desk chairs. He was afraid not to.

"If E. coli is involved with Becky's current problem," Kathleen said, "I'm concerned about the drop in platelets she's had. There was only a slight drop last night, but after she's been rehydrated, the drop is more apparent and statistically significant. It makes me worry about HUS."

"HUS?" Kim questioned. "What in devil's name is HUS?"

"It's the acronym for the Hemolytic Uremic Syndrome," Kathleen said. "It's associated with the shigella-like toxins E. coli O157:H7 is capable of producing. You see, this type of toxin can cause intravascular platelet coagulation as well as red-cell destruction. That, in turn, can lead to multiple-organ failure. Kidneys are the most commonly affected and hence the name uremic syndrome."

Kim's lower jaw slowly dropped. He was stunned. For a moment all he could do was look at Kathleen in a vain hope that she would suddenly smile and say it was all a bad joke. But she didn't.

"You think Becky has HUS?" Kim asked quietly with a calmness he did not feel.

"Let's put it this way," Kathleen said, trying to ease the impact. "It's my concern. There's no proof as of yet. At this moment, it's my clinical intuition that is suggesting it."

Kim swallowed loudly. His mouth had gone dry. "What can we do?" he asked.

"Not a lot, I'm afraid," Kathleen said. "I've sent the sample to the lab looking for the toxin. Meanwhile I will suggest hematology and nephrology consults. I don't think it is premature to get their opinions."

"Let's do it!" Kim blurted.

"Hold on, Dr. Reggis," Kathleen said. "Remember I'm only a consult. Any other consult requests have to go through Claire Stevens. It's her decision. AmeriCare is very clear on this."

"Well, let's call her for chrissake," Kim sputtered. "Let's get the ball rolling."

"You want me to call her this minute?" Kathleen asked.

"Absolutely," Kim said. He reached for the phone and pushed it in front of Kathleen.

While Kathleen used the phone, Kim cradled his head in his hands. He felt weak with sudden anxiety. What had been a nuisance, albeit a bothersome, scary nuisance requiring Becky to suffer and come into the hospital, had now become something else entirely. For the first time in his life, he was on the patient side of a major medical problem; one that he didn't even know much about. He was going to have to learn and learn fast. He quickly thought of ways he could do it.

"Claire's in full agreement," Kathleen announced as she replaced the receiver. "You are lucky to have her. She and I have handled several cases of HUS in the past."

"When will the consults see Becky?" Kim asked urgently.

"I'm sure as soon as Claire can arrange them," Kathleen said.

"I want them right away," Kim stated. "This afternoon!"

"Dr. Reggis, you have to calm down," Kathleen said. "That's why I brought you down here, so that we could talk calmly, one professional to another."

"I can't calm down," Kim admitted. He breathed out noisily. "How common is HUS?"

"Unfortunately it's become relatively common," Kathleen said. "It's usually caused by E. coli O157:H7 of which there are about twenty thousand cases a year. It's become common enough to be the current major cause of acute kidney failure in children."

"Good Lord!" Kim commented. He nervously massaged his scalp. "Twenty thousand cases a year!"

"That's the CDC estimate of the E. coli O157:H7 cases," Kathleen said. "It's only a percentage that go on to HUS."

"Is HUS ever fatal?" Kim forced himself to ask.

"Are you sure we should be talking about this aspect?" Kathleen questioned. "Remember the E. coli diagnosis has not been definitively made. I've just wanted to prepare you for its possibility."

"Answer the question, goddamn it!" Kim said hotly.

Kathleen sighed with resignation. She'd hoped Kim would be smart enough not to want to hear the disturbing details. The fact that he did, left her with no choice. She cleared her throat. "Between two hundred and five hundred people, mostly kids, die from E. coli O157:H7 every year," she said, "and it's usually from HUS."

Perspiration broke out on Kim's forehead. He was stunned anew. "Two to five hundred deaths a year," he repeated. "That's unbelievable, especially since I've never heard of HUS."

"As I said, these are CDC estimates," Kathleen said.

"With that kind of mortality, how come all this isn't better known?" Kim asked. Intellectualization had always been a coping mechanism for Kim in dealing with the emotional burdens of medicine.

"That I can't answer," Kathleen commented. "There's been a couple of high-profile episodes with this E. coli strain, like the Jack-in-the-Box outbreak in 'ninety-two and the Hudson Meat recall in summer 'ninety-seven. Why these and other episodes haven't raised general awareness and concern, I don't know. It is rather mystifying."

"I remember those two episodes," Kim said. "I suppose I just assumed the government and the USDA took care of the problems."

Kathleen laughed cynically. "I'm sure that's what the USDA and the beef industry hoped you'd believe."

"Is this mostly a problem with red meat?" Kim asked.

"Ground meat, to be precise," Kathleen said. "Ground meat that is not cooked through and through. But it's also true that some cases have been caused by such things as apple juice and apple cider and even unpasteurized milk. The key problem is contact with infected cow feces."

"I don't remember this problem as a child," Kim said. "I used to eat raw hamburger all the time."

"It's a relatively new situation," Kathleen said. "It's thought to have

originated in the late seventies, perhaps in Argentina. The belief is that a
shigella bacterium gave an E. coli bacterium the DNA necessary to make
a shigella-like toxin."

"By bacterial conjugation," Kim suggested.

"Precisely," Kathleen said. "Conjugation is bacteria's answer to sexual
reproduction, a method of genetic shuffling. But if conjugation was involved, it's curious since conjugation usually only happens within a
species. But the truly surprising aspect is that once this new strain of E. coli
was formed, it spread extraordinarily rapidly around the globe. Today it
exists in about three percent of bovine intestines."

"Are the infected cows sick?" Kim questioned.

"Not necessarily," Kathleen said. "Although it can cause a bovine di-
arrheal disease, cows seem to be generally immune to the toxin, at least
systemically."

"Strange!" Kim commented. "And ironic! Back when molecular biol-
ogy was in its infancy, a doomsday scenario was envisioned that scared
everybody: a researcher would give an E. coli bacterium the ability to
manufacture the botulism toxin, and then bacteria would inadvertently
get released into nature."

"It's a good analogy," Kathleen said. "Especially considering that with
the emergence of E. coli O157:H7 nature probably didn't do it on its own.
Man helped."

"How so?" Kim asked.

"I believe E. coli O157:H7 has come from the intense farming tech-
niques that are in use today," Kathleen said. "The need for cheap protein
to feed the animals has resulted in creative but disgusting solutions. Cows
are fed rendered animals, including themselves. Even chicken manure is
being widely used."

"You're joking!" Kim said.

"I wish," Kathleen said. "And on top of that, the animals are given antibiotics. It creates a soup within the animals intestines that fosters new
strains. In fact the E. coli O157:H7 was created when the shigella toxin
DNA was transferred along with the DNA necessary for a particular antibiotic resistance."

Kim shook his head in disbelief. He was hearing about an issue of considerable interest, but then, all of a sudden, he remembered the case in point: Becky's situation. The realization was instantly sobering.

"The bottom line of all this is bovine fecal material particularly in ground beef," Kim said. His voice returned to its previous anxious intensity.

"I think that's fair to say," Kathleen said.

"Then I know how Becky got it," Kim said angrily. "She had a rare hamburger at the Onion Ring restaurant Friday night."

"That would be consistent," Kathleen said. "Although the incubation period for E. coli O157:H7 is usually longer, sometimes as much as a week."

The door to the chart room banged open, causing both Kim and Kathleen to start. One of the nurses leaned in. She was flushed.

"Dr. Morgan!" she said urgently. "There's an emergency with your consult Rebecca Reggis!"

Kim and Kathleen raced out of the room and ran headlong down the corridor toward Becky's room.

# CHAPTER 9

As Kim came through Becky's door, he saw a nurse on either side of his daughter's bed. One was taking her blood pressure, the other her temperature. Becky was writhing in pain and whimpering. She appeared as pale as a ghost. Tracy was standing off to the side, with her back against the wall and a hand pressed to her mouth. She was almost as pale as Becky.

"What happened?" Kim demanded.

Kathleen came into the room behind Kim.

"I don't know," Tracy wailed. "Becky and I were just talking when suddenly she cried out. She said she had a terrible pain in her stomach and her left shoulder. Then she had a shaking chill."

The nurse taking the blood pressure called out that it was ninety-five over sixty.

Kathleen went around the left side of the bed and felt Becky's pulse. "Has Dr. Stevens been called?" she asked.

"Yes, immediately," one of the nurses said.

"Her temperature is one hundred and five," the other nurse said with dismay. Her name was Lorraine Phillips. Her colleague was called Stephanie Gragoudos.

Kim nudged Lorraine away from the right side of Becky's bed. Kim was frantic. It was like being stabbed in the heart to see his daughter suffering.

"Becky, what is it?" Kim demanded.

"My stomach hurts me," Becky managed amid groans. "It hurts me bad. Daddy, please!"

Kim pulled down Becky's blanket. He was shocked to see a swath of purplish subcutaneous bleeding on her chest. He raised his eyes to Kathleen. "Were you aware of this purpura?" he asked.

Kathleen nodded. "Yes, I saw it earlier."

"It wasn't there last night," Kim said. Kim looked back at Becky. "Tell Daddy where it hurts."

Becky pointed to her lower abdomen slightly to the right of the midline. She was careful not to touch herself.

Kim gently placed the tips of his index, middle, and ring fingers on Becky's abdomen where she'd pointed. He pressed in enough to barely dimple the skin. Becky writhed.

"Please don't touch me, Daddy," she pleaded.

Kim pulled his hand back sharply. Becky's eyes shot open and a cry of pain issued from her parched lips. Such a response was a sign Kim did not want to see. It was called rebound tenderness, and it was a strong indication of peritonitis, inflammation of the lining of the abdominal cavity. And there was only one thing that could cause such a catastrophe.

Kim straightened up. "She's got an acute abdomen," he yelled. "She's perforated!"

Without a moment's hesitation, Kim pushed up to the head of the bed and released the wheels. "Someone get the rear wheels," he yelled. "We'll use the bed for transport. We've got to get her to surgery."

"I think we should wait for Dr. Stevens," Kathleen said calmly. She motioned for Stephanie to get away from the foot of the bed. Kathleen then stepped to the head next to Kim.

"The hell with Dr. Stevens," Kim snapped. "This is a surgical emergency. The hand-wringing is over. We have to act."

Kathleen put her hand on Kim's arm, ignoring the wild look in his eyes. "Dr. Reggis, you are not in charge. You have to calm . . ."

In his agitated frame of mind Kim perceived Kathleen as an obstacle, not a colleague. Determined to get Becky to surgery as soon as possible, he literally swept her aside. With his strength and Kathleen's small stature, he inadvertently threw her against the bedside table.

Kathleen grabbed the table in a vain attempt to keep her feet but only succeeded in knocking everything off its surface. Water pitcher, glass, flower vase, and thermometer all crashed to the floor beside her.

Stephanie ran out into the hall to scream for help, while Lorraine tried to hold the bed in position. Despite the rear wheels being locked, Kim had managed to push it several feet toward the door.

Tracy recovered from her initial shock to rush to Kim. She tugged on one of his arms to get him to release the bed. "Kim, stop it," she sobbed. "Please!"

Several other nurses arrived, including the head nurse and a brawny male nurse. Everyone converged on Kim, who initially remained intent on pushing the bed into the hall. Even Kathleen pulled herself up from the floor to lend a hand. Finally overwhelmed, Kim let go of the bed, but he wasn't happy. He yelled that anyone who didn't understand that Becky's condition was a surgical emergency was incompetent.

"How will they put me to sleep?" Becky asked, with a voice already thick with sleep.

"They'll just put some medicine in your IV," Kim said. "Don't worry, you won't feel it. The next thing you'll know is that you're awake and all better."

Becky was on a gurney in the anesthesia-holding area of the OR. A surgical cap covered her head. She'd been premedicated, so her pain and discomfort had abated, but she was anxious about facing surgery.

Kim was standing next to her gurney in a clutch of other gurneys with patients waiting to be taken to their respective operating rooms. He was dressed in scrubs, with a hood on his head and booties covering his shoes. He'd recovered his senses after the scene in Becky's room an hour and a half earlier. He'd apologized profusely to Kathleen. She'd graciously said she understood. Claire had arrived soon after and had immediately requested an emergency surgical consult.

"Will I be all right, Daddy?" Becky asked.

"What are you talking about?" Kim asked, trying to make it sound as if it were a ridiculous question. "Of course, you'll be fine. They're just going to open you up like a zipper, patch the little hole, and that will be it."

"Maybe I'm being punished for not signing up for the Nationals," Becky said. "I'm sorry now that I didn't. I know you wanted me to."

Kim choked on tears that threatened to erupt. For a moment he looked off to compose himself and try to think of a response. He found it difficult to tell his daughter about fate when he was grasping for an explanation himself. Only days before, she'd been the very epitome of youthful vigor; now she was poised at the edge of the abyss. Why? he pondered.

"I'll have Mom bring me in the application," Becky added.

"Don't you worry about the Nationals," Kim said. "I don't care about them. I only care about you."

"Okay, Becky," a cheerful voice called out. "Time to fix you up."

Kim raised his head. Both Jane Flanagan, the anesthesiologist, and James O'Donnel, the gastrointestinal surgeon, had appeared from the depths of the OR. They came over to Becky's gurney. Jane went to the head and released the wheel locks.

Becky gripped Kim's hand with surprising strength, considering the amount of pre-op medication she'd had. "Will it hurt?" she asked Kim.

"Not with Jane taking care of you," James said playfully, overhearing the question. "She's the best sandwoman in the business."

"We'll even order you a good dream," Jane joked.

Kim knew and admired both these professionals. He had worked with Jane on numerous cases and had served with James on multiple hospital committees. James had been at Samaritan with Kim and had the reputation of being the best GI surgeon in the city. Kim had felt relieved when he agreed to drop everything that afternoon and come in to operate on Becky.

James grasped the foot of Becky's gurney. With Jane walking backward and James guiding, they maneuvered Becky toward the double swinging doors leading to the OR corridor.

Kim walked along the side. Becky still had a grip on his hand. Jane used her rump to open the doors. As the gurney slid through, James reached out and grasped Kim's arm to keep him from following. The doors closed behind Becky and Jane.

Kim looked down at the hand clasped around his arm and then up into James's face. James was not quite as tall as Kim but bulkier. He had a spattering of freckles across the bridge of his nose.

"What are you doing?" Kim inquired. "Let go of my arm, James."

"I heard what happened downstairs," James said. "I think it's best you don't come into the OR."

"But I want to come in," Kim said.

"Maybe so," James said. "But you're not."

"The hell I'm not," Kim said. "This is my daughter, my only daughter."

"That's the point," James said. "You stay out in the lounge, or I'm not doing the case. It's as simple as that."

Kim's face reddened. He felt panic about being cornered and confused as to what he should do. He desperately wanted James to do the surgery, but he was terrified to be apart from Becky.

"You have to make up your mind," James said. "The longer you agonize, the worse it is for Becky."

Kim angrily snatched his arm free, and, without saying another word, he broke off from staring at James. He strode away toward the surgical locker room.

Kim didn't look at the faces of the people in the surgical lounge as he passed through. He was too distraught. But he didn't pass by unnoticed.

In the locker room, Kim went directly to the sink and filled the bowl with cold water. He splashed it repeatedly onto his face before straightening up to regard himself in the mirror. Over his shoulder, he saw the pinched face of Forrester Biddle.

"I want to talk with you," Forrester said in his clipped voice.

"Talk," Kim said. He took a towel and briskly dried his face. He didn't turn around.

"After imploring you not to go to the media with your opinions, I was appalled to hear Kelly Anderson again quote you on the eleven o'clock news."

Kim let out a short, mirthless laugh. "That's curious, considering that I had refused to talk with her."

"She said it was your feeling that AmeriCare closed the Samaritan ER to cut costs and increase profits by forcing everyone to use the overburdened ER here at the University Med Center."

"I didn't say that," Kim responded. "She did."

"She quoted you," Forrester said.

"A curious situation," Kim said casually. In his current agitated state of mind he was getting perverse pleasure out of Forrester's self-righteous anger. Consequently Kim was not inclined to defend himself, although the incident strengthened his resolve never to talk to the TV journalist again.

"I'm warning you again," Forrester announced. "The administration and myself only have so much forbearance."

"Fine," Kim said. "Consider me warned again."

For a moment Forrester's tight mouth became a grim line without lips. "You can be galling," he spat. "I should remind you that just because you ran the department over at the Samaritan, you should not expect special treatment over here."

"That's apparent," Kim said. He threw the towel into the hamper and walked out, without giving Forrester another glance.

Using the phone in one of the dictation booths to avoid Forrester, Kim called Ginger to tell her that he'd not be coming back to the office. She told him that she'd assumed as much and had sent all the patients home.

"Were they upset?" Kim asked.

"Do you really have to ask?" Ginger said. "Of course they were upset, but they understood when I said it was an emergency. I hope you don't mind that I said it involved your daughter. I knew they'd empathize."

"I suppose that's all right," Kim said, although mixing his private life and professional life bothered him.

"How is Becky?" Ginger asked.

Kim explained what had happened and that Becky was in surgery at that moment.

"I'm so sorry," Ginger said. "Is there anything I can do?"

"I can't think of anything," Kim said.

"Call me," Ginger said. "After aerobics I'll be at home."

"Fine," Kim said. He hung up.

Knowing himself well enough that he could not just sit and wait while Becky was in surgery, Kim went to the hospital library. He had a lot of reading to do. He had to learn what he could about E. coli O157:H7 and HUS.

○   ○   ○

Kim glanced at his watch. It was almost midnight. He looked back at Becky and shuddered. Her image was distorted by a clear plastic tube that snaked out of one of her nostrils and was attached to low suction. Becky's dark hair framed her otherwise angelic, pale face with soft waves. Tracy had combed it for almost an hour. It was something Becky had always liked, and it had done the trick. Becky was fast asleep and appeared for the moment the picture of tranquillity.

Kim was standing next to Becky's bed. The room was awash with the gentle glow of the reflected night-light, just as it had been early that morning. Kim was exhausted mentally and physically.

Tracy was on the other side of the bed, leaning back in one of the two vinyl-covered chairs in the room. She had her eyes closed, but Kim knew she was not asleep.

The door opened on silent hinges. Janet Emery, the corpulent night nurse, pushed through the door. Her permed blond hair glowed in the half light. She didn't speak. She moved to the side of the bed opposite from Kim. Her shoes were soled in a soft crepe so her footfalls were inaudible. Using a small flashlight, she took Becky's blood pressure, pulse, and temperature. Becky stirred but immediately fell back asleep.

"Everything staying nice and normal," Janet said in a low voice.

Kim nodded.

"Maybe you folks should think about going home," Janet added. "I'll be keeping a sharp eye on your little angel here."

"Thanks but I prefer to stay," Kim said.

"Seems to me you could use some rest yourselves," Janet said. "It's been a long day."

"Just do your job," Kim grumbled.

"No question about that," Janet said cheerfully. She went to the door and silently disappeared.

Tracy opened her eyes and glanced over at Kim. He looked wretched under the strain. His hair was a mess and his face covered with stubble. The single night-light near the floor accentuated the gauntness of his cheeks and made his eye sockets look like dark hollows.

"Kim!" Tracy said. "Can't you control yourself? It's not helping any-one not even yourself."

Tracy waited for a response, but it didn't come. Kim appeared like a sculpture depicting anguished frenzy.

Tracy sighed and stretched. "How's Becky doing?"

"She's holding her own," Kim said. "At least the surgery handled the immediate crisis."

The surgery had gone quickly. In fact, James had reported to Kim that what had taken the most time was a painstaking irrigation of Becky's ab-domen to lessen the chances of infection. Following the surgery, Becky had spent a short time in the recovery room before being brought back to the floor. Kim had requested the ICU but again he'd been overruled.

"Tell me again about her colostomy," Tracy asked. "You said it can be closed in a couple of weeks."

"Something like that," Kim said tiredly. "If all goes well."

"It was a major shock for Becky," Tracy said. "As was the tube in her nose. She's having a hard time coping. What's made it worse is she feels betrayed because no one told her these things might happen."

"It couldn't be helped," Kim snapped.

Kim backed up and sank into a chair similar to Tracy's. With his elbows on the hard wooden arms, he buried his face in his hands.

Now all Tracy could see was the top of Kim's head over Becky's bed. He didn't move. The sculpture of anguished frenzy had assumed another, even more expressive pose.

Looking at Kim's dejected posture forced her to think about the situation from Kim's point of view. Drawing on her experience as a therapist, she could appreciate how hard it had to be for him, considering not only his surgical training but, more important, his narcissism. All at once her anger toward him melted.

"Kim," Tracy called. "Maybe you should go home. I think you need some distance as well as rest. Besides, you have to see patients tomorrow. I can stay. I'll just be skipping class."

"I wouldn't be able to sleep even if I did go home," Kim said, without lifting his face from his hands. "Now I know too much."

During the entire time Becky had been in surgery, Kim had researched HUS in the hospital library. What he'd learned had been frighteningly overwhelming. Everything Kathleen had said had been true. HUS could be a horrible illness, and now all he could hope was Becky had something else. The problem was that everything was pointing in the direction of HUS.

"You know, I'm beginning to appreciate how difficult this is for you, above and beyond your medical training," Tracy said sincerely.

Kim lifted his face from his hands and looked over at Tracy. "Please don't patronize me with any of your psychological bullshit. Not now!"

"Call it what you like," Tracy said. "But I'm realizing this is probably the first time in your life that you've been faced with a major problem that your force of will or expertise cannot alter. I think that must make this especially hard for you."

"Yeah, and I suppose all this isn't affecting you at all."

"Quite the contrary," Tracy said. "It's affecting me terribly. But it's different for you. I think you're having to deal with a lot more than Becky's condition. You're having to take a hard look at new limits, new constraints that are impeding your ability to act on Becky's behalf. It's taking a toll."

Kim blinked. He always hated his former wife's psychological theorizing, but at the moment he had to admit she was making a certain amount of sense.

# CHAPTER 10

Kim ended up going home, but as he expected he had not been able to sleep much, and the sleep he did get was marred by disturbing dreams. Several of the dreams he found incomprehensible; they were about being ridiculed for poor performance on tests in college. By far the most horrible nightmare had been about Becky, and it was easy for him to understand. In the dream she had fallen from a jetty into a surging sea. Although Kim was on the jetty, he couldn't reach Becky no matter what he did. When he had awakened, he had been covered with perspiration.

Despite getting little rest, Kim's going home did afford him an opportunity to shower and shave. With at least an improved appearance, he was back in his car just after five in the morning. He drove on mostly deserted streets slick with a dusting of wet snow.

In the hospital he found Becky as he'd left her. She appeared deceptively peaceful in her slumber. Tracy was fast asleep as well, curled in the vinyl chair and covered with a hospital blanket.

At the nurses' station Kim came across Janet Emery dutifully doing her chart work.

"I'm sorry if I was rude last night," Kim said. He sat down heavily in the seat next to Janet. He pulled Becky's chart from the rack.

"I didn't take it personally," Janet said. "I know what kind of stress it is to have a child in the hospital. I experienced it with my own son."

"How was Becky's night?" Kim asked. "Anything I should know?"

"She's been stable," Janet said. "Most important, her temperature has stayed normal."

"Thank God," Kim said. He found the operative note that James had dictated and which had been put into the chart over night. Kim read it but didn't learn anything he didn't already know.

With nothing else to do, Kim went to his office and busied himself with the mountain of paperwork that had accumulated. As he worked, he eyed the clock. When he thought the time appropriate, taking into account the hour difference on the East Coast, Kim gave George Turner a call.

George was enormously sympathetic when he heard about the perforation and the resultant surgery. Kim thanked him for his concern and quickly came to the point of the call: he wanted to ask George's opinion of what to do if the diagnosis of HUS secondary to E. coli O157:H7 was confirmed. Kim was particularly interested in knowing if Becky should be transferred elsewhere.

"I wouldn't recommend it," George said. "You've got an excellent team with Claire Stevens and Kathleen Morgan on board. They've had a lot of experience with this syndrome. Perhaps as much as anybody."

"Have you had any experience with HUS?" Kim asked.

"Just once," George said.

"Is it as bad as it's described?" Kim asked. "I've read just about everything I could find on it, including what's on the Internet. The problem is there's not a lot."

"The case I had was a very unnerving experience," George admitted.

"Could you elaborate?" Kim asked.

"It was unpredictable and relentless," George said. "I'm going to hope that Becky's problem turns out to be something else."

"Can you be more specific?" Kim asked.

"I'd rather not," George said. "It's a protean syndrome. Chances are that even if Becky has it, it will not be anything like my case. My case was quite depressing."

After a few more minutes, Kim brought the conversation to a close. Before hanging up, George asked to be kept informed about Becky's progress. Kim promised to do so.

After disconnecting from George, Kim phoned the nurses' station on Becky's floor. When he got Janet, he asked about Tracy.

"She's up and about," Janet said. "I saw her last time I was down that way taking vital signs."

"Would you mind putting her on the phone," Kim asked.

"Not at all," Janet said agreeably.

While he waited, Kim thought about George's comments. He didn't like the sound of "relentless and unpredictable" and that George's case had been depressing. Such descriptions reminded Kim of his nightmare, and he could feel himself perspire.

"Is that you, Kim?" Tracy asked as she came on the line.

They talked for a few minutes about how they had each passed the previous five hours. Neither had slept well. Then they got around to Becky.

"She seems a bit better than last night," Tracy said. "She's more lucid. I think she's slept off the rest of the anesthesia. Her main complaint is the nasogastric tube. When can that come out?"

"As soon as her whole GI system seems to be working," Kim said.

"Let's hope that can be soon," Tracy said.

"I spoke to George this morning," Kim said.

"What did he say?" Tracy asked.

"He said Claire and Kathleen were a good team, especially if HUS is confirmed. He told me that we couldn't do any better anyplace else."

"That's reassuring," Tracy said.

"Listen, I'm going to stay here," Kim said. "I'll see a few patients, including the pre-ops for tomorrow. I hope you don't mind."

"I don't mind in the slightest," Tracy said. "In fact I think it's a good idea."

"It's hard for me to sit there and do nothing," Kim explained.

"I understand completely," Tracy said. "You do what you have to do. I'll be here, so don't worry."

"Call me if there is any change," Kim said.

"Of course!" Tracy said. "You'll be the first to know."

When Ginger arrived just before nine, Kim told her to cancel whatever patients she could, because he wanted to get back to the hospital sometime in the afternoon.

Ginger asked about Becky, saying she was disappointed Kim hadn't called her the night before. She'd been worrying all night but had been afraid to phone.

Kim told her Becky was doing better following the surgery. He also explained that he'd not gotten home until after midnight and thought it much too late to call.

At first Kim found seeing patients was not easy under the circumstances, but he forced himself to concentrate. Gradually the effort paid off. By noontime, he felt slightly more relaxed although his heart would race every time the phone rang.

He wasn't hungry at lunchtime, and the takeout sandwich Ginger had brought in sat untouched on his desk. Kim preferred to immerse himself totally in his patients' problems. That way he didn't have to deal with his own.

In the middle of the afternoon, Kim was on the phone with a cardiologist from Chicago when Ginger stuck her head in the door. From her expression alone Kim could tell something was wrong. Kim covered the mouthpiece with his palm.

"Tracy was on the other line," Ginger said. "She was very upset. She told me that Becky has taken a sudden turn for the worse and has been moved to the ICU."

Kim's pulse quickened. He quickly wound up the conversation with the Chicago doctor and hung up. He changed his jacket, grabbed his car keys, and ran for the door.

"What should I do with the rest of the patients?" Ginger asked.

"Send them home," Kim said tersely.

Kim drove with determination, frequently barreling along the shoulder to avoid afternoon traffic jams. The closer he got to the hospital the more anxious he became. Although he'd been lobbying to have Becky moved to the ICU, now that she had been he was terrified. Having become all too aware of AmeriCare's cost-saving attitudes, he was certain the move wasn't for prophylaxis; there had to have been a serious emergency.

Eschewing the doctors' parking area, Kim drove right up beneath the hospital's porte cochere. He leaped out and tossed his keys to a surprised hospital security guard.

Kim fidgeted as the elevator rose painstakingly slowly up to the ICU's floor. Once in the corridor crowded with visitors, Kim moved as fast as he could. As he came abreast of a waiting room built specifically for family members of ICU patients, Kim caught sight of Tracy. She stood up when she saw him and came forward.

Tracy threw her arms around Kim, pinning his to his side. For a moment she would not let go. Kim had to forcibly extricate his arms before gently pushing her back. He looked into her eyes, which were brimming with tears.

"What happened?" he asked. He was afraid to hear the answer.

"She's worse," Tracy managed. "Much worse, and it seemed to happen so suddenly, just like with the perforation."

"What was it?" Kim asked with alarm.

"It was her breathing," Tracy said. "All of the sudden she couldn't get her breath."

Kim tried to break away from Tracy, but she held on, clutching his jacket. "Kim, promise me you'll control yourself. You have to, for Becky's sake."

Kim broke Tracy's hold and ran from the room.

"Kim, wait!" Tracy called, running after him.

Ignoring Tracy, Kim dashed across the hall and entered the ICU. Just inside the door, he held up for a moment while he scanned the room. Most of the beds were full. The occupants were all seriously ill patients. Nurses toiled at nearly every bedside. Banks of electronic monitoring equipment beeped and displayed vital data.

The most activity was in one of the small, separate rooms off to the side.

Within its confines was a group of doctors and nurses attending to an acute situation. Kim walked over and stood in the doorway. He saw the respirator and heard its rhythmical cycling.

Judy Carlson, a nurse Kim knew, caught sight of him. She called out his name and all the people surrounding Becky's bed silently stepped back to afford Kim a view. Becky had been intubated. A large tube stuck out of her mouth and was taped to her cheek. She was being breathed by a respirator.

Kim rushed to the bedside. Becky looked up at him with terrified eyes. She'd been sedated but she was still conscious. Her arms were restrained to keep her from pulling out the endotracheal tube.

Kim felt a crushing feeling in his chest. He was revisiting the dream that he'd had the night before; only this time it was real.

"It's okay, Pumpkin, Daddy's here," Kim said, struggling to control his emotions. He was desperate to say something to reassure her. He gripped her arm. She tried to speak but couldn't because of the tube in her throat.

Kim looked around at the people present. He centered his attention on Claire Stevens.

"What happened?" he asked, keeping his voice calm.

"Perhaps we should go outside," Claire said.

Kim nodded. He gave Becky's hand a squeeze and told her he'd be right back. Becky tried to speak but couldn't.

The doctors filed out into the ICU proper and formed a group off to the side. Kim folded his arms to hide his trembling.

"Talk to me!" Kim commanded.

"First let me introduce everyone," Claire said. "Of course you know Kathleen Morgan. We have Dr. Arthur Horowitz, nephrologist; Dr. Walter Ohanesian, hematologist; and Kevin Blanchard, respiratory therapist."

Claire had pointed out each person in turn. All had nodded to Kim, who nodded in return.

"What's the story?" Kim asked impatiently.

"First I have to tell you we're definitely dealing with E. coli O157:H7,"

Claire said. "We'll have an idea of the particular strain tomorrow after pulse field electrophoresis."

"Why is she intubated?" Kim asked.

"The toxemia is affecting her lungs," Claire said. "Her blood gases suddenly deteriorated."

"She's also in kidney failure," Arthur said. "We've started peritoneal dialysis." The kidney specialist was a completely bald man with a full beard.

"Why not a dialysis machine?" Kim questioned. "Aren't they more effective?"

"She should do fine with the peritoneal dialysis," Arthur said.

"But she just had surgery for a perforation," Kim said.

"That was taken into consideration," Arthur said. "But the problem is AmeriCare only offers dialysis machines at Suburban Hospital. We'd have to transfer the patient there, which we surely don't recommend."

"The other major problem is her platelet count," Walter said. The blood specialist was a gray-haired older man who Kim guessed was in his seventies. "Her platelets have fallen precipitously to the point where we feel they must be replenished despite the inherent risks. Otherwise, we might have a bleeding problem on our hands."

"There's also the problem with her liver," Claire said. "Liver enzymes have risen remarkably, suggesting . . ."

Kim's mind was on overload. He was stunned to the extent that he was no longer absorbing the information being presented to him. He could see the doctors talking, but he didn't hear. It was the nightmare all over again, with Becky floundering in the dangerous, surging sea.

A half hour later, Kim stumbled out of the ICU into the ICU waiting room. Tracy got up the moment she saw him. He looked like a broken man.

For a moment they stared into each others eyes. Now it was Kim's turn for tears. Tracy reached out, and they locked in a hug of fear and grief.

# CHAPTER 11

Kim paused for a moment to get his breath. He glanced up at the insti-
tutional clock on the tiled OR wall. It was nearly two o'clock in the afternoon. He was making good progress. This was the last of three cases.

Kim looked back into the depths of the wound. The heart was fully exposed. He was in the process of putting the patient on cardiopulmonary
bypass. As soon as he was finished, the heart could be stopped and opened.
At that point he would replace the damaged valve.

The next step was particularly critical: the placement of the arterial infusion cannula into the aorta to perfuse the coronary arteries. It would be
through this cannula that the cardioplegia solution would be introduced
that would stop the heart with its high potassium, cool it, and nourish it
during the procedure. The problem was that the arterial pressure had to
be dealt with.

"Scalpel," Kim said.

The scrub nurse slapped the scalpel with the appropriate blade into his
waiting palm.

Kim lowered the razor-sharp instrument into the wound and directed
it toward the aorta. The knife trembled in his hand; Kim wondered if
Tom noticed.

Kim made a quick stab into the aorta then covered the incision with the
tip of his left index finger. He did it quickly so that there was little blood
loss. The little blood that appeared was cleared by Tom.

137

"Arterial infusion cannula," Kim said.

The instrument was placed in his waiting hand. He introduced it into the wound and positioned it next to his finger, occluding the stab wound into the aorta. Sliding the tip under his finger, he tried to push it into the pulsating vessel. For reasons not clear to him, the cannula would not penetrate the vessel wall. Arterial blood was now spurting out.

Uncharacteristically, Kim panicked. With blood filling the wound, he pushed too hard with the instrument and tore the aorta, enlarging the opening. Now the stab wound was too big to seal around the cannula's bulbous tip. Blood squirted high enough to splatter against Kim's plastic face shield.

Kim now faced a surgical emergency. Instead of panicking more, his experience kicked in. Rapidly recovering his composure, he reached into the wound with his left hand. Blindly his finger found the hole in the pulsating vessel, and he pressed against it, partially stemming the blood. Tom rapidly sucked out enough of the blood to give Kim a partial view.

"Suture!" Kim barked.

A needle-holder trailing a length of black silk was pressed into his hand. Deftly he passed the needle's tip into the vessel's wall. He did this several times so that when he pulled up on the suture the hole was closed.

With the emergency quickly contained, Kim and Tom eyed each other across the patient. Tom motioned with his head, and Kim nodded. To the surprise of the team, Kim and Tom stepped away from the operative field. They kept their sterile gloved hands pressed against their sterile gowned chests.

"Kim, why don't you let me finish this last case?" Tom whispered. It was a suggestion for Kim's ears only. "I can pay you back for doing the same for me a couple of weeks ago when I was coming down with the flu. Remember?"

"Sure I remember," Kim said.

"You're understandably bushed," Tom said.

It was true: Kim was exhausted. He had spent most of the night in the ICU waiting room with Tracy. When it had become apparent that Becky's condition had stabilized, Tracy convinced Kim to get a few hours' rest in one of the resident on-call rooms. She'd also been the one to convince Kim to go ahead with his planned surgery, arguing that his patients needed him. She'd insisted that it was best for Kim to stay busy since there wasn't anything he could do for Becky besides wait. Her most convincing point had been that he'd be in the hospital and available if needed.

"How did we do this as residents?" Kim asked. "We never had any sleep."

"The benefit of youth," Tom said. "The problem is we're no longer young."

"How true," Kim commented. He paused for a moment. Turning his case over to anyone, even to someone as qualified as Tom, was not an easy decision for him. "All right," he said at length. "You take over. But I'll be watching you like a hawk."

"I wouldn't expect anything different," Tom joked. He knew Kim well enough to recognize his style of humor.

The two surgeons returned to the operating table. This time Tom was on the patient's right.

"All right, everybody," Tom said. "Let's get that cannula in. Scalpel, please!"

With Tom at the helm, the operation went smoothly. Although Kim was on the patient's left, he was the one who positioned the valve and placed the initial sutures. Tom did the rest. As soon as the sternum was closed, Tom suggested Kim should bow out.

"You don't mind?" Kim asked.

"Hell, no," Tom said. "Get over there and check on Becky."

"Thanks," Kim said. He stepped back and pulled off his gown and gloves.

As Kim pulled open the heavy OR door, Tom called out: "Between myself and Jane, we'll write the post-op orders. If there's anything else I can do, just call."

"I appreciate it," Kim said. He hurried into the surgical locker room where he picked up a long white coat to pull on over his scrubs. He was eager to get to the ICU and didn't want to take the time to change back into his street clothes.

Kim had visited the intensive-care unit prior to and between each of his surgeries. Becky had shown some improvement, and there was some talk of trying to wean her off the respirator. Kim hadn't allowed himself to become too hopeful, knowing she'd been on for less than twenty-four hours.

Kim had even found time prior to his first case to phone George again to ask if he could think of anything else they could do for Becky. Unfortunately he hadn't had any suggestions, except for plasmaphoresis, which he didn't recommend.

Kim had come across plasmaphoresis for E. coli O157:H7 toxemia in his research in the library during Becky's surgery. It involved replacing the patient's plasma with pooled fresh frozen plasma. Unfortunately it was a controversial treatment considered experimental with an enormous attendant risk of HIV since the new plasma came from hundreds of different donors.

The doors to the elevator opened and Kim was dismayed to join a group of happy staffers leaving the hospital at the end of the day shift. He knew it was unreasonable of him, but he couldn't help but be annoyed by their cheerful babble.

Getting off the elevator, Kim started down the hall. The closer he got to the ICU, the more nervous he became. He was almost beginning to feel a premonition.

He paused at the waiting-room threshold to see if Tracy was there. He knew she'd planned on going home to clean up and change clothes.

Kim saw her sitting in a chair near the window. She spotted him at almost the same moment and stood up. As she approached, Kim could see there'd been fresh tears. They streaked the side of her face.

"What's wrong now?" he asked with dismay. "Has there been a change?"

For a moment Tracy could not speak. Kim's question brought forth new tears that she had to choke back. "She's worse," Tracy managed. "Dr. Stevens talked about a cascading pattern of major organ failure. It was so much mumbo-jumbo to me, but she said that we should prepare ourselves. I think she was saying that Becky may die!"

"Becky's not going to die!" Kim said with vehemence that bordered on anger. "What happened to make her suggest such a thing?"

"Becky has had a stroke," Tracy said. "They think she's blind."

Kim shut his eyes hard. The idea of his ten-year-old daughter having a stroke seemed beyond any realm of possibility. Yet Kim well understood that her clinical course had been spiraling downward from the outset. That she may have reached the point of no return was not entirely surprising.

Leaving Tracy in the waiting room, Kim strode across the hall and entered the ICU. Mirroring the previous afternoon, a gaggle of doctors were pressed into Becky's cubicle. Kim pushed his way in. He saw a new face: Dr. Sidney Hampton, neurology.

"Dr. Reggis," Claire called.

Kim ignored the pediatrician. He muscled his way to the bedside and looked at his daughter. She was a pitiful shadow of her former self, lost within the wires and tubes, and the technology. Liquid crystal displays and monitor screens flashed their information in the form of digital readouts and tracing cursors.

Becky's eyes were closed. Her skin was a translucent bluish white.

"Becky, it's me, Dad," Kim whispered into her ear. He studied her frozen face. She didn't register any sign of hearing him.

"Unfortunately she's unresponsive," Claire said.

Kim straightened up. His breaths were shallow and rapid. "You think she's had a stroke?"

"Every indication suggests as much," Sidney said.

Kim had to remind himself not to blame the messenger.

"The basic problem is that the toxin seems to be destroying her platelets as fast as we give them," Walter said.

"It's true," Sidney said. "There's no way to know if this was an intracranial hemorrhage or a platelet embolus."

"Or a combination of the two," Walter suggested.

"That's a possibility," Sidney admitted.

"One way or another," Walter added, "the rapid destruction of her platelets must be forming a sludge in her microcirculation. We're into that cascading major organ failure situation that we hate to see."

"Kidney and liver function is definitely going down," Arthur said. "The peritoneal dialysis is not keeping up."

Kim had to steel himself to curtail his anger at this self-serving dialetic. It certainly wasn't helping his daughter. He tried to think and remain rational.

"If the peritoneal dialysis is not working," Kim said in a deceptively calm voice, "perhaps we should transfer her to the Suburban Hospital and get her on a dialysis machine."

"That's out of the question," Claire said. "She's too critical to be transferred."

"Well, it seems to me we have to do something," Kim shot back, his anger bubbling to the surface.

"I think we are doing all we can," Claire said. "We're actively supporting her respiratory and kidney functions, and replacing her platelets."

"What about plasmaphoresis?" Kim said.

Claire looked at Walter.

"AmeriCare is reluctant to authorize it," Walter said.

"Screw AmeriCare," Kim spat. "If there's a chance you think it could help, let's do it."

"Hold on, Dr. Reggis," Walter said. The gray-haired man shifted his weight. He was obviously uncomfortable about this issue. "AmeriCare owns this hospital. We can't just go thumbing our noses at their rules. Plasmaphoresis is expensive and experimental. With lay families, I'm not even supposed to bring it up."

"How do we go about getting them to authorize it?" Kim questioned. "I'll pay for it myself if it can help."

"I'd have to call Dr. Norman Shapiro," Walter said. "He's the chairman of the AmeriCare Review Board."

"Call him!" Kim barked. "Right now!"

Walter looked at Claire. Claire shrugged. "I suppose a call can't hurt."

"Okay by me," Walter said. He left the room to use the phone at the ICU desk.

"Dr. Reggis, plasmaphoresis is grasping at straws," Claire said. "I think it's only fair to tell you and your former wife that you should be preparing yourselves for all eventualities."

Kim saw red. He was in no frame of mind to "prepare himself" as Claire euphemistically suggested. Instead he wanted to strike out at the people responsible for Becky's sorry state, and at that moment his nearest targets were the doctors in that very room.

"You do understand what I'm saying, don't you?" Claire asked gently.

Kim didn't answer. In a suddenly clairvoyant moment, he comprehended the absurdity of blaming these doctors for Becky's plight, especially when he knew where the fault lay.

Without warning, Kim broke away from Claire and rushed out of the ICU. He was beside himself with anger, frustration, and his humiliating sense of impotence. He started down the hall.

Tracy was still in the waiting room. She spotted Kim's hasty exit and immediately knew he was in a rage. When he passed by without a glance, she ran to catch up to him. She was afraid what he might do.

"Kim, stop! Where are you going?" She pulled on his sleeve.

"Out," he said, breaking away.

"Where?"

Tracy had to run merely to keep up with Kim's determined stride. The look on his face frightened her. For the moment she forgot her own grief.

"I've got to do something," he said. "I can't just sit here and wring my hands. Right now I can't help Becky medically, but by God I'm going to find out how she got sick."

"How are you going to find out?" Tracy asked. "Kim, you have to calm down."

"Kathleen told me the E. coli problem is mainly a problem with ground meat," Kim said.

"Everybody knows that," Tracy said.

"Yeah, well, I guess I didn't," Kim said. "And remember when I told you that a week ago I took Becky to the Onion Ring on Prairie Highway? She had a burger, and it was rare. That had to have been when she got sick."

"So you mean to tell me you're going to the Onion Ring restaurant now?" Tracy asked incredulously.

"Obviously," Kim said. "If that's where Becky got sick, that's where I'm going."

"Right now, it doesn't matter where Becky got sick," Tracy said. "What matters is she is sick. We can worry about the how and the why some other time."

"It might not matter to you," Kim said. "But it matters to me."

"Kim, you're out of control," Tracy said with exasperation. "Just once can't you think of someone else besides yourself?"

"What the hell do you mean?" Kim snapped, feeling even more enraged.

"This is about you, not about Becky. It's about you and your doctor ego."

"The hell it is," Kim growled. "I'm in no mood to listen to any of your psychological nonsense. Not now!"

"You're not helping anyone by running off like this," Tracy said. "You're a threat even to yourself. If you have to go, at least wait until you have calmed down."

"I'm going in hopes it can calm me down," Kim said. "And maybe even give me an ounce of satisfaction."

The elevator arrived, and Kim boarded.

"But you haven't even changed out of your scrub clothes," Tracy said, hoping to find some way to delay him for his own good.

"I'm going," Kim said. "Right now. Nobody's going to stop me!"

Kim pulled into the Onion Ring parking lot fast enough to bottom out on the lip of the driveway. There was a muffled thump, and a shudder went through the car. Kim didn't care. He took the first parking spot he came to.

After putting on the emergency brake and turning off the ignition, Kim sat in the car for a moment and looked out the windshield at the restaurant. It was as crowded as it had been a week earlier.

The drive from the hospital had blunted the edge of his anger but not his determination. He thought about what he'd do once he was inside and then got out of the car. Passing through the main entrance, he found the lines at the cash registers stretched almost to the door. Unwilling to wait, he pushed his way to the front. Some of the customers complained. Kim ignored them.

Once at the counter, Kim got the attention of one of the cash-register girls whose name tag said: HI, I'M DEBBIE. She was a nondescript teenager with bleached hair and mild acne. Her facial features were frozen into an expression of absolute boredom.

"Excuse me," Kim said, forcing himself to sound calm even though it was apparent he was not. "I'd like to speak to the manager."

"You have to wait in line to order," Debbie said. She glanced briefly at Kim but was completely insensitive to his state of mind.

"I don't want to order," Kim said slowly and deliberately. "I want to speak to the manager."

"He's like really busy right now," Debbie said. She turned her attention back to the person standing at the head of her line and asked that the order be repeated.

Kim slammed his open palm down on the countertop with such force that it caused several napkin holders to vibrate off and fall with a clatter to the floor. The sound was like a shotgun blast. In an instant the entire restaurant went silent like a freeze-frame in a movie. Debbie turned pearl white.

"I don't want to have to ask again," Kim said. "I want the manager."

A man stepped forward from a position next to the central island behind the row of cash registers. He was dressed in a two-tone Onion Ring uniform. His name tag said: HI, I'M ROGER.

"I'm the manager," he said. His head twitched nervously. "What's the problem?"

"It's my daughter," Kim said. "She happens to be in a coma at the moment, fighting for her life, all from eating a hamburger here one week ago."

Kim was loud enough to make himself heard throughout the restaurant. Those customers who were eating burgers eyed them suspiciously.

"I'm sorry to hear about your daughter," Roger said, "but there's no way she could have gotten sick here, least of all from one of our burgers."

"This is the only place she had ground meat," Kim said. "And she's sick with E. coli and that comes from hamburger."

"Well, I'm sorry," Roger said emphatically. "But our burgers are all cooked well-done, and we've got strict rules about cleanliness. We're inspected regularly by the department of health."

As abruptly as the restaurant had gone silent, it returned to its high level of background noise. Conversations recommenced as if the collective judgment was that whatever Kim's problem was, it didn't concern them.

"Her burger wasn't well-done," Kim said. "It was rare."

"Impossible," Roger contended, with a roll of his eyes.

"I saw it myself," Kim said. "It was pink in the middle. What I'd like to ask . . ."

"It couldn't have been pink," Roger interjected, with a dismissive wave. "It's out of the question. Now, if you'll excuse me, I have to get back to work."

Roger began to turn away from the counter. Kim responded by lashing out and grabbing a handful of Roger's Onion Ring shirt. With his powerful arms, Kim pulled the startled manager over the counter so that his face was inches from Kim's. Instantly it began to empurple. Kim's ironlike grip was restricting blood flow in Roger's neck.

"A little remorse might be appropriate," Kim snarled. "Certainly not uninformed blanket denial."

Roger gurgled incomprehensibly while he ineffectually grappled with Kim's locked fingers.

Kim rudely pushed Roger back over the counter and let go of him, sending him to the floor. The cashiers, the rest of the kitchen staff, and the people waiting in line gasped but stood rooted in shocked immobility.

Kim rounded the end of the counter, intending to talk directly with the chef.

Roger scrambled to his feet, and seeing Kim coming into the kitchen area, he tried to confront him. "You can't come back here," he said gamely. "Only employees are allowed . . ."

Kim didn't give him time to finish. He simply shoved him out of the way, slamming the manager into the counter. The collision displaced a plastic juice machine which crashed to the tiles. Juice sloshed out in a wide arc across the floor. Those nearest jumped out of the way. The restaurant again quieted. A few of the patrons left hurriedly, taking their food with them.

"Call the police!" Roger croaked to the nearest cashier as he scrambled to his feet.

Kim continued around the central island to confront the wizened Paul. Kim took in the leathered face and the tattooed arm and wondered about the man's personal hygiene.

Like everyone else in the kitchen, Paul hadn't moved from the moment Kim had pounded the counter. Some of the burgers on the grill in front of him were smoking.

"My daughter had a rare burger here just about this time a week ago," Kim growled. "I want to know how that could have happened."

Roger came up behind Kim and tapped him on the shoulder. "You're going to have to leave," he said.

Kim spun around. He'd had quite enough of the pesky manager.

Roger wisely backed up. He raised his palms. "Okay, okay," he mumbled.

Kim turned back to Paul. "Any ideas?" he asked.

"No," Paul said. He'd seen people go crazy on oil rigs, and the look in Kim's eyes reminded him of these men.

"Come on," Kim snarled. "You must have been the cook. You have to have some idea."

"Like Roger said," Paul asserted. "It couldn't have been rare. I cook all the burgers well-done. It's policy."

"You people are really starting to piss me off," Kim snapped. "I'm telling you it was rare. I didn't get this secondhand. I was here with my daughter. I saw it."

"But I time them," Paul said. He pointed with his spatula to the smoking patties on the grill.

Kim grabbed one of a half-dozen completed burgers that Paul had put on the shelf above the grill for Roger to place on order trays. Kim rudely broke the burger open and examined the inside of the meat patty. It was well-done. He repeated this three more times, slapping the broken hamburgers back onto the plates.

"You see," Roger said. "They're all well-done. Now, if you'll step out of the kitchen area, we can discuss this more calmly."

"We cook them to an inside temperature higher than the one proposed by the FDA," Paul said.

"How do you know the inside temperature?" Kim asked.

"We gauge it with a special five-pronged thermometer," Roger said. "We take the temperature randomly several times a day, and it's always the same: above a hundred and seventy degrees."

Paul put down his spatula and rummaged in a drawer below the grill. He produced the instrument and offered it to Kim.

Kim ignored the thermometer. He took another hamburger and broke it open. It too was well-done. "Where do you store the patties before they're cooked?"

Paul turned around and opened the refrigerator. Kim bent over and peered inside. He knew he was only looking at a small portion of the meat the Onion Ring had to have on hand.

"Where's the bulk of them?" Kim questioned.

"In the walk-in freezer," Paul said.

"Show me!" Kim commanded.

Paul looked at Roger.

"No way," Roger said. "The walk-in is off limits."

Kim gave Paul a shove in the chest with both hands, propelling the man toward the back of the kitchen. Paul stumbled backward. Then turned and started to walk. Kim followed.

"No you don't," Roger said. He'd caught up to Kim and pulled on his arm. "Only employees are allowed in the freezer."

Kim tried to shake Roger off his arm, but Roger hung on. Frustrated, Kim backhanded the manager across the face with significantly more force than he'd intended. The power of the blow snapped Roger's head around, split his upper lip and sent him crashing to the floor for the second time.

Without even a glance at the fallen manager, Kim followed after Paul who now had the freezer door open. Kim stepped inside.

Fearful of Kim's size and impulsiveness, Paul gave him a wide berth. Paul looked back at his manager, who was now sitting on the rubber kitchen mat dabbing at his bloodied lip. Unsure of what to do, he followed Kim into the freezer.

Kim was looking at the cartons lined up on the left side of the walk-in. Only the first was open. The labels read: MERCER MEATS: REG. 0.1 LB HAMBURGER PATTIES, EXTRA LEAN. LOT 2 BATCH 1-5. PRODUCTION: DEC. 29. USE BY MARCH 29.

"Would a hamburger last Friday night have come from this carton?" Kim asked.

Paul shrugged. "Probably, or one similar."

Kim stepped back into the depths of the freezer and saw another open carton nestled among the sealed ones. He opened it and looked in. He could see that the wrapping was also broken on one of the inner boxes. "How come this carton is open?" he asked.

"It was a mistake," Paul said. "We're supposed to use the oldest patties first so we never have to worry about the 'use by' date."

Kim looked at the label. It was similar to the previous one except for the production date. This one said "Jan. 12" instead of "Dec. 29." "Could a patty have come from this one last Friday?" he asked.

"Possibly," Paul said. "I don't remember the day it was mistakenly opened."

Slipping a pen and piece of paper from the pocket of his white coat,

Kim wrote down the information on the labels of the two open cartons. Then he took a single patty from each. This wasn't easy because the patties were frozen in stacks separated by sheets of waxed paper. He pocketed the patties and the paper.

As Kim exited the freezer, he was vaguely aware of the muffled sound of a siren whining down. In his preoccupied state, he ignored it. "What's Mercer Meats?" he asked Paul.

Paul closed the freezer door. "It's a meat-processing company that supplies us with hamburger patties," he said. "In fact, they supply the entire Onion Ring chain."

"Is it in the state?" Kim asked.

"Sure is," Paul said. "It's right outside of town in Bartonville."

"That's convenient," Kim said.

As Kim walked back into the kitchen area, the front door of the restaurant burst open. Two uniformed police officers came charging in with their hands resting on their holstered revolvers. Their faces were grim. Roger trailed behind them, angrily gesturing toward Kim with his right hand while his left held a bloody napkin against his mouth.

# CHAPTER 12

Weak early-morning sunlight slanted through the mote-filled air of the courtroom and created a swath of light on the floor. Kim was standing in the beam and squinting from the glare. In front of him Judge Harlowe was presiding, in his black judicial robes. Reading glasses were perched precariously on the judge's narrow, knifelike nose. To Kim, he appeared like an enormous black bird.

"After more than twenty years on the bench," Judge Harlowe was saying while glaring down at Kim over the top of his spectacles, "I should not be surprised at what I see and hear. But, this is one strange story."

"It's because of my daughter's condition," Kim said. He was still attired in his long white coat over hospital scrubs, with his surgical mask still tied around his neck. But the coat was no longer crisp and clean. From having slept in it overnight in jail, it was wrinkled and soiled. Below the left pocket was a reddish-brown stain.

"Doctor, I have great sympathy for you given that your daughter is gravely ill," Judge Harlowe said. "What I have trouble understanding is why you are not at the hospital at her side."

"I should be," Kim said. "But her condition is such there is nothing I can do. Besides, I had only intended to be away for an hour or so."

"Well, I'm not here to make value judgments," Judge Harlowe said. "What I am here for is to address your behavior in regard to trespassing, committing battery on a fast-food restaurant manager, and, perhaps most egregious of all, resisting arrest and striking a police officer. Doctor, this is unacceptable behavior no matter the circumstances."

"But, Your Honor, I . . ." Kim began.

Judge Harlowe raised his hand to quiet Kim. "It doesn't matter that you suspect your daughter's illness might have originated at the Onion Ring on Prairie Highway. You of all people should know we have a Department of Health which is mandated to look into this kind of thing, and we have courts of law. Am I making myself clear?"

"Yes, Your Honor," Kim said resignedly.

"I hope you seek some help, Doctor," Judge Harlowe said. "I'm plainly mystified by your actions, knowing that you're a renowned cardiac surgeon. In fact, you operated on my father-in-law, and he still sings your praises. At any rate, I'm releasing you on your own recognizance. You're to return for trial four weeks hence. See the court clerk."

Judge Harlowe struck his gavel and asked for the next case.

On his way out of the courthouse, Kim eyed a public phone. He hesitated for a moment, trying to decide whether or not to call the hospital. The evening before he'd tried to call Tracy, but he'd failed to reach her with the calls he had been allotted. Now, with a phone available, he dithered. He felt guilty about having been gone for so long, as well as embarrassed for what had happened. He was also afraid of what he might find out about Becky. He decided to go rather than call.

At a cab stand just outside the courthouse, Kim caught a cab to the Onion Ring. The deserted restaurant looked completely different in the morning prior to its opening. Kim's aging vehicle was the only one in the parking lot and there wasn't a soul in sight.

Climbing in his car, Kim set out for the hospital. En route he made a detour to Sherring Labs.

Inside he approached a receiving counter and rang a stainless-steel bell. A woman appeared within seconds. She was dressed in a lab coat.

Kim fished the two hamburger patties, now defrosted, out of his left pocket and handed them to the woman. "I'd like these patties tested for E. coli O157:H7," he said. "Also for the toxin."

The technician eyed the discolored meat warily. "I think it might have been better if you'd refrigerated the samples," she said. "When meat's been at room temperature for more than a couple of hours it's going to grow out a lot of bacteria."

"I understand that," Kim said. "But I don't care about other bacteria. I only want to know if E. coli O157:H7 is present."

The woman disappeared for a moment. She returned wearing latex gloves. She took the meat and put each sample into a separate container. Then she took the billing details. Kim used his office account.

"How long will it take?" Kim asked.

"We'll have a final reading in forty-eight hours," she replied.

Kim thanked her, washed his hands in a restroom, and went back out to his car.

As he neared the hospital, Kim became increasingly anxious. He started trembling as he parked his car; the tremors grew worse as he rose up in the elevator. Preferring to face Tracy after checking on Becky, he used a back route to the ICU to avoid the ICU waiting room. As he passed through the halls, people eyed him with curiosity. Kim could well understand, considering his appearance. Besides his soiled attire, he needed a shower and a shave and his hair needed combing.

Within the ICU, Kim nodded to the ward clerk but didn't offer any explanation. Approaching Becky's cubicle, he found himself making a pact with God. *If only Becky could be spared . . .*

Kim slipped in by Becky's bedside. A nurse was changing her IV bottle. Her back was to him. Kim gazed at his daughter. Any faint sliver of hope of improvement he had entertained instantly vanished. Becky was obviously still in a coma. Her eyelids were taped shut and she was still intubated and being respired. What was new were large, deep-purple patches of subcutaneous bleeding under the skin of her face that made her look cadaverous.

"Oh, my goodness, you frightened me," the nurse said when she caught sight of Kim. She put a hand to her chest. "I didn't hear you."

"She doesn't look good," Kim said. He kept his voice even in an attempt to hide the grief, anger, and humiliating impotence he felt.

"I'm afraid not," the nurse said, eyeing Kim with some misgivings. "The poor little angel has been having a terrible time."

Kim's trained ear drew his attention to the cardiac monitor screen. The beeping was irregular as were the blips of the cursor.

"She has an arrhythmia! When did this develop?"

"Relatively recently," the nurse said. "It started last night. She developed a cardiac effusion which quickly brought on symptoms of tamponade. She had to be tapped."

"When?" Kim asked. Now he felt even more guilty for not having been available. Dealing with a cardiac effusion was something he knew about.

"Just after four this morning," the nurse said.

"Are any of her doctors still here?" Kim asked.

"I believe so," the nurse said. "I think they're talking to the patient's mother in the waiting room."

Kim fled. He couldn't stand to see his daughter in such a condition. Out in the corridor, he paused to catch his breath and regain some composure. Then he walked down to the waiting room. He found Tracy talking with Claire Stevens and Kathleen Morgan. As soon as they saw Kim, their conversation stopped.

For a moment there was silence.

Tracy was clearly distraught. Her mouth was a grim line. She had her knees pressed together and her hands clasped. She gazed at Kim with a sad, confused expression reflecting both concern and contempt. She shook her head. "You're in the same clothes. You're a mess. Where on earth have you been?"

"My visit to the Onion Ring took a lot longer than I thought it would." He looked at Claire. "So Becky has now developed pericarditis."

"I'm afraid so," Claire said.

"My God!" Kim exclaimed. "What next?"

"At this stage, just about anything," Kathleen said. "We've confirmed that this is a particularly pathogenic strain of E. coli that produces not one but two extraordinarily potent toxins. What we're seeing is full-blown HUS."

"What about the plasmaphoresis?" Kim asked.

"Dr. Ohanesian made an impassioned plea to the AmeriCare Review Board chairman," Claire said. "But as we warned, the committee probably will not give the okay."

"Why not?" Kim demanded. "We've got to do something, and I said I'll be willing to pay for it."

"Your being willing to pay doesn't matter," Claire said. "From their point of view, it would set a dangerous precedent. They could then be forced to offer it to families that couldn't or wouldn't pay."

"Then let's get Becky to someplace where it is offered," Kim snapped.

"Dr. Reggis," Claire said sympathetically. "Becky is in worse condition today than she was yesterday, and yesterday she was in no condition to be transferred. But plasmaphoresis is not totally out of the question. There's still hope they could give the green light. We'll just have to wait."

"Wait and do nothing," Kim said with a scowl.

"That's not true," Claire said hotly. Then she caught herself and sighed; talking with Kim was a chore she did not relish. "We're supporting her every way possible."

"Meaning you're sitting on your hands and treating complications," Kim spat.

Claire stood up and looked at Tracy and Kathleen. "I think it's time for me to see the rest of my inpatients. But I'll be available if needed: just page me."

Tracy nodded. Kathleen responded that she'd be doing the same thing in a few minutes. Claire left.

Kim collapsed into the chair vacated by Claire and buried his head in his hands. He was struggling with a roller coaster of emotions: first anger and then sadness, then back to anger. Now sadness returned. He fought back tears. He knew he should be seeing his own inpatients, but for the moment he was incapable.

"Why did your visit to the Onion Ring take so long?" Tracy asked. As irritated as she was by his behavior, she couldn't help but be concerned about him. He looked pitiful.

"Actually, I was in jail," Kim admitted.

"Jail!"

"If you want me to tell you that you were right, you were right," Kim said. "I should have calmed down before I went."

"Why were you in jail?" Tracy asked.

"I lost my temper," Kim said. "I went there to find out about the possibility of tainted meat. The manager's self-righteous denial drove me up the wall."

"I don't think it's the fast-food industry's fault," Kathleen offered. "With this E. coli problem the fast-food restaurants are as much a victim as the patrons who are infected. They get contaminated hamburger."

"I figured as much," Kim said, with his face still buried in his hands. "My next visit will be to Mercer Meats."

"With Becky's condition, it's hard for me to think," Tracy said. "But how can there be contaminated meat? Aren't these places continually inspected? I mean, doesn't the USDA certify the meat?"

"They certify it," Kathleen said. "But in this day and age, it's an unfortunate assumption to believe that it's not contaminated."

"How can that be?" Tracy asked.

"For a lot of reasons," Kathleen said, "chief of which is that the USDA has an inherent conflict of interest."

Kim lifted his head out of his hands. "How so?"

"It's because of the USDA's mandate," Kathleen said. "On the one hand, the agency is the official advocate for U.S. agriculture, which includes the powerful beef industry. That's actually the USDA's main job. On the other hand, it has inspectional obligations. Obviously the two roles don't mix. It's a genuine case of asking the fox to guard the henhouse."

"This sounds incredible," Kim said. "Is this something you know for a fact, or is it something you've heard and are just passing it along?"

"I'm afraid it's something I know about firsthand," Kathleen said. "I've been looking into the problem of food contamination for over a year. I've gotten active through a couple of consumer groups who are fighting an uphill battle to do something about it."

"How did you get involved?" Tracy asked.

"It would have been hard for me not to," Kathleen said. "Food contamination and the illness it causes have become a major part of my practice. People in general seem to want to keep their heads in the sand about all this. But it's a problem that is getting worse by the day."

"This is unbelievable!" Kim exclaimed as anger again overcame his sadness.

"There's more," Kathleen said. "Not only is there a conflict of interest with the USDA, but from what I've seen, the USDA and the beef industry are much too close."

"What are you implying?" Kim asked.

"Exactly what I said," Kathleen added. "Particularly in middle-management positions, there's a kind of musical chairs with people moving back and forth to make sure the industry is interfered with as little as possible."

"This is all for profit, no doubt," Kim said.

"To be sure," Kathleen said. "The beef industry is a multibillion-dollar business. Profit maximization is its goal not the public weal."

"Wait a second," Tracy said. "How can all this be true? In the past, the USDA has uncovered problems and has done something about them. I mean, not that long ago with Hudson foods . . ."

"Excuse me," Kathleen interrupted. "The USDA was not responsible for discovering the E. coli contamination involving Hudson Foods. It was an attentive public health official. Normally what happens is the USDA is forced to make a show after an outbreak occurs. Then they make a big deal to the media to give the impression that they are on the job of protecting the public, but unfortunately nothing substantial ever gets done. Ironically enough, the USDA doesn't even have the power to recall meat it finds contaminated. It can only make a recommendation. Nothing it determines is binding."

"You mean like with Hudson Foods?" Tracy asked. "At first they recommended that only twenty-five thousand pounds of meat be recalled."

"Exactly," Kathleen said. "It was consumer groups that forced the USDA to up the recommended recall to over a million pounds. It wasn't the USDA who was the instigator."

"I'd had no idea about any of this," Tracy said. "And I like to think of myself as a reasonably informed person."

"Perhaps the worst part," Kathleen continued, "is that when the USDA talks about contamination with its inspectional services, they're generally talking about gross contamination with visible feces. The industry has fought against any microscopic or bacteriologic inspection for years. Now there is supposed to be some culturing, but it is only a token."

"It's hard to believe," Tracy said. "I guess I've always just assumed that meat was safe."

"It's a sorry situation," Kathleen said. "With tragic consequences."

For a few moments, no one spoke.

"How well we know," Tracy said, as if suddenly realizing this was no idle conversation. Her daughter was no abstraction. A fresh tear streaked down her cheek.

"Well, that settles it," Kim said. He abruptly got to his feet.

"Settles what?" Tracy managed. "Where are you going now?"

"To Bartonville," Kim said. "I'm going to pay a quick visit to Mercer Meats."

"I think you should stay here," Tracy said with exasperation. "You know better than I that Becky's condition is grave. Dr. Stevens and Dr. Morgan have impressed upon me there might be some difficult decisions to be made."

"Of course I know Becky's condition is grave," Kim snapped. "That's why I have so much trouble sitting here doing nothing. It drives me crazy. I have trouble even looking at Becky, knowing there is nothing I can do medically to help. Besides, hearing all this about the beef industry and the USDA makes me furious. I said I was going to find out how she got sick. I'm going to follow this E. coli trail wherever it leads; at least I can do that for Becky."

"What if we need you?" Tracy asked.

"My cellular phone is in my car," Kim said. "You can call me. Anyway, I won't be gone that long."

"Yeah, just like yesterday," Tracy said.

"I've learned my lesson," Kim said. "I'm not going to lose my temper."

Tracy didn't look persuaded. "Go if you have to," she said irritably.

Kim stormed out of the ICU waiting room. Not only was Becky's relentless downward course weighing on him, but so was Tracy's hostility. Just the day before, she'd professed to understand his frustrations. Now it was as if she'd forgotten she'd ever said anything.

Once on the freeway, Kim used his cellular phone to find Tom. He tried him several places before catching him in his lab at the hospital.

"I have to ask another favor," Kim said.

"How's Becky?" Tom asked.

"To be honest, she's very bad," Kim said. "I've been using a lot of denial about her condition, but I can't do that anymore. It doesn't look good. I had no idea this E. coli was so pathogenic and essentially untreatable once the toxin gets into the system. Anyway, I'm not optimistic." Kim paused, fighting tears.

"I'm so sorry," Tom said. "What a tragedy. What can I do to help?"

"Could you follow my inpatients for a couple of days?" Kim managed. "I'm strung out."

"No problem at all," Tom said graciously. "I'll be doing my own rounds when I finish here in the next few minutes, and I'll just add them on. I'll also tell the nurses so they'll call me if there're any problems."

"Thanks, Tom," Kim said. "I owe you."

"I wish I could do more," Tom said.

"Me too, Kim said.

Bartonville was less than forty minutes out of town. Kim cruised down its main street and then followed the directions he'd gotten from a service station at the freeway exit. He found Mercer Meats without a problem.

It was a far bigger plant than he'd expected. The building was all white and modern-looking but otherwise nondescript. The grounds were immaculately landscaped with granite-lined drives and islands of trees in the parking area. The whole complex projected an aura of high profitability.

Kim parked relatively near the front door in one of a half-dozen "visitor" spaces. He slid out from behind the wheel and started toward the entrance. As he walked, he reminded himself not to lose his temper. After the experience at the Onion Ring, he knew that if he did, it would only work against him.

The reception area looked like it belonged at the entrance to an insurance company rather than a meat-packing concern. Plush wall-to-wall carpeting covered the floor, the furniture was richly upholstered, and there were framed prints on the walls. Only the subject matter of the prints gave a hint of the nature of the business: They were prints of various breeds of cattle.

A matronly woman wearing a cordless headset sat at a circular desk in the center of the room.

"May I help you?" she asked.

"I hope so," Kim said. "What's the name of the president of Mercer Meats?"

"That would be Mr. Everett Sorenson," the woman said.

"Would you call Mr. Sorenson and tell him that Dr. Kim Reggis is here to see him?" Kim said.

"Can I tell Mr. Sorenson what this is about?" the woman asked. She eyed Kim skeptically. His appearance was bordering on that of a homeless person.

"Is it necessary?" Kim asked.

"Mr. Sorenson is a very busy man," the woman said.

"In that case," Kim said, "tell him it's about Mercer Meats selling contaminated hamburger patties to the Onion Ring restaurant chain."

"Excuse me?" the woman said. She'd heard Kim, but couldn't quite believe it.

"Or better yet," Kim said, already beginning to forget his promise to himself about maintaining his composure, "tell him I'd like to discuss the fact that my only daughter is fighting for her life after consuming a Mercer Meats patty."

"Perhaps you'd like to sit down," the receptionist said. She swallowed nervously. Kim was now leaning over her desk, resting on his knuckles. "I'll give the president your message."

"Thank you," Kim said. He gave the woman a forced smile and retreated to one of the couches.

The woman spoke into her headset, while casting nervous glances in Kim's direction. He smiled again. He couldn't hear what she was saying, but from the look on her face, he knew it was about him.

Kim had his legs crossed. He bounced his foot. Five minutes dragged by. The more he waited, the more his anger flooded back. Just when he thought he couldn't sit there any longer, a man appeared with a long white coat not dissimilar to the one Kim was wearing, except it was clean and pressed. On his head was a blue baseball hat with MERCER MEATS emblazoned above the bill. He was carrying a clipboard.

He came right up to Kim and stuck out his hand. Kim stood up and shook the man's hand although he'd not intended to.

"Dr. Reggis, I'm Jack Cartwright. I'm glad to meet you."

"Where's the president?" Kim asked.

"He's tied up at the moment," Jack said. "But he asked me to come out and talk with you. I'm one of the vice presidents and among other things I'm in charge of public relations."

Jack was a stocky individual with a doughy face and a slightly up-turned porcine nose. He smiled ingratiatingly.

"I want to talk with the president," Kim said.

"Listen," Jack said without a beat, "I'm truly sorry to hear that your daughter is ill."

"She's more than ill," Kim said. "She's at death's door, fighting for her life against a bacteria called E. coli O157:H7. I imagine this is a bug you've heard of."

"Unfortunately, yes," Jack said. His smile vanished. "Everyone in the meat business is aware of it, especially after the Hudson Meat recall. In fact, we're so paranoid about it, we make an effort to exceed by far all USDA rules, regulations, and recommendations. And as proof of our efforts, we've never been cited for a single deficiency."

"I want to visit the hamburger-patty production area," Kim said. He wasn't interested in Jack's obviously canned spiel.

"Now, that's impossible," Jack said. "We understandably limit access to avoid contamination. But . . ."

"Hold up," Kim interjected as his face reddened. "I'm a doctor. I understand contamination. I'll be willing to put on any suit that's normally worn in the area. Whatever has to be done, I'll do. But I'm not going to take no for an answer."

"Hey, calm down," Jack said good-naturedly. "You didn't let me finish. You can't go onto the production floor, but we have a glassed-in observation walk so you can see the whole process. What's more, you don't have to change out of your street clothes."

"That's a start, I suppose," Kim said.

"Great!" Jack commented. "Follow me."

Jack preceded Kim, leading him along a corridor.

"Are you only interested in hamburger production?" Jack asked. "What about some other meat product, like sausage?"

"Just hamburger," Kim said.

"Fine and dandy," Jack said cheerfully.

They got to a stair and started up.

"I want to emphasize we're tigers about cleanliness here at Mercer Meats," Jack said. "Hell, the entire meat-production area gets cleaned every day, first with high-pressure steam and then with a quaternary ammonium compound. I mean, you could eat off the floor."

"Uh-huh," Kim intoned.

"The whole production area is kept at thirty-five degrees," Jack said as they reached the top of the stairs. He grabbed the handle of a fire door. "It's tough on the workers but tougher on the bacteria. You know what I mean?" Jack laughed; Kim stayed silent.

They went through the door and entered a glass-enclosed corridor perched a floor above the production area. It ran the entire length of the building.

"Pretty impressive, wouldn't you say?" Jack said proudly.

"Where's the patty area?" Kim asked.

"We'll get to that," Jack said. "But let me explain to you what all this machinery is doing."

Below, Kim could see workers going about their business. They were all dressed in white uniforms with white caps that resembled shower hats. They were also wearing gloves and shoe covers. Kim had to admit that the plant looked new and clean. He was surprised. He'd expected something significantly less impressive.

Jack had to speak loudly over the sound of the machinery. The glass on either side of the walkway was single-paned.

"I don't know if you are aware that hamburger is usually a blend of fresh meat and frozen," Jack said. "It's course ground separately over there. Of course, the frozen stuff has to be defrosted first."

Kim nodded.

"After the course grind, the fresh and the frozen meat are dumped into the formulation blender over there to make a batch. Then the batch is finely ground in those big grinders."

Jack pointed. Kim nodded.

"We do five batches per hour," Jack said. "The batches are then combined into a lot."

Kim pointed to a large rubber or plastic bin on wheels. "Does the fresh meat come in those containers?" he asked.

"Yup," Jack agreed. "They're called 'combo bins,' and they hold two thousand pounds. We're very particular with our fresh meat. It has to be used within five days, and it's got to be kept below thirty-five degrees. I'm sure you know that thirty-five degrees is colder than a standard refrigerator."

"What happens to the lot?" Kim asked.

"As soon as it comes out of the fine grinder it goes by this conveyor below us to the patty-formulating machine over yonder."

Kim nodded. The formulating machine was in a separate room, closed off from the rest of the production area. They walked down the glass corridor until they were directly over it.

"An impressive machine, wouldn't you say?" Jack said.

"How come it's in its own room?" Kim asked.

"To keep it extra-clean and protect it," Jack said. "It's the most expensive piece of equipment on the floor and the workhorse of the plant. That baby puts out either regular tenth-of-a-pound patties or quarter-pound jumbos."

"What happens to the patties when they come out of the formulating machine?" Kim asked.

"A conveyor takes them directly into the nitrogen freeze tunnel," Jack said. "Then they are hand-packed into boxes, and the boxes into cartons."

"Can you trace the origin of meat?" Kim asked. "I mean if you know the lot number, the batch numbers, and the production date."

"Sure," Jack said. "That's all recorded in the patty-room log."

Kim reached into his pocket and withdrew the piece of paper on which he'd written the information from the labels in the Onion Ring walk-in freezer. He unfolded it and showed it to Jack.

"I'd like find out where the meat came from for these two dates and lots," Kim said.

Jack glanced at the paper but then shook his head. "Sorry, I can't give you that kind of information."

"Why the hell not?" Kim demanded.

"I just can't," Jack said. "It's confidential. It's not for public consumption."

"What's the secret?" Kim asked.

"There's no secret," Jack said. "It's just company policy."

"Then why keep the logs?" Kim asked.

"They are required by the USDA," Jack said.

"Sounds suspicious to me," Kim said, thinking about some of Kathleen's comments earlier that morning. "A public agency requires logs whose information is not available to the public."

"I don't make the rules," Jack said lamely.

Kim let his eyes roam around the patty room. It was impressive with its polished stainless-steel equipment and lustrous tiled floor. There were three men and one woman tending to the machines.

Kim noticed that the woman was carrying a clipboard on which she scribbled intermittently. In contrast to the men, she did not touch the machinery.

"Who's that woman?" Kim asked.

"That's Marsha Baldwin," Jack said. "She's a looker, isn't she?"

"What's she doing?" Kim asked.

"Inspecting," Jack said. "She's the USDA inspector assigned to us. She stops in here three, four, sometimes five times a week. She's a real hard-ass. She sticks her nose into everything."

"I suppose she could trace the meat," Kim said.

"Sure," Jack said. "She checks the patty-room log every time she's here."

"What's she doing now?" Kim asked. Marsha was bending over, looking into the yawning mouth of the patty-formulating machine.

"I haven't the faintest idea," Jack said. "Probably making sure it was cleaned the way it was supposed to be, which it undoubtedly was. She's a stickler for details, that's all I know. At least she keeps us on our toes."

"Three to five times a week," Kim repeated. "That's impressive."

"Come on," Jack said, motioning with his hand for Kim to follow him. "The only thing you haven't seen yet is the boxes being packed into the cartons, and the cartons being put into cold storage prior to shipping."

Kim knew he'd seen as much as he was likely to see. He was convinced that he would not get to talk with Everett Sorenson.

"If you have any further questions," Jack said back at the reception area, "just give a holler." He gave Kim a business card and flashed a winning smile. Then he pumped Kim's hand, slapped him on the back, and thanked him for his visit.

Kim walked out of the Mercer Meats building and got into his car. Instead of starting the engine, he turned on the radio. After making sure his cellular phone was on, he leaned back and tried to relax. After a few minutes, he rolled the window partly down. He didn't want to fall asleep.

Time moved very slowly. Several times he almost gave up and left. He was feeling progressively guilty about having abandoned Tracy in the ICU waiting room. But a little over an hour later, Kim's patience paid off:

Marsha Baldwin walked out of Mercer Meats. She was dressed in a khaki coat and carried what looked like a government-issue briefcase.

In a mild panic to get to her before she climbed into her car, Kim struggled with his door. It stuck once in a while: a legacy of an old fender bender. Several thumps with his palm got it open, and he leaped out. He sprinted toward the woman. By the time he got to her, she had the back door open of her yellow Ford sedan. She was just straightening up from having stowed her briefcase on the floor of the backseat. Kim was surprised by her height. He estimated she had to be at least five foot ten.

"Marsha Baldwin?" Kim demanded.

Mildly surprised at being accosted by name in the parking lot, Marsha turned to Kim and gave him a once-over with her deep emerald-green eyes. By reflex she swept a lock of her dark blond hair off her forehead and tucked it behind her ear. She was confused by Kim's appearance and immediately put on guard by the confrontational tone of his voice.

"Yes, I'm Marsha Baldwin," she said hesitantly.

Kim took in the whole picture, including the bumper sticker that said "Save the Manatees" on what was obviously a government-issue car and the image of the woman who was, in Jack Cartwright's words, "a looker." Kim estimated she couldn't have been much over twenty-five, with coral-toned skin and cameolike features. Her nose was prominent but aristocratic. Her lips sculpted in sharp relief.

"We have to talk," Kim averred.

"Really?" Marsha questioned. "And what are you, an unemployed surgeon or did you just come from last night's costume party?"

"Under different circumstances I might think that was clever," Kim said. "I was told you are a USDA inspector."

"And who gave you this information?" Marsha asked warily. She'd been warned in her training that occasionally she might have to deal with kooks.

Kim motioned toward the Mercer Meats entrance. "By an unctuous Mercer Meats PR man named Jack Cartwright."

"And what if I was a USDA inspector?" Marsha asked. She closed the rear door of her car and opened the front. She had no intention of giving this strange man much time.

From his pocket Kim extracted the paper with the details from the labels of the patty cartons in the Onion Ring. He held it at the top corner shoulder high. "I want you to find out where the meat came from for these two lots."

Marsha glanced at the paper. "What on earth for?" she questioned.

"Because I believe one of these lots has made my daughter deathly sick with a bad strain of E. coli," Kim said. "Not only do I want to know where the meat came from, but I also need to know where these lots were shipped to."

"How do you know it was one of these lots?" Marsha asked.

"I don't know for sure," Kim said. "At least not yet."

"Oh, really?" Marsha questioned superciliously.

"Yes, really," Kim said hotly, taking offense at her tone.

"Sorry, I can't get you that kind of information," Marsha said.

"Why not?" Kim demanded.

"It's not my job to give such information to the public," Marsha said. "I'm sure it's against the rules."

Marsha started to get into her car.

Picturing his deathly ill daughter in her hospital bed, Kim roughly grabbed Marsha's arm to keep her from getting into the car. "Screw the rules, you goddamn bureaucrat," he snapped. "This is important. You're supposed to be protecting the public. Here's an opportunity to do just that."

Marsha didn't panic. She looked down at the hand gripping her arm, then back up into Kim's indignant face. "Let go of me or I'll scream bloody murder, you crank."

Convinced she was a woman of her word, Kim let go of her arm. He was nonplussed by Marsha's unexpected assertiveness.

"Be nice, now," Marsha said as if she were talking with a juvenile. "I haven't done anything to you."

"Like hell you haven't," Kim said. "If you USDA people weren't acting out a sham and really inspected this meat industry, my daughter wouldn't be sick, nor would some five hundred kids die each year."

"Now, just wait one minute," Marsha shot back. "I work hard at my job, and I take it very seriously."

"Bull," Kim spat. "I've been told that you people work hard at going through the motions. I even hear you're in bed with the industry you're supposed to be inspecting."

Marsha's mouth dropped open. She was incensed. "I'm not going to validate that comment by responding," she said. She climbed in behind the wheel and pulled her door shut. She stuck her key in the ignition.

Kim rapped on her window. "Wait a sec," he yelled. "I'm sorry. Please!" He ran a worried hand through his disheveled hair. "I'm desperate for your help. I didn't mean anything personal. Obviously I don't know you."

After a few seconds' deliberation, Marsha rolled her window down and looked up at Kim. What had appeared to her a moment previously as the visage of an eccentric oddball now looked like the face of a tortured man.

"Are you really a doctor?" she asked.

"Yes," Kim said. "A cardiac surgeon to be exact."

"And your daughter is really sick?"

"Very, very sick," Kim said with a voice that broke. "She has an extremely bad strain of E. coli. I'm almost positive she got it from eating a rare hamburger."

"I'm truly sorry to hear that," Marsha said. "But listen, I'm not the one you should be talking to. I've only been working for the USDA for a short time, and I'm at the bottom of the inspectional service totem pole."

"Who do you think I should contact?" Kim asked.

"The district manager," Marsha said. "His name is Sterling Henderson. I could give you his number."

"Is he sort'a what you'd call middle management?" Kim asked. He could hear Kathleen's voice in the back of his mind.

"I suppose," Marsha said.

"I'm not interested," Kim said. "I've been told there are real problems with the USDA inspectional services in terms of conflict of interest, especially in middle-management positions. Is this something you know anything about?"

"Well, I know there are problems," Marsha admitted. "It's all very political."

"Meaning, a multibillion-dollar industry like the beef industry can throw its weight around."

"Something like that," Marsha said.

"Will you help me for my daughter's sake?" Kim asked. "I can't help her medically, but I'm sure as hell going to find out the how and the why she got sick, and maybe in the process do something about it. I'd love to spare other kids from the same fate. I think one of these lots on this piece of paper has to be contaminated with a particularly dangerous strain of E. coli."

"Gosh, I don't know what to say," Marsha responded. She tapped the steering wheel as she debated with herself. The idea of saving some children from a serious illness had great appeal. But there were risks.

"I don't think there's any way for me to get this material without your help," Kim said. "At least not fast enough to make a difference."

"What about calling the department of public health?" Marsha suggested.

"That's an idea," Kim said. "I'll be willing to try that too on Monday. But, to tell you the truth, I wouldn't be optimistic going that route. I'd just be dealing with another bureaucracy, and it probably would take too long. Besides, I kind'a want to do this myself. It's to make up for not being able to help my daughter medically."

"I might be putting my job on the line," Marsha said. "Although maybe I could enlist the aid of my immediate boss. The trouble with that is that he and I have never had what I would call a good working relationship."

"Would that be the district manager whom you mentioned earlier?" Kim asked.

"That's right," Marsha said. "Sterling Henderson."

"I'd prefer we just kept this between you and me," Kim said.

"That's easy for you to say," Marsha said. "The trouble is, it's my job not yours."

"Tell me," Kim said, suddenly having an idea. "Have you ever seen a child ill with this E. coli problem? The reason I ask is because I never did before my own daughter got sick, and I'm a doctor. I mean I'd read about it, but it was always an abstraction, a statistic."

"No, I never have seen a child sick with E. coli," Marsha admitted.

"Then come with me to see my daughter," Kim said. "After you see her, you can then decide what to do. I'll accept whatever decision you make. If nothing else, it will give added meaning to your work."

"Where is she?" Marsha asked.

"She's at the University Med Center," Kim said. "The same hospital where I'm on the staff." Kim motioned toward Marsha's cell phone that he could see between the two front seats. "Call the hospital if you question what I'm saying. My name is Dr. Kim Reggis. My daughter's name is Becky Reggis."

"I believe you," Marsha said. She wavered. "When do you have in mind?"

"Right now," Kim said. "Come on. My car is right over there." Kim pointed over his shoulder. "You can ride with me. Afterwards I'll bring you back here to get your car."

"I can't do that," Marsha said. "I don't know you from Adam."

"All right," Kim said, warming to the idea of Marsha seeing Becky. "Follow me. I was only worrying about where you'd park once at the hospital, but screw it. Just follow me right into the doctors' lot. What do you say?"

"I'd say you are persistent and persuasive," Marsha said.

"All right!" Kim exclaimed, raising a clenched fist for emphasis. "I'll loop around here, so just follow me."

"Okay," Marsha said warily, unsure of what she'd gotten herself into.

○    ○    ○

Jack Cartwright had had his nose pressed against the window. He'd kept an eye on Kim and had witnessed the entire confrontation between Kim and Marsha Baldwin. Of course he'd not heard what they'd said, but he did see Marsha follow his car out of the lot after the two had seemed to reach some agreement.

Leaving the reception area, Jack hustled down the central corridor, passing the stairwell where he'd taken Kim up to the observation tunnel. At the far end of the hall were the administration offices.

"Is the boss in?" Jack asked one of the secretaries.

"He sure is," she said without interrupting her word processing.

Jack knocked on the president's closed door. A booming voice told him to "come the hell in."

Everett Sorenson had been successfully running Mercer Meats for almost twenty years. It had been under his leadership that the company had been bought out by Foodsmart and that the new plant had been constructed. Sorenson was a big man, even stockier than Jack, with a florid complexion, small ears for his size, and a shiny bald pate.

"What the hell are you all wired up about?" Everett asked as Jack came into the room. Everett had a sixth sense about his minion whom he'd personally elevated right off the patty-room floor into the company's hierarchy.

"We got a problem," Jack said.

"Oh!" Everett said. He tipped forward in his desk chair to lean his bulky torso on his elbows. "What's up?"

Jack took one of the two chairs in front of Everett's desk. "You know that article you pointed out in the paper this morning? The one about the crazy doctor carrying on about E. coli and getting arrested in the Onion Ring restaurant on Prairie Highway?"

"Of course," Everett said. "What about it?"

"He was just here," Jack said.

"The doctor?" Everett asked with disbelief.

"The exact same guy," Jack said. "His name is Dr. Reggis. And I'll tell you straight, this guy is a nutcake. He's out of control, and he's convinced his daughter got her E. coli from one of our patties."

"Damn!" Everett intoned. "This is not what we need."

"And it gets worse," Jack said. "I just watched him have a conversation in our parking lot with Marsha Baldwin. Afterwards they drove away in tandem."

"You mean, you think they drove away together?" Everett asked.

Jack nodded. "That's the way it looked. Before they left, they'd talked for quite a while in the parking lot."

"Jesus Christ!" Everett said, slapping the surface of his desk with one of his shovel-like hands. He pushed back from the desk and got to his feet to pace. "This is not what we need! No way! That goddamn Baldwin bitch has been a thorn in my side from the day she was hired. She's constantly filing these stupid deficiency reports. Thank God Sterling Henderson has been able to can them."

"Can't Sterling do something about her?" Jack asked. "Like get her fired?"

"I wish," Everett said. "I've been complaining until I'm blue in the face."

"With the money we're paying him as if he still works here," Jack said, "you'd think he'd at least get her transferred."

"In his defense, it's a difficult situation," Everett said. "Apparently her father is connected in Washington."

"Which leaves us up the creek without a paddle," Jack said. "Now we've got an overzealous inspector who doesn't play by the rules teamed up with a loose-cannon physician who's willing to get himself arrested at a fast-food restaurant just to make a point. I'm afraid this guy could be like a kamikaze pilot. He'll sacrifice himself, but he's bent on taking us with him."

"I don't like this," Everett said nervously. "Another E. coli fiasco would be devastating. Hudson Meat management didn't survive their run with the bug. But what can we do?"

"We've got to do damage control," Jack said. "And we have to do it quickly. It seems to me that this is the perfect time to call into play the newly formed Prevention Committee. I mean, this kind of situation is exactly what it was formed for."

"You know something," Everett said, "you're right. It would be perfect. I mean, we wouldn't even be involved."

"Why not give Bobby Bo Mason a call," Jack suggested.

"I'll do that," Everett said, warming to the whole idea. This type of tactical thinking and decision-making was why he'd promoted Jack to the vice presidency.

"Time is of the essence," Jack said.

"I'll call right away," Everett said.

"Maybe we can take advantage of Bo's dinner party tonight," Jack said. "That might speed things up. I mean, everybody will be there."

"Good point!" Everett said as he reached for his phone.

Kim parked quickly. He got out in time to direct Marsha into one of the spots reserved for doctors that Kim was relatively confident wouldn't be used on a Saturday. He opened her door the moment she stopped.

"Are you sure this is a good idea?" Marsha asked as she got out. She looked up at the imposing facade of the hospital. After having time to think about the plan during the drive into the city, she was having second thoughts.

"I think it is a masterful idea," Kim said. "I don't know why it took me so long to think of it. Come on!"

Kim took Marsha's arm and guided her toward the entrance. She put up a token resistance at first but then resigned herself to the situation. She'd rarely been in a hospital and didn't know how she'd respond. She was afraid it might upset her more than she bargained back in the Mercer Meats parking lot. To her surprise, while they waited for the elevator in the hospital lobby, she noticed that Kim was trembling, not she.

"Are you all right?" she asked.

"To be truthful, no," Kim admitted. "Obviously I've been in and out of hospitals since medical school, and it's never bothered me even at the beginning. But now with Becky's situation, I get this awful anxiety every time I come through the door. I guess it's the main reason I've not been staying here around the clock. It would be different if there were something I could do. But there isn't."

"It must be heart-wrenching," Marsha said.

"You've no idea," Kim said.

They boarded a crowded elevator and didn't talk until they were in the corridor leading toward the ICU.

"I don't mean to be nosy," Marsha said, "but how is your wife holding up under the strain of your daughter's illness?"

"We're divorced," Kim said. "But we're united in our concern for Becky. Tracy, my ex-wife, is taking it hard, although I sense she's doing better than I. I'm sure she's here. I'll introduce you."

Marsha shuddered. Having to share a mother's anguish was going to make the experience that much more disturbing. She began to question why she'd allowed herself to be dragged into this.

Then, to make matters worse, Marsha saw signs to the ICU that pointed in the direction they were walking.

"Is your daughter in intensive care?" she asked, hoping for a negative response.

"I'm afraid so," Kim answered.

Marsha sighed. This was going to be even worse than she'd feared.

Kim paused at the threshold of the ICU waiting room. He saw Tracy and motioned for Marsha to follow him. By the time he reached Tracy, his former wife had gotten to her feet.

"Tracy, I'd like you to meet Marsha Baldwin. Marsha is a USDA inspector who I'm hoping will help me trace the meat Becky had."

Tracy didn't answer immediately, and seeing her expression, Kim instantly knew that something else had happened. It seemed that every time he came back, Becky got worse. It was like a bad movie playing over and over.

"What now?" Kim asked grimly.

"Why didn't you answer your phone?" Tracy asked with weary exasperation.

"It didn't ring," Kim said.

"I tried to call," Tracy said. "Several times."

Kim realized he'd left his phone in his car when he'd been in Mercer Meats and when he had been with Marsha.

"Well, I'm here now," Kim said disconsolately. "What happened?"

"Her heart stopped," Tracy said. "But they got it going again. I was in the room when it happened."

"Perhaps I should leave," Marsha said.

"No!" Kim said emphatically. "Stay, please! Let me go in and see what's happening."

Kim spun on his heels and ran from the room.

Tracy and Marsha regarded each other uneasily.

"I'm so sorry about your daughter," Marsha said.

"Thank you," Tracy said. She dabbed at the corners of her eyes with a tissue. She'd cried so much in the previous forty-eight hours that she was almost out of tears. "She's such a wonderful child."

"I wasn't aware your daughter was quite this ill," Marsha said. "It must be a terrible burden."

"Unimaginable," Tracy said.

"I feel terrible about intruding at a time like this," Marsha said. "I'm very sorry. Perhaps I should just leave."

"You don't have to leave on my accord," Tracy said. "Kim sounded emphatic that he'd prefer you stay. How he can even think about tracing meat at this juncture, I cannot understand. I'm having difficulty just breathing."

"It must be because he's a doctor," Marsha said. "He made it clear to me he was interested in trying to prevent other children from getting the same problem."

"I suppose I hadn't thought about it from that angle," Tracy said. "Maybe I shouldn't be so quick to judge."

"He's afraid there's a batch of contaminated meat out there," Marsha said.

"I guess that's a real possibility," Tracy said. "But what I don't understand is why he brought you here. I don't mean that to be rude."

"I understand," Marsha said. "He'd asked me to help trace the meat in some specific lots. I was reluctant; it's really not part of my job. In fact, giving out that kind of information might cost me my job if my boss found out. His idea was that seeing your daughter and witnessing firsthand what this E. coli can do might change my mind. At a minimum, he thought seeing her would give added meaning to my work as a meat inspector."

"Seeing Becky's suffering might make you the most conscientious inspector in the world. Are you still interested in knowing how sick she is? It'll take a bit of fortitude."

"I don't know," Marsha said truthfully. "And as I said, I don't want to intrude."

"You're not intruding," Tracy said with sudden resolve. "Come on. Let's make your visit."

Tracy led Marsha out of the waiting room and across the corridor. She paused at the ICU door.

"Stay close," Tracy said. "We're not supposed to be wandering in and out of here unaccompanied."

Marsha nodded. Her heart was beating rapidly, and she was perspiring.

Tracy opened the door and the two women entered. Tracy walked quickly toward Becky's cubicle, with Marsha right behind her. Several of the nurses saw the women but said nothing. Tracy had become a fixture in the ICU over the previous forty-eight hours.

"I'm afraid it's going to be difficult to see much at all," Tracy said as they reached the cubicle's threshold. Besides Kim, there were six doctors and two nurses packed into the tiny room. But it was Kim's voice that could be heard.

"I understand that she has arrested several times," Kim yelled. He was furious from a combination of fear and exasperation. Drawing on his vast clinical experience, he knew his daughter was at death's door, but no one was giving him a straight answer, and no one was doing anything but stand around and figuratively stroke their chins. "What I'm asking is why it's happening."

Kim stared at Jason Zimmerman, the pediatric cardiologist with whom he'd just been introduced. The man looked off, pretending to be absorbed in watching the cardiac monitor that was tracing an erratic rhythm. Something was terribly wrong.

Kim twisted to look at Claire Stevens. Over her shoulder, he caught sight of Tracy and Marsha.

"We don't know what is going on," Claire admitted. "There's no pericardial fluid, so it's not tamponade."

"It seems to me it's something inherent in the myocardium itself," Jason said. "I need a real EKG."

No sooner had these words escaped from the cardiologist's mouth than the monitor alarm sounded. The cursor swept across the screen tracing a flat line. Becky had arrested again.

"Code blue!" one of the nurses shouted to alert the others out in the intensive-care unit proper.

Jason responded by pushing Kim away from the side of the bed. Immediately he began external cardiac massage by putting his hands together and pumping on Becky's frail chest. Jane Flanagan, the anesthesiologist who'd responded to the initial code and who was still there, made sure the endotracheal tube remained in proper place. She also upped the percentage of oxygen delivered by the respirator.

ICU nurses brought the cardiac crash cart on the run. They practically collided with Tracy and Marsha who had to leap out of the way.

Inside the cubicle there was a flurry of activity as the doctors present all lent a hand. It was apparent to everyone that the heart had not just stopped effective beating, but that all electrical activity had ceased.

Tracy clasped a hand to her face. She wanted to flee but she couldn't. It was as if she were frozen in place, fated to watch every agonizing detail.

All Marsha could do was cringe behind Tracy, fearful that she would be in the way.

Kim initially stepped back, recoiling in disbelief and horror. His eyes swept back and forth between the monitor screen to his daughter's pitiful body being savaged by the pediatric cardiologist.

"Epinephrine!" Jason yelled while he continued his efforts.

The nurses at the crash cart responded by efficiently filling a syringe with the medication and handing it off. After several changes of hand, it was given to Jason who stopped his massage long enough to plunge the needle directly into Becky's heart.

Tracy covered her eyes and moaned. Marsha instinctively put her arms around her, but couldn't take her own eyes off the ghastly drama unfolding in front of her.

Jason went back to the massage while he eyed the monitor. There was no change in its relentless tracking straight across the screen.

"Bring the paddles!" Jason yelled. "Let's see if we can get some electrical activity going with a shock. If that doesn't work, we're going to have to pace her, so be prepared."

The experienced nurses had already charged the defibrillator. They handed the paddles forward. Jason stopped his massage to take them.

"Everybody back!" he yelled while he positioned them. When everyone was clear, and the paddles where he wanted them, he pressed the discharge button.

Becky's pale body jerked and her white arms flailed. Everyone's eyes went to the monitor, hoping to see some change. But the cursor was not cooperating. It persisted in its straight, flat line.

Kim pushed forward. He didn't like the way Jason was doing the massage. "You're not getting enough excursion," he said. "Let me take over."

"No," Claire said, coming up behind Kim and pulling him back. "Dr. Reggis, it's not appropriate. We'll handle this. I think you should wait outside."

Kim shook off the pediatrician. His pupils were dilated and his face flushed. He was not going anywhere.

Jason responded to Kim's complaint. As a man of small stature, it was hard for him to develop much force in a standing position. To make it easier for himself, he climbed up onto the bed and assumed a kneeling position. Now he got better chest compression. It was so much better that everyone present could hear several of Becky's ribs snap.

"More epinephrine!" Kim barked.

"No!" Jason managed between pants. "I want calcium!"

"Epinephrine," Kim repeated. His eyes were glued to the monitor cursor. When no syringe was forthcoming, he turned to look at the crash cart. "Where's the epi?" he demanded.

"Calcium!" Jason repeated. "We've got to see some electrical activity. There's got to be an ion imbalance."

"Calcium's coming up," Claire said.

"No!" Kim yelled. He pushed through the group to stand in front of the crash cart. He glared at the nurse.

The nurse looked from Kim's florid face to Claire's. The nurse was confused as to what she should do.

Unaccustomed to being overruled, Kim snapped up a syringe packet and tore it open. Then he grabbed a vial of epinephrine and broke off its top. His trembling fingers dropped the needle. He had to get another.

"Dr. Reggis, no!" Claire said. She grabbed Kim's arm. Walter Ohanesian, the hematologist, tried to help by grabbing Kim's other arm.

Kim easily shook off both of these doctors and filled the syringe unimpeded. Pandemonium ensued as he tried to push his way back to the bedside. Both Kathleen and Arthur, the nephrologist, came to Claire and Walter's aid. The scene devolved to a shoving match with shouts and threats.

"Oh, God!" Tracy moaned. "What a nightmare!"

"Hold it, everybody!" Jane shouted at the top of her lungs to get everyone's attention. The struggle stopped. Then Jane added with urgency but in a more normal volume: "There's something very strange happening. Jason's getting good chest excursion, and I'm up to a hundred-percent oxygen, and yet her pupils are dilating! For some reason, there's no circulation."

Kim shook off the hands that were impeding him. No one moved or spoke except for Jason who kept up with the massage. The doctors were stymied. They were at a temporary loss as to what to do next.

Kim was the first to respond. His training as a surgeon would not allow him to deliberate a moment longer. He knew what he had to do. With no circulation despite good chest excursion, there was only one alternative. He spun around to face the nurses at the crash cart. "Scalpel!" he barked.

"Oh, no!" Claire shouted.

"Scalpel!" Kim repeated more insistently.

"You can't," Claire yelled.

"Scalpel!" Kim screamed. Tossing the syringe of epinephrine aside, he lunged past the others in the direction of the crash cart.

Kim snatched the glass tube containing the scalpel. He unscrewed the top with trembling fingers and extracted the sterile instrument. He tossed the glass tube aside; it shattered on the tile floor. He picked up an alcohol swab and tore open its package with his teeth.

At this point, only Claire was willing to attempt to bar his way. But her efforts were in vain. He pushed her aside with a gentle but firm shove.

"No!" Tracy cried. She wasn't a physician, but her intuition told her what Kim was going to do. She started forward, and Marsha let her go.

Kim reached the bedside and literally knocked Jason off the bed. He swabbed Becky's chest with alcohol. Then, before Tracy could quite get to him, he sliced open his daughter's thorax in one decisive, bloodless sweep.

A collective gasp rose from everyone present except for Tracy. Her response was more of a wail. She staggered back from the appalling scene and would have collapsed if she hadn't been caught by the nephrologist, Arthur.

On the other side of the bed, Jason struggled to his feet. When he saw what was happening he, too, shrank back.

Kim lost no time. Oblivious to the others in the tiny room, the consummate surgeon used both hands to pull Becky's slender ribs apart with a decisive crack. Then he shoved his bare hand into his daughter's open chest and began rhythmically to compress her heart.

Kim's herculean effort was short-lived. After only a few compressions, he could feel that Becky's heart had perforated and was far from normal in texture. It was as if it weren't muscle but rather something much softer which seemed to squish between his fingers. Stunned by this unexpected situation, he withdrew his hand. In the process he also pulled out some of the foreign-feeling tissue. Confused as to what it could be, he brought the bloody material up to his face to inspect it.

A shrill, agonizing whine escaped from Kim's lips when he realized he was holding necrotic shreds of Becky's heart and pericardium. The toxin had been merciless. It was as if his daughter had been eaten from within.

The door to the ICU burst open. Two uniformed hospital security personnel spilled into the room. They had been called by the head nurse after the scuffle over the epinephrine.

As soon as the two men took in the scene, they stopped in their tracks. Becky was still being respired by the ventilator; her pink lungs intermittently filled the gaping incision. Kim stood by her, his hands bloodied, his eyes wild with grief. He tried to gently return the necrotic tissue to Becky's chest cavity. When he was finished with this futile gesture, he put his head back and let out a wail of anguish unlike anything ever heard in the ICU before.

Tracy had recovered enough to step forward. Kim's anguished cry cut her to the quick. She wanted to comfort him and be comforted herself.

But Kim was blind to everyone and anything. He shoved his way out of the cubicle and dashed across the ICU. Before anyone could respond, he was through the door.

In the corridor, Kim went into headlong flight. People who saw him coming got out of the way. One orderly didn't move quickly enough; Kim slammed into him, sending the man and his water cart flying.

Outside of the hospital, Kim ran to his car. Gunning the engine, he shot out of the doctors' lot, leaving a line of rubber in his wake.

Kim drove like a madman out to Prairie Highway. Lucky for him, he encountered no police cruisers. When he turned into the Onion Ring parking lot he was going fast enough to bottom out just as he had on his previous visit. The car bounced violently until he brought it to a screeching stop directly in front of the busy restaurant. Yanking on the emergency brake, he made the motions to get out. Then he hesitated. A glimmer of rationality seeped into the corners of his emotionally overloaded brain. The Saturday afternoon crowd enjoying their burgers, milkshakes, and fries and oblivious to his psychic pain yanked him back to reality.

Kim had raced to the Onion Ring in search of a scapegoat. But now that he was there, he didn't get out of the car.

Instead he raised his right hand and stared at it. Seeing his daughter's dark, dried blood confirmed the awful reality: Becky was dead. And he hadn't been able to do a thing to save her. He began to sob. All he could do was drape himself helplessly over the steering wheel.

Tracy shook her head in disbelief of everything that had happened. She ran her hand through her tangled hair as Marsha Baldwin patted her shoulder. On top of everything else, it was hard to believe she was being consoled by a stranger.

Tracy had responded the opposite of Kim. Instead of flying off in a blind rage, she'd found herself paralyzed, unable to even cry.

Right after Kim's precipitous departure, Claire and Kathleen had accompanied Tracy to the ICU waiting room. Marsha had followed although at the time Tracy was unaware of her presence. Claire and Kathleen had stayed with Tracy for some time to offer their sympathies and to explain what had happened. They had spared no details in response to Tracy's questions, including how the E. coli toxin had obviously attacked both Becky's heart muscle as well as her pericardium, the covering around the heart.

Claire and Kathleen had offered to help get Tracy home, but Tracy had told them that she had her car and that she'd be all right to drive. It wasn't until the two doctors had left that Tracy realized that Marsha was still there, and the two women had begun a long conversation.

"I want to thank you for staying here all this time," Tracy said. "You've been a wonderful support. I hope I haven't bored you with all these Becky stories."

"She sounds like she was a wonderful child."

"The best," Tracy said wistfully. Then she took a fortifying breath and sat up straight in her chair. The two women were sitting in the far corner of the room by the window where they'd pulled two chairs close together. Outside the long shadows of a late, wintery afternoon crept ever eastward.

"You know," Tracy said. "We've been talking all this time and haven't mentioned my ex-husband, the man who's responsible for your being here."

Marsha nodded.

"Life is full of surprises," Tracy said with a sigh. "Here I lose my beloved daughter who was the center of my life, and I surprise myself by worrying about him. I just hope Becky's passing doesn't drive him over the edge."

"What do you mean?" Marsha asked.

"I'm not sure," Tracy admitted. "I guess I'm terrified at what he might do. He's already been arrested for assaulting the manager at the restaurant where he suspects Becky got sick. I just hope he doesn't do something really crazy and end up hurting someone or himself."

"He does seem angry," Marsha said.

"That's putting it mildly," Tracy said. "He was always such a perfectionist. It used to be his anger was directed mostly toward himself. It served as a stimulus for achievement, but that's been changing over the last few years. It's a big reason why we ended up divorcing."

"I'm sorry to hear that," Marsha said.

"He is basically a good man," Tracy said. "Egotistical and self-centered, but still a very good doctor. Certainly one of the best surgeons in his field."

"I'm not surprised," Marsha said. "One of the things that impressed me about him was that in the middle of all this he was still thinking about other children."

"How do you feel about helping him after what you've seen here this afternoon?" Tracy asked. "It would be wonderful if he could channel his anger about Becky in some positive direction."

"I'd like to help very much," Marsha said. "But I guess he scared me. I don't know him the way you do, it's hard to put his actions in any perspective."

"I understand," Tracy said. "But I hope you'll consider it. I'll give you his address. Knowing him as well as I do, I'm sure he'll hole up there until his anger and sense of injustice drive him out to do something. All I can hope is that with your help his energies can be channeled into action that will make a difference."

Marsha climbed into her car. She didn't start it immediately but mulled over the events of this strange day. It had all started when she'd impulsively decided to put in a few hours of overtime at Mercer Meats.

Marsha wondered how to go about getting the information that Kim wanted. The source of meat for the various lots was recorded in the patty-room logs, but reading specific entries was not within her usual province. Her job was just to confirm that the log was being kept. Knowing that someone was always looking over her shoulder, she wondered how she could do it without raising suspicion. The problem was she didn't want her own boss to know what she was up to, and that would be tricky since Mercer Meats was in close contact with her superiors concerning everything she did.

The answer was obvious. She'd go after hours when only the cleaning crew was there. In fact, Saturday was an ideal day for her to try; it would be quieter than usual.

Marsha got out the address Tracy had given her and consulted the city map she had in the car. Kim's house was relatively close; she decided to pay him a visit to see if he were still interested in her help.

It didn't take long for Marsha to find the property, but when she arrived, she was dismayed there wasn't a single light to counteract the gathering gloom. The house was a huge black hulk silhouetted in its dense surround of trees.

Marsha was about to leave, when she caught sight of Kim's car parked in the dark shadows in front of the garage. She decided to get out of her car and go to the front door on the off chance he was there.

Marsha rang the bell. She was surprised at the loudness and clarity of the chimes until she noticed that the front door was not fully closed. When Kim didn't respond to the bell, she rang it again. Again there was no response.

Mystified and concerned by the door being ajar in the middle of the winter, Marsha took a chance and pushed it open farther. She leaned into the front hall and called out Kim's name. There was no answer.

From where she was standing, Marsha's eyes adapted so she could see up the staircase, as well as through the dining room and all the way to the kitchen. She called Kim's name again but again there was no response.

Unsure what to do next, Marsha thought about leaving. But then Tracy's comment about Kim possibly hurting himself came into her mind. She wondered if she should call the police, but that seemed a fairly extreme action to take based on so little evidence. She decided to probe further before deciding what to do.

Marshaling her courage, Marsha stepped into the foyer, intending to go to the base of the stairs. But she didn't get far. Halfway across the hall she stopped dead in her tracks. Kim was sitting in a club chair in an otherwise empty room less than ten feet away. He looked like a specter in the half darkness. His white doctor's coat appeared to glow like the radium dial of an old wristwatch.

"My God!" Marsha exclaimed. "You scared me!"

Kim didn't respond. He didn't even move.

"Dr. Reggis?" Marsha questioned. For a fleeting moment she wondered if he was dead.

"What do you want?" Kim asked in a tired monotone.

"Maybe I shouldn't have come. I just wanted to offer my help."

"And just how do you plan to help?"

"By doing what you'd asked me earlier," Marsha said. "I know it won't bring your daughter back, but I'd like to help you track the meat in those lots you think might be contaminated. Of course, it might be futile. You have to understand that, in this day and age, the meat in a single hamburger patty can come from a hundred different cows from ten different countries. But, be that as it may, I'm willing to give it a try if you still want me to."

"Why the change of heart?" Kim asked.

"Mainly because you were right about the effect of seeing a sick child. But also because you were right to an extent about the USDA. I wasn't willing to admit it earlier, but I know there's foot-dragging by my superiors and too much collusion between the agency and the beef industry. Every one of the deficiency reports I've filed for violations I've uncovered have been suppressed by my district manager. He's all but told me to my face to look the other way when there's a problem."

"Why didn't you say this to me before?" Kim asked.

"I don't know," Marsha said. "Loyalty to my employer, I suppose. You see, I think the system could work. It just needs more people like me who want it to work."

"And meanwhile meat gets contaminated and people get sick," Kim said. "And kids like Becky die."

"Unfortunately that's true," Marsha said. "But we in the business all know where the problem is: it's in the slaughterhouses. It's simply profit over safe meat."

"When are you willing to help?" Kim asked.

"Whenever," Marsha said. "Right now if you're up for it. Actually, tonight would be a good time for me to try because there'll be less risk. The only people at Mercer Meats now would be the overtime cleaning crew. I can't imagine they'd think much if I browse through the patty-room logs."

"All right," Kim said. "You're on. Let's go."

# CHAPTER 13

Tracy felt shell-shocked. Her divorce had been tough, especially the custody battle with Kim, but it was nothing compared to what she was feeling now. Thanks to her experience as a therapist, she recognized clearly the symptoms; she was on the verge of slipping into a serious depression. From having counseled other people in similar circumstances, she knew it wasn't going to be easy, but she wanted to fight it. At the same time, she knew she had to let herself grieve.

As she rounded the final bend in the road and approached her house, she could see Carl's yellow Lamborghini parked at the curb. She didn't know whether she'd be glad to see him or not.

Tracy pulled into her driveway and turned off the engine. Carl came down the steps to meet her, carrying a bouquet of flowers.

Tracy stepped out of her car and into Carl's arms. For a few minutes they didn't talk; he just held her in the late-afternoon darkness.

"How did you find out?" Tracy asked, with her head still pressed against Carl's chest.

"Being on the hospital board, I hear all the news," Carl said. "I'm so sorry."

"Thank you," Tracy said. "God, I feel drained."

"I can imagine," Carl said. "Come on. Let's get you inside."

They started walking up the pathway.

"I hear Kim really lost it. That must make it extra tough on you."

Tracy only nodded.

"The man's clearly out of control. Who does he think he is—God? I tell you, the whole hospital is in an uproar."

Tracy opened the door without responding. She and Carl went in.

"Kim's having a hard time," Tracy said.

"Ha!" Carl commented. He took Tracy's coat and hung it along with his in the hall closet. "That's an understatement. As usual, you're being generous. I'm not nearly so charitable. In fact, I could club him for carrying on the way he did in the Onion Ring restaurant last night about Becky's getting sick there. Did you see the article in the paper? It's had a big effect on the Onion Ring share price. I can't tell you how much of a paper loss I've suffered from his lunacy."

Tracy went into the living room and collapsed on the couch. She felt exhausted and yet wired and anxious at the same time. Carl followed her.

"Can I get you something?" Carl asked. "Like a drink or some food."

Tracy shook her head. Carl sat across from her. "I spoke to some other members of the Foodsmart board," he said. "We're seriously thinking about suing him if the share price continues to fall."

"It wasn't an idle accusation on his part," Tracy said. "Becky had a rare burger there the night before she got sick."

"Oh, come on," Carl said with a dismissive wave of his hand. "Becky didn't get sick there. Hundreds of thousands of burgers are made in the chain. No one gets sick. We cook those burgers to death."

Tracy didn't say anything. Carl quickly realized what he'd said.

"I'm sorry. That was a poor choice of words under the circumstances."

"It's okay, Carl," Tracy said wearily.

"I'll tell you what bugs me about all this," Carl said. "Hamburger has gotten a bad rap with this E. coli brouhaha. It's now like a knee-jerk reaction: E. coli and hamburger. Hell, people have gotten the same E. coli from apple juice, lettuce, milk, even swimming in a contaminated pond. Don't you think it's unfair that hamburger has to take all the crap?"

"I don't know," Tracy said. "I'm sorry I can't be more responsive. I feel numb. It's hard for me to think."

"Of course, dear," Carl said. "I'm the one who should be sorry for carrying on like I am. I think you should eat. When was the last time you had a meal?"

"I can't remember," Tracy said.

"Well, there you go," Carl said. "How about we go out to some quiet place?"

Tracy looked at Carl in total disbelief. "My daughter just died. I'm not going out. How can you even ask?"

"Okay," Carl said, raising his hands in defense. "It was just an idea. I think you should eat. I suppose I could get some takeout food. What about that?"

Tracy lowered her face into her hands. Carl was not helping. "I'm not hungry. Besides, maybe it would be better for me to just be alone tonight. I'm not very good company."

"Really?" Carl questioned. He was hurt.

"Yes, really," Tracy said. She raised her head. "I'm sure there's something you should be doing."

"Well, there is the dinner at Bobby Bo Mason's house," Carl said. "Remember me telling you about that?"

"I can't say that I do," Tracy said tiredly. "Who's Bobby Bo?"

"He's one of the local cattle barons," Carl said. "Tonight's the celebration of his assuming the presidency of the American Beef Alliance."

"Sounds very important," Tracy said in contrast to how she felt.

"It is," Carl said. "It's the most powerful national organization in the business."

"Then don't let me keep you from it," Tracy said.

"You wouldn't mind?" Carl said. "I'll have my cellular phone. You can call me, and I can be back here in twenty minutes tops."

"I wouldn't mind at all," Tracy said. "In fact, I'd feel bad if you missed it on my account."

The car's instrument panel splashed light on Kim's face. Marsha stole glances at him as she drove. Now that she'd had a chance to observe him, she had to admit to herself that he was a handsome man even with his two-day stubble.

They drove in silence for quite a ways. Finally Marsha was able to get Kim talking about Becky. She had a feeling it would be good for him to talk about his daughter and she was right. Kim warmed to the subject. He regaled Marsha with stories of Becky's skating exploits, something Tracy had not mentioned.

When the conversation about Becky lapsed, Marsha had talked a little about herself, explaining that she'd been through veterinary school. She'd described how she and a girlfriend had become interested in the USDA and had vowed to join the agency to make a difference. She'd explained that after graduation, they'd discovered there were obstacles for them to get into the veterinarian side of the USDA. The only entry-level positions available were with the inspectional services. In the end, it had only been Marsha who'd joined. The friend had decided the year or so it would take to be transferred was too big a sacrifice and had opted for private veterinarian practice.

"Veterinary school?" Kim questioned. "I wouldn't have guessed."

"Why not?" Marsha asked.

"I don't know exactly," Kim said. "Maybe you are a little too . . ." Kim paused as he struggled for a word. Finally he said: ". . . too elegant, I guess. I know it's probably unfair, but I'd expect someone to be more . . ."

"More what?" Marsha asked as Kim paused again. She was enjoying Kim's mild discomfort.

"I guess tomboyish," Kim said. He chuckled. "I suppose that's a stupid thing to say."

Marsha laughed too. At least he could hear how ridiculous he sounded.

"If you don't mind my asking," Kim said, "how old are you? I know that's an inappropriate question, but unless you are some kind of child prodigy, you're not in your early twenties like I'd guessed."

"Heavens, no," Marsha said. "I'm twenty-nine, pushing thirty."

Marsha leaned forward and turned on the windshield wipers. It had started to rain. It was already as dark as pitch even though it was only a little after six in the evening.

"How are we going to work this?" Kim questioned.

"Work what?" Marsha asked.

"My getting into Mercer Meats," Kim said.

"I told you, it won't be a problem," Marsha said. "The day shift is long gone along with the supervisors. Only the overtime cleaning crew will be there, along with a security guard."

"Well, the guard's not going to be excited about letting me in," Kim said. "Maybe I should just wait in the car."

"Security is not going to be a problem," Marsha said. "I have both my USDA and Mercer Meats I.D.'s."

"That's fine for you," Kim said. "But what about me?"

"Don't worry," Marsha said. "They know me. They've never once even asked to see my I.D. If it comes up, I'll say you're my supervisor. Or I'll say I'm training you." She laughed.

"I'm not dressed like someone from the USDA," Kim said.

Marsha shot Kim a glance and giggled some more. "What does a night security man know? I think you look bizarre enough to pass for most anything."

"You seem awfully cavalier about this," Kim commented.

"Well, what's the worst-case scenario?" Marsha said. "We don't get in."

"And you get into trouble," Kim said.

"I've already thought of that," Marsha said. "What happens, happens."

Marsha exited the expressway and started through Bartonville. They had to stop at the single traffic light in the town, where Mercer Street met Main Street.

"When I think about hamburger," Marsha said, "I'm surprised anyone eats it. I was a half-ass vegetarian before this job. Now I'm a committed one."

"Coming from a USDA meat inspector, that's not very reassuring," Kim said.

"It turns my stomach when I think of what hamburger has in it," Marsha said.

"What do you mean?" Kim said. "It's muscle."

"Muscle and a bunch of other stuff," Marsha said. "Have you ever heard of the Advanced Meat Recovery System?"

"Can't say that I have," Kim said.

"It's a high-pressure device that they use to clean every scrap off cattle bones," Marsha said. "It results in a gray slurry that they dye red and add to the hamburger."

"That's disgusting," Kim said.

"And central-nervous tissue," Marsha said. "Like spinal cord. That gets into hamburger all the time."

"Really?" Kim asked.

"Absolutely," Marsha said. "And that's worse than it sounds. You've heard of mad cow disease?"

"Who hasn't?" Kim said. "That's an illness that terrifies me. The idea of a heat-resistant protein that you get by eating and that is fatal is the ultimate horror. Thank God we don't have it in this country."

"We don't have it yet," Marsha said. "At least it hasn't been seen so far. But if you ask me, it's just a matter of time. Do you know what is thought to have caused mad cow disease in England?"

"I believe it's thought to have come from feeding rendered sheep to the cows," Kim said. "Sheep that were sick with scrapie, the sheep equivalent."

"Exactly," Marsha said. "And in this country there's supposed to be a ban on feeding rendered sheep to cows. But you know something, there's no enforcement, and I was told by insiders that as many as a quarter of the renderers admit in private they don't pay any attention to the ban."

"In other words, the same circumstances that resulted in mad cow disease in England are present here?"

"Precisely," Marsha said. "And with spinal cord and the like routinely getting into hamburger, the chain to humans is in place. That's why I say it's just a matter of time before we see the first cases."

"Good God!" Kim exclaimed. "The more I hear about this shoddy business, the more appalled I get. I'd no idea about any of this."

"Nor does the general public," Marsha said.

The white hulk of Mercer Meats loomed up, and Marsha turned into its parking area. In contrast to earlier that day, there were few cars. She pulled up close to the front door in the same spot she'd been in that morning. She turned off the engine.

"Ready?" she asked.

"You're sure I should come?" Kim asked.

"Come on!" Marsha said. She opened the door and got out.

The front door was locked. Marsha rapped on it. Inside, the guard was seated at the round reception desk, reading a magazine. He responded by getting up and coming to the door. He was an elderly gentleman with a thin mustache. His security uniform appeared to be several sizes too big.

"Mercer Meats is closed," he said through the glass.

Marsha held up her Mercer Meats I.D. card. The guard squinted at it, then unlocked and opened the door. Marsha immediately pushed in. "Thanks," she said simply.

Kim followed. He could tell the guard looked at him suspiciously, but the man didn't say anything. He merely locked the door.

Kim had to run to catch up to Marsha, who was already beyond the reception desk and briskly walking down the corridor.

"What did I tell you?" she said. "It was no problem at all."

○   ○   ○

The security guard walked over to the end of the reception area and peered down the hall. He watched as Marsha and Kim disappeared into the changing room leading to the production floor. He returned to his desk and picked up the phone. The number he needed was on a Post-it stuck to the edge of the counter.

"Mr. Cartwright," the guard said when the call was answered, "that USDA lady, Miss Baldwin, who you asked me to watch for, just walked in the door with another guy."

"Was her companion dressed in a white lab coat, something like a doctor's?" Jack asked.

"Yup," the security man said.

"When they leave, get them both to sign out," Jack said. "I want proof they were there."

"I'll do that, sir," the guard said.

Jack did not bother to replace the receiver. Instead he pressed the appropriate button on his speed-dialer and waited. A moment later, Everett's stentorian voice reverberated through the line.

"Marsha Baldwin and the doctor are back at the plant," Jack said.

"Good grief!" Everett sputtered. "That's not what I wanted to hear. How the devil did you find out?"

"I left word with security to call if they showed up," Jack said. "Just in case."

"Good thinking," Everett said. "I wonder what on earth they're doing there."

"My guess is they're going to try to trace some meat," Jack said. "That's what he asked me to do this morning."

"Let's not guess," Everett said. "You get the hell over there and see what they're up to. Then get back to me. I don't want this to ruin my evening."

Jack hung up the phone. He didn't want it to ruin his evening either. He'd been looking forward to the dinner at Bobby Bo's for a month and had certainly not anticipated having to go back to the plant. He was in a foul mood when he got his coat and went out to the garage for his car.

○   ○   ○

Kim stamped his feet and flapped his arms. He didn't quite understand it, but the thirty-five-degree temperature of the patty room felt more like twenty-five or even fifteen. He'd pulled on a Mercer Meats white coat over his own hospital coat, but they were just cotton, and underneath he had on only his scrubs. The three layers were not nearly enough insulation against the chill, especially since he was essentially standing around. The showerlike white cap didn't help at all.

Marsha was leafing through the patty-room logbooks, and had been doing so for more than a quarter of an hour. Locating the specific dates, lots, and batches was taking longer than expected. Initially Kim had looked over her shoulder, but the colder he'd become, the less interested he was.

There were two other people in the room besides Marsha and Kim. They were busy pulling hoses around as they cleaned the patty-formulating machine with high-pressure steam. They had been there when Marsha and Kim arrived but hadn't made any attempts at conversation.

"Ah, here we go," Marsha said triumphantly. "Here's December twenty-ninth." She ran her finger down the column until she came to Lot 2. Then moving horizontally, she came to the appropriate batches: one through five. "Uh-oh," she said.

"What's the matter?" Kim asked. He came over to look.

"It's just what I was afraid of," she said. "Batches one through five were a mixture of fresh boneless beef from Higgins and Hancock and imported frozen ground beef. The imported stuff is impossible to trace other than maybe the country. Of course, that would be useless for what you want."

"What's Higgins and Hancock?" Kim asked.

"It's a local slaughterhouse," Marsha said. "One of the bigger ones."

"What about the other lot?" Kim asked.

"Let's check that," Marsha said. She turned the page. "Here's the date. What were the lot and batch numbers again?"

"Lot six, batches nine through fourteen," Kim said, consulting his paper.

"Okay, here it is," Marsha said. "Hey, we're in luck if the January twelfth production is the culprit. Those batches were all from Higgins and Hancock. Take a peek."

Kim looked at where she was pointing. It indicated that the entire lot was made from fresh beef produced on January ninth at Higgins and Hancock."

"Wasn't there some way to narrow it down to one or the other?" Marsha asked.

"Not according to the short-order cook at the Onion Ring," Kim said.

"But I dropped off samples from both production dates at the lab. They should have the result by Monday."

"Until then we'll assume it's the January date," Marsha said. "Because that's the only one that's going to be traceable. Hopefully, we'll be able to go beyond Higgins and Hancock."

"Really?" Kim questioned. "You mean we'll be able to trace the meat back further than the slaughterhouse?"

"That's the way the system is supposed to work," Marsha said. "At least in theory. The trouble is a lot of cows can go into one of those two-thousand-pound combos of boneless beef. But the idea is to be able to trace the animals through purchase invoices back to the ranch or farm they came from. Anyway, the next step is to go to Higgins and Hancock."

"Give me that goddamn book," Jack Cartwright yelled.

Marsha and Kim leaped in fright as Jack lunged around Marsha and snatched up the ponderous logbooks. The noise from the high-pressure steam had kept them from hearing the man enter the patty room and approach them.

"Now you have finally overstepped your bounds, Miss Baldwin!" Jack sneered triumphantly, while pointing an accusatory finger into Marsha's face.

Marsha straightened up and tried to regain her composure. "What are you talking about?" she asked, attempting to sound authoritative. "I have a right to examine the logs."

"The hell you do," Jack said, while continuing to poke his finger at Marsha. "You have the right to ascertain we keep the logs, but the logs themselves are private property of a private company. And more important, you do not have the right to bring in the public under the authority of the USDA to look at these logs."

"That's enough," Kim said. He stepped between the two. "If anybody is to blame here it's me."

Jack ignored Kim. "One thing I can assure you, Miss Baldwin, is that Sterling Henderson, the district USDA manager, is going to hear about this violation of yours ASAP."

Kim batted Jack's brutish finger to the side and grabbed a handful of the man's white coat. "Listen, you oily bastard . . ."

Marsha gripped Kim's arm. "No!" she cried. "Leave him alone. Let's not compound this."

Reluctantly Kim let go.

Jack smoothed his lapels. "I want you two out of here," he snarled, "before I call the police and have you arrested."

Kim glared back at the Mercer Meats vice president. For a blind instant the man was the embodiment of all Kim's anger. Marsha had to pull on his sleeve to get him to leave.

Jack watched them go. As soon as the door closed, he hoisted the logs up to chest height and slipped them into their appropriate shelves. Then he followed them into the changing room. Marsha and Kim were already gone. Out in the hall he walked down to the reception area. He got there in time to see Marsha's car leaving the lot and accelerating up the street.

"They didn't pay me no attention," the guard said. "I tried to tell them they had to sign out."

"It doesn't make any difference," Jack said.

Jack walked back to his office and phoned Everett.

"Well, what did you learn?" Everett demanded.

"It was just as I suspected," Jack said. "They were in the patty room, looking at the patty-room logs."

"They weren't looking at the formulation logs?" Everett asked.

"The guard said they hadn't gone anyplace but the patty room," Jack said. "So they couldn't have looked at the formulation logs."

"At least that's a blessing," Everett said. "The last thing I want is for someone to find out we're recycling outdated frozen patties. And that might happen if someone were to snoop around in the formulation logs."

"That's not a worry with this crisis," Jack said. "What is a worry is that this duo might end up at Higgins and Hancock. I heard them talking about Higgins and Hancock before I surprised them. I think Daryl Webster should be warned."

"An excellent idea," Everett said. "We can mention it to Daryl when we see him tonight. Better yet, maybe I'll give him a quick call."

"The sooner the better," Jack said. "Who knows what these two might do, as crazy as that doctor seems to be."

"See you at Bobby Bo's," Everett said.

"I might be a tad late," Jack said. "I've got to go all the way back home to change before I drive over there."

"Well, get a move on," Everett said. "I want you there for the Prevention Committee meeting."

"I'll do what I can," Jack said.

Everett hung up the phone and then searched for Daryl Webster's phone number. He was in his upstairs study off his dressing room, half-dressed in his tuxedo. When Jack had called he'd been struggling with his shirt studs. Formal attire was not a common requirement in Everett's life.

"Everett!" Gladys Sorenson called from the master bedroom. Gladys and Everett had been married for more years than Everett wished to acknowledge. "You'd better shake a leg, dear. We're due over at the Masons' in half an hour."

"I gotta make a quick call," Everett yelled back. He found the number and quickly dialed. The phone was answered on the first ring.

"Daryl, Everett Sorenson here," Everett said.

"This is a surprise," Daryl said. The two men not only had traveled similar career paths; they even resembled each other physically. Daryl was equally heavyset, with a thick neck, shovel-like hands, and a ruddy, plethoric face. The difference was that Daryl had a full head of hair and normal-sized ears. "The Mrs. and I are just about to walk out the door on our way to the Masons'."

"Gladys and I are about to do the same," Everett said. "But something's come up. You know that young, pain-in-the-ass inspector, Marsha Baldwin, who's been causing me grief?"

"Yeah, Henderson told me about her," Daryl said. "A real independent troublemaker as I understand it."

"Well, she's hooked up with that raving maniac doctor who got himself arrested last night at an Onion Ring restaurant. Did you see that in today's paper?"

"Who could miss it?" Daryl said. "It gave me a cold sweat with him carrying on about E. coli."

"You and me both," Everett said. "And now it's gotten worse. A little while ago she snuck into my plant with the doctor. Somehow he's got her to help him trace meat."

"Presumably looking for E. coli," Daryl said.

"Undoubtedly," Everett said.

"This is very scary," Daryl said.

"I couldn't agree more," Everett said. "Especially since Jack Cartwright overheard them talking about Higgins and Hancock. We're concerned they may show up at your establishment on the same crusade."

"This I don't need," Daryl said.

"We're going to be talking about a long-term solution tonight," Everett said. "Did you get the message?"

"I did," Daryl said. "Bobby Bo called me."

"In the meantime, maybe you should take some precautions," Everett said.

"Thanks for the tip," Daryl said. "I'll call my security and alert them."

"That's exactly what I would have suggested," Everett said. "See you in a little while."

Daryl disconnected. He held up a finger to indicate to his wife, Hazel, that he had one more quick call to make. Hazel, dressed to the nines, was impatiently waiting at the front door. While she tapped her toe, Daryl dialed the main number at the slaughterhouse.

○    ○    ○

Marsha turned into Kim's driveway and stopped directly behind Kim's car. She left the motor running and the headlights on.

"I appreciate what you've done," Kim said. He had his hand on the door, but he didn't open it. "I'm sorry it didn't go more smoothly."

"It could have been worse," Marsha said brightly. "And who knows what's going to happen? We'll just have to see how it plays out."

"Would you like to come in?" Kim asked. "My house is a wreck, but I could use a drink. How about you?"

"Thanks, but I think I'll take a rain check," Marsha said. "You've got me started on something I intend to finish. By the time you get the lab results on Monday, I'd like to have the meat traced as much as possible. That way we'd be that much farther ahead of the game when we try to make an argument for a recall."

"Are you planning on doing something now?"

"Yup," Marsha said, with a nod. She glanced at her watch. "I'm going to head directly out to Higgins and Hancock. This might be my only chance. As I said earlier, the district USDA manager and I have never gotten along. Come Monday, when he hears about our little escapade from Jack Cartwright, I might be out of a job. Of course, that would mean I'd lose my I.D. card."

"Gosh," Kim remarked. "If you lose your job, I'm going to feel terrible. It's certainly not what I intended."

"There's no need for you to feel responsible," Marsha said. "I knew the risk I was taking. Even in retrospect, I think it was worth it. Like you said, I'm supposed to be protecting the public."

"If you're going to the slaughterhouse now, then I'm coming along," Kim said. "I'm not going to let you go alone."

"Sorry, but it's out of the question," Marsha said. "I didn't think there'd be a problem at Mercer Meats and there was. It's a different story at Higgins and Hancock. I know there'd be a problem. Heck, it might be tough for me to get in there even with my USDA card."

"How can that be?" Kim asked. "As a USDA inspector, can't you visit any meat establishment?"

"Not where I'm not assigned," Marsha said. "And especially not a slaughterhouse. They have their own full-time contingent of USDA people. You see, slaughterhouses are akin to nuclear installations as far as visitors are concerned. They don't need them, and they don't want them. All they can do is cause trouble."

"What are the slaughterhouses hiding?" Kim asked.

"Their methods, mostly," Marsha said. "It's not a pretty sight in the best of circumstances but particularly after the deregulation of the eighties, slaughterhouses have all pushed up the speed of their lines, meaning they process more animals per hour. Some of them run as much as two hundred fifty to three hundred animals an hour. At that speed contamination can't be avoided. It's inevitable. In fact, it is so inevitable that the industry sued the USDA when the agency considered officially calling meat with E. coli contaminated."

"You can't be serious," Kim said.

"Trust me," Marsha said. "It's true."

"You're saying the industry knows that E. coli is in the meat?" Kim said. "They're contending it can't be helped?"

"Exactly," Marsha said. "Not in all meat, just some of it."

"This is outrageous," Kim said. "This is something the public has to find out about. This can't continue. You've convinced me I've got to see a slaughterhouse in operation."

"Which is exactly why the slaughterhouses don't like visitors," Marsha said. "And that's why you'd never get in. Well, that's not entirely true. Slaughtering has always been a labor-intensive business, and one of their biggest headaches is a constant shortage of help. So I suppose if you got tired of being a cardiac surgeon, you could get a job. Of course, it would help if you were an illegal alien, so they could pay you less than the minimum wage."

"You're not painting a very flattering picture," Kim said.

"It's reality," Marsha said. "It's hard, undesirable work, and the industry has always relied heavily on immigrants. The difference is that today the workers come from Latin America, particularly Mexico, rather than Eastern Europe, where they came from in the past."

"This is all sounding worse and worse," Kim said. "I can't imagine that I've never given it any thought. I mean, I eat meat, so in some ways I'm responsible."

"It's the downside of capitalism," Marsha said. "I don't mean to sound like a radical socialist, but this is a particularly flaming example of profit

over ethics: greed with a complete disregard for consequence. It's all part
of what prompted me to join the USDA, because the USDA could change
things."

"If change was considered desirable by those in power," Kim added.

"True," Marsha agreed.

"Putting this all in perspective," Kim said, "we're talking about an industry that exploits its workforce and feels no compunction about killing
hundreds of kids a year." Kim shook his head in disbelief. "You know, the
total lack of ethics that this represents makes me worry even more about
you."

"How do you mean?" Marsha asked.

"I'm talking about your going off right now to visit Higgins and Hancock essentially under false pretenses," Kim said. "By using your USDA
I.D., you'll be suggesting you're there on official business."

"Obviously," Marsha said. "That's the only way I could get in."

"Well, as security-minded as they are," Kim said, "won't you be taking
a risk? And I'm not talking about your job security."

"I see what you mean," Marsha said. "Thank you for being concerned,
but I'm not worried about my well-being. The worst that could happen
is that they'd complain to my boss, like Jack Cartwright has threatened
to do."

"Are you sure?" Kim asked. "If there were any danger, I wouldn't
want you to go. To tell you the truth, after the episode in Mercer Meats,
I feel uncomfortable about you doing any more on my behalf. Maybe you
should just let me do what I can. If you go out there tonight, I'll be nervous the entire time."

"I'm flattered by your concern," Marsha said. "But I think I should just
go and see what I can. I'm not going to get hurt or in any more trouble
than I already am. I might not even get in. And as I said, you wouldn't be
able to do anything on your own because you certainly wouldn't be able
to get in."

"Maybe I could get a job," Kim said. "Like you suggested."

"Hey, I was only kidding," Marsha said. "I was just trying to make a
point."

"I'm willing to do what I have to do," Kim said.

"Listen," Marsha said, "what if I take my cellular phone with me and call you every fifteen or twenty minutes? Then you won't have to worry, and I can keep you posted about what I'm finding. How's that?"

"It's something, I guess," Kim said without a lot of enthusiasm. But the more he thought of the idea, the better it began to sound. The concept of his getting a job in a slaughterhouse was far from appealing. But most important was Marsha's adamant assurances about the lack of risk.

"I'll tell you what," Marsha added. "This visit won't take me that long, and after I'm done, I'll come back and have that drink you offered. That is, if the invitation is still open."

"Of course," Kim said. He nodded as he went over the plan one last time. Then he gave Marsha's forearm a quick squeeze before getting out of the car. Instead of closing the door, he leaned back in. "You better take my phone number," he said.

"Good thinking," Marsha said. She fumbled for a pen and a piece of paper.

Kim gave her the number. "I'm going to be waiting right by the phone, so you'd better call."

"No need to worry," Marsha said.

"Good luck," Kim said.

"I'll be talking with you soon," Marsha said.

Kim slammed the car door. He watched as she backed up, turned, and accelerated down the street. He watched until the red taillights and their reflection in the rain-slicked street were swallowed by the night.

Kim turned and looked up at his dark, deserted house. Not a single light relieved its somber silhouette. He shuddered. Suddenly left by himself, the reality of Becky's loss descended. The crushing melancholy he'd felt earlier flooded back. Kim shook his head in despair at how tenuous his world had been. His family and his career had seemed so substantial, and yet within a relative blink of the eye, it had all disintegrated.

○   ○   ○

Bobby Bo Mason's house was lit up like a Las Vegas casino. To provide the proper gala atmosphere for his inaugural dinner celebration, he'd retained a theatrical lighting specialist to do the job. And to make the scene even more festive, he'd hired a mariachi band to play under a tent on the front lawn. A little rain certainly wasn't going to dampen his affair.

Bobby Bo was one of the largest cattle barons in the country. In keeping with his image of himself as well as his position in the industry, he'd built a house whose flamboyant style was a monument to Roman Empire kitsch. Columned porticos stretched off in bewildering directions. Plaster-cast, life-sized, imitation Roman and Greek statues dotted the grounds. Some were even painted in realistic skin tones.

Liveried valet parkers lined up at the head of the circular drive to await the arrival of the guests. Six-foot-high torches bordering the drive sputtered in the light rain.

Everett Sorenson's Mercedes beat Daryl Webster's Lexus but only by less than a minute. It was as if they'd planned it. As they exited their cars they embraced as did their wives.

The cars were whisked away by the valets, while other staff protected the guests with large golf umbrellas. The foursome started up the grand staircase leading to the double front doors.

"I trust you called your security," Everett said sotto voce.

"The moment after I spoke with you," Daryl said.

"Good," Everett said. "We can't be too careful, especially now that the beef business is back to being relatively healthy."

They reached the front door and rang. While they waited, Gladys reached over and straightened Everett's clip-on tie.

The double doors were whisked open. The light from within was enough to make the newly arrived guests squint as it reflected off the white marble foyer. In front of them stood Bobby Bo framed by the massive granite jambs and lintel.

Bobby Bo was heavyset, similar to Everett and Daryl, and, like his colleagues, he believed in his product enough to eat staggeringly large steaks. He had a lantern jaw and a barrel chest. He was impressively attired in a custom-tailored tuxedo, a hand-tied bowtie edged with gold thread, and diamond studs and cuff links. His fashion idol had been the "Dapper Don" prior to his conviction and incarceration.

"Welcome, folks," Bobby Bo beamed. His smile revealed several gold molars. "Coats to the little lady and please help yourself to champagne."

Music and gay laughter floated out from the living room; the Sorensons and the Websters were not the first to arrive. In contrast to the outside mariachis, the inside music was more restrained and emanated from a string quartet.

After the coats had been taken, Gladys and Hazel strolled arm in arm into the thick of the party. Bobby Bo held back Everett and Daryl.

"Sterling Henderson's the only one not here yet," Bobby Bo said. "As soon as he is, we'll have a short meeting in my library. Everyone else has been alerted."

"Jack Cartwright's a bit delayed as well," Everett said. "I'd like him to sit in on it."

"Fine by me," Bobby Bo said. "Guess who else is here?"

Everett looked at Daryl. Neither one wanted to guess.

"Carl Stahl," Bobby Bo said triumphantly.

A shadow of fear fell over Everett and Daryl.

"That makes me feel uncomfortable," Everett said.

"I'd have to say the same," Daryl said.

"Come on, you guys," Bobby Bo teased. "All he can do is fire you." He laughed.

"I don't think getting fired is something I want to joke about," Daryl said.

"Nor I," Everett said. "But thinking about it is all the more reason we have to nip this current problem in the bud."

# CHAPTER 14

The windshield wipers tapped out a monotonous rhythm as Marsha rounded the final bend and got her first view of Higgins and Hancock. It was a sprawling, low-slung plant, with a vast, fenced-in stockyard in the rear. It looked ominous in the cold rain.

Marsha turned into the large, deserted parking lot. What cars that were there were widely scattered. When the three–to–eleven cleaning crew had arrived, the lot had been jammed with the day workers' vehicles.

Having visited the plant once during her orientation to the district, Marsha knew enough to drive around to the side. She recognized the unmarked door that was the employee entrance. Above it was a single caged light fixture which dimly lit the area.

Marsha parked, set the emergency brake, and turned off the engine; but she didn't get out. For a moment she sat and tried to bolster her confidence. After the conversation with Kim, she felt nervous about what she was about to do.

Prior to Kim's mentioning physical danger, Marsha had not considered it. Now she wasn't so sure. She'd heard plenty of stories of the industry's use of strong-arm tactics in its dealings with its immigrant employees and with union sympathizers. Consequently, she couldn't help but wonder how they might respond to the kind of threat her unauthorized activities would surely pose.

"You're being overly melodramatic," Marsha said out loud.

With sudden resolve, Marsha unhooked her cellular phone from its car cradle. She checked its battery.

"Well, here goes," she said as she alighted from the car.

It was raining harder than she expected, so she ran for the employee entrance. When she got there, she tried to yank open the door but found it locked. Next to the door was a button with a small plaque that said: AFTER HOURS. She pushed it.

After a half a minute and no response, Marsha rang the bell again and even rapped on the solid door with her fist. Just when she was thinking of returning to her car and calling the plant with her cell phone, the door swung open. A man in a brown-and-black security uniform looked out at her with a confused look on his face. Visitors were obviously a rarity.

Marsha flashed her USDA card and tried to push into the building. The man held his position, forcing her to remain in the rain.

"Let me see that," the guard said.

Marsha handed the man the card. He inspected it carefully, even reviewing the back.

"I'm a USDA inspector," Marsha said. She feigned irritation. "Do you really think it's appropriate to make me stand out here in the rain?"

"What are you doing here?" the man asked.

"What we inspectors always do," Marsha said. "I'm making sure federal rules are being followed."

The man finally backed up enough to allow Marsha to enter. She wiped moisture off her forehead and then shook it free from her hand.

"There's only cleaning going on now," the guard commented.

"I understand," Marsha said. "Could I please have my I.D.?"

The guard handed back the card. "Where are you going?"

"I'll be in the USDA office," Marsha said over her shoulder. She was already on her way. She walked with determination and didn't look back, even though the guard's reaction had surprised her and added to her unease.

○  ○  ○

Bobby Bo Mason pulled the library's paneled mahogany door closed. The sound of merriment from the rest of the house was cut off abruptly. He turned to face his tuxedoed colleagues who were sprinkled around the library's interior. Represented were most of the city's businesses associated with beef and beef products: cattlemen, slaughterhouse directors, meat-processor presidents, and meat-distributor heads. Some of these men were sitting on dark-green velvet chairs; others were standing with their champagne glasses held close to their chests.

The library was one of Bobby Bo's favorite rooms. Under normal circumstances, every guest was made to come into it to admire its proportions. It was clad entirely in old-growth Brazilian mahogany. The carpet was an inch-thick antique Tabriz. Oddly, this "library" contained no books.

"Let's make this short so we can get back to more important things like eating and drinking," Bobby Bo said. His comment elicited some laughter. Bobby Bo enjoyed being the center of attention and was looking forward to his year as the president of the American Beef Alliance.

"The issue here is Miss Marsha Baldwin," Bobby Bo continued when he had everyone's attention.

"Excuse me," a voice said. "I'd like to say something."

Bobby Bo watched as Sterling Henderson got to his feet. He was a big man, with coarse features and a shock of startlingly silver hair.

"I'd like to apologize right from the top," Sterling said in a sad voice. "I've tried from day one to rein this woman in, but nothing's worked."

"We all understand your hands have been tied," Bobby Bo said. "I can assure you this little impromptu meeting is not to cast blame but rather to solve a problem. We were perfectly happy letting you deal with it until just today. What's made the Miss Baldwin issue a crisis is her sudden association with this crank doctor who got the media's attention with his ruckus about E. coli."

"It's an association that promises trouble," Everett said. "An hour ago we caught her and the doctor inside our patty room going through our logs."

"She brought the doctor into your plant?" Sterling questioned with horrified surprise.

"I'm afraid so," Everett said. "It gives you an idea of what we're up against. It's a critical situation. We're going to be facing another E. coli fiasco unless something is done."

"This E. coli nonsense is such a pain in the ass," Bobby Bo sputtered. "You know what really irks me about it? The goddamn poultry industry puts out a product that's almost a hundred percent swimming in either salmonella or campylobacter and nobody says boo. We, on the other hand, have a tiny problem with E. coli in what . . . two to three percent of our product and everybody's up in arms. What's fair about that, will someone tell me? What is it? Do they have a better lobby?"

The hushed jingle of a cellular phone resounded in the silence following Bobby Bo's passionate philippic. Half the occupants in the room reached into their tuxes. Only Daryl's unit was vibrating in sync with the sound. He withdrew to the far corner to take the call.

"I don't know how the poultry business gets away with what they do," Everett said. "But that shouldn't divert our attention at the moment. All I know is that the Hudson Meat management didn't survive their E. coli brouhaha. We have to do something and do it fast. That's my vote. I mean, what the hell did we form the Prevention Committee for anyway?"

Daryl flipped his phone closed and slipped it back into his inner jacket pocket. He rejoined the group. His face was more flushed than usual.

"Bad news?" Bobby Bo inquired.

"Sure as hell is," Daryl said. "That was my security out at Higgins and Hancock. Marsha Baldwin is there right now going through USDA records. She came in flashing her USDA card, saying she was there to make sure federal rules were being followed."

"She's not authorized even to be in there," Sterling asserted indignantly, "much less look at any records."

"There you go," Everett said. "Now I don't even think it's a topic for debate. I think our hand is forced."

"I'd tend to agree," Bobby Bo said. He gazed out at the others. "How does everyone else feel?"

There was a universal murmur of assent.

"Fine," Bobby Bo said. "Consider it done."

Those who were sitting stood up. Everybody moved toward the door that Bobby Bo threw open. Laughter and music and the smell of garlic wafted into the room.

Except for Bobby Bo, the men filed out of the room and went in search of their consorts. Bobby Bo went to his phone and placed a quick internal call. Hardly had he replaced the receiver, when Shanahan O'Brian leaned into the room.

Shanahan was dressed in a dark suit and muted tie. He was sporting the kind of earphone a Secret Service agent might wear. He was a tall Black Irish fellow, a refugee of the turmoil in Northern Ireland. Bobby Bo had hired him on the spot, and for the past five years, Shanahan had been heading up Bobby Bo's security staff. He and Bobby Bo got along famously.

"Did you call?" Shanahan asked.

"Come in and close the door," Bobby Bo said.

Shanahan did as he was told.

"The Prevention Committee has its first assignment," Bobby Bo said.

"Excellent," Shanahan said with his soft Gaelic accent.

"Sit down and I'll tell you about it," Bobby Bo said.

Five minutes later, the two men walked out of the library. In the foyer they parted company. Bobby Bo went to the threshold of the sunken living room and looked out over the crowd of revelers. "How come it's so quiet in here!" Bobby Bo shouted. "What is this, a funeral? Come on, let's party!"

From the foyer, Shanahan descended into the underground garage. He got into his black Cherokee and drove out into the night. He took the ring road around the city, pushing his car as much as he thought he could get away with. He exited the freeway and drove due west. Twenty minutes later he pulled into a rutted, gravel parking lot of a popular nightspot called El Toro. On top of the building was a life-sized red neon outline of a bull. Shanahan parked at the periphery, leaving a wide space between his vehicle and the other mostly broken-down pickup trucks. He didn't want anybody opening their doors and denting his new car.

Even before he got near the entrance to the bar, he could hear the thundering bass of the Hispanic music; inside it was just shy of overpowering. The popular watering hole was crowded and smoke-filled. The patrons were mostly men, although there were a few brightly dressed, raven-haired women. There was a long bar on one side and a series of booths on the other. In the middle were tables and chairs and a small dance floor. An old-fashioned, brightly illuminated jukebox was against the wall. In the back was an archway through which a series of pool tables could be seen.

Shanahan scanned the people at the bar. He didn't see whom he was looking for. He walked down the bank of booths with no success. Giving up, he approached the busy bar. He literally had to squeeze between people. Then there was the problem of getting the bartender's attention.

Waving a ten-dollar bill finally succeeded where shouts did not. Shanahan handed the bill to the man.

"I'm looking for Carlos Mateo," Shanahan yelled.

The money disappeared as if it were a magic trick. The bartender didn't speak. He merely pointed to the back of the room and mimed the motion of shooting pool.

Shanahan weaved his way across the small dance floor. The backroom was not quite as crowded as the front. He found the man he was searching for at the second table.

Shanahan had spent a good deal of time and effort recruiting for the proposed Prevention Committee. After following up multiple leads and after a lot of interviewing, he'd settled on Carlos. Carlos had escaped from prison in Mexico and had been on the run. Six months previously, he'd managed to cross into the United States on his first attempt. He'd come to Higgins and Hancock in desperate need of a job.

What had impressed Shanahan about the man was his cavalier attitude toward death. Although Carlos was reticent concerning the details, Shanahan learned that the reason he'd been imprisoned in Mexico was because he had knifed to death an acquaintance. In his job at Higgins and

Hancock, Carlos was involved in the deaths of more than two thousand animals per day. Emotionally he seemed to view the activity of killing on par with cleaning his truck.

Shanahan stepped into the cone of light illuminating the second pool table. Carlos was in the process of lining up a shot and didn't respond to Shanahan's greeting. Shanahan had to wait.

*"Mierda!"* Carlos exclaimed when his ball refused to drop. He slapped the table's rail and straightened up. Only then did he look at Shanahan.

Carlos was a dark-haired, dark-complected wiry man with multiple flamboyant tattoos on both arms. His face was dominated by bushy eyebrows, a pencil-line mustache, and hollow cheeks. His eyes were like black marbles. Over his torso he was wearing a black leather vest that showed off his lean musculature as well as his tattoos. He was not wearing a shirt.

"I've got a job for you," Shanahan said. "A job like we talked about. You interested? It's got to be now."

"You pay me, I'm interested," Carlos said. He had a strong Spanish accent.

"Come with me," Shanahan directed. He pointed through the archway toward the front door.

Carlos handed off his cue stick, gave a couple of crumpled bills to his complaining opponent, then followed Shanahan.

The two men didn't try to talk until they were outside.

"I don't know how you can stand that noise in there for more than five minutes," Shanahan remarked.

"How come, man?" Carlos asked. "It's good music."

With the rain falling steadily, Shanahan brought Carlos to his Cherokee and the two men climbed inside.

"Let's make this fast," Shanahan said. "The name is Marsha Baldwin. She's an attractive, tall blonde who's about twenty-five."

Carlos's face twisted into a grin of pleasure, making his mustache look like two dashes under his narrow nose.

"The reason you got to move fast," Shanahan explained, "is because at this very moment she's where you work."

"She's at Higgins and Hancock?" Carlos asked.

"That's right," Shanahan said. "She's in the admin section looking into records she's not supposed to. You won't be able to miss her. If you have trouble finding her, ask the guard. He's supposed to keep his eye on her."

"How much you pay?" Carlos asked.

"More than we talked about, providing you do it now," Shanahan said. "I want you to go this minute."

"How much?" Carlos asked.

"A hundred now and two hundred later if she disappears without a trace," Shanahan said. He reached into his jacket pocket and withdrew a crisp hundred-dollar bill. He held it up so Carlos could see it. It was bathed in red light from the neon bull.

"What about my job?" Carlos asked.

"Like I promised," Shanahan said. "I'll get you off the kill floor by the end of the month. Where do you want to go, the boning room or the carcass room?"

"The boning room," Carlos said.

"So we have a deal?" Shanahan.

"Sure," Carlos said. He took the bill, folded it, and slipped it into his jeans pocket. He started to get out of the car. It was as if he'd been asked to rake leaves or shovel snow.

"Don't screw it up," Shanahan said.

"It's going to be easy with her in Higgins and Hancock," Carlos said.

"That's what we figured," Shanahan said.

Lifting her arms over her head, Marsha stretched. She'd been bending over the open file-cabinet drawer long enough to make her back stiff. She used her hip to close the drawer, and it made a definitive click as it slid home. Picking up her cellular phone, she headed for the USDA office door. While she walked, she punched in Kim's phone number.

As the call went through, she opened the door and looked up and down the silent hall. She was pleased not to see anyone. While she'd been going through the files, she'd heard the guard pass by and even hesitate outside the door on several occasions. He'd not bothered her, but his loitering had raised her anxiety level. She knew that if he approached her, she'd feel trapped in the seemingly deserted building. She'd not seen a single one of the cleaning people who were supposed to be there.

"This better be you," Kim said without saying hello.

"That's a strange way to answer the phone," Marsha said with a nervous laugh. She closed the USDA office door and started up the deserted hall.

"It's about time you called," Kim said.

"I haven't had any luck so far," Marsha said, ignoring Kim's complaint.

"What's taken you so long to call?" Kim demanded.

"Hey, cool it," Marsha said. "I've been busy. You have no idea how much paperwork the USDA requires. There's daily sanitation reports, disposition records, livestock slaughter reports, process deficiency records, kill-order reports, and purchase invoices. I've had to go through all of it for January ninth."

"What did you find?" Kim asked.

"Nothing out of the ordinary," Marsha said. She came to a door with a frosted-glass panel. Stenciled on the glass was the word: RECORDS. She tried the door. It was unlocked. She stepped inside, closed the door, and locked it behind her.

"Well, at least you looked," Kim said. "Now get yourself out of there."

"Not until I look at the company records," Marsha said.

"It's eight–fifteen," Kim said. "You told me this was going to be a quick visit."

"It shouldn't take me that much longer," Marsha said. "I'm in the record room right now. I'll call you back in a half hour or so."

Marsha disconnected before Kim had a chance to object. She put the phone down on a long library table and faced a bank of file cabinets along one wall. The opposite wall had a single window against whose panes the rain was beating. It sounded like grains of rice. At the far end of the room was a second door. Marsha went to it and made sure it was locked.

Feeling relatively secure, she walked back to the file cabinets and yanked out the first drawer.

○   ○   ○

After several minutes, Kim finally withdrew his hand from the receiver. He'd hoped that Marsha would have called right back. The conversation had ended so abruptly he'd thought they'd been cut off. Eventually he had to accept the fact that she'd hung up.

Kim was sitting in the same club chair Marsha had found him in. The floor lamp next to the chair was the only light on in the house. On the side table was a glass of neat whiskey that he'd poured for himself and then had not touched.

Kim had never felt worse in his life. Images of Becky kept flooding his mind and bringing forth new tears. The next instant, he found himself denying the whole, horrid experience and attributing it to an extension of his nightmare where Becky had fallen into the sea.

The sound of the refrigerator kicking on in the kitchen made him think he should try to eat. He couldn't remember the last time he'd put anything significant in his stomach. The trouble was he wasn't hungry in the slightest. Then he thought about taking himself upstairs to shower and change clothes, but that sounded like too much effort. In the end, he decided he'd just sit there and wait for the phone to ring.

○   ○   ○

The old Toyota pickup had no heat and Carlos was shivering by the time he turned off the paved road onto the gravel track that led around the Higgins and Hancock stockyard. He switched off the single functioning headlight and proceeded by knowledge of the route and shadowy glimpses of the fence posts to his right. He drove all the way around to the point where the stockyard funneled into the chute leading into the plant. During the day, this was where all the luckless animals entered.

He parked the truck in the shadow of the building. He took off the heavy mittens he used to drive and replaced them with tight-fitting black leather gloves. Reaching under his seat, he extracted a long, curved kill knife, the same kind he used during the day. By reflex he tested its edge with his thumb. Even through the leather he could tell it was razor-sharp.

He climbed from the cab. Blinking in the rain, he quickly climbed the fence and dropped into the trampled mud of the stockyard. Mindless of the cow dung, he sprinted down the chute and disappeared into its dark depths.

○    ○    ○

With an oyster fork in one hand and a cut-crystal glass of bourbon in the other, Bobby Bo mounted his coffee table and drew himself up to his full height. In the process, he knocked over an hors d'oeuvre plate of marinated shrimp to the delight of his two professionally cut standard poodles.

Bobby Bo loudly clanged the the fork against the glass. No one heard until the quartet stopped playing.

"All right, everyone," Bobby Bo yelled over the heads of his guests. "Dinner is served in the dining room. Remember to bring the number you drew out of the bucket. That will be your table. If you haven't drawn a number, the bucket will be in the foyer."

The crowd began to move out of the living room en masse. Bobby Bo managed to step down from the coffee table without further mishap other than to scare one of the dogs, which yelped and fled into the kitchen.

Bobby Bo was on his way to the dining room, when he caught sight of Shanahan O'Brian. Excusing himself, he stepped over to stand beside his head of security.

"Well?" Bobby Bo whispered. "How did it go?"

"No problem," Shanahan said.

"Is it going to happen tonight?" Bobby Bo asked.

"As we speak," Shanahan said. "I think Daryl Webster should be told, so he can tell his security not to interfere."

"Good idea," Bobby Bo said. He smiled happily, patted Shanahan on the shoulder, then hurried after his guests.

O   O   O

The doorbell shocked Kim out of his melancholic stupor. For the moment, he was disoriented as to the origin of the noise. He even started to reach for the phone. He'd expected the phone to ring and certainly not for the door to chime. When he realized it was the door, he looked at his watch. It was quarter to nine. He couldn't believe that someone would be ringing his doorbell at such a time on Saturday night.

The only person he could imagine it might be was Ginger, but she never came over without calling. Then Kim remembered he'd failed to listen to his answering machine, so she could have called and left a message. While Kim considered the possibilities of this, the doorbell sounded again.

He did not want to see Ginger, but when the doorbell sounded for the third time followed by some knocking, Kim pushed himself out of the chair. He was just thinking of what he could say, when to his utter surprise, he found himself looking at Tracy, not Ginger.

"Are you okay?" Tracy asked. She spoke quietly.

"I guess," Kim said. He was nonplussed.

"Can I come in?" Tracy asked.

"Of course," Kim said. He stepped back to give Tracy room. "Sorry! I should have invited you in immediately. I'm just surprised to see you."

Tracy stepped into the dimly lit foyer. She could see that the only light in the house was in the living room, next to an easy chair. She slipped out of her coat and rain hat. Kim took them.

"I hope you don't mind my coming over here like this," Tracy said. "I know it was a little impulsive on my part."

"It's okay," Kim said. He hung up Tracy's things.

"I didn't want to be with anyone," Tracy explained. She sighed. "But then I started thinking about you and worrying, especially with how agitated you were when you ran out of the hospital. I thought that since we've both lost the same daughter, we're the only ones that could have any idea of how we feel. I guess what I'm saying is I need some help and imagine you do too."

Tracy's words snatched away any remnants of denial Kim was entertaining. He felt a keen wave of grief he'd been doing his best to avoid. He breathed out heavily and swallowed as he choked back tears. For a moment he couldn't speak.

"Have you been sitting here in the living room?" Tracy asked.

Kim nodded.

"I'll get a chair from the dining room," Tracy said.

"Let me," Kim volunteered. He appreciated having something physical to do. He brought the chair into the living room and placed it within the penumbra of light from the floor lamp.

"Can I get you something to drink?" Kim managed. "I poured myself some scotch."

"Thank you, but no," Tracy said. She sat down heavily, then leaned forward, cradling her chin in her hands with her elbows on her knees.

Kim lowered himself in the club chair and looked at his former wife. Her dark hair, which was always wavy and full, was matted against the top of her head. The small amount of makeup she normally wore was streaked. She was clearly pained, yet her eyes were as bright and sparkly as Kim remembered.

"There's also something I wanted to tell you," Tracy said. "After I had a little time to think, I believe what you did today to Becky took a lot of courage." She paused for a moment while she bit her lip. "I know I couldn't have done it even if I was a surgeon," she added.

"I appreciate your saying that," Kim said. "Thank you."

"I was appalled at first," Tracy admitted.

"Open-heart massage is a desperate act in any circumstance," Kim said. "Doing it on your own daughter is . . . well, I'm sure the hospital isn't looking at it the same way you are."

"You did it out of love," Tracy said. "It wasn't hubris like I thought at first."

"I did it because it was clear to me the external massage wasn't working," Kim said. "I couldn't let Becky just fade away like it seemed she was doing. No one knew why she was arresting. Of course, now I know why and why the external massage wasn't working."

"I had no idea this E. coli could be such an awful illness," Tracy said.

"Nor did I," Kim said.

The phone's jangle startled both people. Kim snapped up the receiver. "Hello," he barked.

Tracy watched as Kim's face registered first confusion, then irritation.

"Hold it," Kim snapped into the receiver. "Cut the spiel. I'm not interested in your company's Visa card, and I want you off this line." He hung up forcibly.

"It looks like you are expecting a call," Tracy said captiously. She stood up. "I'm intruding. Maybe I should go."

"No," Kim said. But then he immediately corrected himself. "I mean, yes, I'm expecting a call, but no, you shouldn't leave."

Tracy cocked her head to the side. "You're acting strange," she said. "What's going on?"

"I'm a basket case," Kim admitted. "But . . ."

The phone interrupted Kim's explanation. Again he snatched the receiver off the hook and said a frantic hello.

"It's me again," Marsha said. "And this time I've found something."

"What?" Kim asked. He motioned for Tracy to sit down.

"Something potentially interesting," Marsha said. "On January ninth there is a discrepancy between the USDA paperwork and Higgins and Hancock's."

"How so?" Kim asked.

"There was an extra animal slaughtered at the end of the day," Marsha said. "In the company's records it's designated lot thirty-six, head fifty-seven."

"Oh?" Kim questioned. "Is an extra animal significant?"

"I would think so," Marsha said. "It means the animal wasn't seen by the USDA vet."

"So you mean it could have been unhealthy?" Kim questioned.

"That's a distinct possibility," Marsha said. "And it's supported by the the purchase invoice. This final animal wasn't a steer raised for beef. It was a dairy cow bought from a man named Bart Winslow."

"You're going to have to explain," Kim said.

"Well, dairy cows often go for hamburger," Marsha said. "So that's one thing. The other thing is that I recognize the name, Bart Winslow. He's a local guy who's what they call a 'Four-D' man. That means he goes around and picks up downers. Those are dead, diseased, dying, and disabled farm animals. He's supposed to take them to the renderer to be turned into fertilizer or animal feed."

"I'm not sure I want to hear the rest," Kim said. "Don't tell me that they sometimes sell them to the slaughterhouse instead of the renderer."

"Apparently that's what happened with this last animal," Marsha said. "Head fifty-seven in lot thirty-six must have been a downer, probably sick."

"This is disgusting," Kim commented.

"It gets worse," Marsha said. "I found a company deficiency report on the same animal that had nothing to do with its being sick or not having been seen by the vet. Are you ready for this . . . it's revolting."

"Tell me!" Kim urged.

"Uh-oh!" Marsha said. "Somebody is at the door. I got to get these papers back in the file!"

Kim heard a loud thump. In the background he could hear the rustling of papers and then the distinctive sound of a file cabinet drawer being slammed shut.

"Marsha!" Kim yelled.

Marsha didn't come back on the line. Instead Kim heard the sound of shattering glass. It was loud enough to make him jump. For a split second he reflexively pulled the phone away from his ear.

"Marsha!" Kim shouted again. But she didn't answer. Instead he heard the unmistakable sound of furniture being upended and crashing to the floor. Then there was a heavy silence.

Kim pulled the phone away from his ear and looked at Tracy. His eyes reflected the terror he felt.

"What's going on?" Tracy questioned with alarm. "Was that Marsha Baldwin?"

"I think she's in danger!" Kim blurted. "My God!"

"Danger from what?" Tracy demanded, sensing Kim's frenzy.

"I have to go!" Kim cried. "It's my fault!"

"What is your fault?" Tracy cried. "Please, what's going on?"

Kim didn't answer but rather spun on his heels and dashed from the house. In his haste, he left the front door ajar. Tracy ran after him, demanding to know where he was going.

"Stay here," Kim yelled, just before jumping into his car. "I'll be right back." The driver door slammed. A moment later the engine roared to life. Kim gunned the car backward out into the street. Then he raced off into the night.

Tracy ran a hand through her matted hair. She had no idea what was going on nor what she should do. At first she entertained the idea of getting into her car and driving home. But Kim's frenzy worried her, and she wanted to know what it was all about. Besides, the thought of being home was not appealing; she'd already fled from there.

The cold rain finally made up Tracy's mind for her. She turned around and went back into the house. As Kim had suggested, she'd wait there.

○     ○     ○

The chase had started with the shattering of the door's glass panel. A gloved hand had reached in through the jagged edges and unlocked the door. The door had then burst open, slamming against the wall.

Marsha had let out a short shriek. She'd found herself facing a gaunt, dark-complected man wielding a long knife. The man had taken a step toward her, when she'd turned and fled, tipping over chairs behind her in hopes of hindering the man's pursuit. She instinctively knew he was there to kill her.

Frantically she unlocked the rear door. Behind her she could hear cursing in Spanish and the crashing of chairs. She didn't dare look back. Out in the hall, she ran headlong in search of anyone, even the intimidating guard. She tried to yell for help, but, in the effort of flight, her voice was hoarse.

She dashed past empty offices. At the end of the hall, she hurried into a lunchroom. One of the many long tables held a small collection of lunchboxes and thermos bottles, but their owners were nowhere in sight. Behind her, she could hear running footfalls gaining on her.

At the far end of the lunchroom, a door stood open. Beyond it was a half flight of stairs that terminated at a stout fire door. With little choice, Marsha ran across the room, strewing her path with as many of the lunchroom chairs as she could. She mounted the stairs two at a time. By the time she got to the fire door, she was seriously sucking air. Behind her, she could hear her pursuer struggling with the upturned chairs.

Yanking open the fire door, Marsha darted into the vast, cold room beyond. This was the kill floor, and in the semidarkness created by widely spaced night-lights, it had a ghastly, alien look, especially since it had been recently steam-cleaned. A cold, gray mist shrouded the ghostly, metal catwalks, the sinister hooks hanging from the ceiling rails, and the stainless-steel abattoir equipment.

The maze of machinery hindered Marsha's pace. Her run became a walk. Desperately she screamed for help only to hear her voice reverberate against the cold, lonely, concrete walls.

Behind her, the fire door banged open. She was close enough to hear the panting breaths of her pursuer.

Marsha took refuge behind a monstrous piece of equipment and pressed herself into the shadows created by a metal-grate stair. She tried vainly to control her own breathing.

There was no sound save for the slow drip of water someplace near. The cleaning people had to be somewhere. She just had to find them.

Marsha hazarded a glance back at the fire door. It was closed. She didn't see the man.

A sudden loud click made Marsha start. An instant later, the room was flooded with harsh light. Marsha's heart fluttered in her chest. With the lights on she was sure to be found.

One more glance back at the fire door was enough to make up her mind. Her only chance was to flee back the way she'd come.

Pushing off from her hiding place, Marsha sprinted to the fire door. Grabbing its handle, she yanked it.

The heavy door began to open, but almost immediately she could move it no further. Marsha looked up. Over her shoulder was a tattooed arm bracing the door from opening.

Marsha spun around and pressed her back against the door. With abject fear, she stared into the man's cold, black eyes. The monstrous knife was now in his left hand.

"What do you want from me?" Marsha screamed.

Carlos didn't answer. Instead he smiled coldly. He tossed the knife from one hand to the other.

Marsha tried to flee again, but in her desperate haste she lost her footing on the wet, stained cement. She sprawled headfirst on the cold floor. Carlos was on her in an instant.

Rolling over, Marsha tried to fight by grabbing for the knife with both hands, but its razor-sharp edge sliced into her palm down to the bone. She tried to scream, but Carlos clasped his left hand over her mouth.

When Marsha tried to dislodge his hand, Carlos quickly raised his weapon and dealt her a vicious blow to the head with the heavy haft. Marsha went limp.

Carlos stood up and took a couple of deep breaths. Then he crossed Marsha's arms so that her cut hands were on her stomach. Picking up her feet, he dragged her across the kill-room floor to the grate at the termination of the cattle chute. He stepped over to an electrical junction box and threw the switch, activating the room's machinery.

Kim drove like a madman, oblivious to the rain-slicked streets. He agonized about what could have happened to Marsha in the Higgins and Hancock record room. He found himself hoping that she had been surprised by a security guard, even if it meant her arrest. Any fate worse than that he didn't want to consider.

As he turned into the parking area in front of the immense plant, Kim noticed there were only a few parked cars scattered through the lot. He saw Marsha's car at one end, nowhere near the entrance.

Kim pulled up directly opposite the front door. He leaped out. He tried the door. It was locked. He banged on it with his fist. Cupping his hands around his face, he peered inside. All he could see was a dimly lit, deserted corridor. There was no security guard in sight.

Kim listened. There was no sound. His anxiety mounted. Stepping back from the door, he surveyed the front of the building. There were a number of windows facing the parking lot.

Kim stepped off the concrete entrance slab and quickly moved north along the side of the building. He looked into each window he came to and tried it. They were all locked.

When he peered into the third window, he saw file cabinets, upended chairs, and what he guessed was Marsha's phone on the table. Like the others, the window was locked. Without a second's hesitation, he bent down and picked up one of the stout rocks lining the edge of the parking area. Hefting it up to shoulder height, he tossed it through the window. The sound of shattering glass was followed by a tremendous crash as the rock bounced off the wooden floor and collided with a number of the up-ended chairs.

Carlos paused and listened. From where he was standing in the head-boning room, the place where cattle heads were stripped of their cheeks and tongues, the sound of Kim's rock came through as merely a muffled thump. Yet as an experienced burglar, he knew he could not ignore any unexpected noises; invariably they spelled trouble.

Carlos closed the top of the combo bin then turned out the light. He slipped out of the bloody white coat and pulled off the gauntlet-length, yellow rubber gloves he was wearing. He stowed these items under a sink. Picking up his knife, he moved silently but swiftly from the boning room out into the kill floor. There he doused the light as well. Once again he stopped to listen. He would have retreated up the cattle chute except he wasn't quite finished.

O    O    O

Kim had climbed through the window headfirst. He did his best to avoid the shards of broken glass on the floor but wasn't entirely successful. As he got to his feet he had to brush a few small slivers gingerly from his palms. With that accomplished, he scanned the room. He saw a blinking red light on a motion detector high in one corner but ignored it.

The abandoned cell phone, the upended chairs, as well as a broken panel of glass in the door to the front hall immediately convinced Kim that he was standing in the room where Marsha had been when she called him. He also noticed the open door at the rear of the room and guessed after being surprised she'd fled in that direction.

Dashing to this second door, Kim looked down the length of a deserted back hallway. He paused to listen. There wasn't a sound, a fact which only fanned his ever-building anxiety.

Kim started down the corridor, rapidly opening each door he came to. He glanced into storerooms, cleaning closets, a locker room, and several restrooms. At the far end of the hall, he came to a lunchroom. He paused at the threshold. What caught his attention was the trail of overturned chairs leading to a rear door. Kim followed the trail out the rear door and up a half flight of steps. He yanked open the fire door and stepped through.

Kim again paused. He didn't know what to do. He found himself in a room filled with a labyrinth of machinery and raised metal platforms that cast grotesque shadows.

Kim noticed a cloyingly fetid smell that was vaguely familiar. His mind struggled to make the association. Within seconds he had the answer. The odor reminded him of observing an autopsy as a second-year medical student. He shuddered against the mostly suppressed, unpleasant memory.

"Marsha!" Kim yelled in desperation. "Marsha!"

There was no response. The only thing Kim could hear were the numerous echoes of his own frantic voice.

To Kim's immediate right was a fire station with an extinguisher, a long, heavy-duty flashlight, and a cabinet with glass-paneled doors that revealed a canvas fire hose and long-handled firefighter's axe. Kim snatched the flashlight from its bracket and turned it on. Its concentrated beam illuminated narrow conic sections of the room and cast even more grotesque shapes onto the walls.

Kim set out into the alien world, shining the light in fast-moving arcs. He proceeded in a clockwise direction, skirting past the machinery to explore more thoroughly.

After a few minutes, he paused and again yelled out Marsha's name. Besides his echoes, all he could hear was the sound of dripping water.

Ahead the flashlight beam swept across a grate. Kim moved it back. Over the center of the grate was a dark smear. Advancing to the grate, he bent down, and shined the light directly on the smear. Hesitantly he reached out with his index finger and touched it. A chill went down his spine. It was blood!

Carlos had pressed himself against the wall of the head-boning room, at the very lip of the doorless opening to the kill-room floor. He'd been retreating from Kim's relentless advance. Carlos had first seen Kim as he'd come down the back hallway clearly on a searching mission.

Carlos had no idea who this stranger was and had first hoped the man would content himself with wandering around the office area of the plant. But once Kim had come into the kill floor and had yelled out Marsha's name, Carlos knew he'd have to kill him.

Carlos was not dismayed. Contingencies were a factor in such work. Besides, Carlos figured he'd be paid more, maybe even double. He also wasn't concerned about the stranger's size and probable strength. Carlos had experience and the benefit of surprise, and, most important, he had his favorite knife, which at the moment he was holding in his right hand up alongside his head.

Cautiously Carlos eased his head out into the opening so he could see into the kill-floor area. It was easy to keep track of the stranger now, thanks to the flashlight. Carlos saw the man straighten up from the grate at Carlos's workstation.

All at once the flashlight shined directly at Carlos. He retreated from the beam, careful to keep the knife blade from flashing in the darkness. He held his breath as the stranger edged closer, again probing the kill floor with sweeping motions of his shaft of light.

Carlos flattened himself against the wall and tensed his muscles. The stranger was coming into the boning room as Carlos had anticipated. The searching flashlight beam flickered around the room in a progressively brighter fashion. Carlos could feel his pulse sky rocket as adrenaline coursed around his body. It was a sensation he loved. It was like popping speed.

$\circ$    $\circ$    $\circ$

Kim knew he was in a slaughterhouse that had been in operation that day, so finding blood shouldn't have come as a surprise. Yet the blood he'd found was unclotted and appeared fresh. He hated to think it could have been Marsha's; the chance that it was brought back his familiar fury. Now he wanted to find her with even more urgency than earlier, and if she were indeed injured, he wanted to find the individual responsible.

After having searched the kill floor, Kim decided to widen his search to other areas of the huge plant. He headed to the only open passageway he'd seen, on guard against the person or persons who had already spilled blood.

In the next instant it was his wariness that saved him. Out of the corner of his eye, he detected sudden movement coming at him from the side. Reacting by reflex, he leaped ahead and used the long flashlight to parry what he perceived as a thrust.

Carlos had lunged from the shadows, hoping to skewer Kim in the side with a quick stab, withdraw the knife, and retreat. He'd planned to finish Kim off once Kim had been weakened. But the knife missed its mark and only succeeded in producing a shallow cut across the top of Kim's hand.

As Carlos tried to regain his balance, Kim hit him with the flashlight. It was a glancing blow to the shoulder that didn't hurt Carlos although, catching him off balance, it knocked him to the ground. Before Carlos could scramble to this feet, Kim took off. He ran through the head-boning room into the main boning room. This next room was almost the size of the kill floor and somewhat darker. It was filled with a maze of long stainless-steel tables and conveyer belts. Above was a web of metal-grate catwalks where supervisors could survey the butchering of the carcasses into known cuts of meat on the tables below.

Kim searched frantically for some kind of weapon to counter the long knife. Having turned off the flashlight and afraid to turn it back on, he could only grope blindly along the tables. He found nothing.

A large, empty, plastic trash barrel fell over when Kim stumbled against it. Desperately, he reached out to keep it from rolling around and further giving away his position. Looking back at the passageway into the head-boning room, Kim could see the silhouette of the man with the knife. He was backlit for a brief instant before silently slipping into the shadows.

Kim trembled with fear. He was being stalked by an obvious killer armed with a knife in a dark, totally alien environment with no way to protect himself. He knew he had to stay hidden. He could not let this man get near him. Although he'd managed to elude the first thrust, Kim was smart enough to understand that he probably wouldn't be so lucky a second time.

The sudden high-pitched sound heralding the start-up of electronic equipment made Kim jump. All around him the tangle of conveyer belts commenced their noisy operation. Simultaneously the room was flooded with bright, fluorescent light. Kim's heart leaped into his throat. Any chance of remaining hidden in the mazelike room evaporated.

Kim crouched as best he could behind the plastic trash barrel. By looking beneath the boning tables he saw the tattooed man pursuing him.

The stranger was advancing slowly along the back aisle with both hands held up in the air. His right hand clasped the knife that looked to Kim to be about the size of a machete.

Kim panicked. Carlos was only one aisle away. Kim knew the man would see him the moment he looked down the aisle Kim was in. It was only a matter of seconds.

Impulsively Kim leaped to his feet while grasping the plastic trash barrel with both hands. Shouting like a Celtic warrior commencing battle, he charged directly at his stalker. Using the plastic barrel like a shield, Kim collided with the knife-wielding Mexican.

Carlos was bowled over. Although shocked by the unexpected charge and powerful impact, Carlos had the presence of mind to hold on to the knife.

Kim's momentum carried him well beyond Carlos. He tossed aside the plastic container and sprinted the length of the main boning room. Kim knew he'd only succeeded in knocking his pursuer down; he'd by no means put him out of commission. Sensing his best chance was to again flee, he passed through a second doorless opening to find himself in a cold, misty, dimly lit forest of cattle carcasses. Each had been sawed in half and hung from a hook attached to a roller system in the ceiling. The only light came from widely spaced ceiling lights along a central corridor separating the long rows of cooling carcasses.

Kim sprinted along the central corridor desperately looking for a place to hide. The chill room was cold enough so he could see his breath as he panted. He hadn't gone far when he came to a cross aisle down which he caught a welcome glimpse of the green glow of an exit sign. He made a beeline for it only to discover that the door was secured with a chain and a heavy-duty padlock.

Kim then heard the distant but unmistakable sound of his pursuer's heels clicking against the concrete floor. Kim could tell he was approaching, and Kim panicked again. Moving as quickly as he could along the narrow periphery of the carcass room, Kim hunted for another exit. Unfortunately when he found it, it too was chained shut.

Discouraged, Kim continued on. The room was gargantuan. Squeezing between the outer wall and the hanging carcasses, it took Kim several minutes to reach the corner, where he turned ninety degrees. Here his progress was faster. Just before he reached the central corridor that ran the length of the room, he came to an interior door. He tried it, and to his relief, it opened into a dark room. Next to the door was a light switch. Kim flipped it on. The room was a large storeroom with steel shelving.

Kim ducked into the room with the desperate hope of finding something to use as a weapon. He made a quick circuit of the space but had no luck. All he found were small, spare parts including replacement ball bearings for the overhead rail system plus a cardboard box of rubber stamps used by the USDA inspectors to grade meat "select," "choice," or "prime." The only sizable object was a broom.

Thinking the broom might be better than nothing, Kim picked it up. Returning to the front of the room, he was about to exit, when he again heard the footfalls of his pursuer. The man was close, no more than twenty feet away, approaching along the nearby central aisle!

Panicking again, Kim pulled the storeroom's door closed as quickly and as silently as possible. Holding the broom in both hands by the tip of its handle, he flattened himself against the wall just to the right of the door.

The sound of the footsteps stopped. Kim could hear the man cursing. Then the footfalls recommenced, increasing in intensity until they stopped just outside the door.

Kim held his breath. He gripped the broom handle harder. For an agonizing moment, nothing happened. Then he saw the door handle begin to turn. The man was coming in!

Kim's heart raced. The door was yanked open. As soon as Kim sensed the man was starting in, he gritted his teeth and swung the broom at chest height with all the strength he could muster. By chance he hit the man full in the face, knocking him back through the door. The surprise and the force of the impact dislodged the knife, and it tumbled to the floor.

Still holding the broom in his left hand, Kim leaped for the knife. He seized it, only to discover it was a flashlight, not a knife.

"Freeze!" a voice commanded.

Kim straightened up and looked into the blinding glare of another flashlight. Instinctively he raised his hand to shield his eyes. Now he could make out the man on the floor. It wasn't the Mexican but rather a man dressed in a brown Higgins and Hancock shirt. It was a security guard, and he had both hands clasped to his face. Blood was coming out of his nose.

"Drop the broom," a voice behind the glare commanded.

Kim let go of both the flashlight and the broom. Both fell to the floor with a clatter.

The bright beam of the flashlight was lowered, and to Kim's utter relief, he found himself facing two uniformed policemen. The one without the flashlight was holding his pistol in both hands, pointed directly at Kim.

"Thank God!" Kim managed, despite looking down the barrel of a gun less than ten feet away.

"Shut up!" the policeman with the gun commanded. "Get out here and face the wall!"

Kim was only too happy to comply. He stepped out of the storeroom and put his hands against the wall as he'd seen done in movies.

"Frisk him," the policeman said.

Kim felt hands run up and down his arms, legs, and torso.

"He's clean."

"Turn around!"

Kim did as he was told, keeping his hands raised to avoid any confusion as to his intentions. He was close enough to read the officers' name tags. The man with the gun was Douglas Foster. The other was Leroy McHalverson. The security guard had gotten up and was dabbing at his newly bent nose with a handkerchief. The metal portion of the whisk had hit him with enough force to break it.

"Cuff him," Douglas said.

"Hey, hold on!" Kim said. "I'm not the one you should be cuffing."

"Really?" Douglas questioned superciliously. "Who would you suggest?"

"There's someone else in here," Kim said. "A dark, wiry-looking guy with tattoos and a huge knife."

"And wearing a hockey mask, no doubt," Douglas said scoffingly. "And his name is Jason."

"I'm serious," Kim said. "The reason I'm here is because of a woman named Marsha Baldwin."

The two policemen exchanged glances.

"Honest!" Kim maintained. "She's a USDA inspector. She was here doing some work. I was talking with her by phone when someone surprised her. I heard breaking glass and a struggle. When I got here looking for her to help her, I was attacked by a man with a knife, presumably the man who attacked Ms. Baldwin."

The policemen remained skeptical.

"Look, I'm a surgeon at the University Med Center," Kim said. He fumbled in the pocket of his soiled white coat. Douglas's grip on his pistol tightened. Kim produced his laminated hospital I.D. card and handed it to Douglas. Douglas motioned for Leroy to take it.

"It looks authentic," Leroy said after a quick inspection.

"Of course it's authentic," Kim said.

"Have you doctors given up on personal hygiene?" Douglas asked.

Kim ran a hand through his scruffy beard and glanced down at his dirty coat and scrubs. He'd not showered, shaved, or changed clothes since early Friday morning. "I know I look a little worse for wear," he said. "There's an explanation. But for the moment I'm more concerned about Ms. Baldwin and the whereabouts of that man with a knife."

"What about it, Curt?" Douglas asked the security man. "Was there a woman USDA inspector here or a strange, dark, tattooed man?"

"Not to my knowledge," Curt said. "At least they didn't come in while I've been on duty. I came on at three o'clock this afternoon."

"Sorry, fella," Douglas said to Kim. "Nice try." Then to Leroy he added: "Go ahead and cuff him."

"Wait a sec," Kim said. "There's blood in the other room that I'm afraid might have come from Ms. Baldwin."

"Where?" Douglas asked.

"It's on a grate," Kim said. "I can show you."

"This is a slaughterhouse," Curt said. "There's always blood."

"This looked like fresh blood," Kim said.

"Cuff him and we'll go see," Douglas said.

Kim allowed his wrists to be handcuffed behind his back. Then he was made to walk ahead of the others the full length of the central aisle of the chill room. In the main boning room. Curt asked the policemen to wait while he turned off the lights and the conveyer belts.

"The man with the knife turned this machinery on," Kim said.

"Yeah, sure he did," Douglas said.

Kim didn't try to argue nor did he point out the plastic trash barrel which had rolled against one of the boning tables. He was sure the blood would convince these cops he was telling the truth.

Kim directed them to the proper grate. When Curt shined his flashlight, Kim was disappointed to see that the blood was gone.

"It was here!" Kim contended, shaking his head. "Somebody hosed it off."

"Undoubtedly the man with the knife," Leroy said with a chuckle.

"Who else?" Douglas questioned facetiously.

"Wait a second," Kim said urgently. He was desperate. He had to get them to believe him. "The telephone! She was talking to me on her cell phone. It's in the record room."

"That's creative," Douglas commented. "I have to give you credit for that." He looked at Curt. "Do you think we could take a look? I mean it's on our way out."

"Of course," Curt said.

While Curt led the way to the record room with Kim and Douglas in tow, Leroy went out to the squad car to make contact with the station. At the record-room threshold, Curt stepped aside and let the others enter. Once inside, Kim was immediately crestfallen. The chairs had been righted; more important, the phone was gone. "It was here, I swear," he said. "And a number of these chairs were upended."

"I didn't see any phone when I came in here to investigate the break-in," Curt said. "And the chairs were as you see them now."

"What about the broken glass-door panel?" Kim said excitedly. He pointed at the door to the front hall. "I'm sure that was the shattering noise I heard while I was on the phone with her."

"I assumed the door was just part of the break-in," Curt said. "Along with the window."

"It couldn't be," Kim said. "I broke the window, but the door panel was already broken when I got here. Look, all the glass from the door panel is on the inside. Whoever did it was in the hall."

"Hmm," Douglas said. He stared down at the broken glass at the base of the door. "He does have a point."

"Her car!" Kim said, getting another idea. "It has to be outside still. It's a yellow Ford sedan. It's parked at the end of the building."

Before Douglas could respond to this new suggestion, Leroy returned from the squad car. A wry smile lit up his broad face. "I just got off the radio with the station," he said. "They ran a quick check for me on the good doctor, and guess what? He's got a sheet. He was arrested just last night for trespassing, resisting arrest, striking a police officer, and assault and battery on a fast-food manager. Currently he's out of the slammer on his own recognizance."

"My, my," Douglas said. "A repeat offender! Okay, Doc, enough of this nonsense. You're going downtown."

# CHAPTER 15

It was déjà vu all over again for Kim. He was back in the same courtroom with the same judge. The only real difference was the weather outside. This time there was no sun; the day was cloudy with scattered snow flurries, and Judge Harlowe's mood matched the gray day.

Kim was seated at a scarred library table alongside Tracy. Standing before them and directly below the bench was Justin Devereau, a lawyer and longtime friend of Kim's. He was aristocratic in appearance, a Harvard-trained lawyer who'd followed the old adage: "Go West, young man." He'd started what had become one of the largest and most successful law firms in the city. His case success rate was unrivaled. Yet, on this particular morning, he looked concerned. He'd been fighting an uphill battle against Judge Harlowe's ire.

Kim looked worse than ever, having spent yet another night in jail in the same outfit. He still hadn't shaved or showered. He was also clearly anxious about the outcome of the current proceedings. The last thing he wanted to do was go back to jail.

Justin cleared his throat. "Allow me to reiterate that Dr. Kim Reggis has truly been the proverbial pillar of society up until the tragic affliction of his only daughter."

"His daughter's illness was the excuse for his appearance before this court yesterday, Counselor," Judge Harlowe said with impatience. "For my weekend on call, I don't like to see the same face twice. It's an insult to my judgment for having allowed the individual his freedom after the first infraction."

"Dr. Reggis's daughter's recent death has caused him monumental stress, Your Honor," Justin persisted.

"That's apparent," Judge Harlowe said. "What's in question is whether he is a threat to society in his current state of mind."

"These were aberrant episodes that will not be repeated," Justin asserted. "As you have heard, Dr. Reggis is full of remorse for his rash actions."

Judge Harlowe toyed with his glasses. His eyes wandered to Kim's. He had to admit the man did look penitent. As well as pitiful. The judge looked at Tracy. The woman's presence and testimony had impressed him.

"All right," Judge Harlowe said. "I'll allow bail, but what has swayed me is not your Ivy League bombast, Counselor, but rather the fact that Dr. Reggis's former wife has graciously consented to come before this court to attest to his character. With my probate experience, I find that a convincing testimonial. Five thousand dollars bail and trial in four weeks. Next case!"

Judge Harlowe struck his gavel and picked up the next set of papers.

"Excuse me, Your Honor," Justin said. "There's no question of flight here, so five thousand dollars is blatantly excessive."

The judge peered down over the tops of his reading glasses. He raised his eyebrows. "I'm going to pretend I didn't hear that," he said. "And I advise you not to push your client's luck, Counselor. Next case, please!"

Justin shrugged and beat a hasty retreat back to Kim and Tracy. After gathering his things, he motioned for them to follow him out of the courtroom.

With Justin's help the bail was quickly posted. In less than a half hour the group emerged from the courthouse out into the overcast, wintery morning. They paused at the base of the courthouse steps. A few isolated snowflakes drifted down from the sky.

"At first I was afraid Harlowe wasn't going to give you bail," Justin said. "As the judge implied, consider yourself lucky."

"Under the circumstances I have a hard time considering myself lucky," Kim said with little emotion. "But thanks for your help. I apologize for getting you out on a Sunday morning."

"Glad to do it," Justin said. "And I'm terribly sorry about Becky. My heartfelt sympathies to you both."

Kim and Tracy echoed their thanks.

"Well, I better be going," Justin said. He touched the brim of his hat. "I'll see you two. My best to you both at this difficult time."

Justin gave Tracy a peck on the cheek and Kim a handshake before starting off. He got only a few paces away, when he stopped. "A word of advice to you, Kim. Don't get arrested again. If you do, I can guarantee you won't get bail. Back-to-back arrests like you've managed obviously puts you in a special category."

"I understand," Kim said. "I'll be careful."

Kim and Tracy watched Justin walk away until he was completely out of earshot. They turned to each other.

"Now I want you to tell me really what happened," Tracy said.

"I'll tell you as much as I know," Kim said flatly. "But I have to get my car. Would you mind giving me a ride out to Higgins and Hancock?"

"Not at all," Tracy said. "I'd planned as much."

"We'll talk in the car," Kim said.

They started across the street in the direction of the parking lot.

"I'm living a nightmare," Kim confessed.

"As I said last night," Tracy responded, "we both need help, and we might be the only people who can give it to each other."

Kim sighed. "It must seem crazy to you that I've plunged headlong into this E. coli crusade. Our daughter is dead and all I want to do is race around like some cloak-and-dagger sleuth." He shook his head. "All these years I prided myself on being the strong one, but now I see that, really, you're the one with the inner strength. I know I can't avoid the fact of Becky's death forever, but I just can't look at it now. I hope you can understand that I'm just not ready to deal with it."

Tracy was silent for a while. Then she reached out and put a hand on Kim's arm. "I understand," she said. "And I won't rush you. I'll even support you in your quest. But you won't be able to deny Becky's death forever."

Kim nodded his head. "I know," he whispered. "And thank you."

The ride went quickly. Kim gave Tracy all the details from the time Marsha showed up at his house until the police booked him and put him in jail. When he described the attack by the man with the knife, Tracy was aghast. He even showed her the shallow slice across the top of his hand.

"What did this man look like?" Tracy asked. She shuddered. She couldn't imagine the horror of being attacked in a dark slaughterhouse.

"It happened so fast," Kim said. "I wouldn't be able to describe him very well."

"Old, young?" Tracy asked. "Tall, short?" For some inexplicable reason she wanted an image of this individual.

"Dark," Kim said. "Dark skin, dark hair. I think he was Mexican or at least Latin American. Slender but well-muscled. He had a lot of tattoos."

"Why didn't you tell all this to Justin?" she asked.

"What good would it have done?" Kim said.

"He could have said something to the judge," Tracy persisted.

"But it wouldn't have changed anything," Kim maintained. "In fact, it might have made things worse. I mean, it sounds so improbable, and I just wanted to get away from there so I could think of what to do."

"So you believe Marsha Baldwin is still in Higgins and Hancock?" Tracy asked. "Possibly being held against her wishes?"

"That or worse," Kim said. "If it were human blood I found, she could have been killed."

"I don't know what to say," Tracy admitted.

"Nor do I," Kim said. "I keep hoping she got out. Maybe I should call my answering machine. Maybe she called."

Tracy pulled the phone from its car cradle and handed it to Kim. He dialed and listened. After a couple of minutes, he put the phone back.

"Well?" Tracy asked.

Kim shook his head dejectedly. "No luck," he said. "Just Ginger."

"Tell me again exactly what you heard when you were talking with her the last time," Tracy asked.

"I heard the sound of breaking glass," Kim repeated. "It came right after she said someone was at the door. Then I heard a series of crashes, which I believe were from chairs falling over. I think whoever came through the door chased her out of the room."

"And you told all this to the police?" Tracy asked.

"Of course," Kim said. "But a lot of good that did! Yet it's understandable. They think I'm some kind of nut. When I tried to show them the blood, it had been washed away. When I tried to show them her cell phone, it was gone. Even her car wasn't in the parking lot where it had been when I got there."

"Could she have taken the phone?" Tracy asked. "And driven away in the car?"

"I hope to God she did," Kim said. "I hate to think of any alternative, and I feel so responsible. She'd gone there because of me."

"You didn't force her to do anything she didn't want to do," Tracy said. "In the short time I had with her, I could tell she wasn't the kind of person people could push around. She definitely had a mind of her own."

"What I'd like to do is get my hands on the guard," Kim said. "He had to know Marsha was there, even though he denied it."

"If he lied to the police, he certainly isn't going to tell you anything," Tracy said.

"Well, I've got to do something," Kim said.

"Do you know anything about her?" Tracy asked. "Like where she lives, or where she's from, or whether she has any family in the area?"

"I know almost nothing about her," Kim admitted. "Except that she's twenty-nine, and she went to veterinary school."

"Too bad," Tracy commented. "It would be a help if you could establish for sure whether or not she's missing. If she is, then the police would have to listen to you."

"You just gave me an idea," Kim said. He straightened up from his slouch. "What do you think of my going to Kelly Anderson and getting her to help?"

"Now, that's not a bad idea," Tracy said. "The question is, would she do it?"

"There's no way of knowing unless I approach her," Kim said.

"She's caused you enough grief," Tracy said. "It seems to me she owes you something."

"Gosh, the media could be a big help," Kim said. "Not only with the Marsha problem, but also with the whole meat-contamination issue."

"The more I think about this, the better I like it," Tracy said. "Maybe I can help you convince her."

Kim looked appreciatively at his former wife. With the bitterness of the divorce and the rancor of the custody issues he'd forgotten how warmly attractive she was. "You know, Trace," he said, "I'm really thankful that you came to court this morning and not just because you made the effort to raise the bail. I'm just thankful you're willing to be with me after all that's happened."

Tracy looked over at Kim. The remark was so out of character for him, yet seeing his eyes she knew he was sincere. "That's a very nice thing to say," she told him.

"I mean it," Kim said.

"Well, I appreciate your saying it," Tracy said. "I can't remember the last time you thanked me for anything. In fact, it must have been before we were ever married."

"I know," Kim admitted. "You're right. I had a little time to think last night in jail, and I have to say that the events over the last twenty-four hours, particularly concerning Becky, have opened my eyes."

"Opened your eyes to what?" Tracy asked.

"To what's really important in life," Kim said. "I suppose that sounds melodramatic, but I've realized I've made a terrible mistake. I've focused too much on career and competition, at the expense of family. And us."

"I'm impressed to hear you say such a thing," Tracy said. This did not sound like the Kim she'd divorced.

"I'm afraid I've been selfish all my adult life," Kim continued. "It's a little ironic since the whole time I've been hiding behind the facade of the charitable, selfless physician. Like a child, I've needed constant praise and constant reinforcement, and being a surgeon was a perfect fit.

"All this makes me feel sad and ashamed. It also makes me want to apologize to you and wish I could take back a number of wasted years."

"I'm surprised and overwhelmed," Tracy said. "But I accept. I'm impressed by your insight."

"Thanks," Kim said simply. He stared out the windshield. They had turned onto the side road and were approaching Higgins and Hancock. The building looked peaceful and clean under the dusting of snow.

"Is this it?" Tracy asked.

Kim nodded. "The entrance to the parking lot is coming up," he said. "My car should be right in front of the main door. At least that's where I left it."

Tracy turned where Kim indicated. Kim's car was immediately apparent. It was standing in total isolation. There were only two other cars in the lot, but they were all the way at the end of the plant.

"Marsha's car was parked where those two cars are," Kim mentioned. "Maybe there's an employee entrance over there."

Tracy pulled up alongside of Kim's car. She stopped and set the emergency brake.

Kim pointed to the record-room window that he'd smashed to gain entrance into the building. It had been boarded up. He explained to Tracy he'd done it with one of the large rocks lining the parking lot.

"What's the plan?" Tracy asked when Kim paused.

Kim sighed. "I've got to get to the hospital. Tom's agreed to look in on my patients, but I have to see them too. Then I'll go see Kelly Anderson. I happen to know where she lives."

"We have some decisions to make concerning Becky," Tracy said.

Kim nodded but looked off in the distance.

"I know it is difficult," Tracy said. "But we have to make funeral arrangements. It might even help us accept her death."

Kim bit his lip.

"Anger and denial are part of the grieving process," Tracy said when Kim didn't respond. "I'm guilty of using them as well as you, but we do have responsibilities."

Kim turned to face Tracy. There were tears in the corners of his eyes. "You're right," he admitted. "But, as I said, I need a little more time because of what's happened. Would it be too much to ask for you to go ahead and make the arrangements without me? I know it's asking a lot. I'll certainly agree to anything you decide, and, of course, I'll be there for the service. I'd just like to follow up on this Kelly Anderson idea immediately."

Tracy tapped her fingers against the steering wheel while she stared at Kim and pondered his request. Her first thought was to say no and to tell him that he was just being selfish again. But then she reconsidered. Although she didn't want to make the arrangements by herself, she knew that the service itself was far more important than making the arrangements. She also recognized that at the moment she was probably more capable than he was.

"You won't mind what day I pick?" Tracy questioned. "Or where a service might be?"

"Not at all," Kim said. "Whatever you decide."

"All right," she said. "But you have to promise to call me as soon as you get home."

"I promise," Kim said. He reached over and gave Tracy's forearm a squeeze before getting out of the car.

"I'll wait to make sure your car starts," Tracy said.

"Good idea," Kim said. "And thanks." He shut the door. He waved before heading over to his car.

Tracy waved back and wondered if she was doing the right thing.

Kim opened his car door, but didn't get right in. He looked at Higgins and Hancock and shuddered at the memory of the previous night. The terror he'd felt running from the man with the knife came flooding back. It was an experience he knew he'd never forget.

Kim started to get into the car but hesitated again. For a brief moment, he entertained the idea of talking with the guard on duty to find out how to get in touch with Curt, the guard from the previous night. But

Tracy's admonition immediately came to mind, and Kim decided she was right. If Curt were willing to lie to the police about Marsha's presence, he certainly wouldn't be apt to tell the truth to Kim. And the fact that he probably was lying meant there was more to this affair than might appear on the surface.

Kim's car started with ease, and he waved at Tracy who waved back before preceding him out of the parking lot. Kim followed at a distance, rethinking their recent conversation. He thought it was ironic that the awful events of the last few days—Becky's death and his having come close to being murdered—could end up making him feel closer to Tracy than he had in years, maybe even ever.

They parted company on the freeway. Kim beeped his horn in farewell. Tracy beeped back as she sped away toward her neighborhood. Kim took the exit appropriate for the med center.

On Sundays the doctors' parking lot was almost empty, and Kim was able to park close to the front entrance. As he climbed out of his car he told himself the first order of business was for him to go directly up to the surgical locker room. He wanted to clean up, shave, and change into the street clothes he'd left there Friday morning.

○   ○   ○

Martha Trumbull and George Constantine were both in their early seventies, and both had been faithful volunteers at the University Medical Center long enough to have been awarded the prestigious Friends of the Hospital service pins. Martha proudly wore hers on the front of her pink volunteer smock, whereas George wore his on the lapel of his cerulean volunteer blazer.

Martha and George's favorite assignment was manning the information desk in the hospital lobby. They particularly liked to work there on Sunday when they had it to themselves. On the other days of the week, a paid hospital employee was in charge.

Taking their roles seriously, they not only knew the layout of the hospital with the same detail as the floor plans of their own homes, but they also knew the names of the entire hospital professional staff. When Kim came through the door on his way to the elevator, they both thought they recognized him yet they weren't a hundred-percent certain.

Martha glanced at George. "Is that Dr. Reggis?" she whispered.

"I think so," George said. "But I can't imagine what he's been doing in that white coat, unless he had to change a tire."

"I think the beard looks worse than the coat," Martha said. "Someone should tell him, because he's such a nice-looking man."

"Wait a second," George said. "Weren't we supposed to call Dr. Biddle if we saw Dr. Reggis?"

"That was yesterday," Martha said. "You think it's the same today?"

"Why take a chance?" George said as he reached for the phone.

To Kim's relief the elevator was empty when he boarded it on the ground floor, and he was able to ride solo all the way to the surgical floor. He wasn't quite as lucky on his transit of the surgical lounge. There were a number of the OR nurses and on-call anesthesiologists having coffee. Although no one said anything, those assembled eyed him with curiosity.

Kim was glad to get into the surgical locker room and away from the inquiring faces. He was particularly pleased to find it vacant, and he lost no time. After rescuing his hospital I.D., a few papers and pens, plus some surgical tape from the pockets, he pulled off the coat, the scrubs, and even his underwear. Everything went into the laundry hamper.

Completely naked, Kim was shocked to catch his reflection in the mirror. His visage was far worse than he imagined. His ratty whiskers were significantly more than a five o'clock shadow but far from being a beard. And his hair was a mess, plastered down across his forehead yet standing straight up in the back, suggesting he'd just gotten out of bed.

Opening his combination lock, Kim got out the toiletries he kept in his locker and quickly shaved. Then he got into the shower with a vial of shampoo.

Kim had his head under the jet of water when he thought he heard his name called. Leaning out from the stream but with his eyes closed tightly against the suds, he listened. Someone repeated his name. The voice was definitely more authoritative than friendly.

Kim rinsed off the soap, then looked toward the shower entrance. He was in a common shower with four heads. Standing on the tiled threshold were Dr. Forrester Biddle, Chief of Cardiac Surgery, and Dr. Robert Rathborn, Acting Chief of the Medical Staff. They made a curious pair. In contrast to Forrester's ascetic gauntness, Robert was the picture of self-indulgent obesity.

"Dr. Reggis," Robert repeated when he was confident of Kim's attention. "As the current head of the medical staff, it is my duty to inform you that your hospital privileges have been temporarily revoked."

"This is a curious conversation to have while I'm in the shower," Kim said. "Or was it your specific intent to catch me naked?"

"Your glibness has never been more inappropriate," Forrester spat. "I've been warning you, Dr. Reggis."

"You couldn't wait for five minutes?" Kim questioned.

"We felt it was important enough to inform you as soon as possible," Robert said.

"What are the grounds?" Kim asked.

"For obstructive behavior during your daughter's cardiac resuscitation attempt," Robert said. "Three doctors and two nurses have filed formal complaints of physical intimidation by you that precluded them from carrying out their duty."

"And I am appalled at your decision to perform open-heart cardiac massage on your own daughter," Forrester said. "In my opinion, it is beyond the pale of acceptable professional behavior."

"She was dying, Robert," Kim hissed. "The closed chest massage wasn't effective. Her pupils were dilating."

"There were other qualified people on the scene," Robert said sanctimoniously.

"They weren't doing crap!" Kim snapped. "They didn't know what the hell was going on. Nor did I until I got a look at her heart." Kim's voice broke, and he looked away for a moment.

"There'll be a hearing," Robert said. "The issue here is whether you are a threat to patients or even yourself. You'll have an opportunity to present your side of this unfortunate episode. Meanwhile, you are not to practice any medicine within these walls, and you are specifically forbidden to do any surgery whatsoever."

"Well, it's good of you gentlemen to come into my office like this with such good news," Kim said.

"I wouldn't be so glib if I were you," Forrester warned.

"Nor would I," Robert said. "This incident and our action will be communicated to the Board of Medicine. You could very well find your medical license in jeopardy."

Kim turned around so that he could present what he thought was the most appropriate part of his anatomy to his two guests. Bending forward, he went back to completing his shampoo.

The El Toro bar looked like a completely different establishment in the daylight. Without the red glow of the neon bull and without the lively, percussive sound of the Hispanic music, the ramshackle building looked abandoned. The only evidence it wasn't were the freshly discarded beer cans scattered about the deserted parking lot.

Shanahan shook his head at the miserable scene as his black Cherokee navigated the pockmarked parking area. The rainy, foggy weather didn't help as it blanketed the area with a dense pall. Shanahan pulled alongside Carlos's truck whose condition matched the surroundings.

Carlos climbed out of his truck and came around to Shanahan's driver's-side window. It was heavily tinted, and Carlos could only see his own reflection until Shanahan lowered it.

With no greeting and no explanation, Shanahan handed Carlos a hundred-dollar bill.

Carlos looked at the money then back at Shanahan. "What's this?" he said. "You told me two hundred. The woman's been taken care of just like we talked about."

"You messed up," Shanahan said. "It wasn't clean. We heard about the doctor. You should have done him. You knew he was there looking for the woman."

"I tried," Carlos said.

"What do you mean, tried?" Shanahan asked with derision. "You're supposed to have this great reputation with a knife. The guy was unarmed."

"I didn't have time," Carlos said. "He set off the silent alarm when he broke in, and the police got there before I could finish him. I was lucky to get rid of her blood and stuff."

"What did you do with her car?" Shanahan asked.

"It's in my cousin's garage," Carlos said.

"We'll pick it up," Shanahan said. "I don't want anybody using it. It's got to be junked."

"Nobody's going to use it," Carlos said.

"What about her phone?" Shanahan asked.

"I got that in my truck," Carlos said.

"Get it!" Shanahan ordered.

Dutifully Carlos returned to his truck. A minute later he was back at Shanahan's window. Carlos handed the cell phone to the security man.

Shanahan tossed the phone onto the passenger seat. "I hope I don't have to ask you if you made any calls."

Carlos raised his dark eyebrows innocently but didn't respond verbally.

Shanahan closed his eyes, put a hand to his forehead, and shook his head in dismay. "Please tell me you didn't use the phone," he said through clenched teeth, although he already knew the answer.

When Carlos still didn't respond, Shanahan opened his eyes and stared dumbfounded at his accomplice. He tried to control his rage. "All right, who did you call? Don't you know they'll be able to trace the call? How can you be so stupid?"

"I called my mother in Mexico," Carlos admitted guiltily.

Shanahan rolled his eyes and started to worry that he would now have to get rid of Carlos. The trouble with this kind of work was that when things started to go wrong, they had a way of quickly getting out of hand.

"But my mother has no phone," Carlos said. "I called a phone in a store where my sister works."

"What kind of a store?" Shanahan asked.

"A big store," Carlos said. "It sells all sorts of things."

"Like a department store?" Shanahan asked.

"Yeah, like a department store," Carlos said.

"When did you call?" Shanahan asked.

"Last night," Carlos said. "The store is open late on Saturday night, and my mother always goes to walk my sister home."

"Where in Mexico?" Shanahan asked.

"Mexico City," Carlos said.

Shanahan felt relieved. An anonymous call to a large store in the most populous city in the world wasn't much of a lead.

"And that was the only call?" Shanahan asked.

"Yeah, man," Carlos said. "Just one call."

"Let's get back to the doctor," Shanahan said. "Does he know what happened to the woman?"

"Probably," Carlos said. "He saw her blood."

"One way or the other, he's a threat," Shanahan said. "He's got to go. We'll pay you the other hundred plus three hundred extra to do the job. What do you say?"

"When?" Carlos asked.

"Tonight," Shanahan said. "We know where he lives, and he lives alone. It's in the Balmoral section of town."

"I don't know," Carlos said. "He's a big guy."

"With the reputation you have, I didn't think that would matter," Shanahan said.

"It's not the killing that will be hard," Carlos said. "It's getting rid of the body and the blood."

"You don't have to worry about that," Shanahan said. "Just do the trick and walk out. Maybe you could make it look like a robbery by taking money and valuables. Just don't take anything that can be traced."

"I don't know," Carlos said. "The police don't like us Mexicans driving around in the Balmoral neighborhood. I've been stopped up there."

"Listen, Carlos," Shanahan said. He was quickly losing his patience. "You don't have a lot of choice at this juncture. You screwed up last night. As I understand it you had plenty of time to kill the doctor. Besides, you don't even have a green card."

Carlos shifted his weight and rubbed his upper arms against the damp cold. He had no coat and was still wearing his leather vest without a shirt.

"What's the address?" Carlos asked with resignation.

"That's more like it," Shanahan said as he handed over a typed three-by-five card.

○    ○    ○

Defying the revocation of his hospital privileges by the medical staff as delivered by Robert Rathborn, Kim went around the hospital and visited all his in-patients. He spent the most time with Friday's post-ops. As Tom Bridges had promised, he'd been following all the patients closely. Kim was pleased that all were doing well and without complications. By the time Kim left the hospital it was mid-afternoon.

Kim had considered trying to call Kelly Anderson to arrange a meeting but then decided it would be better just to drop in. Besides, he didn't have her phone number, and he rationalized it was undoubtedly unlisted.

Kelly Anderson lived in a prairie-style house in the Christie Heights section of town. It wasn't quite as upscale as Balmoral but it was close. Kim pulled to the curb and stopped. He turned off the ignition and gazed at the house. It took him a moment to build up his courage. For Kim, coming to Kelly Anderson was akin to conniving with the devil herself. He felt he needed her but certainly didn't like her.

Kim trudged up to the front door; realizing that there was a very good chance he would not even make it across the threshold.

Caroline, Kelly's precocious daughter, opened the door. For a moment, Kim could not find his voice. The child brought back the unwelcome image of Becky in the ICU.

Kim heard a man's voice from inside the house, asking Caroline who was there.

"I don't know," Caroline yelled back over her shoulder. "He won't talk."

"I'm Doctor Reggis," Kim managed.

Edgar Anderson appeared behind his daughter. He was an academic-appearing fellow, with heavy dark-rimmed glasses. He was wearing an oversized, elbow-patched cardigan sweater. A pipe hung from the corner of his mouth.

"Can I help you?" Edgar inquired.

Kim repeated his name and asked to speak to Kelly Anderson.

Edgar introduced himself as Kelly's husband and invited Kim inside. He showed him into the living room, which had the appearance of never being used.

"I'll let her know you are here," Edgar said. "Please sit down. Can I offer you anything? Coffee?"

"No, thank you," Kim said. He felt self-conscious, as if he were a mendicant. He lowered himself onto an immaculate couch.

Edgar disappeared, but Caroline stayed to stare at Kim from behind a club chair. Kim could not look at her without thinking about Becky.

Kim was relieved when Kelly swept into the room.

"My, my," she intoned. "This is curious. The fox chasing the hound. Sit down, please!" Kim had gotten to his feet when she'd entered. She plopped into the club chair. "And to what do I owe the pleasure of this unexpected visit?" she added.

"Could we speak alone?" Kim asked.

Acting as if she had been unaware Caroline was in the room, Kelly told her daughter to find something entertaining to do.

As soon as Caroline had left, Kim started by telling about Becky's death. Kelly's glib demeanor changed immediately. She was obviously deeply moved.

Kim told Kelly the whole story, including the details of the discussions he'd had with Kathleen Morgan and Marsha Baldwin. He told her about his visit and arrest at the Onion Ring restaurant. He even told her about the harrowing episode in Higgins and Hancock, culminating in his second arrest.

When Kim fell silent, Kelly exhaled and leaned back. She shook her head. "What a story," she said. "And what a tragedy for you. But what brings you to me? I assume there is something you want me to do."

"Obviously," Kim said. "I want you to do a story about all this. It's something the public needs to know. And I want to get out the message about Marsha Baldwin. The more I think about it, the more I'm convinced there's a conspiracy here. If she's alive, the sooner she's found the better."

Kelly chewed the inside of her cheek while she pondered Kim's request. There were some intriguing elements to the story, but there were also some problems. After a few moments, she shook her head. "Thank you for coming by and telling me all this, but I'm not interested from a professional point of view: at least not at this time."

Kim's face fell. As he'd told the story, he'd become progressively convinced of its merit, and Kelly's rapid negative decision came as a disappointing surprise. "Can you tell me why?" he questioned.

"Sure," Kelly said. "As much as I sympathize with you about the tragic loss of your darling, talented daughter, it's not the kind of TV journalism I generally do. I go after harder, bigger stories, if you know what I mean."

"But this is a big story," Kim complained. "Becky died of E. coli O157:H7. This has become a worldwide problem."

"True," Kelly admitted. "But it's only one case."

"That's the point," Kim said. "Only one case so far. I'm convinced she got it at the Onion Ring restaurant on Prairie Highway. I'm afraid she's going to turn out to be the index case of what could be a big outbreak."

"But an outbreak hasn't happened," Kelly said. "You said yourself your daughter got sick over a week ago. If there were going to be an outbreak, there would have been more cases by now, but there haven't been."

"But there will be," Kim said. "I'm convinced of it."

"Fine," Kelly said. "When there are more cases, I'll do a story. I mean, one isolated case is not a story. How can I say it more clearly?"

"But hundreds of kids die each year from this bacteria," Kim said. "People don't know that."

"That might be true," Kelly said. "But these hundreds of cases are not related."

"But they are," Kim said with exasperation. "Almost all of them get it from ground beef. The meat industry that produces the hamburger is a threat to everyone who eats ground beef. It's a situation that has to be exposed."

"Hey, where have you been?" Kelly asked with equal exasperation. "It's already been exposed, particularly by the Jack-in-the-Box outbreak and the Hudson Meat recall. This E. coli has been in the news just about every month."

"It's been in the news but the media has been giving the wrong message," Kim said.

"Oh, really?" Kelly questioned superciliously. "I suppose that in addition to being a cardiac surgeon you're also a media expert?"

"I don't profess to be a media expert," Kim said. "But I do know that the media coverage of this issue has given two important false impressions: one, that the presence of this dangerous E. coli in ground meat is unusual; and two, that the USDA is on the job inspecting meat to guarantee its safety. Both these messages are false as evidenced by the deaths of up to five hundred kids a year."

"Whoa!" Kelly commented. "Now you're out on very thin ice. I mean, now you're making a couple of major accusations. How can you back it up? What kind of proof do you have?"

"My daughter's death," Kim said with obvious anger. "And the CDC's reports of the other deaths."

"I'm talking about the accusation you made about E. coli being so common and the USDA failing to inspect the meat."

"I don't have specific proof right now," Kim said. "That's what I expect you to find when you do the story. But so many kids wouldn't be dying if it wasn't true. And all this was substantiated by Marsha Baldwin."

"Ah, of course," Kelly said dubiously. "How could I forget. The mysterious USDA inspector who you say has been missing for less than twenty-four hours. The one you feel has fallen victim to foul play."

"Exactly," Kim said. "They had to silence her."

Kelly cocked her head to the side. She wasn't a hundred-percent sure she shouldn't be afraid of Kim, especially considering his double arrests. She had the sense his daughter's death had done something to his mind. He seemed paranoid, and she wanted him out of the house.

"Tell me again," Kelly said. "The reason you think Miss Baldwin is missing is because of the interrupted telephone call and the blood you found in the slaughterhouse?"

"Exactly," Kim repeated.

"And you told all this to the police who arrested you?" Kelly asked.

"Of course," Kim said. "But they didn't believe me."

"And I can see why," Kelly said silently to herself. All at once she stood up. "Excuse me, Dr. Reggis," she said out loud. "I'm afraid we're going around in circles. This is all hearsay and therefore smoke and mirrors as far as I'm concerned. I'd like to help you, but I can't at the moment, at least not until you have something tangible, something that a story could be based on."

Kim pushed himself up off the low couch. He could feel his anger returning, but he fought against it. Although he didn't agree with Kelly's position, he had to admit he understood, and the realization only renewed his determination. "All right," Kim said resolutely. "I'll get something substantive, and I'll be back."

"You do that," Kelly said, "and I'll do the story."

"I'm going to hold you to that," Kim said.

"I always keep my word," Kelly said. "Of course, I have to be the one who decides if the evidence is sufficient."

"I'll make sure there're no ambiguities," Kim said.

Kim exited the house and ran down to his car parked at the curb. He wasn't running because of the rain, although it had increased in intensity while he had been in the Anderson house. He was running because he'd already decided what he was going to do to satisfy Kelly's need for proof. It wasn't going to be easy, but Kim didn't care. He was a man with a mission.

Kim made a U-turn and stomped on the accelerator. He didn't notice Kelly standing in the doorway of her house or see her shake her head one final time as he sped away.

As soon as Kim made it onto the freeway he punched in Tracy's phone number on his cellular phone.

"Trace," Kim said with no preamble when she answered. "Meet me at the mall."

There was a pause. At first Kim thought the connection had been broken. Just when he was about to resend the call, Tracy's voice came over the line: "I took you at your word. I've made arrangements for a funeral service."

Kim sighed. At times he was able to put Becky entirely out of his mind. Thank God for Tracy. She was so strong. How could he face this tragedy without her? "Thank you," he said at last. It was hard to find the words. "I appreciate your doing it without me."

"It will be at the Sullivan Funeral Home on River Street," Tracy said. "And it will be on Tuesday."

"That's fine," Kim said. He just couldn't bring himself to think too long or hard about it. "I'd like you to meet me at the mall."

"Don't you want to hear the rest of the details?" Tracy asked.

"At the moment, meeting me at the mall is more important," Kim said. He hoped he didn't sound too cold. "Then I'd like to ask if you'd come back with me to our old house."

"How can going to the mall be more important than our daughter's funeral?" Tracy asked with exasperation.

"Trust me," Kim said. "You can give me the details of the arrangements when I see you."

"Kim, what's going on?" Tracy asked. She sensed an excited anticipation in his voice.

"I'll explain later," Kim said.

"Where at the mall?" Tracy asked with resignation. "It's a big place."

"Connolly Drugs," Kim said. "Inside the store."

"When?" Tracy asked.

"I'm on my way," Kim said. "Get there as soon as you can."

"It will take me more than a half hour," Tracy said. "And you know they close at six tonight."

"I know," Kim said. "That's plenty of time."

Tracy hung up the phone. She wondered if she was hurting Kim more than she was helping him by having let him avoid participating in the funeral arrangements. But she didn't have much time to dwell on it just then.

Despite their bitter divorce, thinking about Kim brought out the mother in Tracy. She found herself wondering when Kim had eaten last. She knew she wasn't hungry, but guessed it would be best if they both had something. So before leaving for the mall, Tracy threw some food into a bag and carried it out to the car.

On the way to the mall, Tracy decided that she would insist that Kim participate in finalizing the plans for Becky's service. It would be best for both of them.

Since it was late afternoon on a cold, rainy Sunday, there was no traffic, and Tracy made it to the mall faster than she estimated. Even the parking area was relatively empty. It was the first time Tracy had ever been able to get a spot within a few steps of the main entrance.

Inside, the mall was more crowded than she expected given the number of cars outside. Just beyond the door she was confronted by a group of senior citizens bearing down on her while doing their version of power-walking. Tracy had to step into the lip of a shop for a moment to avoid being trampled. Walking on to the center of the mall, she assiduously avoided looking at the skating rink for fear of the memories it would invariably evoke.

Connolly Drugs was as busy as ever, particularly at the prescription counter where there were upwards of twenty people waiting. Tracy made a rapid trip around the store but didn't see Kim. On a slower transit, she located him in the hair-products section. He was carrying a box containing a pair of hair clippers and a bag from one of the mall's trendy clothing stores.

"Ah, Tracy," Kim said. "Just in time. I want you to help me pick out a hair rinse. I've decided to go blond."

Tracy lifted her hands onto her hips and regarded her former husband with bewilderment. "Are you all right?" she asked.

"Yeah, I'm fine," Kim said. He was preoccupied looking at the panoply of hair products.

"What do you mean you want to go blond?" Tracy asked.

"Just what I said," Kim asserted. "And not just dirty blond. I want to be very blond."

"Kim, this is crazy," Tracy said. "You have to know it. And if you don't, I'm even more worried."

"There's nothing to worry about," Kim said. "I'm not decompensating if that's what you think. All I want to do is disguise myself. I'm going undercover."

Tracy reached out and grabbed Kim by the shoulder to steady him. She leaned forward, suddenly transfixed by his earlobe. "What's this?" she questioned. "You're wearing an earring!"

"I'm pleased you noticed," Kim said. "I had a little time before you got here, so I got an earring. I thought it was sufficiently out of character. I also got a leather outfit." He held up the shopping bag.

"What are the hair clippers for?" Tracy asked.

"Those are for you to give me a haircut," Kim said.

"I've never cut anyone's hair," Tracy said. "You know that."

"That doesn't matter," Kim said with a smile. "I'm aiming for a skinhead look."

"This is bizarre," Tracy complained.

"The more bizarre, the better," Kim said. "I don't want to be recognized."

"Why?" Tracy asked.

"Because I visited Kelly Anderson," Kim said. "And she refuses to lend us her investigative journalistic skills until I supply her with some incontrovertible proof."

"Proof of what?" Tracy asked.

"Proof of the allegations Kathleen Morgan and Marsha Baldwin made about the meat industry and the USDA."

"And how is a disguise going to help you do that?" Tracy asked.

"It's going to help me get a job," Kim said. "Marsha Baldwin told me slaughterhouses like Higgins and Hancock don't allow visitors, but she suggested I could get a job, especially if I were an illegal alien. I don't mean to say I'm trying to look like an illegal alien, just some marginal member of society who needs to earn some money."

"I can't believe this," Tracy said. "You mean you are going to go into Higgins and Hancock to try to get a job after someone tried to kill you in there?"

"I'm hoping the employment officer and the man with the knife are two different people," Kim said.

"Kim, this is no laughing matter," Tracy said. "I don't like the idea at all, especially if your fears about Marsha are true."

"It might be a little dicey if they recognize me," Kim admitted. "That's why I want the disguise to be good. Marsha contended that Higgins and Hancock is always in need of help because turnover is so high. So I'm counting on their not being particularly choosey."

"I don't like this one bit," Tracy said. "I think it's too risky. There's got to be another way. What if I talk to Kelly Anderson?"

"She's not going to budge," Kim said. "She was clear about that. I've got to go in Higgins and Hancock, risk or not. Even if there is risk, I think it is worth it for Becky's sake. For me, it's a way to make her loss less meaningless."

Kim felt tears spring to his eyes. "Besides," he managed to add, "I have the time now that I'm unemployed. I'm on a forced, temporary leave from the hospital."

"Because of what happened in the ICU?" Tracy questioned.

"Uh-huh," Kim said. "Apparently you were the only person who thought my action was courageous."

"It was courageous," Tracy asserted. She was impressed. Kim had come around one-hundred-eighty degrees. He really wanted to do something for Becky's sake and was willing to risk his career and reputation to do so. She couldn't argue with his motives or his goal. Without another word, Tracy turned to the shelving and walked along the aisle until she found what she considered the best bleaching rinse.

○   ○   ○

Carlos had waited until dusk before driving his dilapidated pickup into the Balmoral neighborhood. He liked the fact that the streets were dark. The only lights were at the corners over the street signs. Having looked at a map, it didn't take him long to find Edinburgh Lane and eventually Kim's house.

Carlos turned off his single working headlight before gliding to a stop in the shadow of some trees lining the street. He switched off the ignition and waited. From where he was parked he could see the silhouette of Kim's house against the darkening sky. Carlos was pleased. The lack of light suggested that Kim was not home. Once again Carlos would have the benefit of surprise, only this time it would be even better. Kim would be caught totally off-guard.

Carlos waited in his truck for twenty minutes before he felt comfortable enough to get out. He heard a dog bark, and he froze. The dog barked again, but it sounded farther away. Carlos relaxed. He reached into his truck and extracted one of the long kill-floor knives from beneath the seat. He slipped it under his coat.

Skirting around the front of his aged Toyota, Carlos entered the trees that separated Kim's house from its neighbor. Wearing a black leather coat and dark trousers, Carlos was all but invisible as he silently slipped through the thicket.

Carlos was pleased when he got a full view of the back of Kim's house. Like the front, there wasn't a light on in any window. Now he was certain the house was empty.

Hunched over, Carlos ran from the protection of the trees across Kim's backyard and flattened himself against the house. Again he waited for any suggestion that his presence was known. The neighborhood was deathly quiet. Even the dog that he'd heard earlier had fallen silent.

Staying within the shadow of the house, Carlos approached Kim's screened back porch. The knife flashed briefly in the dim light as Carlos cut a slit in the screen just long enough for him to silently slip through.

Burglary was Carlos's true forte; the killing talent had been born of ne-
cessity.

O    O    O

Kim turned off the main road and drove through the gate marking the
boundary of Balmoral Estates. He glanced in the rearview mirror to see
Tracy's car follow suit. He was pleased that she was willing to help him
with his hair, more for her company than from need. He was also pleased
about her offer to make them something to eat. Kim couldn't remember
the last time he had an actual meal although he guessed it had been
Thursday night.

After parking his car in front of his garage, Kim gathered his bundles
and went back to meet Tracy as she climbed from her car. It was raining
harder than ever. In total darkness, they navigated the black pools that
had formed along the front walk.

When they reached the cover of the porch, Tracy offered to hold the
packages while Kim got out his key.

"No need," Kim said. "The door's unlocked."

"That's not very wise," Tracy commented.

"Why not?" Kim said. "There's not much in the house to take, and it
makes it easier for the realtor."

"I suppose," Tracy said, unconvinced. She opened the door, and they
entered the foyer.

They took off their coats and wiped the moisture from their foreheads.
Then they carried their parcels into the kitchen.

"I'll tell you what," Tracy said while putting her bag of groceries onto
the countertop, "I'm happy to make us something to eat and help you with
your hair, but first I'd really like to take a shower and warm up. Would
you mind?"

"Mind?" Kim questioned. "Not at all. Help yourself."

"It's sad to say," Tracy added, "but the shower is the only thing I miss
about this house."

"I understand completely," Kim said. "It was the only thing we made our own. There's a robe in with the towels if you'd like. Of course you also have some clothes here, but I moved them out to the hall closet."

"Don't worry, I'll find something," Tracy said.

"I had a shower at the hospital," Kim said. "So I'll start a fire in the fire-place here in the family room. Maybe it will make this empty house a lit-tle less depressing."

While Tracy headed upstairs, Kim got out a flashlight from the kitchen junk drawer, and headed down to the basement where the firewood was stored. He turned on the light, but the single bulb had never been ade-quate to light the huge, cluttered cellar.

Kim had never felt comfortable in basements because of a disturbing experience he'd had in the basement of the home where he'd grown up. When Kim was six, his older brother had locked him in an unused wine cellar and then forgot about him. With the insulated door, no one had heard Kim's hysterical cries or his frantic pounding. It was only after his mother became worried he'd not appeared for dinner that his brother had remembered where he was.

Kim could not go down to the basement without remembering the terror he'd felt thirty-eight years previously. When he heard a thump in a neighboring storeroom as he loaded wood in his arms, the hairs on the back of his neck stood up. He froze and listened. He heard the noise again.

Steeling himself against the desire to flee, Kim put the wood down. Taking the flashlight, he walked over to the door to the storeroom. It took strength of will to make himself push the door open with his foot and shine the light in. A half dozen pairs of tiny red rubylike points of light stared back at him before scampering off.

Kim breathed a sigh of relief. He went back to the woodpile to finish loading up.

Tracy had climbed the stairs, feeling a twinge of nostalgia. It had been some time since she'd been on the second floor of the house. Outside of Becky's room, she'd paused, gazing at the closed door and wondering if she dare enter. Compromising, she merely opened the door and stood on the threshold.

Becky's room had not changed. Since Tracy and Kim shared custody, Tracy had gotten new furniture for her daughter and left the old where it was. Becky didn't mind and preferred to leave what she considered her childhood objects in her old room. She'd not even taken her stuffed animal collection.

The idea that Becky was gone was inconceivable to Tracy. She'd been the center of Tracy's life, particularly after Tracy's relationship with Kim had deteriorated.

Tracy took a deep breath and pulled the door closed. As she walked down toward the master suite, she wiped the tears from the corners of her eyes with her knuckle. She knew from her professional experience how difficult the next few months would be for her and for Kim.

Tracy entered the master bath directly from the hall instead of going around through the bedroom. Once inside, she flicked on the light and closed the door behind her. She surveyed the room. It wasn't nearly as clean as it had always been when she lived in the house, yet it was still beautiful, with its granite-topped vanity and marble shower.

Leaning into the shower stall, she turned on the water and adjusted the showerhead to deliver a pulsating jet. Then she opened the generous closet and got out a large bath towel along with a Turkish robe. Placing them on the vanity, she began to remove her damp clothes.

Carlos heard the shower and smiled. This job was going to be easier than he'd imagined. He was standing in the walk-in closet in the master bedroom, intending to wait until Kim unknowingly opened the door. But hearing the shower running, he thought it would be better to corner the doctor in such a conveniently confined space. Escape would be impossible.

Carlos cracked the door and a sliver of pale light fell across his face. He looked out. The bedroom was still mostly dark with the only light coming from the bathroom. Carlos was pleased about this as well. It meant he would not have to worry about being seen as he approached the bathroom. For what he had to do, surprise was an important element.

Carlos opened the door wide enough to step out into the room. He had his knife in his right hand.

Moving like a cat advancing on its prey, Carlos inched forward. With each step, he could see progressively more of the bathroom's interior through the open passageway connecting the rooms. He saw a hand flash by and drop clothing onto the counter.

Taking one more step, Carlos had a full view of the bathroom, and he froze. It wasn't Kim. It was a strikingly lithe, sexy woman in the process of unhooking her bra. In an instant, her soft, white breasts were revealed. The woman then hooked her thumbs beneath the elastic of her panties and pulled them off.

Carlos was transfixed by this unexpected but welcome spectacle, as Tracy turned her back toward him and climbed into the billowing mist coming from the shower stall. She closed the moisture-streaked glass door behind her, and threw her towel over a bar at the shower's rear.

Carlos moved forward as if drawn to a siren. He wanted a better view.

○　　○　　○

Tracy put her hand under the water spray then pulled it clear. It was much too hot, which was what she expected. It had been her intent to turn the shower stall into a modified steam bath.

Reaching behind the stream of water, she adjusted the mixing valve. While she waited for the water temperature to change, she glanced at the soap dish and noticed it was empty. The bar was out at the sink.

Tracy opened the door to get the soap when a flicker of light caught her attention. It had come from the bedroom. At first she couldn't believe her eyes, and she blinked. There was the spectral image of a man in black standing just within the penumbra of the bathroom light. The flash had come from the blade of an enormous knife in the man's right hand.

For a beat the two people stared at each other, Tracy in shocked horror and Carlos in libidinous interest.

Tracy was the first to react. She let out a horrendous scream as she yanked the shower door shut. Then she snatched the tubular towel bar from its brackets and passed it through the U-shaped handle of the heavy glass door to prevent it from opening.

Carlos reacted by springing forward into the bathroom. He wanted to get to her before her scream brought Kim. Switching the knife to his left hand, he grasped the handle of the shower door and yanked. Frustrated by not being able to get inside, he put up a foot to give himself more leverage. The light tubular towel bar slowly dented under his effort and began to bend.

When Tracy's scream sounded through the house, Kim was on his way up the cellar stairs with his armload of firewood. Already on edge from the run-in with the mice, Kim's heart leaped into his throat. He dropped the firewood with a tremendous clatter as the logs tumbled back down the stairs, knocking all sorts of things off the steps that had been inappropriately stored there.

Afterward Kim would not even remember how he got through the kitchen, dining room, foyer, and up the stairs. As he reached the upper hallway, he heard Tracy scream again, and he redoubled his efforts. He hit the thin, paneled bathroom door at a full run and shattered it on his way through.

Kim burst into the bathroom and skid on the shag rug as he tried to stop. He saw Carlos with his foot up against the glass shower stall, apparently trying to open it. He saw the knife and immediately realized he should have brought something to defend himself.

Carlos reacted by spinning around and slashing out with the knife. The tip of the blade caught Kim across the bridge of his nose as he backed up.

Carlos tossed the knife into his right hand and turned his full attention to Kim. Kim's eyes were glued to the knife as he backed up toward the broken door to the hall.

Tracy struggled with the dented towel bar to extract it from the shower-door handle. When she finally was able to do it, Kim and Carlos had disappeared out into the hallway. She grasped the towel bar at one end and frantically pushed out of the shower. Naked, she rushed after the two men.

Carlos was still forcing Kim to back up by menacing him with his blade. Kim had picked up a broken door stile and was using it in a vain attempt to counter Carlos's repeated thrusts. Blood from the cut over Kim's nose was running down his face.

Without hesitation, Tracy ran up behind Carlos and clubbed him several times over the head with the towel bar. The hollow tube was not enough to hurt Carlos, but he had to defend himself against the repeated blows. He turned around to take a few swipes at Tracy who immediately backed up.

Kim took the opportunity to grab the leg of a small console table. He ripped the table from the wall and then smashed it over the banister to free the leg. By the time Carlos turned to face him, Kim was brandishing the leg like a truncheon.

With Kim on one side and Tracy on the other, Carlos decided that his lethal weapon was trumped. He bolted down the stairs.

Kim followed, with Tracy close behind.

Carlos threw open the front door and ran down across the front lawn. Kim was close behind, but he stopped when Tracy yelled for him. He looked back. She was standing in the doorway.

"Come back," Tracy yelled. "It's not worth it."

Kim turned in time to see Carlos leap into a truck parked in the shadows. An instant later, exhaust billowed out of the tailpipe, and the vehicle lurched forward and picked up speed.

Kim hurried back up to the house and pushed open the door. Tracy was standing in the foyer. She'd pulled on her coat to cover her nakedness.

Kim enveloped her in his arms. "Are you okay?" he asked urgently.

"You're the one who's hurt," Tracy said. The laceration that stretched across Kim's nose and into one eyebrow was gaping and still bleeding.

Kim let go of Tracy to step into the powder room where he examined himself in the mirror. He was surprised to see how much blood was involved. Over his shoulder, he saw Tracy's face. She'd come up behind him.

"Gosh, it was close," Kim said, redirecting his attention to his wound. "This could have been serious. First he cut my hand, and now right between the eyes."

"Are you suggesting this was the same man who attacked you last night?" Tracy asked with astonishment.

"There's no doubt," Kim said. "I would have had trouble describing him, but I didn't have any trouble recognizing him."

Tracy shuddered and then couldn't stop. Kim could see in the mirror that she was shivering despite her coat.

Kim spun around and grasped her shoulders. "What's the matter? You're okay, aren't you? I mean, you didn't get cut or anything?"

"Physically I'm all right," Tracy managed. "It's just the reality of what happened is finally dawning on me. That man wanted to kill us."

"He wanted to kill me," Kim said. "I have a feeling you were a surprise, and enough of one to have saved my life. Thank God you weren't hurt."

Tracy twisted out of Kim's grasp. "I'll call the police," she said on her way to the family room.

Kim caught up to her, and grabbing her arm, he pulled her to a stop. "Don't bother to call the police," he said.

Tracy eyed Kim's hand clasped around her upper arm then looked up into his face. She was incredulous. "What do you mean, don't bother?" she questioned.

"Come on," Kim urged, gently pulling her back toward the stairs. "Let's get my gun. I doubt the guy will be back, but there's no sense in taking any chance of not being prepared."

Tracy held back. "Why don't you want to call the police?" she questioned. "It doesn't make any sense."

"They won't do anything," Kim said. "We'll end up spending a lot of time for nothing. Undoubtedly they'll attribute this episode to a failed burglary, whereas we know what it is about."

"We do?" Tracy asked.

"Of course," Kim said. "I said it was the same guy from Higgins and Hancock. Obviously what I was afraid had happened to Marsha, did happen, and the people responsible, whether they're from Higgins and Hancock or the meat industry in general, are afraid of me."

"That seems like all the more reason to call the police," Tracy said.

"No!" Kim said emphatically. "Not only won't they do anything, they might cause trouble. Above all, I don't want them interfering in my attempt to get evidence for Kelly Anderson. In their eyes, I'm already a felon. They think I'm a nutcase."

"They don't think I'm a nutcase," Tracy said.

"They might," Kim said. "As soon as you tell them you've been spending time with me."

"You think so?" Tracy questioned. That was a point she'd not considered.

"Come on," Kim urged. "Let's get the gun."

Tracy followed Kim out to the foyer. They started up the stairs. She was confused but for the moment allowed Kim's determination to sway her. Yet the attack by the man with the knife terrified her.

"I'm having serious second thoughts about your getting more involved in all this," Tracy said.

"Not me," Kim said. "I feel even more committed. Any residual benefit of doubt I'd felt has flown out the window now that I know what they're willing to do to protect themselves."

They passed the broken door to the bathroom. Tracy could hear the shower still running. She shuddered anew at the image of the killer separated from her by a mere layer of glass.

Tracy followed Kim into the bedroom. He went directly to the bedside table and took out a small Smith & Wesson. thirty-eight-calibre pistol. He checked the cylinder. It was loaded. He slipped the gun into his jacket pocket and looked over at the open door to the walk-in closet.

"That prick must have been hiding in there," Kim said. He walked over and switched on the light. Most of the drawers had been emptied onto the floor. Kim pulled out the drawer where he kept his minimal jewelry. "That's nice," he added. "He helped himself to my father's Piaget."

"Kim, I think we should forget about this whole thing," Tracy said. "I don't think you should try to get a job in Higgins and Hancock."

"I don't have any choice at this point," Kim said. "I'm not going to give up my father's watch without a fight."

"This is no time for jokes," Tracy said. "I'm being serious. It's too dangerous."

"What would you have us do?" Kim asked. "Move away to some foreign country?"

"That's a thought," Tracy said.

Kim laughed mirthlessly. "Wait a sec," he said, "I was just kidding. Where would you want to move?"

"Someplace in Europe," Tracy said. "I had another conversation with Kathleen after the three of us talked. She told me there were some countries, like Sweden, where the food is not contaminated."

"Seriously?" Kim questioned.

"That's what she said," Tracy offered. "They may pay a little more for the extra scrutiny, but they've decided it's worth it."

"And you'd seriously think of going to live in another country?" Kim asked.

"I hadn't thought about it until you mentioned it," Tracy said. "But yes, I'd consider it. Given what happened to Becky, I'd like to be public about it—use the move to make a statement about the food situation in this country. And it certainly would be a lot less risky."

"I suppose," Kim said. He thought about the idea for a moment, but then shook his head. "I think running away is too much of a cop-out. For Becky's sake, I'm going to see this to the bitter end."

"Are you sure you're not doing this just to avoid coming to grips with Becky's death?" Tracy asked. She took a nervous breath. She knew she was touching a sensitive area. The old Kim would have reacted with rage.

Kim didn't answer immediately. When he did, his voice didn't sound angry. "I've admitted as much already, but I think I'm doing this for Becky's memory as well. In that sense, part of her legacy would be preventing other kids from sharing her fate."

Tracy was touched. She went up to Kim and put her arms around him. He truly seemed to be a different man.

"Come on," Kim urged. "Get out of that coat and back into your clothes. We'll get the stuff we bought and get the hell out of here."

"Where will we go?" Tracy asked.

"First to the hospital," Kim said. "I have to get this laceration sutured up, or I'll be looking at it the rest of my life. Once that's done, we can go on to your house if you wouldn't mind. I think we'll feel a lot safer there than we will here."

○    ○    ○

"Now, who the hell is that?" Bobby Bo Mason asked. He and his wife, along with their two children, were having a small Sunday night dinner of sirloin steaks, double-baked potatoes, peas, and corn muffins. Their chewing concentration had been broken by the front-door chimes.

Bobby Bo lifted the tip of his napkin to blot the corners of his lips. The other end of the napkin was tucked into his shirt just below his sizable Adam's apple. He looked up at the clock. It was just a few minutes shy of seven.

"Want me to get it, dear?" Darlene asked. Darlene was Bobby Bo's third wife and mother of his youngest children. He also had two kids at the state agricultural school.

"I'll get it," Bobby Bo grumbled. He pushed back from the table, stuck out his lantern jaw, and headed for the front door. He wondered who had the nerve to ring his bell during dinner, but he guessed it had to be important because whoever it was had gotten through security down at the gate.

Bobby Bo pulled open the door. It was Shanahan O'Brian. The man was literally holding his hat in his hand.

"You don't look happy," Bobby Bo said.

"I'm not," Shanahan admitted. "It's not good news."

Bobby Bo glanced over his shoulder to make sure Darlene hadn't followed him to the door.

"Come on into the library," Bobby Bo said. He stepped aside to let Shanahan enter. Then he preceded his security head into the library. He closed the door after them.

"All right," Bobby Bo said. "What's the scoop?"

"I just had a call from Carlos," Shanahan said. "He didn't get the doctor."

"I thought this guy was supposed to be some kind of ace with a knife," Bobby Bo complained.

"That's what I'd been told," Shanahan said. "Carlos insists this doctor is just lucky. He broke into the doctor's house. He'd been told that the doctor lived alone, but when the doctor came home this time he apparently had a woman with him."

"Big deal," Bobby Bo said. "This Carlos is supposed to be a killer. What difference does it make if a woman was there?"

"She apparently confused him," Shanahan said. "He caught her naked and . . ."

"Enough," Bobby Bo said, raising his hand. "I don't want to hear any more details. The fact of the matter is this amateur wetback botched it up."

"That's the long and short of it," Shanahan said.

"Damn!" Bobby Bo said. He slapped the edge of his desk and began to pace and loudly curse.

Shanahan let his boss blow off some steam. He'd learned over the years it was best to say as little as possible when Bobby Bo was irritated.

"Well," Bobby Bo said, while still walking back and forth in front of the fireplace. "This all goes to show how stupid it is to save a few bucks by relying on a novice. So much for the vaunted Protection Committee. Let's call the professional up in Chicago and get him down here ASAP to straighten out this mess. What's his name again?"

"Derek Leutmann," Shanahan said. "But he is expensive. I think we should let Carlos have one more crack at it."

"How expensive?" Bobby Bo asked.

"At least five K," Shanahan said.

"Hell, five K is cheap if it prevents another major meat recall," Bobby Bo said. "I mean, we're talking about hundreds of millions of dollars, if not the viability of the industry as we know it, if the public learns the true extent of this E. coli problem. It'll be a thousand times worse than James Garner having to have bypass surgery after touting meat for us." Bobby Bo giggled at his own joke.

"I'm worried about the doctor causing trouble in relation to Marsha Baldwin," Shanahan said.

"Yeah, well, that too," Bobby Bo said.

"What about Carlos?" Shanahan asked. "He's really angry at this point. He's willing to do it for nothing. It's become a matter of pride."

"What's been the upshot of this last botched attempt?" Bobby Bo asked. "Have the police been called? Do I have a lot of media nonsense to look forward to?"

"Apparently not," Shanahan said. "We've monitored the scanner all afternoon and evening. There's been nothing."

"Thank God for small favors," Bobby Bo said. "I'll tell you what. Make the arrangements with Leutmann, but if the situation presents itself, let Carlos have one more chance. What do you think?"

"Leutmann will demand a down payment just to come here," Shanahan said. "It's not the kind of thing we can get back."

"So we save two and a half K," Bobby Bo said. "Plus we have our bases covered. One way or the other, we'll be rid of this pesky doctor."

"Okay," Shanahan said. "I'll get right on it."

"Good," Bobby Bo said. "Just make sure that the next time you talk to me, it's good news."

"I'll make it my personal responsibility," Shanahan said.

"One other thing," Bobby Bo said. "Get some bio on this doctor. When Leutmann gets here, I want him to know how to find him without screwing around."

○    ○    ○

The emergency room at the University Medical Center was as busy as usual. Kim and Tracy were in the waiting room, sitting in seats close to where they'd been when they'd waited with Becky. Kim was holding a sterile four-by-four gauze pad against his laceration.

"This is a rather unpleasant déjà vu," Kim commented.

"Seems like a year ago since we were here," Tracy said wistfully. "I can't believe so much could happen in so few days."

"In some respects it seems like a long time and in others like a blink of the eye," Kim said. He gritted his teeth. "I can't help but wonder if things wouldn't have turned out much differently if Becky had been seen quicker on that first visit and cultures taken."

"I posed that question to Dr. Morgan," Tracy said. "She didn't think it would have mattered that much."

"It seems hard to believe," Kim said.

"Why didn't you want to call one of your surgical friends to sew you up?" Tracy asked.

"For some of the same reasons I didn't want to call the police," Kim said. "I just want to have it stitched and be done with it. I don't want there to be a big rigmarole. With a friend there'd be questions, and I'd feel guilty about lying."

"They'll undoubtedly ask you how it happened even here," Tracy said. "What will you tell them?"

"I don't know," Kim said. "I'll think of something."

"How long do you think we'll have to wait?" Tracy asked.

"According to David Washington, not long," Kim said.

By chance they'd run into the evening ER head when they'd first arrived. He'd heard about Becky's passing and had offered his deepest sympathies. He'd also promised to get Kim in and out of the ER as soon as possible and was unconcerned when Kim told him he wanted to use an alias.

For a while they sat in silence while mindlessly watching the pathetic parade of the sick and injured that passed in front of them. Tracy was the one who broke the silence. "The more time I have to think about what we just experienced, the less inclined I am to allow you to go through with what you're planning. I mean, it's plainly self-destructive for you to even consider going into Higgins and Hancock after everything that's occurred."

"What do you mean, allow me?" Kim questioned irritably while still musing about the ER visit with Becky. "What are you going to do, physically stand in my way?"

"Please, Kim," Tracy said. "I'm trying to have a conversation with you. Because of what's happened to Becky, I'm worried about whether you're capable of making reasonable decisions. It seems clear to me that getting a job in Higgins and Hancock is too risky."

"It might be risky," Kim said. "But there's no other choice. It's the only way to get the media involved, and the media is our only hope of doing anything about this sorry situation."

"What can you hope to accomplish in Higgins and Hancock to justify the risk?" Tracy said. "I mean specifically."

"That I can't say until I get in there," Kim admitted. "Never having been in a slaughterhouse, I don't know what to expect. But I know what I'm interested in and what the issues are. The first concerns how Becky got sick. Marsha Baldwin discovered something about the head of the last animal slaughtered on January ninth. I want to find out what it was. The second issue is Marsha Baldwin's disappearance; somebody's got to know something. And lastly there is the issue about how E. coli generally gets into the meat. Marsha suggested it has something to do with the way they slaughter the animals. I want to see it with my own eyes and then document it. Once I have, I'll get Kelly Anderson involved. Exposing the USDA angle will be up to her."

Tracy stared off in the middle distance.

"You're not going to respond?" Kim commented after a short silence.

"Sure," Tracy said, as if waking from a minitrance. "You make it all sound so reasonable. But I'll tell you something. I'm not going to allow you to go by yourself. I've got to be involved in some form or fashion so that I can help if need be, even if I have to get a job too."

"You're serious!" Kim said. He was amazed.

"Of course I'm serious," Tracy said. "Becky was my daughter too. I don't think you should be the only one taking the risk."

"Well, that's an interesting idea," Kim said. Now it was his time to stare off while he pondered.

"I wouldn't even have to worry about a disguise," Tracy added. "They've never seen me."

"I don't know whether you could get a job," Kim said. "At least not easily."

"Why not?" Tracy asked. "If you could get a job, why couldn't I?"

"Marsha said they were in constant need of help but only in the actual slaughtering side of the business," Kim said. "I don't think you're ready for that."

"No, but maybe they could use me as a secretary or something along those lines," Tracy said. "We don't know unless I try."

"I've got a better idea," Kim said. "Remember Lee Cook who worked for me back at the Samaritan?"

"I think so," Tracy said. "Wasn't he that clever technician who could fix anything electronic and who kept all the sophisticated electronic equipment functioning at the hospital?"

"You got it," Kim said. "After the merger, he retired. He's building his own airplane in his basement and doing other odd jobs. But I'm sure he could wire me up with a bug. In that way you can be in the car in the parking lot listening in real time. Then, if need be, you can use your cell phone to call for the cavalry."

"You mean so I could hear you all the time?" Tracy asked.

"Yeah, continuously," Kim said.

"Could I talk with you?" Tracy asked.

"Well, I don't know about that," Kim said. "I'd have to have an earphone of some kind. That might be a giveaway. I can't imagine too many Higgins and Hancock employees wear earphones."

"I could even record what you say," Tracy said, warming to the idea.

"That's true," Kim agreed.

"What about video?" Tracy asked.

"Hey, maybe so," Kim said. "I know they have some tiny cameras nowadays. Maybe that could be the documentation we'll need for Kelly Anderson."

"Mr. Billy Rubin!" a voice called out over the heads of the waiting crowd.

Kim raised his free hand and stood up. Tracy did likewise. An ER resident dressed in all white saw them and walked over. He was carrying a clipboard with Kim's ER registration sheet attached.

"Mr. Billy Rubin?" the resident repeated. His name tag said: DR. STEVE LUDWIG, EMERGENCY MEDICINE RESIDENT. He was a brawny fellow with a ready smile and closely cropped, thinning, dirty-blond hair. "Did you know that bilirubin is a medical term?"

"No," Kim said. "I didn't have any idea."

"It is," Steve commented. "It comes from the breakdown of hemoglobin. Anyhow, let's take a look at your laceration."

Kim pulled away the four-by-four. Due to swelling, the wound was more gaping now than earlier.

"Whoa!" Steve intoned. "That's one nasty cut. We'd better get that sewn up. How did it happen?"

"Shaving," Kim said.

Tracy couldn't help but repress a smile.

# CHAPTER 16

Tracy shifted her weight impatiently. She had her arms folded and was leaning against the plaster wall of the upstairs hall. She'd positioned herself directly across from the door into the guest bath. She'd been there for almost five minutes.

"Well?" Tracy called through the door.

"Are you ready?" Kim's voice answered.

"I've been ready," Tracy answered. "Open the door!"

The door squeaked open. Tracy's hand shot to her mouth and she let out an involuntary giggle.

Kim looked completely different. His hair was unevenly cut short, teased to stand mostly upward, and bleached platinum blond. His eyebrows matched his hair in color and formed a stark contrast with the dark stubble-covered face. The sutured laceration wrapping over the bridge of his nose and extending through one blond eyebrow gave him a Frankenstein look. He was dressed in a black, double-flap pocket corduroy shirt over a black T-shirt with black leather pants. He had a black leather belt and matching bracelet decorated with stainless-steel rivets. The outfit was topped off with a fake diamond-stud earring in his left earlobe and a tattoo of a wolf with the word "lobo" on his right upper arm.

"So what do you think?" Kim asked.

"You look bizarre!" Tracy said. "Especially with the black silk stitches. I'd hate to run into you in a dark alley."

"That sounds like the effect I was striving for," Kim said.

"You certainly don't look like anybody I'd want to know," Tracy added.

"In that case maybe I should swing by the hospital," Kim suggested. "Maybe with this outfit they'll reinstate my privileges without a hearing."

"A doctor is the last thing I'd suspect you were," Tracy said with another laugh. "I particularly like the tattoo."

Kim lifted his arm to admire his handiwork. "Pretty cool, huh?" he said. "The directions guaranteed it would last for three or four days, provided I don't shower. Can you imagine?"

"Where's the microphone?" Tracy asked.

"Right here under my collar," Kim said. He rolled over the upper edge of the shirt. A tiny microphone was safety-pinned to the underside.

"Too bad video was out of the question," Tracy said.

"Hey, remember it's not completely out of the question," Kim said. "Lee said he'd work on it, and when he says that, nine times out of ten he comes through. It just won't be for a few days."

"Let's test the audio system," Tracy suggested. "I want to make sure it's working as well as it did last night in Lee's garage."

"Good idea," Kim said. "You hop in your car and drive down to the corner. That should be just about right. Lee said it would work up to two hundred yards."

"Where will you be?" Tracy asked.

"I'll move around inside the house," Kim said. "I'll even try going down into the basement."

Tracy nodded and went down to the hall closet. She got out her coat, then called back up the stairs. "Don't forget to put in your earphone, too."

"I already have it in," Kim yelled.

Tracy went out into the crisp morning. A wind had come up during the night, blowing the storm clouds to the East. In their place was pale blue sky.

Tracy got into her car, started it, and drove to the corner as they'd discussed. She pulled to the side of the road and turned off the engine. Next she opened her driver's-side window and put a makeshift antenna on the roof of her car.

Inside the car, Tracy slipped on a pair of stereo earphones that were attached to an old-style reel-to-reel tape recorder. The tape recorder was wired to an amplifier, which in turn was connected to a transformer sitting on top of a freestanding car battery.

A red light on the front panel of the amplifier illuminated when Tracy turned the unit on. She heard some brief static in her earphones, but it cleared quickly. On top of the amplifier was a microphone. Tracy picked it up.

After glancing outside her car to make sure none of her neighbors were watching, she spoke into the microphone.

"Kim, can you hear me?" she asked.

Kim's voice came back so loud, Tracy winced. "I can hear you like you were standing right next to me," he said.

Tracy quickly turned down the volume and pressed the start button on the tape recorder.

"How's your volume?" Tracy asked. "You were much too loud on this end."

"It's fine," Kim said.

"Where are you?" Tracy asked.

"I'm in the back part of the basement," Kim said. "If it works here, I'm pretty sure it's going to work anyplace."

"It is surprisingly clear," Tracy admitted.

"Well, come on back," Kim said. "Let's get this show on the road."

"Ten-four," Tracy said. She had no idea what the expression meant but had heard it in lots of movies and TV shows.

She took off the headphones and stopped the tape. She rewound it and then played it. She was pleased that both sides of the conversation came through perfectly clearly.

By the time Tracy got back to the house, Kim had everything they intended to take waiting by the front door. They'd packed lunches and filled thermos bottles, banking on Kim being hired on the spot. They also had a blanket and extra sweaters for Tracy. Kim was sure it would be cold sitting in the car all day.

They stowed everything in the backseat. Kim climbed in the back, too, since the front passenger seat was taken up by the electronic equipment.

Tracy slid behind the wheel and was about to start the car when she thought of something else.

"Where's your gun?" she asked.

"It's upstairs in the guestroom," Kim said.

"I think you should have it," Tracy said.

"I don't want to carry a gun in the slaughterhouse," Kim said.

"Why not?" Tracy asked. "God forbid, what if you have to face that creep with the knife again?"

Kim considered the suggestion. There were reasons against taking it. First, Kim was afraid the gun might somehow be discovered. Second, he'd never once fired it and didn't know if he could actually shoot someone. But then he remembered the panic he'd felt when he'd been chased by the man with the knife and how he'd wished he'd had some kind of weapon.

"All right," Kim said. He opened the door, took Tracy's keys, and returned to the house. A few minutes later, he climbed back into the car and handed the keys to Tracy.

Tracy started the car and was about to back up.

"Wait a sec," Kim said. "There's something else."

Tracy turned the ignition key. The engine coughed and died. With a confused expression, she faced around at Kim. "What now?" she asked.

Kim was staring up at the house. "I was just thinking about that creep being in my house when we arrived last night," Kim said. "I don't want to be surprised like that again. It's not entirely inconceivable that they could trace me here."

"What do you propose?" Tracy asked with a shudder.

"Are any of your neighbors particularly nosy?" Kim asked. "These houses are all pretty close together."

"There's Mrs. English across the street," Tracy said. "She's an elderly widow who I swear must spend the whole day looking out the window."

"That's a start," Kim said. "Let's ask her to keep an eye out until we get back. Would you mind?"

"Not at all," Tracy said.

"But that's not enough," Kim said. "We got to have backups. It's got to be one-hundred-percent sure. How many doors into the house?"

"Just the usual front door and back door," Tracy said.

"What about the basement?" Kim asked.

"The only way into the basement is through the house," Tracy said.

"The guy last night came through the back sliders," Kim said, while thinking out loud.

"This house has no sliders," Tracy said.

"Good." He got out of the car. Tracy did the same.

"Why not do something to the doors so we'd know if they'd been opened," Tracy suggested. "I mean for someone to get in, they'd have to break a window or go through one of the doors. When we get back we can check."

"That's a good idea," Kim said. "But then what would we do?"

"Well, we sure as hell won't go in the house," Tracy said.

"Where would we go?" Kim asked. "We wouldn't want to be followed."

Tracy shrugged. "A motel, I guess."

"I know what we'll do," Kim said. "On the way out to Higgins and Hancock, we'll stop by the bank. We'll pull out our savings as a fallback. If we're really worried about being followed, credit cards aren't the best idea."

"Wow, you really are thinking ahead," Tracy said. "In that case, we might as well grab our passports too."

"Listen, I'm being serious," Kim complained.

"So am I," Tracy said. "If it gets to the point that we're that worried, I want the option of going far away."

"Fair enough," Kim said. "Let's do it."

It took them a half hour to do everything they had in mind around the house and another half hour to stop at the bank. They used separate tellers to speed things up, but it didn't work. Kim's teller had been nonplussed by his appearance and had to go back to a manager to get the signature authenticated.

"I feel a little like a bank robber," Tracy said as they walked out to the car. "I've never carried this much cash."

"I was afraid they weren't going to give me my money," Kim said. "Maybe I've overdone it a little with this disguise."

"The fact that they didn't recognize you is the important point," Tracy said.

It was mid-morning by the time they got on the freeway en route to Higgins and Hancock. The day that had started out so clear was already becoming veiled with high cirrus clouds. Midwestern winter weather rarely saw long periods of sunlight.

"What did you say to Mrs. English?" Kim asked from the backseat.

"I didn't have to say much," Tracy said. "She was delighted with the task. It's nasty to say, but I think we've given her life new meaning."

"When did you say you'd be back?" Kim asked.

"I didn't," Tracy said.

"Let's review our high school Spanish," Kim said out of the blue.

Surprised at this suggestion, Tracy glanced at Kim's reflection in the rearview mirror. In the last twenty-four hours she couldn't tell when he was kidding and when he was being serious.

"I want to try to speak with a Spanish accent," Kim explained. "Marsha said that a lot of the slaughterhouse workers are Hispanic, mostly Mexican."

For the next few minutes, they counted in Spanish and constructed simple sentences. Neither could remember much vocabulary. They soon fell silent.

"Let me ask you something," Tracy said after they'd driven for a few miles without conversation.

"Shoot," Kim said.

"If all goes well," Tracy said, "and we succeed in getting Kelly Anderson to cover the story and make it a big exposé, what would you hope would happen?"

"I'd like to see no market for the twenty-five billion pounds of ground meat produced each year," Kim said.

"And then what?" Tracy asked.

"Well," Kim said while he put his thoughts in order. "I'd want the public to demand that meat and poultry inspection plus farm-animal feed approval be taken away from the USDA. It would be better if it were given to the FDA, which doesn't have a conflict of interest. Or better still, I'd like to see the system privatized so that there'd be a true competitive incentive for finding and eliminating contamination."

"You don't put much stock in this new meat irradiation movement?" Tracy asked.

"Hell, no," Kim said. "That's just the industry's way of copping out. Allowing meat irradiation is just an invitation for the industry to allow that much more contamination to get in during processing in the hopes it will all be killed with the gamma rays at the end. You'll notice even with irradiation the industry insists the onus is on the consumers to handle and cook the meat in a way the industry considers proper."

"That was Kathleen Morgan's position as well," Tracy said.

"It should be any thinking person's position," Kim said. "We've got to get the media to make people understand that contamination must not be tolerated even if it means the product will cost a little more."

"This is all a very tall order," Tracy commented.

"Hey, we might as well aim high," Kim said. "And it's not impossible. After all, meat and poultry weren't always contaminated. It's a relatively recent phenomenon."

In the distance, stockyards came into view. Consistent with its being a workday, herds of cattle could be seen milling about the muddy enclosure.

"It's kinda sad," Tracy said, looking out over the sea of animals. "It's like they're all facing the death penalty."

Tracy turned into the Higgins and Hancock parking lot. In contrast with their visit the previous morning, it was mostly full. A large proportion of the vehicles were aged pickup trucks.

"How about dropping me off near the front entrance," Kim said.

"Then I suggest you drive over to the end of the building. You won't be so noticeable there and the entire plant will be well within two hundred yards."

Tracy pulled over to the curb. She and Kim looked at the building. The record-room window that Kim had broken was unboarded, and its missing glass and mullions were apparent. Standing in the flowerbed in front of the window was a man in overalls and a red plaid shirt, taking measurements.

"I feel like I should offer to help," Kim said.

"Don't be silly," Tracy said.

The front door opened. Tracy and Kim instinctively slid down low in their seats. Two men came out of the front door, engrossed in conversation. Then the pair walked away. The plant was obviously in operation.

Tracy and Kim straightened up. They looked at each other and smiled nervously.

"We're acting like a couple of teenagers preparing to pull off a prank," Kim said.

"Maybe we should talk this over some more," Tracy said.

"Time for talk is over," Kim said. He leaned toward Tracy and gave her a kiss. It was the first time they'd kissed for longer time than either cared to remember. "Wish me luck," Kim added.

"I don't know why I agreed to all this," Tracy said. She looked out at the slaughterhouse with misgivings.

"You agreed out of civic responsibility," Kim said with an impish smile. "Hell, if we can pull this off, we'll be saving a million times more lives than I could with a lifetime of surgery."

"You know what I find the most amazing about all this?" Tracy said, looking back at Kim. "Within a couple of days, you've gone from a narcissist to an altruist, from one extreme to another. I used to be under the impression that personalities couldn't change."

"I'll let you psychologists worry about that," Kim said as he opened the car door.

"Be careful," Tracy admonished.

"I will," Kim said. He climbed out of the car but then leaned back inside. "Remember, I'm only going to put my earphone in my ear on rare occasions. For the most part this is going to be a one-way conversation."

"I know," Tracy said. "Good luck."

"Thanks," Kim said. "See ya!" He waved goodbye.

Tracy watched Kim saunter toward the door in character with his outrageous disguise. Despite her apprehensions, she had to smile. He had the carefree, brazen look of a punk-rock drifter.

With the car back in gear, Tracy drove down to the end of the plant as Kim had suggested and parked behind a van. After rolling down the window, she put the antenna on top of the car. With the stereo headphones in place, she turned on the amplifier. After the experience that morning with the volume, she had the dial all the way down. Carefully she turned it up. When she did, she immediately heard Kim's voice with an overdone Spanish accent.

"I need a job, any job," Kim was saying, drawing out his vowels. "I'm flat broke. I heard in town you were hiring."

Tracy hit the start button on the tape recorder, then tried to make herself comfortable.

○   ○   ○

Kim had been both impressed and encouraged by the speed with which he'd been escorted into the office of the kill-floor supervisor. His name was Jed Street. He was a nondescript man with a slight paunch bulging his long white, bloodstained coat. On the corner of his desk was a yellow plastic construction helmet. In front of him was a large stack of cattle purchases receipts.

Jed had looked quizzically at Kim when Kim had first come through the door. But after a few moments, he'd seemingly accepted Kim's appearance and made no mention of it whatsoever.

"Have you ever worked in a slaughterhouse before?" Jed asked. He rocked back in his desk chair and played with a pencil with both hands.

"No," Kim said casually. "But there's always the first time."

"Do you have a Social Security number?" Jed asked.

"Nope," Kim said. "I was told I didn't need one."

"What's your name?" Jed asked.

"José," Kim said. "José Ramerez."

"Where are you from?"

"Brownsville, Texas," Kim said with more of a southern drawl than a Spanish accent.

"Yeah, and I'm from Paris, France," Jed said, seemingly oblivious to Kim's verbal faux pas. He rocked forward. "Look, this is hard, sloppy work. Are you ready for that?"

"I'm ready for anything," Kim said.

"Do you have a green card?" Jed asked.

"Nope."

"When are you willing to start?"

"Hey, I'm ready to start right now," Kim said. "I haven't eaten anything for a day and a half."

"That's probably a good thing," Jed said, "considering you've never been working in a slaughterhouse before. I'm going to have you start out sweeping the kill-room floor. It's five bucks an hour, cash. With no Social Security card, that's the best I can do."

"Sounds good," Kim said.

"One other thing," Jed said. "If you want to work, you gotta work the three-to-eleven cleanup shift too, but just for tonight. One of the guys called in sick. What do you say?"

"I say okay," Kim responded.

"Good," Jed said. He got to his feet. "Let's get you outfitted."

"You mean I have to change clothes?" Kim asked anxiously. He could feel the gun pressing up against his thigh and the audio system's battery packs pressing against his chest.

"Nah," Jed said. "You only need a white coat, boots, hard hat, gloves, and a broom. The only thing you have to change are your shoes to get the boots on."

Kim followed Jed out of the supervisor's office and along the back corridor. They went into one of the storerooms Kim had looked into Saturday night. Kim got everything Jed had mentioned except the broom. For the boots, he had to settle for elevens. They were out of ten and a halfs. They were yellow rubber and came to midcalf. They weren't new and didn't smell good.

Jed gave Kim a combination lock and took him to the locker room off the lunchroom. He waited while Kim changed into the boots and stored his shoes. Once Kim had on the hard hat, the yellow gauntlet-length gloves, and the white coat, he looked like he belonged.

"That's quite a cut you got on your nose," Jed commented. "What happened?"

"A glass storm door broke," Kim said evasively.

"Sorry to hear that," Jed said. "Well, you ready for the plunge?"

"I guess," Kim said.

Jed led Kim out through the lunchroom and up the half flight of stairs to the fire door. There he paused and waited for Kim to catch up. He took something out of his pocket and extended his hand to Kim.

"I almost forgot these buggers," Jed said. He dropped two small, weightless objects into Kim's waiting palm.

"What are these?" Kim asked.

"Earplugs," Jed said. "There's a lot of noise out on the kill floor from the overhead rails and the power skinners and saws."

Kim examined one of the small, cone-shaped, sponge-rubberlike earplugs. They too were yellow.

"Listen," Jed said. "Your job is to move around the floor and push the shit on the floor into the grates."

"Shit?" Kim asked.

"Yeah," Jed said. "You have a problem with that?"

"Real shit?"

"Well, a mixture of cow shit, barf, and gore," Jed said. "Whatever falls down from the line. This isn't a tea party. And, by the way, watch out for the moving carcasses suspended from the rails, and, of course, watch out for the slippery floor. Falling down is no picnic." Jed laughed.

Kim nodded and swallowed. He was really going to have to steel himself for the gruesome aspects of this job.

Jed checked his watch. "It's less than an hour before we stop the line for the lunch break," he said. "But no matter. It'll give you a chance to get acclimated. Any questions?"

Kim shook his head.

"If you do," Jed said, "you know where my office is."

"Right," Kim said. It seemed Jed was waiting for an answer.

"Aren't you going to put in those earplugs?" Jed said.

"Oh yeah," Kim said. "I forgot." Kim pushed the little spongy plugs into his ear and gave a thumbs-up sign to Jed.

Jed threw open the door. Even with the earplugs, Kim was initially bowled over by the cacophony of noise that exploded into the stairwell.

Kim followed Jed out onto the kill floor. It was a far different place than it had been on Saturday night. Kim thought he'd prepared himself for the experience awaiting him, but he hadn't. Instantly he turned green at the sight of the overhead conveyer carrying the suspended, hot, thousand-plus-pound carcasses combined with the whine of all the power machinery, and the horrid smell. The thick, warm air was laden with the stench of raw flesh, blood, and fresh feces.

Kim was equally overwhelmed by the visual impact of the spectacle. The powerful roof air conditioners, vainly struggling to keep the room temperature down, caused the fifty or so skinned dead animals currently in Kim's line of sight to steam. Hundreds of workers in blood-spattered white coats were standing on the raised metal-grate catwalks elbow to elbow, laboring on the carcasses as they streaked by. Powerlines draped about the space in a bewildering fashion, like pieces of a huge spiderweb. It was a surreal, Dantesque image of the inferno: a hell on earth.

Jed tapped Kim on the shoulder and pointed at the floor. Kim's eyes lowered. The kill floor was a literal sea of blood, pieces of internal organs, vomitus, and watery cow diarrhea. Jed tapped Kim again. Kim looked up. Jed was about to hand him a broom, when he saw the color of Kim's face and that Kim's cheeks were involuntarily billowing outward.

Jed took a cautionary step backward while hastily pointing off to the side.

Kim retched but managed to slap a hand to his face. He followed Jed's pointing finger and saw a door with a crudely painted sign that read: GENTS.

Kim made a beeline for the bathroom. He yanked open the door and dashed to the sink. Leaning forward on the cold porcelain, he convulsively vomited up the breakfast he'd shared with Tracy that morning.

When the retching finally stopped, he rinsed out the sink and raised his head to look at himself in the cracked, dirty mirror. He was paler than he'd ever remembered, emphasized by his reddened, congested eyes. Beads of perspiration rimmed his forehead.

Supporting his torso against the sink, he fumbled with the earphone that he had coiled beneath his shirt. With trembling fingers he plucked out one of the earplugs Jed had given him and pushed in the earphone.

"Tracy, are you there?" Kim questioned with a raspy voice. "I've got my earphone in. You can talk."

"What happened?" Tracy asked. "Was that you coughing?"

"It was more than coughing," Kim admitted. "I just lost my breakfast."

"You sound terrible," Tracy said. "Are you all right?"

"I'm not great," Kim admitted. "I'm embarrassed at my reaction. With all my medical training, I didn't think I'd react quite so viscerally. This place is . . . well, it's indescribable." He looked around the room, which was the filthiest men's room he'd ever been in. The walls were covered with stains and smutty graffiti, mostly in Spanish. The tiled floor looked like it had never been mopped and was covered with a film of blood and other debris tracked in from the kill floor.

"You want to call it quits?" Tracy asked. "I can't say I'd mind."

"Not yet," Kim said. "But I'll tell you; I was only out on the kill floor for twenty seconds, and I think I've become an instant vegetarian."

The sudden sound of a flushing toilet in one of the two stalls lining the side of the men's room made Kim jump. He'd not bothered to check if either of the toilets was occupied. He yanked out the earphone, tucked it and its wire back under his shirt, and turned to the sink to pretend he was washing. Behind him he heard the stall door bang open.

Kim worried what the stranger had heard, and for the moment he didn't look in the man's direction. In the mirror he saw the man pass slowly behind him, studying him quizzically; and Kim's heart leaped up into his throat. It was the man who'd attacked him, first there at Higgins and Hancock and then again in his own home!

Slowly Kim turned around. The man had proceeded to the door but hadn't opened it. He was still staring at Kim inscrutably.

For an instant, Kim locked eyes with the stranger. Kim tried to smile as he pretended to look for paper towels. There was a dispenser but its front was ripped away and its interior was empty. Kim hazarded another glance at the stranger. His enigmatic expression had not changed. Kim's right hand sought the comfort of the gun in his pocket.

Seconds seemed like minutes to Kim. The man's cold, black impenetrable eyes remained riveted on him. The man was like a statue. It took all of Kim's self-control not to say something to break the uncomfortable silence.

To Kim's utter relief, the man suddenly broke off the confrontation, pushed open the door, and disappeared.

Kim exhaled. He'd not even been aware that he'd been holding his breath. Bending his head down, he whispered into his concealed microphone: "Good Lord, the knife-wielding madman was in one of the toilet stalls. I don't know what he heard. He stared at me but didn't say anything. Let's hope to hell he didn't recognize me."

After splashing some cold water on his face, and replacing the earplug, Kim took a deep breath and pushed out through the bathroom door to return to the kill floor. He tried to breathe shallowly through his mouth to avoid the smell. His legs felt a little rubbery. Just in case the stranger was waiting for him, he had a hand in his pocket, gripping the snub-nosed pistol.

Jed was standing close by, obviously waiting for Kim. Kim looked for the stranger, and he thought he caught sight of him off to the side, just disappearing around the edge of a distant piece of machinery.

"You all right?" Jed shouted over the din.

Kim nodded and tried to smile.

Jed gave him a wry smile in return and handed him the long-handled, stiff-bristled broom. "You must have had more in your stomach than you thought," he said. Then he patted Kim on the back before walking off.

Kim swallowed and shuddered to stave off another wave of nausea. He put his head down to avoid looking at the line of headless, skinless carcasses moving rapidly in front of him on their way to the cooler. Grasping the broom in both hands, he tried to concentrate on pushing the offal that covered the floor toward one of the many grates.

"I don't know if you can hear me with all this noise," Kim said with his mouth close to his microphone. "Obviously the guy with the knife works here, which, when I think about it, doesn't surprise me. I think I better locate him."

Kim ducked as one of the thousand-plus-pound, steaming carcasses brushed by him. By not looking where he was moving, he'd inadvertently gotten in the way of the overhead conveyer. Now his white coat had a blood stain just like everyone else's in the vast room.

Kim straightened up, and after judging the speed of the carcasses, stepped through the line. He was intent on following the route taken by the man who'd attacked him.

"Obviously I've been given the worst job in the place," Kim commented, hoping that Tracy could hear him despite the general racket. "I'm the lowest of the low but at least it gives me the opportunity to move around. It's like an assembly line for all the other workers. They stay in the same place while the carcasses move."

Kim moved around the monstrous piece of machinery he'd seen the stranger disappear behind. The floor in this area of the room was relatively clean. There was only a small amount of blood that had seeped beneath the equipment. To Kim's left was a wall.

Kim continued forward. Ahead, in a darker area of the room where there were no ceiling fluorescent lights, he could see several men working. A new sound emerged from the general background noise. It was an intermittent percussive sound that made Kim think of the kind of air gun used in carpentry to shoot nails.

Kim continued to sweep with his broom although there was little debris on the floor. After another twenty feet and rounding another piece of equipment, he could see what part of the room he was in.

"I've come to where the live animals enter the building," Kim said into his microphone. "They're funneled into single file. When the lead animal comes abreast of an elevated platform, a man presses what looks like a jackhammer against the top of its head. It sounds like a nail gun. It must shoot a bolt into their skulls because I can see brain tissue spatter out."

Kim looked away for a moment. As a man who'd dedicated his life to saving lives, this unabated carnage made him feel weak. After a moment, he forced himself to look back.

"The cows immediately collapse onto a large rotating drum that throws them forward and upends them," Kim continued. "Then a worker hooks them behind the Achilles tendon, and they are hoisted up onto the overhead conveyer.

"If and when we get mad-cow disease in this country, killing the animals like this will not be a good idea. It's undoubtedly sending emboli of brain tissue throughout the cow's body since the cows' hearts are still beating."

Despite his revulsion about what he was witnessing, Kim forced himself to move forward. He now had an unobstructed view.

"You know something?" Kim said. "These hapless steers somehow know what's coming. They must smell death in here. They're defecating all over each other as they come down the chute. That certainly can't help the contamination . . ."

Kim stopped in midsentence. To his right and only twenty feet away was the knife-wielding stranger. Instantly he knew why the man favored knives. He was one of two people who stepped beneath the newly killed animal as it was hoisted up. With a deft flick of the wrist, he or his partner slit the throat of the animal and then jumped free of the ten-gallon shower of hot cow blood. The blood came in giant pulsating squirts as the animal's heart pumped out its life force. The blood then disappeared into a grate in the floor.

In the next second, Kim's heart leaped in his chest. Already tense from seeing his attacker so close, he overreacted when someone tapped him on the shoulder. Before he could stop himself he threw an arm up defensively.

Luckily it was Jed, and he didn't look happy. Kim's reaction had scared him as much as he had scared Kim.

"What the hell are you doing over here?" Jed shouted over the noise. The repeated concussion of the high-pressure killing instrument sounded like an evil metronome.

"I'm just trying to get oriented," Kim yelled. He shot a glance back at his attacker, but the man either hadn't seen Kim or didn't care about him. He'd stepped off to the side and was in the process of sharpening his knife with a grindstone while his partner took over the throat-slitting. Kim could see the knife clearly. It was similar to the one the man had used when he'd attacked Kim.

"Hey, I'm talking to you," Jed yelled irritably. He poked at Kim with an insistent finger. "I want you to get your ass around to where they're eviscerating. That's where the shit is, and that's where I want you to be."

Kim nodded.

"Come on, I'll show you," Jed said. He motioned for Kim to follow him.

Kim cast one last look at his attacker, who was holding up the knife to inspect its razor edge. A flash of light glinted off the blade. He didn't look in Kim's direction.

Kim shuddered and rushed after Jed.

They soon came to the moving line of carcasses. Kim was impressed by Jed's nonchalance. When he ducked through he actually pushed the bodies aside like clothes on a rack rather than waiting for a moment to dart through an opening. Kim was reluctant to touch the hot bodies. He had to hesitate like a jumper waiting to enter a jump rope that was being rapidly whipped around by two friends.

"This is where I want you," Jed yelled when Kim caught up to him. Jed made a sweeping motion with his hand. "Here's where the dirty work is done, and this is where you and your broom should hang out. Understand?"

Kim nodded reluctantly, while fighting against another wave of nausea. He was now in the area where the internal organs were being re-moved. Huge snakelike coils of intestines were sloshing out of the sus-pended carcasses onto stainless-steel tables along with quivering masses of liver, grapefruit-sized kidneys, and friable strips of pancreas.

Most of the intestines appeared to be tied off, but some weren't. Either they hadn't been tied or the tie had come loose. One way or the other, there were also a lot of cow feces on the tables and on the floor mixing with the rivers of blood.

Kim lowered the head of his broom to the floor and started pushing the slop toward one of the many grates. As he worked, he was reminded of the myth of Sisyphus and the cruel king's terrible fate. No sooner had Kim cleared an area of its filth than it became refouled with a fresh deluge of blood and offal.

Kim's only solace was the fact that his disguise must have been ade-quate. He was relatively confident that the man with the knife had not recognized him.

Kim tried his best to ignore the more grisly aspects of this ghostly workplace. Instead he concentrated on his immediate task at hand. For the next step in his undercover investigation, he'd wait until the lunch break.

○   ○   ○

Out the window, Shanahan could see a jumbo jet laboriously lumber down the runway and then ever so hesitantly lift its nose. Seemingly going much too slowly it became airborne and headed off toward a distant des-tination.

Shanahan was at Gate Thirty-two on Concourse B, waiting for the flight from Chicago. It had not been easy getting there. The people at se-curity had tried to deny him access to the concourse without a ticket. Since he'd made specific plans to meet Leutmann at the gate, Shanahan knew he had to get there. Unfortunately no amount of arguing or cajol-ing had swayed the security people. To solve the dilemma, Shanahan had had to purchase a ticket on a flight he didn't intend to take.

Shanahan and Derek had never met. To overcome that difficulty Shanahan had described himself so that Derek might recognize him. But to make certain Derek would identify him, Shanahan had also said he'd carry a bible. Derek had said he'd thought a bible was a nice touch. He added that he'd be carrying a black briefcase.

The door to the jetway for the Chicago flight opened and was secured by an agent. Almost immediately the passengers began disembarking. Shanahan picked up the bible and stood. He gazed at each passenger expectantly.

The tenth person looked promising, although the individual's appearance was not anything like Shanahan had expected. The man was thirty-ish, slender, blond, and deeply tanned. He was dressed in a pinstriped business suit and carried a black ostrich briefcase. Sunglasses were perched on top of his carefully coiffed head. The man halted just inside the terminal and swept the area with his blue eyes. Spotting Shanahan, he walked directly over.

"Mr. O'Brian?" Derek questioned. He had a slight English accent.

"Mr. Leutmann," Shanahan said. He was taken aback. From Derek's phone voice he'd expected a dark, heavyset, physically imposing individual. The man in front of him resembled an English aristocrat more than a hired killer.

"I trust you brought the money," Derek said.

"Of course," Shanahan said.

"Would you mind handing it over," Derek said.

"Here in the terminal?" Shanahan questioned. He looked over his shoulder nervously. Shanahan had hoped to discuss the money issue in the privacy of his car in the parking garage. He was supposed to try to negotiate down both the down payment and the fee.

"Either we're in business or not," Derek said. "It's best to find out immediately to avoid hard feelings."

Shanahan removed the envelope he had in his inner jacket pocket and gave it to Derek. It contained five thousand dollars, half of the ten K the killer had demanded. There was no way Shanahan was going to try to bargain in public.

To Shanahan's horror, Derek put down his briefcase, blithely tore open the envelope, and counted the money. Shanahan anxiously looked around. Although no one appeared to be paying them any attention, Shanahan was acutely uncomfortable.

"Excellent," Derek commented, before pocketing the cash. "We're in business. What are the details you are supposed to provide me?"

"Could we at least start walking?" Shanahan managed to say despite a dry throat. Derek's nonchalance was unnerving.

"Of course," Derek said. He gestured down the concourse. "Why don't we proceed to baggage claim?"

Thankful to at least be moving, Shanahan started out. Derek stayed abreast, treading lightly on crepe-soled loafers.

"You have checked baggage?" Shanahan asked. It was something else he didn't expect.

"Of course," Derek said. "The airlines frown on firearms in the cabin. In my line of work, one has little choice."

They were walking along with a stream of other arriving passengers. To their left passed an equal number of people clutching tickets and hurrying in the opposite direction. There was no privacy.

"We have a car for you," Shanahan said.

"Excellent," Derek said. "But at the moment I'm more interested in the identity of the quarry. What's the name?"

"Reggis," Shanahan said. "Dr. Kim Reggis." Once again he scanned the faces around them. Thankfully there were no signs of interest or recognition. "Here's a recent photo," Shanahan said. He handed the picture to Derek. It wasn't very good. It had been copied from a newspaper article.

"This is quite grainy," Derek said. "I'm going to need more information."

"I've put together a bio," Shanahan said. He handed the paper to Derek. "You'll notice it has a physical description of the man. There's also the year, model, and type of his car along with the tag number. You have his address, but we have reason to believe he's not staying there at the moment."

"This is more like it," Derek said as he scanned the sheet. "Yes, indeed. Very complete."

"We believe Dr. Reggis spent last night at his former wife's residence," Shanahan said. "She bailed him out of jail yesterday morning."

"Jail?" Derek questioned. "Sounds like the doctor has been misbehaving."

"That's an understatement as far as we are concerned," Shanahan said.

They reached the baggage carousel and pressed in among the other passengers. The baggage from Derek's flight was just beginning to appear.

"There's one thing that I think you ought to know," Shanahan said. "There was a botched attempt on the doctor's life last night."

"Thank you for your forthrightness," Derek said. "That is indeed an important point. What you mean to say, of course, is that the man will be highly vigilant."

"Something like that," Shanahan said.

A shrill beeping sound made the tense Shanahan jump. It took him a moment to realize it was his pager. Surprised at being paged since Bobby Bo knew where he was and what he was doing, Shanahan snapped the pager off his belt and glanced at the small LCD screen. He was further confused because he didn't recognize the number.

"Would you mind if I used a phone?" Shanahan said. He pointed to a bank of pay phones lining a nearby wall.

"Not at all," Derek said. He was contentedly studying the information sheet on Kim.

Finding a few coins in his pocket en route to the phone, Shanahan quickly dialed the mysterious number. The phone was picked up on the first ring. It was Carlos.

"The doctor is here!" Carlos said in an excited, forced whisper.

"Where the hell are you talking about?" Shanahan asked.

"Here at Higgins and Hancock," Carlos said, keeping his voice low. "I'm using the phone in the lunchroom. This has to be fast. The doctor is working here as a slop boy. He looks crazy, man."

"What are you talking about?" Shanahan asked.

"He looks weird," Carlos said. "He looks like an old rock singer. His hair's cut short and what's left is blond."

"You're joking," Shanahan said.

"No, man!" Carlos insisted. "He's also got stitches on his face where I cut him. It's him, I know it is, although I had to look at him for a couple of minutes before I was sure. Then he came all the way around to my station and stood there for a couple of minutes until the boss came and dragged him away."

"What boss?" Shanahan asked.

"Jed Street," Carlos said.

"Did the doctor recognize you?" Shanahan asked.

"Sure, why not?" Carlos said. "He was staring at me. For a minute I was thinking he might come after me, but he didn't. If he had I would have done him in. You want me to do it anyway? I can get him while he's here?"

"No!" Shanahan shouted, losing control of himself for a moment. He knew that if Carlos killed Kim in the middle of the day with a hundred witnesses it would be a disaster. Shanahan took a deep breath and then spoke quietly and slowly. "Don't do anything. Pretend you don't recognize him. Just stay cool. I'll get word to you. Understand?"

"I want to do this guy," Carlos said. "I told you I don't want the money."

"That's very generous of you," Shanahan said. "Of course, you were the one who screwed up to begin with, but that's not the point at the moment. I'll get word to you, okay?"

"Okay," Carlos said.

Shanahan hung up the phone. He kept his hand on the receiver while he looked over at Derek Leutmann. This was a quandary. For the moment he didn't know what to do.

An unexpected tapping on the driver's-side window made Tracy's heart skip a beat. During the time that she'd been parked at the end of the slaughterhouse, she'd seen occasional people coming and going from their vehicles. But no one had come near her car. Hastily Tracy pulled off the stereo headphones and turned to look out the window.

Standing next to the car was a grisly man clad in soiled overalls and a dirty turtleneck. On his head was a baseball hat turned backwards. Glued to his lower lip was an unlit cigarette that bobbed up and down as he breathed through his open mouth.

Tracy's first impulse was to start the car and drive away. That idea was abandoned when she remembered the antenna teetering on the roof. Feeling she had little choice, she cracked the window.

"I saw you from my truck," the man said. He pointed over his shoulder at a neighboring van.

"Oh, really," Tracy responded anxiously. She didn't know what else to say. The man had a vivid scar that ran down the side of his face onto his neck.

"Whatcha listening to?" the man asked.

"Not much," Tracy said. She looked over at the tape recorder. It was still rolling. "Just some music."

"I like country music," the man said. "You listening to country music?"

"No," Tracy said with a weak smile. "This is more New Age. Actually, I'm waiting for my husband. He's working here."

"I've been doing some plumbing work here myself," the man said. "They got more drains and pipes here than anyplace in the county. Anyhow, I was wondering if you've got a light. I can't find my lighter noplace."

"Sorry," Tracy said. "I wish I could help you, but I don't smoke, and I don't have any matches."

"Thanks anyway," the man said. "Sorry to bother you."

"No bother," Tracy said.

The man walked away, and Tracy breathed a sigh of relief. She rolled up the window. The episode made her realize how tense she was. She'd been on edge from the moment Kim had disappeared inside, but her anxieties had skyrocketed ever since Kim's confrontation with the killer in the bathroom. The fact that she'd not been able to talk to Kim didn't help. She truly wanted to tell him to get out of there: It just wasn't worth it.

After a furtive glance around to make sure no one else was watching her, Tracy slipped the stereo headphones back on and closed her eyes. The problem was she had to concentrate to hear what Kim was saying. The general din inside the plant had forced her to turn the volume down quite low.

○   ○   ○

Kim had moved all the way around the eviscerating area and now had a view of the whole slaughtering process. He could see the cows being killed, hoisted up, and their throats being slit. Next they were skinned and decapitated with the heads going off on a separate overhead conveyer system. After the evisceration the carcasses were sawed in half lengthwise by a frightful saw far beyond the gruesome conceptions of Hollywood horror movie producers.

Kim glanced at his watch to time the rapidity with which the wretched animals were killed. He was astonished. With his chin down on his chest he spoke into his microphone.

"Let's hope Lee Cook can come up with an appropriate video system," he said. "It's going to be a snap to document Marsha's major point. She said the problem concerning contamination in the meat industry was in the slaughterhouse. She said it was simply profit over safety. I just timed the activity here. They're slaughtering the cattle at the unbelievable rate of one every twelve seconds. At that speed, there's no way to avoid gross contamination.

"And talk about collusion between the USDA and the industry; it's even evident on this operational level. Up on the catwalks there are a few inspectors. They stand out like black sheep. They wear red hard hats instead of yellow and their white coats are comparatively clean. But they're doing more laughing and joking with the workers than inspecting. I mean the inspecting is pure sham. Not only is the line moving too fast; these guys are hardly even looking at the carcasses as they whip by."

Kim suddenly caught sight of Jed Street nosing around the eviscerating tables and sinks. Kim recommenced his sweeping with his push broom. He moved away from Jed in a counterclockwise direction and soon found himself in the decapitation area. The beheading was done by another saw only slightly less appalling than the saw used to cut the carcasses in two. Just before the spine was completely severed by the man wielding the saw, another man caught the hundred-plus-pound head with a hook dangling from the head conveyer rail. It was a process that required coordination and teamwork.

Continuing his cleaning efforts, Kim followed the line of the skinned heads. With their lids gone the lifeless eyes gave the heads a curiously surprised look as they clanked along.

Kim followed the head conveyer to a point where it disappeared through an aperture into an adjoining room. Kim immediately recognized the room as the place where he'd been attacked Saturday night.

Glancing over his shoulder, he looked for Jed. When he didn't see him in the pandemonium, Kim took a chance that Jed wouldn't miss him and walked through the doorless opening into the head-boning room.

"I've come into the room where the heads go," Kim said into his microphone. "This is potentially important in how Becky happened to get sick. Marsha had found something in the paperwork about the head of the last animal on the day the meat for Becky's hamburger might have been slaughtered. She said it was 'revolting,' which I now find curious, since I find the whole process revolting."

Kim watched for a moment as the head conveyer dumped a head every twelve seconds onto a table where it was attacked by a team of butchers. Knives similar to the ones used to slit the animals' throats quickly cut out the huge cheek muscles and the tongues. The workers took this meat and tossed it into a two-thousand-pound combo bin similar to those Kim had seen at Mercer Meats.

"I'm learning something every minute," Kim said. "There must be a lot of cow cheeks in hamburger."

Kim noticed that after the cheeks and tongues were removed, the cow heads were pushed onto a flat conveyer belt that dumped them ignominiously into a black hole that presumably led to the basement.

"I think I might have to visit the basement," Kim said reluctantly. He had the sense that his childhood fear of basements would be put to the test.

○    ○    ○

So far it had been a good day as far as Jed Street was concerned, despite its being Monday. He'd had a great breakfast that morning, had gotten to work early enough to sit and have a second cup of coffee with several of the other supervisors, and had had to face fewer absenteeisms than usual. Finding and keeping decent help was Jed's biggest headache.

With none of his key day employees having called in sick, Jed was confident that his team would have processed close to two thousand head by the lunch break. That made Jed happy because he knew it would make his immediate boss, Lenny Striker, happy.

Jed slipped out of his white coat and hung it up. Wanting to catch up on his paperwork, he'd retreated to his office with his third cup of coffee of the day. He walked around his desk and sat down. Pen in hand, he went to work. He had a considerable number of forms that had to be filled out each and every day.

Jed hadn't been working long when his phone rang. He reached for his coffee before picking up the receiver. He was relatively unconcerned about getting a call so late in the morning and could not imagine it would be particularly serious. At the same time he knew there was always a chance. Being in charge of something as potentially dangerous as a kill floor, he knew that disaster was never far away.

"Hello," Jed said, overemphasizing the first syllable. He took a sip of coffee.

"Jed Street, this is Daryl Webster. Do you have a moment to speak with me?"

Jed spat out his coffee, then scrambled to wipe the brew off his forms. "Of course, Mr. Webster," Jed sputtered. He'd worked for Higgins and Hancock for fourteen years, and during that time the real boss had never called him.

"I got a call from one of Bobby Bo's people," Daryl explained. "He told me that we've employed a new slop boy just today."

"That's correct," Jed said. He felt his face heat up. Hiring illegal aliens was tacitly condoned while the official policy was that it was forbidden. Jed hoped to God he wasn't going to end up being a scapegoat.

"What's this man's name?" Daryl asked.

Jed frantically searched through the papers on his desk. He'd written the name down, although not on any employment forms. He breathed a sigh of relief when he found it.

"José Ramerez, sir!" Jed said.

"Did he show you any identification?" Daryl asked.

"Not that I recall," Jed said evasively.

"What did he look like?"

"He is a little strange-looking," Jed said. Jed was confused. He couldn't fathom what difference it made what the man looked like.

"Could you give me an idea?" Daryl asked.

"Kind of punk," Jed said, trying to think how his fourteen-year-old son would describe the man. "Bleached hair, earring, tattoos, leather pants."

"Is he a fairly big guy?" Daryl asked.

"Yeah, over six feet for sure."

"And he has some stitches on his face?"

"Yeah, he did," Jed said. "How did you know that, sir?"

"Did he say where he was living?" Daryl asked.

"No, and I didn't ask," Jed said. "I have to say he's been quite appreciative of getting the work. He's even agreed to work a shift and a half."

"You mean he's working tonight?" Daryl asked. "As part of the cleanup crew?"

"Yup," Jed said. "We had someone call in sick just this morning."

"That's good," Daryl said. "That's very good. Good job, Jed."

"Thank you, sir," Jed said. "Is there something you'd like me to do or to say to Mr. Ramerez?"

"No, nothing at all," Daryl said. "In fact, keep this conversation of ours confidential. Can I count on you for that?"

"Absolutely, sir," Jed said.

Jed recoiled when he heard the line disconnected. It had been so pre-cipitous. He looked quizzically at the phone for a second before hang-ing up.

O    O    O

Not wanting to be caught in the head-boning room where there was noth-ing to sweep, Kim had retreated back to the main kill floor. He still had no clue as to what Marsha was talking about when she mentioned that last head now that he'd followed the trail through most of the plant. The only unknown was what happened to the heads after disappearing down the black hole.

Kim went back to the evisceration area and reswept parts of the floor he'd already cleaned several times. The frustrating part was that in cer-tain areas, it only took about fifteen minutes to look like he'd never been there.

Despite his earplugs, he suddenly could hear a sustained raucous buzz. He straightened up from his work and looked around. He immediately saw that the cattle had been halted in the chute. No more animals were being killed. The pitiable cows close to the executioner had been given a momentary reprieve. The executioner had put aside his tool and was in the process of coiling the high-pressure hose.

The animals that had already been killed advanced through the line until the final one had been eviscerated. At that point the line was stopped, and the tremendous din was replaced by an eerie silence.

It took Kim a few moments to realize that part of the silence was due to his earplugs. When he took them out, he heard the noises of the power tools being stowed and a buzz of animated conversation. Workers started swinging down from the catwalks, while others used stairs and ladders.

Kim stopped one of the workers and asked him what was going on.

"No speak English," the worker said, before hurrying off.

Kim stopped another. "Do you speak English?" he asked.

"A little," the man said.

"What's happening?" Kim asked.

"Lunch break," the man said, before hurrying after the first.

Kim watched as the hundred or so workers streamed from the catwalks and lined up to pass through the fire door. They were en route to the lunchroom and the locker area. An equal number of employees came from the main boning room via the head-boning room. Despite the pall of death and the stench, the camaraderie was evident. There was much laughter and friendly jostling.

"How anyone could eat is beyond me," Kim said into his microphone.

Kim saw the man who'd attacked him, along with his partner. They walked by without a glance to join the ever-lengthening queue. Kim felt even more confident about his disguise.

Kim stopped one of the eviscerators whose damp white coat had become variegated with shades of pink and red. He asked the man how to get to the basement. In return, Kim got a look that suggested he was crazy.

"Do you speak English?" Kim inquired.

"Sure, man, I speak English," the eviscerator said.

"I want to go below," Kim said. "How do I get there?"

"You don't want to go downstairs," the man said. "But if you did, you'd go through that door." He pointed to an unmarked door with an automatic closer mounted on its upper edge.

Kim continued sweeping until the last worker had passed through the fire door. After all the noise and chaotic activity when the line was in operation, it was strange for Kim to be alone with forty or fifty suspended, steaming carcasses. For the first time since Kim had arrived, the floor around the evisceration area was free of gore.

Putting his broom aside, Kim walked over to the unmarked door the man had pointed out. After a quick glance over his shoulder to make sure he wasn't being observed, he pulled the door open and stepped inside. The door closed quickly behind him.

The first thing that Kim was aware of was the smell. It was ten times worse than the kill floor, which had sickened him so quickly earlier. What made it so awful was the added stench of putrefaction. Although he

retched a few times, he didn't vomit. He assumed it was because his stomach was empty.

Kim was standing on a landing above a flight of cement stairs that descended into utter blackness. Over his head was a single, bare lightbulb.
On the wall behind him was a fire extinguisher and an industrial-sized,
emergency flashlight.

Kim yanked the flashlight from its brackets and turned it on. He aimed
the concentrated beam down the stairs, revealing a long flight descending
to a deep cellar. The walls were stained with large, Rorschach-like
blotches in brown. The distant floor looked smooth and black like a pool
of crude oil.

Kim got one hand free from his rubber glove and located his earphone.
After removing his earplug, he slipped it into his ear.

"Can you hear me, Trace?" Kim said. "If you can, say something. I just
put in my earphone."

"It's about time!" Tracy said irritably. Her voice was loud and clear despite Kim's being surrounded by reinforced concrete walls. "I want you
to come out here immediately."

"Whoa," Kim said. "What are you all wound up about?"

"You're in this slaughterhouse with someone who has tried to kill you
twice," Tracy said. "This is ridiculous. I want you to give up this mad-
ness."

"I've got a little more investigating to do," Kim said. "Besides, the
knife guy hasn't recognized me, so calm down!"

"Where are you?" Tracy asked. "Why haven't you put your earphone
in until now? It's been driving me crazy not to be able to talk to you."

Kim started down the stairs. "I can't risk the earphones except when
I'm alone," he said. "As to where I am at the moment, I'm heading down
into the basement, which I have to admit is no picnic. It's like descending
into the lower circles of hell. There's no way I could describe the smell."

"I don't think you should go into the basement," Tracy said. "I like
being able to talk with you, but it's safer if you stay in a group. Besides,
you're probably not supposed to be in there, and if someone catches you,
there'll surely be trouble."

"Everybody's at lunch," Kim said. "Being caught down here is not my worry."

Breathing through his mouth to help avoid the stench, Kim reached the bottom of the stairs. He shined the flashlight beam around the vast, pitch-black space. It was a warren of vats and Dumpster-like containers. Each was connected with a duct that led upward through the ceiling to catch the blood, unwanted guts, and discarded bones and skulls.

"This is where they store everything until it gets trucked to the rendering plant," Kim said. "Obviously from the odor it's all in various stages of decay. There's no refrigeration down here. Although it's hard to imagine as bad as it smells now, it must be worse in the summertime."

"It sounds disgusting," Tracy said. "It's hard to believe that waste like that would have any use."

"The renderer turns it into fertilizer," Kim said. "And, disgustingly enough, cattle feed. The industry has forced our unwitting cattle into becoming cannibals."

"Uh-oh!" Kim mumbled as he felt a shiver descend his spine.

"What's the matter?" Tracy demanded anxiously.

"I just heard a noise," Kim said.

"Then get yourself out of there," Tracy said anxiously.

Kim shined his light in the direction of the noise. In a fashion strikingly similar to the episode in his own basement the night before, a number of pairs of diabolically ruby eyes stared back at him. A second later the eyes disappeared, and Kim caught sight of a group of animals the size of house cats scampering off. Unlike the night before, they weren't mice.

"It's okay," Kim said. "It's just some monster rats."

"Oh, that's all," Tracy said sarcastically. "Just a group of friendly monster rats."

Kim stepped out onto the cellar floor and discovered that not only did the floor surface look like crude oil, it had approximately the same consistency. His boots made a rude sucking sound each time he picked up his feet.

"This is certainly a nightmare image of post-industrialization," Kim commented.

"Cut the philosophizing," Tracy snapped. "Come on, Kim! Get out of there! What on earth are you doing down there anyway?"

"I want to find the chute for the heads," Kim said.

He slogged forward among the tanks and vats, trying to estimate where the head-boning room lay above. He came to a concrete block wall which he assumed was contiguous with the wall above. That meant the chute he was looking for would be on the other side.

Kim shined his light along the wall until he located an opening. Walking down to it, he ducked through. He shined his light around this second space. It was smaller than the first and cleaner. It also had what he'd guessed. To his immediate right was a chute connected to a particularly large Dumpster.

"This looks promising," Kim said. "I think I found it. It's about the size of a construction Dumpster." With the flashlight beam, he followed the chute up to where it penetrated the ceiling. He estimated the diameter of the chute to be about the same as the aperture he'd remembered above.

"Okay, wonderful!" Tracy said. "Now come out of there."

"In a second," Kim said. "I'm going to see if I can look inside."

Kim stepped over to the rusted, filthy Dumpster-like container. In this area of the basement there was no sucking sound as he walked. Around the side of the container near where the chute was attached was a small metal platform accessible by four steps. Kim climbed up. He could now see the top of the Dumpster. Right in front of him was a hatch secured with a metal latch. He moved the latch to the side but then couldn't open the hatch. At least not with one hand.

Putting the flashlight between his knees, he got both hands under the edge of the hatch. With a squeak, it lifted. Holding it with his left hand, he raised the flashlight with his right and shined it inside. It was not a pretty image.

The container was almost brimming with rotting, skinned cattle heads. In contrast with the newly slaughtered, bloody heads upstairs, here the eyes were shriveled and the attached shards of gristle were black. In many of the heads the gaping hole made by the air gun was plainly visible.

Disgusted by the view as well as the smell, Kim was about to lower the hatch into place, when an involuntary cry of horror escaped from his lips. The flashlight beam had found a particularly gruesome sight. Partially buried by a subsequent avalanche of fresh cow skulls was Marsha's severed head!

The shock caused Kim to let go of the heavy hatch, and it slammed shut with a deafening crash in the confined space. The booming sound echoed repeatedly off distant, unseen concrete walls.

"What happened?" Tracy demanded frantically.

Before Kim could respond, a horrid screeching noise tortured both Kim's and Tracy's ears. The crashing hatch had activated some automatic machinery.

Kim snatched up the light and shone it in the direction of the dreadful noise. He saw a rusted steel overhead door rising.

Kim could hear Tracy repeatedly demand to be told what was going on, but he couldn't answer her, he truly didn't know. Behind the rising door was a filthy, forklift vehicle that suddenly came to life like a horrible, futuristic mechanical creature. Red lights on its front began to flash, washing the room with the color of blood.

As soon as the overhead door reached its apogee, the driverless vehicle began to give off high-pitched, intermittent beeps as it rolled forward in a thunderous, jerky fashion. Terrified of the imminent collision, Kim leapt from the platform and pressed himself against the wall.

The forklift crashed into the Dumpster, causing a boom even louder than the sound of the slamming hatch. The Dumpster shuddered and then raised. As the forklift backed up, the chute connecting the container with the head-boning room above became detached. When the Dumpster was completely free from the space, a second, empty Dumpster waiting next to the first slid into place with another thunderous crash. The chute automatically snapped into place.

The forklift stopped, pivoted, then rumbled off into the inky blackness.

"Kim, I don't know if you can hear me or not," Tracy shouted, "but I'm coming in!"

"No!" Kim cried into his microphone. "I'm okay. I inadvertently activated some automatic removal equipment. I'm coming out, so don't come in."

"You mean you're coming out here to the car?" Tracy asked hopefully.

"Yes," Kim said. "I need a breather."

○    ○    ○

It wasn't that Derek Leutmann didn't trust Shanahan O'Brian, but he knew there was more to this aggravating story than he'd been told. Besides, Derek had a set methodology in his work. Killing people was a business in which one could not be too careful. Rather than going directly to Kim's former wife's house as Shanahan had initially suggested, Derek went to Kim's. He wanted to test the reliability of Shanahan's information as well as learn more about his supposed quarry.

Derek drove into Balmoral Estates and directly to Kim's property without hesitation. He knew from experience that such behavior was far less suspicious than cruising the neighborhood.

Derek parked in the driveway in front of the garage. He opened his metal Zero Halliburton valise that was resting on the passenger seat next to him. Reaching in, he pulled out a nine-millimeter automatic from its custom-cut pocket in Styrofoam. With trained ease, he attached a silencer and then slipped the gun into the right pocket of his camel-hair coat. The pocket had been altered to accommodate the long weapon.

Derek got out of the car, holding his ostrich briefcase. He took a quick peek into the garage. It was empty. Then he strode up the front walk, appearing for all the world like a successful businessman or an elegant insurance adjuster. He rang the bell. Only then did he glance around at the neighborhood. From Kim's porch he could see only two other houses. Both appeared unoccupied at that moment.

He rang the bell again. When no one answered, he tried the door. He was surprised but pleased to find it unlocked. Had it not been, it wouldn't have made much difference. Derek had the tools and the expertise to handle most locks.

Without a moment's hesitation, Derek entered the house and closed the door behind himself. He stood for a moment, listening. There wasn't a sound.

Still carrying his briefcase, Derek made a rapid, silent tour of the first floor. He noticed some dirty dishes in the sink. They looked as though they'd been sitting awhile.

Climbing up to the second floor, Derek saw the splintered door leading into the master bath. He took in the broken console table. Stepping into the bath, he felt the towels. It was clear that none had been recently used. So at least that much of Shanahan's information seemed accurate.

In the walk-in closet in the master bedroom he glanced down at all the clothes littering the floor. He couldn't help but wonder exactly what had gone on during the botched hit that Shanahan had mentioned.

Back down on the first floor Derek entered the study and sat down at Kim's desk. Without removing his gloves, he began to go through some of the correspondence to see what he could learn about the man he had been brought all the way from Chicago to kill.

○    ○    ○

Tracy had backed up so that she could see along the front of Higgins and Hancock. She'd thought about driving back to the entrance but was afraid to do so because she and Kim had not discussed where she'd be when he came out. She was afraid Kim might come out one of the other doors and then be searching for her.

But she soon saw him emerge from the front door and jog in her direction. He was dressed in a white coat and had a yellow plastic construction helmet on his head. He ran up to the car, and after glancing back over his shoulder, he climbed into the backseat.

"You're paler than I've ever seen you," Tracy said. She was turned around in her seat as much as the steering wheel would allow. "But I guess the blond hair emphasizes it."

"I've just seen one of the worst things in my life."

"What?" Tracy asked with alarm.

"Marsha Baldwin's head!" Kim said. "It's probably all that's left of her, along with a few bones. As disgusting as it sounds, I'm afraid most of her must have gone for hamburger."

"Oh, God!" Tracy murmured. Her eyes locked with Kim's. She saw tears appear, and it made her respond in kind.

"First Becky and now this," Kim managed. "I feel so damn responsible. Because of me, one tragedy had to lead to another."

"I can understand how you feel," Tracy offered. "But as I've already said, Marsha was doing what she wanted to do, what she thought was right. It doesn't justify her death, but it's not your fault."

Tracy reached out toward Kim. He took her hand and squeezed it. For a few moments a wordless but powerful communication passed between the two people.

Tracy sighed, shook her head in despair, then took her hand back. She twisted around in the seat and started the engine. Before Kim had gotten to the car, she'd already hauled in the antenna.

"One thing is for sure," Tracy said, while putting the car into gear. "We're getting out of here."

"No!" Kim said. He reached forward and put a restraining hand on her shoulder. "I've got to go back. I'm going to see this to the end. Now it's for both Becky and Marsha."

"Kim, this now involves proven murder!" Tracy said evenly. "It's time for the police."

"It's only one murder," Kim said. "And one murder pales against the murder of up to five hundred kids a year that this industry is guilty of in the name of increased profit."

"Responsibility for the children might be hard to prove in court," Tracy said. "But finding the head of a person makes a startlingly clear case."

"I found the head, but I don't know where it is now," Kim said. "It was in with the cow heads, but when I slammed the cover, I activated the system to take them away. It's on its way to the renderer. So there'd be no corpus delicti even if we wanted to blow the whistle on Marsha's death. Obviously my word at the moment means nothing to the police."

"They can start their own investigation," Tracy said. "Maybe they'll find other bones."

"Even if they did," Kim said, "the issue here is not to prosecute one low-level thug like the guy who tried to kill me. It's the industry I want to do something about."

Tracy sighed again and turned off the engine. "But why go back now? You've accomplished what you set out to do. You've learned that it will be easy to document how the meat gets contaminated." Tracy tapped the tape recorder. "This tape alone might be almost as good as a video. I can tell you it's powerful stuff the way you described what's going on in there. I'm sure Kelly Anderson will jump on it."

"I want to go back mainly because I'll be working the three-to-eleven cleanup as you heard," Kim said. "I'm hoping that sometime during that shift I can get into the record room. Marsha found what she called a 'deficiency report' that involved the head of a sick animal. She said she was putting it back into the file, and I heard her do it. I want to find that paper."

Tracy shook her head in frustration. "You're taking too much of a risk," she said. "If Kelly Anderson gets on the case, let her find the deficiency report."

"I don't think I'm taking any risk at this point," Kim said. "The guy with the knife looked me right in the eye in the men's room. If I were to be recognized, that would have been the moment. In fact, I don't even want this gun anymore."

Kim struggled to get the pistol out of his pants pocket. He handed it to Tracy.

"At least keep the gun," Tracy said.

Kim shook his head. "No, I don't want it."

"Please," Tracy said.

"Tracy, I'm carrying enough stuff with these battery packs," Kim said. "And I think having it is more of a risk than a comfort."

Reluctantly Tracy took the gun and put it down on the car floor. "I can't talk you out of going back in there?"

"I want to follow this through," Kim said. "It's the least I can do."

"I hope you understand that sitting here while you are taking all this risk is driving me crazy."

"I can understand," Kim said. "Why don't you go home and just come back for me at eleven?"

"Oh, no!" Tracy said. "That would be worse. At least this way I can hear what's going on."

"Okay," Kim said. "It's your call. But I'd better get back. The lunch break is almost over."

Kim got his legs out of the car before leaning back inside. "Can I ask you to do something sometime this afternoon?" he said.

"Of course," Tracy said. "As long as I don't have to leave the car."

"Would you call Sherring Labs with your cell phone?" Kim asked. "Ask about the results on the meat I dropped off. They should be ready about now."

"Fine," Tracy said.

Kim gave her shoulder a squeeze. "Thanks," he said before climbing out. He closed the door, waved, and walked away.

○    ○    ○

Derek Leutmann slowed down as he neared Tracy's house. The numbers on some of the neighboring houses were not very apparent, and he did not want to drive by. As the house came into view he saw the Mercedes parked at the head of the drive. Not wishing to block it, Derek did a U-turn and parked across the street.

Taking out the information sheet given to him by Shanahan, Derek checked the license number of the Mercedes. His suspicions were substantiated. It was the doctor's car.

After going through the same preparations as he'd done outside of Kim's house, Derek emerged into the light rain that had begun to fall. He snapped open a small, collapsible umbrella before taking out his briefcase. With the briefcase in one hand and the umbrella in the other, he crossed the street and glanced into the car. He was surprised to see it there, thinking that it should have been with Kim at his office. Of course that suggested Kim was not at his office.

Derek knew a lot more about Kim now than he did earlier. He knew that he was a cardiac surgeon who was extremely well regarded. He knew that he was divorced and was paying considerable alimony and child support. What he didn't know was why O'Brian and his boss in the cattle business wanted the man dead.

Derek had asked Shanahan that very question and had gotten a vague answer. Derek never wanted to know the details of any of his client's dealings with a potential mark, but he wanted to know the generalities. It was another way of reducing risk not only during the hit but after. He'd tried to press Shanahan but to no avail. All he was told was that it involved business. The curious thing was that Derek had found no connection between the doctor and cattle or beef, and Derek had found a lot of information in the doctor's desk.

Most of Derek's work stemmed from problems involving money in some form or fashion with competition, gambling, divorce, and unpaid loans leading the list. Most of the people were scum whether they were clients or marks, and Derek liked it that way. This case seemed significantly different, and a sense of curiosity was added to Derek's other strong emotions. What Derek disliked the most was to be underestimated and taken advantage of. He'd not gotten into the business in the usual way via mob association. He'd been a mercenary in Africa back in the days when there had been good guys and bad guys, before any of the national armies had had any training.

Derek climbed the steps to the porch and rang the bell. With Kim's car in the drive he expected an answer, but there wasn't any. Derek rang again. He turned and surveyed the neighborhood. It was quite different from Kim's. From where Derek was standing he had a good view of five houses and a reasonable view of four more. But there was not a lot of activity. The only person he saw was a woman pushing a stroller, and she was heading away from him.

Despite a painstaking search of Kim's correspondence and records, Derek had failed to come up with any evidence suggesting the doctor had a gambling problem, so Derek reasoned that gambling couldn't have been the stimulus for Shanahan's offering him the contract. Divorce was out because the former wife had gotten a good settlement. Besides, she and the doctor were apparently getting along fine. Otherwise she certainly wouldn't have bailed him out of jail as Shanahan reported. A loan seemed equally unlikely since there had been no indication in Kim's records that he needed money, and even if he had, why would he borrow from a cattleman? That left competition. But that was the most unlikely of all. Kim didn't even own any stock in the beef industry except for a few shares in a fast-food hamburger chain. It was indeed a mystery.

Derek turned around and examined the door. It was secured with a standard throw-bolt and lock, a mere inconvenience given his experience. The question was whether there was an alarm.

Putting down his briefcase, Derek cupped his hands to peer through the sidelight. He saw no keypad. Taking out his locksmith tools from his left pocket, he made quick work of the locks. The door opened and swung inside. He looked along the inside of the jamb. There were no contacts. Stepping within the small foyer, he looked for a keypad on the portion of the walls that he'd not been able to see from the porch. There was none. Then he glanced up around the cornice for motion detectors. He relaxed. There was no alarm.

Derek retrieved his briefcase before closing the door. He made a rapid tour of the first floor before climbing to the second. In the guestroom he found a small overnight bag with a shaving kit and clothes he guessed belonged to Kim. In the only bathroom he found several sets of damp towels.

Derek went back downstairs and made himself comfortable in the living room. With Kim's car in the driveway and his things in the guestroom, Derek knew that the doctor would be back. It was only a matter of waiting.

○   ○   ○

Carlos butted the unsuspecting Adolpho out of the way and got his time card into the time clock before his partner. It was an ongoing joke they'd been playing for months.

"I'll get you next time," Adolpho joked. He made a point of speaking in English because Carlos had told him he wanted to learn to speak better.

"Yeah, over my dead body," Carlos replied. It was one of his favorite new phrases.

It had been Adolpho who'd gotten Carlos to come to Higgins and Hancock and then helped him bring his family. Adolpho and Carlos had known each other since they were kids back in Mexico. Adolpho had come to the United States several years before Carlos.

The two friends emerged into the afternoon rain arm-in-arm. Along with an army of other workers, they headed for their vehicles.

"You want to meet tonight at El Toro?" Adolpho questioned.

"Sure," Carlos said.

"Bring a lot of pesos," Adolpho advised. "You're going to lose a lot of money." He mimed using a cue stick to shoot pool.

"It will never happen," Carlos said, slapping his partner on the back. It was at that moment that Carlos saw the black Cherokee with its darkly tinted windows. The vehicle was next to his own and fumes were rising languidly from its exhaust pipe.

Carlos gave Adolpho a final pat on the back. He watched his partner get into his truck before Carlos headed for his own. Carlos took his time and waved to Adolpho as he drove by. At that point, he detoured toward the Cherokee and approached the driver's-side window.

The window went down. Shanahan smiled. "I got some good news," he said. "Come around and get in."

Carlos did as he was told. He shut the door behind him.

"You're going to have another chance to do the doctor," Shanahan said.

"I'm very happy," Carlos said. He smiled too. "When?"

"Tonight," Shanahan said. "The doctor is working here."

"I told you," Carlos said. "I knew it was him."

"There's been a bit of luck," Shanahan said with a nod. "And best of all he's working the cleanup tonight. It will be arranged that he will clean the men's room next to the record room. Do you know where that is? I don't. I've never been in Higgins and Hancock."

"Yeah, I know where it is," Carlos said. "We're not supposed to use that room."

"Well, tonight you will," Shanahan said with a wry smile. "It will be late, probably after ten. Make sure you're there."

"I'll be there," Carlos promised.

"It should be easy," Shanahan said. "You'll be dealing with an unarmed, unsuspecting person in a small room. Just make sure the body disappears like Marsha Baldwin."

"I do what you say," Carlos said.

"Just don't screw up this time," Shanahan said. "I've gone out on a limb for you, and I don't want to be embarrassed again."

"No problem!" Carlos said with emphasis. "Tonight I keeelll him!"

# CHAPTER 17

Straightening up with a groan, Kim stretched his back. Abandoning his heavy wooden-handled mop, he put his hands on his hips to get maximum extension.

Kim was by himself mopping the front hall, starting from the reception area. He'd had his earphone in for the last ten minutes, complaining to Tracy how exhausted he was. Tracy was sympathetic.

The cleaning had been extensive. The whole crew had started with high-pressure steam hoses on the kill floor. It was backbreaking work, since the hoses weighed several hundred pounds and had to be hauled up onto the catwalks.

After the kill floor, they had moved into the boning rooms. Cleaning them had taken the rest of the shift up until the dinner break at six. At that time Kim had gone back out to the car and even had had the stomach for some of the lunch he and Tracy had packed that morning.

After the dinner break, Kim had been sent out on his own on various jobs around the plant. As the others had slowed down, he'd volunteered to mop the front hall.

"I'm never going to complain about surgery being hard work again," he said into his microphone.

"After all this experience, I'll hire you to do my house," Tracy quipped. "Do you do windows?"

"What time is it?" Kim asked. He was in no mood for humor.

**319**

"It's a little after ten," Tracy said. "Less than an hour to go. Are you going to make it?"

"I'll make it, all right," Kim said. "I haven't seen any of my cleaning colleagues for the last hour. It's time for the record room."

"Be quick!" Tracy urged. "Your being in there is going to make me anxious all over again, and I don't think I can take too much more."

Kim stuck the heavy-duty mop into his bucket and pushed the contraption down the hall to the record room door. Its broken central panel was covered by a piece of thin plywood.

Kim tried the door. It opened with ease. He reached in and turned on the light. Except for a larger sheet of the same plywood over the sashless window facing the parking lot, the room looked entirely normal. The broken glass and the rock he'd tossed in had all been taken away.

The left side of the room had a long line of file cabinets. At random, Kim yanked out the nearest drawer. It was jammed full of files so tightly that not another sheet of paper could have been added.

"Gosh," Kim said. "They sure do have a lot of paperwork. This isn't going to be as easy as I'd hoped."

The end of an El Producto cigar burned brightly for a few moments and then faded. Elmer Conrad held the resulting smoke in his mouth for a few pleasurable moments and then blew it contentedly at the ceiling.

Elmer was the three-to-eleven cleaning crew supervisor. He'd held the job for eight years. His idea of work was to sweat like crazy for the first half of the shift and then coast. At that moment he was in the coasting mode, watching a Sony Watchman in the lunchroom with his feet up on a table.

"You wanted to see me, boss?" Harry Pearlmuter asked, poking his head into the lunchroom from the back hall. Harry was one of Elmer's underlings.

"Yeah," Elmer said. "Where's that queer-looking temp guy?"

"I think he's out in the front hall mopping," Harry said. "At least that's what he said he was going to do."

"Do you think he cleaned those two bathrooms out there?" Elmer asked.

"I wouldn't know," Harry said. "You want me to check?"

Elmer let his heavy feet fall to the floor with a thump. He pushed himself up to his full height. He was over six-feet-five and weighed two hundred forty pounds.

"Thanks, but I'll do it myself," Elmer said. "I told him twice he had to clean those heads before eleven. If he hasn't done them, he will! He's not leaving here until they're done."

Elmer put down his cigar, took a swig of coffee, and set out to find Kim. What was motivating him was that he'd received specific instructions from the front office that Kim was to clean the bathrooms in question, and he was to clean them alone. Elmer had no idea why he'd gotten such an order, but he didn't care. All he cared about was that it was carried out.

$$\circ \qquad \circ \qquad \circ$$

"This isn't going to be so hard after all," Kim said into his microphone. "I found a whole drawer of Process Deficiency Reports. They go from nineteen eighty-eight to the present. Now, all I have to do is find January ninth."

"Hurry up, Kim," Tracy said. "I'm starting to get nervous again."

"Relax, Trace," Kim said. "I told you I haven't seen a soul in an hour. I think they're all back in the lunchroom watching a ball game. . . . Ah, here we are, January ninth. Hmmm. The folder's jammed full."

Kim pulled a clutch of papers from the folder. He turned around and put them down on the library table.

"Pay dirt!" Kim said happily. "It's the whole group of papers Marsha talked about." Kim spread the papers out so that he could see them all. "Here's the purchase invoice from Bart Winslow for what must have been a sick cow."

Kim glanced through the other papers, finally picking one up. "Here's what I'm looking for. It's a Process Deficiency Report on the same cow."

"What does it say?" Tracy asked.

"I'm reading it," Kim said. After a moment he added: "Well, the mystery has been solved. The last cow's head fell off the rail onto the floor. Of course, I know what that means after the work I've been doing today. It probably fell in its own manure and then went in to be butchered for hamburger meat. This cow could have been infected with the E. coli. That's consistent with what you found out from Sherring Labs this afternoon indicating that the patty made from the meat butchered on January ninth was heavily contaminated."

In the next instant, Kim was startled enough to let out a whimper. To his utter shock the Process Deficiency Report was ripped from his hands. He spun around to find himself facing Elmer Conrad. While he'd been talking, he'd not heard the man come into the room.

"What the hell are you doing with these papers?" Elmer demanded. His broad face had become beet-red.

Kim felt his heart race. Not only had he been caught looking at confidential documents, but he had the microphone in his right ear. To try to keep the wire out of Elmer's line of sight, he kept his head turned to the right, looking at Elmer out of the corner of his eye.

"You better answer me, boy," Elmer growled.

"They were on the floor," Kim said, desperately trying to think of something. "I was trying to put them back."

Elmer glanced at the open drawer to the file cabinet, then back at Kim. "Who were you talking to?"

"Was I talking?" Kim asked innocently.

"Don't mess with me, boy," Elmer warned.

Kim put his hand on his head then gestured ineffectually at Elmer, but no words came out of his mouth. He was trying to think of something clever to say but couldn't.

"Tell him you were talking to yourself," Tracy whispered.

"Okay," Kim said. "I was talking to myself."

Elmer looked askance at Kim, almost the same way Kim was looking at Elmer.

"You sounded like you were having a goddamn conversation," Elmer said.

"I was," Kim offered. "Just with myself. I do it all the time when I'm alone."

"You're one weird dude," Elmer said. "What's wrong with your neck?"

Kim rubbed the left side of his neck with his left hand. "It's a little stiff," he said. "Too much mopping, I guess."

"Well, you got some more to do," Elmer said. "Remember those two restrooms next door here. Remember I told you that you had to clean them."

"I guess that did slip my mind," Kim said. "Sorry, but I can get right to it."

"I don't want you doing a crappy job," Elmer said. "So take your time even if you have to work past eleven. Understand?"

"They'll be pristine," Kim promised.

Elmer tossed the Process Deficiency Report onto the table and roughly pushed all the papers together. While he was occupied, Kim pulled the earphone out of his ear and tucked it under his shirt. It felt good to straighten his neck out.

"We'll leave these papers for the secretaries to deal with," Elmer said. He reached over to the file cabinet and pushed the open drawer shut. "Now get the hell out of here. You're not supposed to be in here in the first place."

Kim preceded Elmer out of the room. Elmer hesitated at the door to look around one final time. Only then did he put out the light and close the door. Taking out a large ring of keys, he locked it.

Kim was busy rinsing out his mop when Elmer turned to him. "I'm going to keep my eye on you, boy," Elmer warned. "And I'm going to come back and inspect these two restrooms after you're done. So don't cut corners."

"I'll do my best," Kim said.

Elmer gave him one final disapproving look before heading back toward the lunchroom.

Kim slipped his earphone back into his ear as soon as Elmer disappeared from view.

"Did you hear that whole exchange?" Kim asked.

"Of course I heard it," Tracy said. "Have you had enough of this nonsense now? Come on out!"

"No, I want to try to get those papers," Kim said. "The problem is the bum locked the door."

"Why do you want them?" Tracy asked with exasperation.

"It's something more to show Kelly Anderson," Kim said.

"We already have the results from the lab," Tracy said. "That should be enough for Kelly Anderson to make a case for a recall. That's what you want, isn't it?"

"Of course," Kim said. "At a minimum, Mercer Meats' entire January twelfth production has to be recalled. But those papers also show how the industry is willing to buy sick cows, avoid inspection, and then allow a grossly soiled cow head to continue in production."

"Do you think that was how Becky got sick?" Tracy asked emotionally.

"There's a good chance," Kim said with equal emotion. "That and the fact that her burger wasn't cooked through."

"It makes you realize how tenuous life is that it could be snuffed out by something so trivial as a cow's head falling on the floor and a hamburger not cooked enough."

"It also underlines the importance of what we're doing here," Kim said.

"How do you think you can get the papers now that the record-room door is locked?" Tracy asked.

"I don't know exactly," Kim admitted. "But the door has a thin piece of plywood covering a hole. It probably wouldn't be too hard to knock it off. But it will have to wait until I make a stab at these two restrooms. I expect Elmer to wander back here in a few minutes, so I better get busy."

Kim looked at the two doors. They faced each other across the hall. He pushed open the men's room door. Careful to avoid tipping over his bucket, he maneuvered it over the raised threshold and onto the tile. He gave it a shove into the room and let the door close behind him.

The room was a generous size with two toilet stalls and two urinals on the right and two sinks with mirrors over them to the left. There was a series of coat hooks just inside the door. The only other objects in the room were two paper towel dispensers and a trash container.

In the middle of the far wall was a window that looked out onto the parking lot.

"At least this men's room isn't very dirty," Kim said. "I had fears that it was going to look like the one on the kill floor."

"I wish I could come in there and help," Tracy said.

"I wouldn't mind that at all," Kim said.

Kim grabbed the handle of the mop. Stepping on the wringer's foot pedal, he wrung out the mop head. Then he walked over to the window and started mopping.

The door to the bathroom burst open with enough force for its knob to crack the wall tile. The sound and the movement shocked Kim, and his head shot up. To his utter dismay he now found himself staring at the man who had attacked him previously. Once again the man was brandishing a kill-floor knife.

The man's lips slowly curled back into a cruel smile. "We meet again, Doctor. Only this time there will be no police and no woman to help you."

"Who are you?" Kim demanded, eager for the man to continue talking. "Why are you doing this to me?"

"My name is Carlos. I've come to kill you."

"Kim, Kim!" Tracy shouted in Kim's ear. "What's going on?"

To help him think, Kim tore the earphone from his ear. Now Tracy's frantic voice sounded as if she were yelling from a great distance.

Carlos took a step into the room, while holding up the knife so that Kim could appreciate its size and curving shape. The abused door swung shut.

Kim had a hold of the mop and he instinctively raised it.

Carlos laughed. To him the idea of a mop against a kill-floor knife was ludicrous.

With no other alternative, Kim dashed into one of the open toilet stalls and bolted the door. Carlos lunged forward and kicked the door fiercely.

The stall shuddered under the impact, but the door held. Kim frantically backed up and straddled the toilet. Beneath the stall door, he could see Carlo's feet as he prepared to kick the door again.

O    O    O

Tracy panicked. She fumbled with the ignition key before getting the car started. Throwing the vehicle into gear, she stomped on the accelerator. The car shot forward with enough speed to press her into the seat. The antenna she'd balanced on top skidded off the back of the car and bounced along the pavement on its wire tether.

Tracy fought with the steering wheel to bring the speeding car around a tight turn. Misjudging the closeness of a neighboring vehicle, she ricocheted off its side, throwing her own car up onto two wheels for a split second. The car thudded to earth and with squealing tires rocketed along the front of Higgins and Hancock.

Tracy had no plan initially. Her only thought was to try to get to the men's room where Kim was cornered, apparently by the same man who'd been in Kim's house the night before. She knew she had little time. She could see the man's horrid face in her mind's eye as he'd tried to force his way into her shower stall with his knife.

For a moment Tracy contemplated crashing her car into the front entrance of the building, but she decided it wouldn't necessarily do the trick. She had to get into the men's room itself. That was when she remembered the gun and swore at Kim for not having kept it with him.

Slamming on the brakes, Tracy brought her car to a shuddering halt just opposite the window to the record room. She reached down onto the floor and snatched up the gun. Clutching it in her hand, she jumped from the car and ran over to the record-room window.

Remembering how Kim had gained entry, she put down the gun and picked up one of the rocks edging the pavement. Using both hands, she threw it against the plywood. It took two smacks, but she succeeded in knocking the plywood free of its temporary nails. Then she yanked it off.

Tracy snatched up the gun and tossed it through the window. Then she followed it headfirst. Once inside the dark room, she had to grope around for the gun on her hands and knees. As she searched she could hear intermittent thumps behind the wall to the right as if a metal partition was being kicked repeatedly. The noise increased her frenzy.

Her fingers finally brushed up against the weapon where it had come to rest at the base of a table leg. She seized it and then moved as fast as the darkness would allow to the vaguely illuminated door to the hall.

Tracy unlocked the door. From having listened to the conversation between Kim and Elmer she knew the men's room had to be close to the record room. She decided to follow the sound of the thumping. She made a right. After running only a few steps, she saw the men's room sign.

Without a second's hesitation, Tracy crashed through the door using her shoulder. She had the gun clasped in both hands and pointed it into the depths of the room.

She'd had no idea what to expect. What she saw was Carlos less than ten feet away with one leg raised in preparation for kicking a toilet stall door in. The door was already bent.

As soon as he spotted her, Carlos made a flying leap for Tracy. Like the night before, he had a large knife clasped in his hand.

Tracy had no time to think. Closing her eyes against the hurling figure she pulled the trigger in quick succession. Two shots rang out before Carlos careened into her, slamming her against the door and knocking the gun from her hand. She felt a stabbing pain in her chest as she crumbled beneath the man's weight.

Tracy desperately tried to breathe and to wriggle free as the man's weight settled on top of her. But he had her easily pinned.

To Tracy's surprise the killer moved off her. She looked up, expecting to see him standing over her with his knife raised for a deadly stab. Instead she was looking at Kim's distraught face.

"Oh, God!" Kim cried. "Tracy!" He'd pulled the killer off her and had thrown him aside as if the man were no more than a sack of potatoes. Frantic over the amount of blood spreading across Tracy's chest, he dropped to his knees and ripped open her blouse. As a thoracic surgeon, he'd treated stab wounds to the chest, and he knew what to expect. But what he found was a blood-soaked bra; Tracy's skin was intact. There was no sucking chest wound with air rushing in as he'd feared.

Kim leaned closer to Tracy's face. She was still struggling to catch the breath that had been knocked out of her.

"Are you all right?" Kim demanded.

Tracy nodded but still couldn't speak.

Kim turned his attention to the killer. The man was writhing and groaning and had managed to turn himself over on his stomach. Kim rolled him back over and recoiled.

At such close range, both of Tracy's wild shots had found their mark. One had gone through Carlos's right eye to exit out the back of his skull. The other had hit him in the right chest, which explained the blood all over Tracy.

The man was foaming at the mouth and jerking uncoordinatedly. It was clear to Kim he was about to die.

"Is he hurt?" Tracy managed. Wincing against the pain in her chest, she pushed herself to a sitting position.

"He's as good as dead," Kim said. He stood up and began searching for the gun.

"Oh, no!" Tracy moaned. "I can't believe it. I can't believe I killed someone."

"Where's the gun?" Kim demanded.

"Oh, God!" Tracy managed. She couldn't take her eyes off Carlos who was agonally choking.

"The gun!" Kim snapped. He got down on his hands and knees. He found Carlos's knife but not the gun. Moving over to the stalls, he bent down again. At last he saw it behind the first toilet. Reaching in, he pulled it out.

Stepping over to the sink, he grabbed a paper towel and wiped the weapon clean.

"What are you doing?" Tracy asked through anguished tears.

"Getting rid of your fingerprints," Kim said. "I want only my prints on this thing."

"Why?" Tracy demanded.

"Because whatever comes of this mess, I'm taking responsibility," Kim said. He gripped the weapon, then tossed it aside. "Come on! We're getting out of here!"

"No!" Tracy said. She went after the gun. "I'm in this as much as you."

Kim grabbed her and pulled her upright. "Don't be foolish! I'm the accused felon here. Let's go!"

"But it was in self-defense," Tracy complained tearfully. "It's terrible, but it's justifiable."

"We can't trust what kind of spin the legal profession might put on this," Kim said. "You're trespassing and I'm here under false pretenses. Come on! I don't want to argue now!"

"Shouldn't we stay here until the police come?" Tracy asked.

"No way," Kim said. "I'm not going to sit in jail while this all gets sorted out. Come on now, let's go before anybody gets here."

Tracy doubted the wisdom of fleeing the scene but she could also tell that Kim's mind was made up. She let herself be led from the men's room. Kim looked up and down the hall, surprised that the shots had not brought any of his cleaning crew colleagues.

"How did you get in here?" Kim whispered.

"Through the record-room window," Tracy said. "The same window you broke."

"Good," Kim said. He took Tracy's hand. Together they dashed to the record-room door. Just as they were entering, they heard approaching voices.

Kim motioned for Tracy to be silent as he quietly closed and locked the door. In the darkness they first went to the library table, where Kim snatched up the incriminating papers. Then they made their way to the window. Through the wall, they heard commotion in the men's room followed by running footsteps down the hall.

Kim climbed out first. Then he helped Tracy. Together they dashed for Tracy's car.

"Let me drive," Kim said. He jumped behind the wheel while Tracy got into the backseat. He started the car and drove quickly out of the parking lot.

For a while they drove in silence.

"Who could have guessed it would have turned out like this," Tracy said at last. "What do you think we should do?"

"Maybe you had the right idea back there," Kim said. "Maybe we should have called the police ourselves and faced the consequences. I suppose it's not too late to turn ourselves in, although I think we should call Justin Devereau first."

"I've changed my mind," Tracy said. "I think your first instinct was correct. You'd certainly go to jail and probably me too, and it would probably be a year before there even was a trial. And then who knows what would happen? After the O.J. Simpson case I have zero confidence in the American court system. We don't have a million dollars to throw away on Johnny Cochrane or Barry Scheck."

"What are you implying?" Kim asked. He cast a quick glance at Tracy in the rearview mirror. She never failed to surprise him.

"What we talked about last night," Tracy said. "Let's go far away and deal with this mess from abroad. Someplace where the food is uncontaminated so we could continue our fight against that issue as well."

"Are you serious?" Kim asked.

"Yes, I'm serious," Tracy said.

Kim shook his head. They'd mentioned the idea and even had their passports, but he'd truly not taken it seriously. In his mind it had been more of a desperate scheme of last resort, something to consider in a worst-case scenario. Of course, thanks to the killing, he had to admit things couldn't have turned out much worse than they had.

"Of course we should call Justin," Tracy added. "He'll have some good suggestions. He always does. Maybe he'll know where we should go. There are probably some legal issues relating to extradition and all that."

"You know what I like best about the idea of us going to a foreign country?" Kim said after a few minutes of silence. He looked up to make eye contact with Tracy in the rearview mirror.

"What's that?" Tracy asked.

"That you're suggesting we do it together," Kim said.

"Well, of course," Tracy said.

"You know," Kim said. "Maybe we shouldn't have gotten divorced."

"I have to admit the idea has crossed my mind," Tracy said.

"Maybe something good will come from all this tragedy," Kim said.

"If we did get remarried, I know we couldn't have another Becky, but it would be nice to have another child."

"You'd really want to?" Kim asked.

"I'd like to try."

Silence again reigned for a time as the former lovers struggled with their emotions.

"How long do you think we will have before the authorities catch up with us?" Tracy asked.

"It's hard to say," Kim said. "If you're asking to know how long we have before we have to make up our minds about what we're going to do, I'd say we don't have much time. I think we have to decide in twenty-four to forty-eight hours."

"At least that allows us time for Becky's services tomorrow," Tracy said, choking up all over again.

Kim felt tears arise in his own eyes with the mention of Becky's imminent funeral. Despite his best efforts to avoid facing it, Kim could no longer deny the horrible fact that his beloved daughter was gone.

"Oh, God!" Tracy whimpered. "When I close my eyes I can see the face of the man I shot. It's something I'll never be able to forget. It'll haunt me the rest of my life."

Kim wiped the tears off his cheek and took an uneven breath to pull himself together. "You have to concentrate on what you said back in the men's room. It was justified. If you hadn't pulled the trigger and shot him, he would surely have killed you. And then he would have killed me. You saved my life."

Tracy closed her eyes.

It was after eleven o'clock when they pulled into Tracy's driveway and parked behind Kim's car. They were both completely drained: physically, mentally, and emotionally.

"I hope you're planning on staying here tonight," Tracy said.

"I was hoping I was still invited," Kim said.

They got out of the car. Arm-in-arm they walked up the path toward the house.

"Do you think we should call Justin tonight?" Tracy asked.

"Let's wait until morning," Kim said. "As wired as I am, I don't know whether I'll be able to sleep, but I need to try. At this point I really can't think much beyond taking a long, hot shower."

"I know what you mean," Tracy said.

They climbed onto the porch. Tracy got out her key and opened the door. She stepped inside and made way for Kim. She closed the door and locked it. Only then did her hand grope for the light switch.

"Wow, that seems bright," Kim said, squinting at the overhead light.

Tracy used the dimmer to cut the glare.

"I'm a basket case," Kim admitted. He slipped out of his Higgins and Hancock white coat and held it out at arm's length. "This thing should be burned. It's probably got E. coli plastered all over it."

"Just throw it away," Tracy said. "But it's probably best to throw it in the trash barrel outside in the back. I can only imagine what it's going to smell like in the morning." She took off her own coat and winced at the pain in her chest. Something hard had struck her just to the left of her sternum when Carlos had collided with her. At the time the pain had been so acute she'd thought she'd been stabbed.

"Are you all right?" Kim asked seeing her reaction.

Gingerly Tracy felt along the edge of her breastbone. "Is there anything that can break in here?" she asked.

"Of course," Kim said. "You could have fractured either a rib or the sternum itself."

"Oh, great!" Tracy said. "What should I do, Doctor?"

"Some ice wouldn't hurt," Kim said. "I'll get some after getting rid of this white coat."

Kim started for the back door via the kitchen. Tracy opened the hall closet and hung up her coat and kicked off her shoes. After closing the door, she started for the stairs. Halfway she suddenly froze and let out a screeching gasp.

Kim had only made it to the threshold of the kitchen when he heard Tracy's cry. He came running back. He was relieved to discover her unharmed in the center of the front hall. She was calm, but she seemed oddly transfixed at something in the living room. Kim tried to follow her line of sight. At first he saw nothing and was perplexed. But then he too saw what she was looking at. He was equally as startled.

In the shadows of the half-darkened room was a man. He was sitting motionless in the wing chair next to the fireplace. He was dressed in a dark suit and tie. A camel-hair coat was draped carefully over the back of the chair. His legs were casually crossed.

The man reached up and turned on a floor lamp.

Tracy let out another plaintive whine. On the coffee table in plain sight and within the man's easy reach was a black automatic pistol with an attached silencer.

The man was the picture of serenity, which only made him that much more terrifying. After turning on the light, his hand returned to the armrest. His expression was stern, almost cruel.

"You have made me wait much longer than I had intended," he said suddenly, breaking the silence. His voice was angrily accusatory.

"Who are you?" Tracy asked hesitantly.

"Come in here and sit down!" he snapped.

Kim looked to his left, judging how quickly he might be able to shove Tracy behind the arched wall of the foyer and possibly out of harm's way. He didn't see how he could be quick enough especially since she'd then have to get out the front door.

Derek responded to their hesitation by snapping up the handgun and training it on them.

"Don't aggravate me further!" he warned. "This has been a bad day, and I'm in a cross mood. I'll give you two seconds to come in here and sit on the couch."

Kim swallowed hard, but his voice came out in a hoarse whisper. "I think we'd better sit down."

Kim urged Tracy forward while he berated himself for not having checked the house when they'd arrived. He'd made the effort that morning to be able to tell if anyone had come in while they were away, but then after the death of Carlos, he'd not even thought of it.

Tracy sat down first. Kim took a seat next to her. They were on the couch diagonally opposite the wing chair.

Derek calmly replaced his gun on the coffee table and leaned back. His hands returned to the upholstered arms of the chair with his fingers slightly curled like a gunfighter ready to draw. It was as if he were daring the people in the room to try to flee or take the gun, thereby giving him an excuse to shoot them.

"Who are you?" Tracy repeated. "What are you doing in my house?"

"My name is immaterial," Derek said. "Why I'm here is another matter. I was brought to this city to kill the doctor."

Both Kim and Tracy swayed slightly. Derek's frightening revelation made them momentarily dizzy. They were speechless in their terror. The man was a hired killer.

"But something went wrong," Derek said. "They brought me all the way to this godforsaken city and then withdrew the contract without any real explanation other than to say they had someone else who was going to do the job. They even had the gall to ask for the down payment back after I flew all the way out here."

Derek leaned forward and his eyes blazed. "So not only am I not going to kill you, Dr. Reggis, I'm going to do you a favor. Now, I cannot figure out why these beef people want you dead."

"I can tell you," Kim offered anxiously. He was more than willing to cooperate.

Derek raised his hand. "There's no need for me to know the details at this point," he said. "I tried to find out, but I gave up. It's your business. What you should know is that these people want you dead enough to hire me or someone like me. My way of getting back at them for taking advantage of me is to tell you that you are in grave danger. What you do with the information is entirely up to you. Am I making myself clear?"

"Perfectly," Kim said. "Thank you."

"No reason to thank me," Derek said. "I'm not doing this for altruistic reasons."

Derek stood up. "The only thing I ask in return is that you keep this conversation just between us. Otherwise I might have to come back and visit either one of you again, and I hope that's just as clear. I should warn you that I am very good at what I do."

"Don't worry," Kim said. "We won't discuss this with anyone."

"Excellent," Derek said. "Now, if you will excuse me, I am going to try to get home."

Kim made a move to get up from the couch.

"Don't bother," Derek said, motioning Kim to stay put. "I saw myself in; I'll see myself out."

Kim and Tracy watched dumbfounded as Derek slipped on his camel-hair coat. He picked up his handgun and slipped it into his pocket. Then he picked up his briefcase.

"I wouldn't have been quite so rude if you'd gotten home at a decent hour," Derek said. "Good night."

"Good night," Kim said.

Derek walked out of the living room.

Kim and Tracy heard the door open and then slam closed.

For several minutes neither spoke.

"This is all so incredible. It's as if I'm in a nightmare and just can't wake up," Tracy said.

"It's a nightmare that keeps on going," Kim agreed. "But we have to do what we can to end it."

"Do you still think we should go to a foreign country?" Tracy asked.

Kim nodded. "At least I should. It seems I'm a marked man. In fact, let's not even stay here tonight."

"Where will we go?" Tracy asked.

"Hotel, motel, what does it matter?" Kim asked.

# CHAPTER 18

As soon as early-morning daylight began to creep around the edges of the cheap curtains, Kim gave up trying to fall back asleep. He eased out of bed to avoid disturbing Tracy, gathered up his clothes, and padded silently into the Sleeprite Motel's bathroom. He closed the door as quietly as possible, then turned on the light.

Kim looked at himself in the mirror and cringed. Between his ridiculous blond hair and sutured laceration framing sunken, red eyes, he hardly recognized himself. Despite his exhaustion, he'd slept fitfully and had awakened for the final time just after five. All night he'd reviewed the previous days' horrific events, agonizing over what to do. The idea of being pursued by hired killers was almost too much to comprehend.

Kim shaved and showered, thankful for simple tasks to divert his mind for a few moments. Brushing his hair down flat, he thought he appeared significantly more presentable.

After pulling on his clothes, Kim cracked the door. He was glad to see that Tracy had not budged. He knew she'd slept equally poorly and was pleased that she was now getting some real sleep. Kim was thankful for her presence but ambivalent about allowing her to share the current risk.

Kim went to the desk and used the pad by the phone to scribble a short note to tell Tracy that he'd gone to bring back some breakfast. He put the note on the blanket on his side of the bed. Then he picked up the car keys.

It was more difficult to get the entrance door open silently than it had been with the bathroom door because the entrance door was metal, and it had a chain-lock and a throw-bolt in addition to its regular lock.

Once outside, Kim reminded himself that he was being pursued by hired killers. The thought made him acutely paranoid despite being relatively certain he was safe for the moment. He and Tracy had used assumed names when they had checked in at the motel and had paid in cash.

Kim went to the car and climbed in. He started the engine but didn't pull out immediately. He watched the man who'd checked them in six hours earlier. He'd seen Kim come out of the room but had gone back to his chores. He was busy sweeping in front of the office. Kim wanted to make sure the man didn't do anything suspicious before he left Tracy alone, like suddenly run back inside the office to use the phone.

Recognizing his paranoia, Kim chided himself. He knew he was going to have to pull himself together or risk making the wrong decisions. Putting the car in gear, he backed up before driving out of the parking lot.

A few miles down the road was a donut shop where Kim ordered two coffees, two orange juices, and an assortment of donuts. The place was nearly full of truckers and construction men. While Kim stood in line at the cash register, many of them eyed him skeptically. From their point of view, no doubt he was quite a sight.

Kim was happy to leave. As he stepped off the curb on his way to his car his eye saw the headlines of the paper placed behind the window of the dispenser. It said in bold, capital letters: "BERSERK DOCTOR SEEKS REVENGE BY MURDER!" Then along the bottom of the page in smaller print was: "THE ONCE RESPECTED PROFESSIONAL NOW A FUGITIVE FROM JUSTICE."

A shiver of fear descended down Kim's spine. He quickly went to the car and deposited the food and drink. Heading back to the dispenser he sought the proper coins from his pocket. With a trembling hand he got out one of the papers. The door to the dispenser clattered shut.

Any lingering hope the story did not concern him was dashed when Kim saw a photo of himself below the headlines. It was several years old with his normal shock of dark hair.

Ducking back into the car, Kim turned back the front page of the newspaper. The story was on page two:

## EXCLUSIVE TO THE MORNING SUN TIMES:

Dr. Kim Reggis, a respected cardiac surgeon and the former head of the department at the Samaritan Hospital and now on staff at the University Medical Center, has taken the law into his own hands vigilante style. In response to the tragic death of his daughter on Saturday, he allegedly disguised himself with blond hair color, got a job at Higgins and Hancock under a false name, and then brutally murdered another worker by the name of Carlos Mateo. It is thought that the motive for this unprovoked killing is that Dr. Reggis believed his daughter died of meat slaughtered at Higgins and Hancock.

Mr. Daryl Webster, the president of Higgins and Hancock, has told the Times that this is a preposterous allegation. He also said that Mr. Mateo was a valued worker and a devoted Catholic, who tragically leaves behind an invalid wife and six young children. . . .

Kim angrily tossed the paper onto the passenger seat. He didn't have to read any further to be disgusted—and concerned. He started the car and drove back to the motel. Carrying the food and the paper, he entered.

Tracy heard him come in and poked her head around the bathroom door. She was toweling her wet head, having just gotten out of the shower.

"You're up," Kim commented. He put down the food on the desk.

"I heard you go out," Tracy said. "I'm glad to see you back. I was a little afraid you might leave me here with the idea of sparing me. Promise me you won't do that."

"The idea crossed my mind," Kim admitted. He sank dejectedly into the only chair.

"What's the matter?" Tracy asked. Although she knew there was more than enough on Kim's mind, he seemed far more despondent than she expected.

Kim held up the newspaper. "Read this!" he said.

"Is it about the man at Higgins and Hancock?" Tracy asked fearfully. She wasn't sure she wanted to read the details.

"Yes, and about me, too," Kim said.

"Oh, no!" Tracy cried with dismay. "You're already associated with it?" She stepped into the room while wrapping herself in the thin towel. She took the paper and read the headlines. Slowly she sank onto the edge of the bed, turning the page to read the rest.

It didn't take Tracy long. When she was finished, she closed the paper and put it aside. She looked at Kim. "What a character assassination," she said somberly. "They even included mention of your recent arrests and that your hospital privileges have been suspended."

"I didn't get that far," Kim said. "I only read the first two paragraphs, but it was enough."

"I can't believe this has all happened so quickly," Tracy said. "Someone must have recognized you at Higgins and Hancock."

"Obviously," Kim said. "The man we killed wasn't trying to kill José Ramerez. And when he failed to kill me, the people who were paying him opted to destroy my credibility and possibly send me to jail for life." Kim laughed mirthlessly. "And to think I was worried about the legal ramifications. I never even considered the media. It surely gives you an idea of the money and power of this industry in this town that they can manage to distort the truth like this. I mean, there was no investigative reporting in this article. The paper just printed what the meat industry told them. They have me murdering a God-fearing family man in cold blood in a fit of revenge."

"This means we don't have twenty-four to forty-eight hours to decide what we're going to do," Tracy said.

"I should say not," Kim said. He stood up. "It means we should have decided last night. And for me it also means there's no longer a question. I'll fight this travesty but definitely from afar."

Tracy stood up and stepped over to Kim. "There's no longer a question for me either," she said. "We'll go together and fight this together."

"Of course it will mean we'll miss Becky's service," Kim said.

"I know," Tracy said.

"I think she'll understand."

"I hope so," Tracy managed. "I miss her so much."

"Me too," Kim said.

Kim and Tracy looked into each other's eyes. Then Kim reached out and put his arms around his former wife. Tracy put hers around Kim, and they hugged, pressing themselves against each other as if they'd been involuntarily separated for years. Another long moment passed until Kim leaned back to look Tracy in the eye. "It's like old times to feel close to you like this."

"Very old times," Tracy agreed. "Like in a previous life."

○   ○   ○

Kelly Anderson looked at her watch. It was almost one-thirty. She shook her head. "He's not coming," she said to Brian Washington.

Brian adjusted the TV camcorder on his shoulder. "You really didn't expect him to, did you?" he asked.

"He loved his daughter," Kelly said. "And this is her funeral."

"But there's a policeman right outside," Brian said. "They'd arrest him on the spot. The guy would have to be crazy to come."

"I think he is a little crazy," Kelly said. "When he stopped in to my house to get me interested in his crusade, he had a wild look in his eye. He even scared me a little."

"That I doubt," Brian said. "I've never seen you scared. In fact, I think you have ice in your veins, especially with as much ice tea you drink."

"You more than anyone should know it's just an act. I'm scared every time I go on the air."

"Bull," Brian said.

Kelly and Brian were standing in the foyer of the Sullivan Funeral

Home. There were a few other people milling about and whispering discreetly. Bernard Sullivan, the proprietor, was standing near the door. He was clearly anxious and glanced repeatedly at his watch. The funeral service had been booked for one o'clock, and he had a tight schedule for the day.

"Did you think Dr. Reggis was crazy enough to kill someone like they said in the paper?" Brian asked.

"Let's put it this way," Kelly said, "I think he was pushed to his limit."

Brian shrugged. "I guess you just never know," he said philosophically.

"Maybe the good doctor's absence is understandable," Kelly said. "But, for the life of me, I can't understand where Tracy is. She was Becky's mother, for God's sake. And she has no reason to avoid the law. I'll tell you: this has me worried."

"What do you mean?" Brian asked.

"If the good doctor has really lost it," Kelly said, "it wouldn't be so farfetched to think that he might blame his former wife in some twisted way for his daughter's death."

"Oh, geez," Brian said. "I never thought of that."

"Listen," Kelly said, suddenly making up her mind. "You go call the station to get Tracy Reggis's address. I'll go have a chat with Mr. Sullivan and ask him to page us if Tracy Reggis shows up."

"You got it," Brian said.

Brian headed back to the funeral-home office, while Kelly walked over to the funeral director and tapped him on the arm. Twenty minutes later, Kelly and Brian were in Kelly's car, gliding to a stop in front of Tracy's house.

"Uh-oh," Kelly said.

"What's the matter?" Brian asked.

"That car," Kelly said. She pointed to the Mercedes. "I think that's the doctor's car. At least it's the car he was driving when he came to visit me."

"What should we do?" Brian asked. "I don't want any madman running out of the house with a baseball bat or a shot gun."

Brian had a point. Following her scenario, Reggis could very well be in the house holding his former wife as a hostage or even worse.

"Maybe we should go around and talk to the neighbors," Kelly suggested. "Somebody might have seen something."

At the first two houses they approached, no one responded to the front doorbell. The third bell they rang was Mrs. English's, and she answered the door promptly.

"You're Kelly Anderson!" Mrs. English said excitedly, after taking one look at Kelly. "You're wonderful. I see you on TV all the time." Mrs. English was a diminutive, silver-haired lady who looked like the quintessential grandmother.

"Thank you," Kelly said. "Would you mind if we asked you a few questions?"

"Am I going to be on TV?" Mrs. English asked.

"It's a possibility," Kelly said. "We're researching a story."

"Ask away," Mrs. English said.

"We're curious about your neighbor across the street," Kelly said. "Tracy Reggis."

"There's something strange going on there," Mrs. English said. "That's for sure."

"Oh?" Kelly questioned. "Tell us about it."

"It started yesterday morning," Mrs. English said. "Tracy came over and asked me to watch her house. Now, I watch it anyway, but she was very specific. She wanted me to tell her if any strangers came by. Well, one did."

"Someone you've never seen before?" Kelly asked.

"Never," Mrs. English said unequivocally.

"What did he do?" Kelly asked.

"He went inside."

"When Tracy wasn't here?"

"That's right."

"How did he get in?"

"I don't know," Mrs. English said. "I think he had a key because he opened the front door."

"Was he a big man with dark hair?"

"No, he was average-height with blond hair," Mrs. English said. "Very well dressed. Like a banker or lawyer."

"And then what happened?" Kelly asked.

"Nothing. The man never left and when it got dark, he didn't even turn on a light. Tracy didn't come back until late with another blond man. This man was bigger and had on a white coat."

"You mean like a doctor?" Kelly asked. She winked at Brian.

"Or a butcher," Mrs. English said. "Anyway, Tracy didn't come to talk with me like she said she would. She just went into the house with the second man."

"And then what happened?"

"They were all inside for a while. Then the first man came out and drove away. A little while later, Tracy and the other man came out with suitcases."

"Suitcases like they were going on a trip?"

"Yes. But it was a strange time to go on a trip. It was nearly midnight. I know because it was the latest I've stayed up for as long as I can remember."

"Thank you, Mrs. English," Kelly said. "You've been most helpful." Kelly motioned for Brian to leave.

"Am I going to be on TV?" Mrs. English asked.

"We'll let you know," Kelly said. She waved and walked back to her car. She climbed in. Brian got into the passenger seat.

"This story keeps getting better," Kelly said. "I wouldn't have guessed in all the world, but Tracy Reggis has apparently decided to go on the lam with her fugitive former husband. And to think she seemed like such a sensible person. I'm blown away!"

By three o'clock the chaos of the lunchtime rush finally faded in the Onion Ring restaurant on Prairie Highway, and the exhausted day shift gathered up their things and left: everyone except for Roger Polo, the manager. As conscientious as he was, he couldn't leave until he was sure there was a smooth transition to the evening shift. Only then would he turn things over to Paul, the cook, who acted as the supervisor in Roger's absence.

Roger was busy installing a new tape in one of the cash registers when Paul arrived at his station behind the grill and began arranging the utensils the way he liked them.

"Much traffic today?" Roger asked while snapping the register's cowling shut.

"Not bad," Paul said. "Was it a busy day here?"

"Very busy," Roger said. "There must have been twenty people waiting to get in when I opened the doors, and it never let up."

"Did you see the morning's paper?" Paul asked.

"I wish," Roger said. "I didn't even have a chance to sit down to eat."

"You better read it," Paul said. "That crazy doctor that came in here Friday murdered a guy out at Higgins and Hancock last night."

"No kidding!" Roger blurted. He was genuinely dumbstruck.

"Some poor Mexican guy with six kids," Paul said. "Shot him through the eye. Can you imagine?"

There was no way Roger could imagine. He leaned on the countertop. His legs felt wobbly. He'd been mad about being struck in the face; now he felt lucky. He shuddered to think of what might have happened had the doctor brought a gun when he'd come to the Onion Ring.

"When your time's up, it's up," Paul said philosophically. He turned around and opened the refrigerator. Looking into the patty box, he could see it was almost empty.

"Skip!" Paul yelled. He'd seen Skip out in the restaurant proper emptying the trash containers.

"Do you have the newspaper?" Roger asked.

"Yeah," Paul said. "It's on the table in the employee room. Help yourself."

"What's up?" Skip asked. He'd come to the outer side of the counter.

"I need more burgers from the walk-in," Paul said. "And while you're at it, bring a couple of packages of buns."

"Can I finish what I'm doing first?" Skip asked.

"No," Paul said. "I need 'em now. I only have two patties left."

Skip muttered under his breath as he rounded the counter and headed to the restaurant's rear. He liked to finish one job before starting another. It was also beginning to bug him that everybody in the whole place could boss him around.

Skip pulled open the heavy, insulated door to the freezer and stepped into the arctic chill. The automatic door closed behind him. He pushed back the flaps of the first carton on the left but found it was empty. He cursed loudly. His colleague equivalent on the day shift always left him things to do. This empty carton would have to be cut down for recycling.

Skip went to the next carton and found that one empty as well. Picking up both cartons, he opened the door and threw them out of the freezer. Then he walked into the depths of the walk-in to locate the reserve patty cartons. He scraped the frost off the label on the nearest one he could find. It said: MERCER MEATS. REG. 0.1 LB HAMBURGER PATTIES, EXTRA LEAN. LOT 6 BATCH 9-14. PRODUCTION: JAN. 12, USE BY: APR. 12.

"I remember this baby," Skip said out loud. He checked the flaps. Sure enough, the carton had been opened.

To be certain there weren't any older patties, Skip scraped off the frost from the label of the final carton. The date was the same.

Grabbing the first carton by its flaps, Skip dragged it to the front of the freezer. Only then did he reach inside to pull out one of the interior boxes. As he'd expected this box had been opened as well.

Skip carried the patty box back to the kitchen, and after squeezing by Paul who was busy scraping the residue off the grill, Skip put the patty box in the refrigerator.

"We're finally using those burgers I opened by accident a week or so ago," Skip said as he slammed the refrigerator door.

"That's cool as long as the other ones are finished," Paul said, without looking up from his labors.

"I checked," Skip said. "The older ones are all gone."

○   ○   ○

The large wall clock on the wall of the WENE newsroom gave Kelly the exact time. It was 6:07. The local news had been on since five-thirty. Her segment was scheduled to begin at 6:08, and the technician was still fumbling with her microphone. As usual Kelly's pulse was racing.

One of the large TV cameras suddenly was rolled into place directly in front of her. The cameraman was nodding and speaking softly into his headphone. Out of the corner of her eye she saw the director pick up his microphone wire and head in her direction. In the background she could here the anchor, Marilyn Wodinsky, finishing a wrap-up of the national news.

"Good grief," Kelly snapped. She pushed away the technician's hand and rapidly secured the microphone herself. It was a good thing because within seconds the the director held up five fingers and gave the countdown, ending by pointing at Kelly. Simultaneously the camera in front of Kelly went live.

"Good evening, everyone," Kelly said. "We have an in-depth report this evening concerning a sad local story; a story that plays like a Greek tragedy. A year ago we had a picture-perfect family. The father was one of the country's most renowned cardiac surgeons; the mother, a psychotherapist, highly regarded in her own right; and the daughter, a darling, talented ten-year-old, considered by some as a rising star in figure skating. The denouement started presumably with the merger of the University Hospital and the Samaritan. Apparently, this put pressure on the marriage. Soon after, a bitter divorce and custody battle ensued. Then a few days ago, on Saturday afternoon, the daughter died of a strain of E. coli which has surfaced in intermittent outbreaks around the country. Dr. Kim Reggis, the father, pushed to the limit by the sad disintegration of his life, decided that the local beef industry was responsible for his daughter's death. He became convinced that his daughter had contracted the toxin from an Onion Ring restaurant in the area. The Onion Ring chain gets its burgers from Mercer Meats, and Mercer Meats gets a significant amount of its beef from Higgins and Hancock. The distraught Dr. Kim Reggis disguised himself as a blond drifter, obtained employment under an alias at Higgins and Hancock, and shot dead another Higgins and Hancock employee. The deceased is Carlos Mateo, who leaves behind a disabled wife and six young children.

"WENE has learned from the authorities that a gun left at the scene had been registered to the doctor and that his fingerprints were found on it.

"Dr. Reggis is now a fugitive and is being actively sought by the police. In a bizarre twist to the story, his former wife, Tracy Reggis, has apparently joined him in flight. At this time it is unknown if she is being coerced or acting under her own volition.

"To follow up on this story, WENE interviewed Mr. Carl Stahl, CEO of Foodsmart, Incorporated. I asked Mr. Stahl if Becky Reggis could have contracted her E. coli from an Onion Ring restaurant."

Kelly breathed a sigh of relief. A makeup person appeared from behind the background screen and adjusted a few wisps of hair and powdered her forehead. Meanwhile Carl Stahl's face appeared on the studio's monitor.

"Thank you, Kelly, for this opportunity to speak with your listeners," Carl said solemnly. "First let me say that having known Tracy and Becky Reggis personally, I'm crushed by this sad affair. But to answer your question, there is no way Miss Reggis could have contracted her illness from an Onion Ring restaurant. We cook our burgers to 178 degrees interior temperature, which is higher than what is recommended by the FDA, and we insist our chefs check this temperature twice a day."

The director again pointed at Kelly, and the red light on top of the camera in front of her blinked on.

"I posed the same question to Jack Cartwright of Mercer Meats," Kelly said, looking directly into the camera.

Once again Kelly visibly relaxed as the monitor came back to life. This time it was Jack Cartwright's image.

"Mercer Meats supplies the Onion Ring chain with their hamburger patties," Jack said. "They are made from the finest 'extra lean' ground beef, so there is no way that someone could have gotten sick from one of their burgers. Mercer Meats adheres to, in fact, surpasses all USDA requirements for meat processing in terms of sanitation and sterilization.

The Onion Ring restaurants have the finest ingredients that money and technology can buy."

Without a second's hesitation Kelly cut in at the conclusion of Jack Cartwright's taped interview. "And finally I posed the identical question to Mr. Daryl Webster, acting head of Higgins and Hancock."

The monitor came alive for the third time. "The Onion Ring makes its burgers from the best meat in the world," Daryl said contentiously, poking his finger at the camera. "And I dare anyone to dispute that. We here at Higgins and Hancock are proud to provide their supplier, Mercer Meats, with their fresh beef. And let me say this, I think it's a tragedy that one of our best employees has been murdered in this cold-blooded fashion. All I can hope is that this fruitcake is brought to justice before he kills someone else."

Kelly raised her eyebrows as the camera in front of her went live again. "As you can see, emotions are running high in the aftermath of this murder and a young girl's tragic death. So there you have it, the story of the Reggis family, and its tragic consequences. WENE will bring you more as soon as it is available. Over to you, Marilyn."

Kelly exhaled loudly and detached her microphone. In the background Marilyn's voice could be heard: "Thank you, Kelly, for that heartbreaking and disturbing story. Now on to other local news . . ."

Kelly activated the automatic garage door and then stepped out of her car as it began to shut. She slung her shoulder bag over her shoulder and climbed the three steps from the garage into the house.

The house was quiet. She had expected to see Caroline sitting on the gingham couch watching her half hour of allotted television, but the TV was off and Caroline was nowhere in sight. All Kelly could hear was the faint clicking of a computer keyboard coming from the library.

Kelly opened the refrigerator and poured herself some juice. Glass in hand, she passed through the dining room and poked her head into the library. Edgar was at the computer. Walking in, she gave him a peck on the cheek, which he accepted without taking his eyes off the monitor.

"That was an interesting piece you did on Dr. Reggis," Edgar said. He double-clicked his mouse and looked up.

"You think so?" Kelly said without a lot of enthusiasm. "Thanks."

"A sad story for everyone involved," Edgar said.

"To say the least," Kelly said. "A year ago he could have been a poster-boy for American success. As a heart surgeon, he had it all: respect, a beautiful family, a big home, all the trappings."

"But it was a house of cards," Edgar said.

"Apparently," Kelly said. She sighed. "What's with Caroline? Did she get her homework done?"

"Mostly," Edgar said. "But she wasn't feeling too good and wanted to go to bed."

"What's the trouble?" Kelly asked. It was rare for Caroline to miss her TV.

"Nothing overwhelming," Edgar assured her. "Just some stomach upset with cramps. She probably ate too much and too quickly. She insisted we stop at an Onion Ring restaurant after her skating practice, and the place was mobbed. I'm afraid her eyes were bigger than her stomach. She ordered two burgers, a shake, and a large fries."

Kelly felt an uncomfortable stirring in the pit of her stomach.

"Which Onion Ring?" Kelly asked hesitantly.

"The one out on Prairie Highway," Edgar said.

"Do you think Caroline is already asleep?" Kelly asked.

"I wouldn't know for sure," Edgar said. "But she hasn't been up there very long."

Kelly put down her juice. She left the room and climbed the stairs. Her face reflected her anxiety. She stopped to listen outside of Caroline's room. Once again, all she could hear was the clicking of the computer keyboard drifting up from downstairs.

Quietly Kelly cracked the door. The room was dark. Opening the door further, she stepped inside and silently walked over to her daughter's bedside.

Caroline was fast asleep. Her face looked particularly angelic. Her breathing was deep and regular.

Kelly resisted the temptation to reach out and hug her daughter. Instead she just stood there in the semidarkness, thinking about how much she loved Caroline and how much Caroline meant to her. Such thoughts made her feel acutely vulnerable. Life was indeed a house of cards.

Backing out of the room, Kelly closed the door and descended the stairs. She returned to the library, collected her juice glass, and sat down on the leather couch. She cleared her throat.

Edgar looked over. Knowing Kelly as well as he did, he knew she wanted to talk. He switched off his computer.

"What is it?" he asked.

"It's the Dr. Reggis story," Kelly said. "I'm not satisfied with it. I said as much to the news director, but he overruled me, saying it was tabloid fodder not hard news and that I wasn't supposed to waste any more time on it. But I'm going to do it anyway."

"Why do you feel this way?" Edgar asked.

"There are some gnawing loose ends," Kelly said. "The biggest one involves a USDA inspector by the name of Marsha Baldwin. When Kim Reggis stopped here on Sunday, he told me that he thought the woman had disappeared. He implied that foul play may have been involved."

"I assume you have been looking for her," Edgar said.

"Sort of," Kelly admitted. "I really didn't take Kim Reggis too seriously. As I told you, I thought he'd gone over the edge after his daughter's death. I mean, he'd been acting bizarre and according to him the woman had only been missing for a few hours. Anyway I attributed his allegations to raving paranoia."

"So you haven't found the woman," Edgar said.

"No, I haven't," Kelly said. "Monday I made a few isolated calls, but I wasn't really into it. But today I called the USDA district office. When I asked about her, they insisted I talk to the district manager. Of course I didn't mind talking to the head honcho, but then he didn't give me any information. He just said that they hadn't seen her. After I hung up, I thought that it was curious that I had to speak to the head of the office to get that kind of information."

"It is curious," Edgar admitted.

"I called up later and asked specifically where she'd been assigned," Kelly said. "Guess where?"

"I haven't a clue," Edgar said.

"Mercer Meats," Kelly said.

"Interesting," Edgar said. "So how are you going to go about investigating all this?"

"I don't know yet," Kelly said. "Of course I'd love to find the doctor. Seems like I've always been chasing him."

"Well, I've learned to respect your intuition," Edgar said. "So go for it."

"One other thing," Kelly said. "Keep Caroline out of the Onion Ring restaurants, particularly the one on Prairie Highway."

"How come?" Edgar asked. "She loves the food."

"For the moment, let's just say it's my intuition."

"You'll have to tell her yourself," Edgar said.

"I don't have a problem with that," Kelly said.

The door chimes surprised both of them. Kelly glanced at her watch. "Who's here ringing our bell at eight o'clock on a Tuesday?" she questioned.

"Beats me," Edgar said, while getting to his feet. "Let me get it."

"Be my guest," Kelly said.

Kelly rubbed her temples as she gave more thought to Edgar's question about how she would look into this Reggis situation. Without the doctor, it wasn't going to be easy. She tried to remember everything Kim had said when he'd visited on Sunday.

Out in the front hall she heard Edgar talking with someone and being told where to sign. A few minutes later, he returned. He was clutching a manila envelope, staring at the label.

"You got a package," he said. He shook it. Something was moving around freely inside.

"Who's it from?" Kelly asked. She didn't like getting mystery packages.

"There's no return address," Edgar said. "Just the initials KR."

"KR," Kelly repeated. "Kim Reggis?"

Edgar shrugged. "I suppose it's possible."

"Let me see it," Kelly said.

Edgar handed her the package. She felt through the paper. "Well, it doesn't feel dangerous. It feels like a reel of something padded with paper."

"Go ahead and open it," Edgar said.

Kelly tore open the envelope and pulled out a bunch of official-looking forms and a recording tape. Attached to the top of the tape was a Post-it. On it was written: *Kelly, You asked for documentation, and here it is. I'll be in touch. Kim Reggis.*

"These are all papers from Higgins and Hancock," Edgar said. "With attached descriptions."

Kelly shook her head as she scanned the material. "I have a feeling my investigation just got off to a flying start."

# EPILOGUE

The dilapidated, recycled UPS van coughed and sputtered, but the engine kept going. The van climbed a gradual incline after fording across a small stream.

"By golly, that's the deepest that crick's been since I've been in these parts," Bart Winslow said. He and his partner, Willy Brown, were driving along an isolated country road, trying to get back to the main road after picking up a dead pig. It had been raining for almost two days, and the road was awash and the potholes full of muddy water.

"I been thinking," Bart said, after spitting some tobacco juice out the driver's-side window. "Benton Oakly's not going to have much of a farm if his cows keep getting the runs like the one we picked up before the pig."

"Sure as shootin'," Willy said. "But you know, this one's not much sicker than the one we picked up a month ago. What do you say we take it to the slaughterhouse like we did the other one?"

"I suppose," Bart said. "The problem is we gotta drive all the way out to the VNB slaughterhouse in Loudersville."

"Yeah, I know," Willy said. "That TV lady got Higgins and Hancock to close for a couple of weeks for some kind of investigation."

"Well, the good part is that VNB is a hell of a lot less choosey than Higgins and Hancock," Bart said. "Remember that time we sold them those two cows deader than a Thanksgiving turkey right out of the oven?"

355

"Sure do," Willy said. "When you reckon Higgins and Hancock gonna reopen?"

"I hear by Monday next 'cause they didn't find nothing but a handful of illegal aliens," Bart said.

"Figures," Willy said. "So what you think about this cow we got?"

"Let's do it," Bart said. "Fifty bucks is better'n twenty-five in anybody's book."

# AFTERWORD

A basic requirement for the pursuit of happiness is good health, and the minimum requirement for good health is clean water and uncontaminated food. Human beings as a civilization have been struggling with the former since urbanization. Only in recent times has civil engineering led to sustainable solutions. Tragically, the circumstance with the latter is the opposite. After significant technological progress with food preservation, particularly in regard to refrigeration, we have been losing ground due to the pressure for increased food quantity and lower prices. Intensive farming and animal rearing practices have actually created new, frightful forms of contamination and threaten to spawn more. It is a problem that cries out for attention. For those people who would like to learn more about this serious situation and the havoc it wreaks, I strongly recommend they read:

> Fox, Nicols, *Spoiled: What Is Happening to Our Food Supply and Why We Are Increasingly at Risk* (Basic Books, 1997; Penguin, 1998).